About the Author

Kay Patrick won a scholarship to RADA at sixteen. She acted in Theatre and Television, most notably in *Dr Who* alongside William Hartnell. She later switched to behind the camera, script editing, directing and producing in radio, theatre and television. Over a period of twenty years she has directed Coronation Street. She wrote an historical documentary -"A Strange and Fearful Thing" – for BBC Radio 4, but *The Trial of Marie Montrecourt* is her first novel.

The Trial of Marie Montrecourt

Kay Patrick

Matador
9 Priory Business Park,
Wistow Road, Kibworth Beauchamp,
Leicestershire. LE8 0RX
Tel: 0116 279 2299
Email: books@troubador.co.uk
Web: www.troubador.co.uk/matador
Twitter: @matadorbooks

ISBN 978 1785891 977

British Library Cataloguing in Publication Data.
A catalogue record for this book is available from the British Library.

Printed and bound in the UK by TJ International, Padstow, Cornwall
Typeset in 11pt Aldine401 BT by Troubador Publishing Ltd, Leicester, UK

Matador is an imprint of Troubador Publishing Ltd

To June, Maisie and Wendy

OCTOBER 1905

Armley Gaol – Leeds

It was so dark in the cell. One of the wardresses had taken pity on her and allowed her a candle, a pen and paper. Marie could only hope that the woman knew how much the gesture had meant. She'd been so taken aback by this unexpected act of kindness that she hadn't been able to find the words to say thank you. During the trial, she'd faced nothing but hostility.

She glanced up at the small window that was set close to the ceiling. A thin shaft of moonlight struggled to make its presence felt. It barely illuminated the low wooden bench and the small bed with its one blanket, which she now pulled around her for warmth. A distant clock struck one. In a few hours she might know the verdict. She might know what the future held for her – or if she even had a future. She couldn't bear this waiting. She wanted it to be over, one way or the other. She struggled to her feet, her legs stiff with cold, and began to pace the cell. She must try to focus on something. The letter; she must write the letter.

The candle on the bench flickered, threatened by the many draughts that entered crevasses that were invisible to her. When the flame was finally still again, it created a tiny circle of light that was just bright enough to enable her to see. She sat back on the bed and stared at the blank paper in front of her.

If she did write, should it be to Daphne or Evelyn? What would she say to them? What *could* she say to them? After a moment, she pushed the paper aside. Their faith in her was so strong that even if the jury found her guilty, she knew they would never accept the verdict. Others might say: "Let her hang, it's all she deserves." She realised she had spoken the words aloud.

Marie lay back on the bed wearily and closed her eyes. Some of the newspapers had accused her of being degenerate, printing headlines that said she was a monster. Was it true? Is that what she had become, and is that how she would be remembered?

The distant clock struck again. Perhaps none of that would matter soon. There might not even be a future to worry about. Even if she did survive, would she be able to live with the past?

CHAPTER ONE
November - 1899

Harrogate

Marie perched nervously on the edge of her bed, waiting for him. Was it fear or excitement that made her shiver? A nearby church clock struck ten. Mr Pickard would be arriving soon, so she must get ready.

There was no difficulty in choosing what to wear. It would have to be the hated grey serge skirt and white blouse that she'd arrived in, because those were the only clothes she had. Both were too big for her. She must pin up her hair, too. With practiced ease she coiled it on top of her head, jabbing pins in to hold it in place. She was quite proud of her hair. It was probably her best feature. One of the nuns had once described it as being the colour of burnt sugar. She'd never seen burnt sugar, so she didn't know if that was true.

What had Mr John Pickard made of her when he had first seen her? Whatever it was, it didn't seem to please him. Perhaps he hadn't been expecting to escort a young woman who looked little more than a child from Chartres. If that was the case, he didn't mention it. He didn't mention anything really. They travelled mainly in silence.

There was a knock at the door and her stomach leapt.

"Come in." She tried to keep her voice steady as she stood up to receive Mr Pickard.

She'd forgotten what a large man he was – rotund, perhaps, rather than large. She gave a small curtsy and, after a polite exchange of greetings, he settled his huge frame with some difficulty onto the narrow seat of the only armchair in the room. Marie perched on the window seat facing him, impatient to hear what he had to say.

"It was a relief to find you spoke such perfect English," he said, which wasn't exactly the information she was longing to hear.

"I speak both French and English fluently." She couldn't help boasting a little, although Reverend Mother didn't approve of pride. "The convent of Our Lady is called the English convent, because it takes in a great many pupils from England. Why am I here?" If it sounded rude, she hadn't meant it to. She'd accepted the decision to go to England unquestioningly, but surely now she deserved some answers. "Have I family here in Harrogate? Someone has discovered a relative – a distant relative?"

He raised a hand to silence her and took a handkerchief out of his pocket to mop his brow. "I must say, I was startled by the suddenness of your departure from the convent."

"Yes, well…" She hesitated for a moment. He would never understand her true reasons, so she concentrated on the practical. "On my eighteenth birthday, Reverend Mother told me that the money left for my keep had come to an end. There was nothing remaining. I'm not sure why *you* were approached though. "

"I am a solicitor." John Pickard appeared to believe that would suffice as an answer. "What do you imagine your future will be now?"

"I don't know."

She'd always assumed she would just go on helping Sister Grace in the infirmary when she had finished her education. A thought struck her. "Is it Sister Grace who got in touch with you? Reverend Mother said I had no living relatives, but Sister Grace has. She was born in England. Are they offering me a home?"

He observed her for a moment in silence. "Trying to starve yourself was a very foolish thing to do, you know."

So, he'd been told. He would never understand what had driven her to do it, but Sister Grace did. Marie had heard an argument between her and Reverend Mother about it.

"Is it Sister Grace who arranged for me to come here?" She repeated her question. "Please tell me."

"I'm in no position to answer anything, Miss Montrecourt. I simply follow orders."

She was astonished. "You mean I'm not to be told anything?"

"All I *can* tell you is that provision has been made for you to stay here in England until your future has been decided. A small allowance has been arranged – by whom I am not at liberty to say – I have been appointed as your guardian to administer it. It will be paid until your future is settled. And because Harrogate is where I live, and I have been made legally responsible for you, Harrogate will be your new home. Reverend Mother has made her enquiries about my standing and has accepted that I am in a position to deal fairly with you. Have you any objections?"

She was at a loss how to respond.

"I know it must seem strange," said John Pickard, with unexpected sympathy, "but if you accept this allowance then I'm afraid you have to accept the terms that come with it. You must not question the source and you must obey my instructions. Do you accept these terms?"

A thought occurred to her. If Sister Grace *was* involved in making these arrangements, she wouldn't want Reverend Mother to know about it. That had to be the reason for this secrecy. She realised John Pickard was waiting impatiently for her reply.

"Have you any objections? If you're not happy with the arrangement, then I will have to return you to the convent."

She could never go back there. "I accept," she replied quickly.

He looked relieved. "I want your word that you will not do anything impetuous or rash, nor involve yourself with anything or anyone without first discussing it with me. Will you agree to that?"

"Yes." Marie looked out of the window. It had begun to snow. There was a piece of waste ground on the opposite side of the road and its grass was already hidden by a layer of white. She could see trees on the horizon, and in the foreground people were hurrying home to escape the weather. Carriages were driving past. It was a strange and beautiful world that she was about to enter. "I will place myself entirely in your hands, Mr Pickard. I will do as you wish. Where will I live?"

"Here, in this lodging house. It is run by Isabelle and Geoffrey Minton."

So she wouldn't be staying with the family of Sister Grace! When they'd arrived last night she'd been greeted by a woman with a kind face, but she'd been too tired to take much notice of her. The woman must have been Isabelle Minton.

"Geoffrey is a client of mine, and they are both very reliable and honest people. Please turn to Isabelle if you want to ask anything. She will advise you." He regarded her with a critical eye. "The first thing we must do is to send you to Leyland's department store to buy some new clothes. Isabelle Minton tells me the only garments you have with you are those you arrived in, which are most unsuitable. Isabelle will go with you. The bill will come directly to me. She has instructions not to spend beyond the limit I've set."

As he made a move to pick up his hat, Marie impetuously caught hold of his arm. "Will you promise to tell my benefactor how grateful I am?" She hoped he could at least do that.

He patted her hand awkwardly. "The only people who are now concerned in this matter are the two of us. I will be in touch, Miss Montrecourt, to further discuss your future when you've had time to settle in."

After John Pickard had left, Isabelle Minton called on Marie to make sure she was comfortable with the room. After sharing a dormitory with eleven other girls, having a room of her own was a luxury. She was to eat her meals downstairs in the dining room with the other guests. "And I would also ask you not to wander around Harrogate by yourself. We can walk out together, but it isn't acceptable for a young woman to go around unescorted."

Marie said she understood.

"Tomorrow I will take you to Leylands."

Marie found it impossible to sleep that night. So many questions and so few answers.

The next morning, excitement took over from anxiety as Marie and Isabelle walked to the department store.

"It isn't far," said Isabelle, finding it difficult to keep pace, "but slow down a little or I'll run out of breath before we get there!" She laughed.

Not knowing what to expect, having never been to a department store before, Marie was astonished by the palatial building. The entrance doors, guarded by a man in green and silver livery, opened out onto a richly carpeted salon that was lit by chandeliers. Glass cases displaying gloves, fans, hats, capes and muffs were placed on counters that overflowed with vases of flowers. A staircase led to the floor above, where fashionable gowns were on show. The floor above that was the furnishing and carpet department, but Marie had little interest in it.

She had never had new clothes before – just second-hand cast-offs from pupils who had outgrown them – and she was overwhelmed by the choice before her. Even when Isabelle made it clear that their budget was limited, she was still at a loss where to begin.

When she finally found her voice, she drove the shop assistants demented by darting around the store and trying on everything that was presented to her. Isabelle trailed behind, unsuccessfully attempting to curb her excitement. Eventually, however, Isabelle's calm guidance prevailed and, with her help, Marie became the proud owner of four dresses, a coat, a hat with feathers, boots, gloves, a chemise, corsets, nightdresses – in fact, everything that a young woman might need. She was frustrated when she learnt that the dresses and coat would have to be altered to fit, as she was small for her age. There would be a delay of a few days before they were delivered.

"Just a few days," Isabelle said, patting her hand. "Not so very long to wait."

Back in her room at Devonshire Place, Marie decided to occupy her time by finally unpacking the few possessions she'd brought with her. The most treasured of these was a notebook that Sister Grace had given her for helping in the infirmary. It contained recipes of herbal remedies. Sister Grace had also given her bottles of rare herbs and oils, and a Bunsen burner for heating up the ingredients if needed. There was also a battered tin box that had once belonged to her mother. She ran her fingers over its worn surface. All she knew about her mother was her name – Hortense Montrecourt – and that she'd arrived at the convent unexpectedly, giving birth to Marie within a week. She'd died without ever holding her baby.

Marie opened the lid, savouring the faint perfume of patchouli and lavender that it still released after all these years. Inside was Marie's only inheritance: a small piece of rock; a tarnished silver button, which had an engraved design that was far too worn to register anymore; and some scribbled words on a scrap of paper that had been found beside her mother after she died.

I cannot forget what I have done, what I have been made to do, it read. *May God forgive me, and forgive him too for making me do it. Protect my child.* Writing these words must have been her mother's last act, but Marie had never understood their meaning. She returned everything to the box and closed the lid.

*

Marie sat on the window seat and gazed out at the snow, which was now laying thickly over everything. Her clothes had arrived and she longed to show them off, but Isabelle was busy with her new baby and wanted to wait until the weather was more clement before going out.

"If you want to go to mass, Saint Peter's is just around the corner. Mr Pickard said he would be quite happy for you to go there unaccompanied. As long as you go straight there and come straight back again. We're chapel, I'm afraid."

Marie could see the church tower from her window, with its grey, stone spire pointing up to the sky. It was a reminder of the life she'd just escaped and brought back memories she'd rather forget. She told Isabelle she had no need for mass.

Still, she was very eager to explore her new surroundings. Being shut away in her room made her feel as if she was back behind the grey stone walls of the convent. She felt she would die if she didn't breathe fresh air soon. She could remember the route she and Isabelle had taken to the department store, which was in the middle of Harrogate. It wasn't far, and she'd seen one or two young women walking alone across The Stray unaccompanied. Surely there could be no harm in venturing out by herself. No one need know and, anyway, she wouldn't be away long. She slipped out unnoticed, her promise to Isabelle forgotten.

Despite the snow, Harrogate was crammed with visitors. Isabelle Minton had told her that the spa was a popular destination for the wealthy and fashionable, with its curative waters and brisk climate. She was excited by the energy of the place – the colour, the noise, the swirl of people pushing past her.

She suddenly caught sight of her reflection in a shop window. Gone was the child in the grey serge skirt and white blouse. Now, looking back at her, was an elegant and fashionable young woman – from the top of her hat, with its feathered brim set at a jaunty angle on her piled-up hair, to the tip of the brown leather boots that were peeping out from underneath the swirling skirts of her checked coat.

She glanced up and saw a man on a ladder. He was draping a gold banner over his shop front with the words: *HAPPY YULETIDE – WELCOME TO 1900 – THE NEW CENTURY* picked out in red. He saw Marie staring up at him and shouted "Happy Christmas" to her. She waved in reply and was so distracted that she was nearly mown down by one of the new automobiles, its approach having been muffled by the thick layer of snow covering the road. It was the sudden blare of the klaxon that finally drew her attention to it, making her leap for the safety of the pavement.

The sky now clouded over and it started to snow again. Marie took shelter in the doorway of a large shop, Ogden's the Silversmiths, just as a young man emerged from it with his arms full of parcels. He somehow managed to raise his hat to her.

"Hiding from the snow or waiting for me?"

She just had time to notice the lock of blond hair falling over his forehead and a pair of smiling blue eyes, before she lowered her gaze and quickly left the protective shelter of the doorway to avoid having to reply. Isabelle had warned her to beware of young men who tried to engage her in conversation.

The snow had started to fall faster now, turning the fur of her collar into a sparkling white. She was beginning to tire. Surely this was the second time she'd passed by the Royal Baths? She struggled to get her bearings. The gilded cupolas of the Grand Hotel were to her left, and dominating the skyline to the right was the Hotel Majestic. However, this was of very little help seeing as she had no clear idea of where she was heading. She began to think that she had been foolish to go out on her own.

"You do keep cropping up, don't you?"

She glanced behind her, startled by the unexpected voice. It was the man who had raised his hat to her in Ogden's doorway. Had he been following her?

"You look lost," he said. "Can I help?"

"No. No, thank you."

The man interpreted her response as an invitation to join her, however, and fell into step by her side. Alarmed, she took the first turning right and found herself in a dark alleyway. It was deserted.

She started to walk faster. Was he still following? She could hear footsteps. Was it him? She glanced around and saw a figure, but couldn't see who it was. The footsteps were getting closer. She quickened her pace, her heart beating painfully. There was a shop straight ahead. Increasing her speed until she was almost running, she shot through the shop door with little thought for dignity – her hat was awry and her coat was slipping from her shoulders. Weak with relief, she collapsed against some shelving behind her.

"Can I help you?"

The brisk query, which had come so unexpectedly out of the gloom, startled her. Marie turned around to find a woman looking at her enquiringly. She was wearing a plain white blouse with leg of mutton sleeves and a severely cut black skirt. Marie knew she was being rude, but she couldn't help staring at the woman's hair. It was extremely short. It wasn't roughly cut like the nuns' hair but had been tailored into the nape of the neck like a man's. Her expression was severe and unwelcoming.

"I… I just…" Marie glanced around her. What kind of place was this? There were ancient looking prints on the walls and shelf upon shelf of old books. It must be a bookshop.

The woman raised a quizzical eyebrow. "The cat appears to have got your tongue."

Marie made some attempt to straighten her hat and regain her composure. "No. Not at all. I didn't know; I didn't realise. I came..." She was beginning to find the woman's steady gaze unnerving.

"You're very welcome to just look around, you know." An unexpected smile softened the woman's face, making it a great deal less severe. Her tone was abrupt, but her voice was low and that counteracted its harshness. "I'm Daphne Senior. I own the shop." She held out her hand.

"Marie Montrecourt." The woman's handshake was firm and businesslike.

"So, got your breath back yet? What brought you in? You're very young to be wandering around on your own."

"I'm eighteen," said Marie, taking offence.

Daphne made a mock gesture of apology. "I didn't realise."

"And I just took shelter in here."

"Really? Shelter from the snow?" The woman seemed to be teasing her. "You catapulted in here as though all the hounds of Hell were after you."

"I was being followed. By a man."

Daphne crossed swiftly to the door and peered out. "Can't see anyone. Whoever it was, he appears to have thought better of coming in here after you." She closed the door and returned to Marie. "So, Montrecourt – that's a French name, isn't it? And if I'm not mistaken there's the slightest hint of an accent."

"I'm told my English is very good." The woman was still regarding her quizzically. "I think I must go."

"No, Marie Montrecourt, I won't let you go. You're brightening up an extremely dull day for me. I won't let you just slip away. After all this excitement, you need a cup of tea. The English remedy for everything. And then you can tell me more about yourself."

"Oh no, really..." Marie had no wish to be cross-examined.

"I insist. Follow me." It was a command, not a request, so Marie obeyed as Daphne led the way into a small backroom that was separated from the shop by a curtain.

By the time the second cup of tea had been poured, the atmosphere between the two women had become much more relaxed. Daphne had done most of the talking and Marie was astonished by the breadth of her knowledge about, what seemed like, everything.

"Do you smoke?"

Marie realised with a shock that she was being offered a cigarette. "My goodness! No. No, thank you." She'd never seen a woman smoke before. Fascinated, she watched as Daphne placed the cigarette in an amber holder. After lighting it, she blew out a perfect smoke ring.

"You look like one of Mesmer's patients. Quite transfixed," said Daphne with a laugh and she inhaled deeply again.

Marie, embarrassed to appear so naive, stood up. "I think I'd better go."

"Have I upset you? I'm sorry." Daphne quickly stubbed out the cigarette in her saucer. "It's childish of me, but I can't resist shocking people. Stay a little longer. I'd rather enjoy your company than smoke a cigarette, believe me. It's surely better sitting in here with me than walking the streets of Harrogate in the snow?" Marie hesitated. "I have an idea. Instead of rushing off, why don't you look around the shop? I have books on everything and anything. You'd enjoy that, wouldn't you? Won't say another word, I promise."

"I haven't... I didn't bring any money with me." Marie had only intended to walk around the town and not go into any of the shops. Besides, she had no money of her own.

"Choose any book you like. Call in another day to pay me. In fact, choose two books. I'm feeling generous."

The sight of so many books had the same effect on Marie

that a casket of jewels would have on a thief. She couldn't resist them, and she could always ask Mr Pickard if he would pay Miss Senior for them later. He had said there was a small sum set aside in the allowance for necessities. Surely he would agree that those necessities included books. She wandered along the shelves, pulling out novels, books of poetry, biographies. Two books! Only two!

The shop bell clattered and Marie turned to see two young women enter arm in arm. They were coarse-featured and loud-voiced, with shawls over their heads and clogs on their feet. They were hardly dressed for the cold. She watched them curiously, as they seemed completely out of place. Daphne appeared to know them. She crossed over to them and words were exchanged between the three of them in whispers. Daphne then glanced towards Marie and again said something to the women that Marie couldn't hear. Whatever it was, it prompted them to disappear into the back of the shop.

Daphne walked over to her. "I need to close now. Found anything you like yet?"

Marie held out a book of poems by the Romantics and a short history of Harrogate. It was obvious that she was being dismissed because there was no comment on her choice from Daphne and the books were swiftly turned into a parcel.

"Now, tell me where you're staying, Marie Montrecourt, and I'll give you directions on how to get back there."

"Devonshire Place."

"That's not very far away at all – almost around the corner. Five minutes is all it should take." She quickly scribbled down directions and almost bundled Marie out into the snow, turning the 'Open' sign to 'Closed' and locking the door.

Curiosity overcame Marie and she couldn't help glancing back. Through the glass panel, she saw the two women emerge from the back of the shop. Daphne crossed over to them and embraced them both warmly. Their heads drew close together and the trio seemed locked in a deep conversation. But then the snow began to fall heavily again and curtained them from view.

As Marie entered Devonshire Place, she almost bumped into a man who was standing in the hallway. He was handing his damp overcoat to the Minton's housekeeper and stared at her as she passed. She then saw Geoffrey Minton come out of the parlour to greet the man, before she scurried up the stairs, anxious to avoid any awkward questions as to where she had been.

When she reached the door to her room, she turned and saw that the man was still staring after her. For a moment, she was silhouetted in the doorway. Then she closed the door, shutting out the light and leaving only darkness behind.

CHAPTER TWO

Nothing would have dragged Evelyn Harringdon back to the country today, except his need to settle some of his more pressing gambling debts. He was therefore left with no option but to travel to the family home outside London, throw himself on his father's mercy and endure the contempt he knew would rain down on him. Eventually, only once he'd been made to crawl, his father would give him the money he so needed. The family name must not be sullied by scandal.

Evelyn acknowledged that his feelings towards his father were complex. He admired him and he was in awe of him, but he didn't *love* him. What he found inexplicable then was that, despite everything, he still craved his approval. He was twenty-five years old and should have grown out of that by now. His father was, and always had been, a cold, unemotional man who claimed the moral high ground and defended it with zeal. Evelyn had struggled to please him for years, even when it had become obvious he'd never succeed. So, instead, he had created a new life for himself in London where he had become a prominent member of the fashionable set. They valued him for his charm and his skill at the gambling tables. At home, he was viewed as a failure.

As he turned his motor car into the drive of Ardington Hall, the house came into sight through the snow-covered birch trees and he was again struck by its beauty. The creamy Cotswold stone suddenly turned gold as it was lit by an unexpected burst of winter sunlight. The house had been a gift to the Harringdon family from a grateful William of Orange, but no one was very clear what exactly the family had done to deserve it. The sprawling mansion, with its graceful arches and soaring towers, had been gratefully received.

The gift had also included acres of rolling Cotswold countryside. Evelyn's mother ran the land with such efficiency that his father was able to spend most of his time in London carrying out his duties in the House of Lords. However, over the last few weeks, he'd been absent from the Lords.

Evelyn swung the bright blue Renault in a wide circle and pulled up at the stone steps that swept in an arc to the front door. He wondered why Wilson hadn't come out to greet him. He then noticed that the shutters were still closed even though it was already midday. Once out of the car, he walked up the steps and pushed open the heavy front door. It took him some time to adjust to the darkness of the hallway.

"Wilson?"

He looked around for the butler. He then heard a flurry of movement upstairs, followed by voices. One of these he recognised as belonging to his mother, but the other voices were male and unfamiliar. He took the stairs two at a time and realised they were coming from his father's bedroom. He knocked on the door.

"Mother? Father?"

There was a sharp intake of breath and then silence. After some time, his mother finally spoke behind the door: "You weren't expected, Evie."

"No. I wanted to surprise you." He had obviously managed to do that.

She still didn't open the door. "Go downstairs, Evelyn. I'll join you in the blue drawing room."

He frowned. Her voice sounded strained. "Is everything all right?"

"I'll join you in the drawing room," she repeated.

He did as he was told and poured himself a brandy. He heard the front door open. Curiously, he crossed to the window that overlooked the drive. He saw his mother on the steps, talking to a man with his back to the window. He was a large man and wore a greatcoat to protect him from the cold. He turned, and Evelyn caught a glimpse of the round circle of his face that was set on the even larger circle of his body – a child's representation of a figure. One of the servants was helping him into a carriage. As it pulled away, his mother turned and saw that he'd been observing them. She headed inside.

He wasn't particularly close to his mother. She once told him she could never forgive him for his reluctance to emerge into the world. Harriet, his younger sibling, had been much more amenable, and her birth had been far less traumatic.

As she entered the drawing room, she closed the door behind her. "I'm sorry, Evie. You've arrived at a very distressing time. There is no easy way to tell you this, so I will simply come to the point." She seemed to be struggling with her emotions, which was something Evelyn had rarely witnessed. "I'm sorry to inform you that your father is dying."

"Good God." His exclamation was involuntary and his mother chose to ignore it. He'd always thought of his father as indestructible. "I suppose I should go to him." He started towards the hall.

"No." Her voice stopped him. "No, Evie. He's dying of typhoid. It's highly contagious. Dr Oliver is with him. On his instructions no one else is to be allowed into the room. He was very clear about it."

"You were in there, Mother, and that gentleman who left in such a hurry. Who was he?"

She ignored his question. "I'm his wife, Evie. It's my duty to be with him. I am nursing him with the doctor's help. No one else needs to take the risk."

"I'm his son. I have a duty to him, too."

His only son and heir. It would be foolish to risk the

contagion. I would ask you to accept my decision – it is your father's, too, of course."

Evelyn nodded his head obediently and she swept out of the room. There was a discreet knock on the door and the butler, Wilson, entered. He'd been with the family ever since Evelyn could remember. He looked distressed and weary.

"Can I get you something, sir? I apologise for not being in the hall when you arrived."

Evelyn waved aside his apology. "Is it serious with my father?"

"It seems so, sir."

"Have you seen him?"

"Not since he was taken ill. Can I get you something, sir?" he repeated.

"No. No, thank you, but perhaps you can ask one of the servants to collect my case from the motor car. I'll go up to my room."

The eyes of his ancestors watched impassively from their carved frames as he climbed past them to the first floor. He heard the murmur of voices from his father's room again. This time, he knew it was Dr Oliver who was in there with his mother. Suddenly, someone else spoke.

"He is watching. Bury – deep…"

Surely that couldn't be his father? The voice was too querulous – too feeble.

Evelyn hesitated outside the door of the bedroom, then quietly tried the handle. It was locked. He slipped into the antechamber next to it, but the connecting door to the bedroom was also locked. Uncertain what to do next, he glanced around. Something caught his attention, something out of place. He stood up and walked to the sofa. One of his father's shoes was lying abandoned on the floor, just the one. One single, solitary shoe – black and highly polished, with the lace neatly tied. His father was such a meticulous man. It was absurd, but the sight of it brought Evelyn close to tears.

His father had begun speaking again. It was painful to listen to. "Montre…" What was he struggling to say? Silence fell.

After a moment, the door from the bedroom was unlocked and his mother emerged into the antechamber looking pale and worn. "It's over. He died in peace. You can see him now. Dr Oliver has said not to touch him or to go too close." She followed her son back into the room.

It was dark, so dark that Evelyn could barely see his father. What he did see, however, shocked him. The face that had inspired a generation had, in death, collapsed into the lined face of a defenceless old man. The nation's hero, whose approval *he* had longed for, was now nothing more than an empty shell, and his approval would never be won.

On the table beside the bed, there was a letter. It was in his father's hand. He could just make out a name. Montrecourt, was it? Was that what his father had been trying to say – the name Montrecourt?

He glanced at Dr Oliver. "Was he in pain?"

"I increased his intake of morphine," replied the doctor.

"He had been on it before?"

"Ever since he was wounded at Majuba."

Evelyn glanced back at his father. He hadn't realised. He frowned – something was missing from the table by the bedside. The letter he'd just seen wasn't there anymore. He looked enquiringly at his mother, but her face was expressionless.

"I suggest you go to your room, Evie, and tidy up after your journey," she said. "Dinner will be served at the usual time. I'm afraid you will be on your own. I have no appetite."

"No, neither have I," said Evelyn. She nodded and left. He

turned to Dr Oliver. "Was there a letter on the table beside my father's bed?"

Dr Oliver looked nonplussed. "I'm so sorry, I have no idea."

"It's not important."

With one last glance towards his father, Evelyn left the room.

CHAPTER THREE

"No matter how brightly the sun shines, its warmth and light never penetrates any of the shops in Market Alley, does it?"

In the small backroom of the bookshop, standing in front of the cracked mirror over the sink, Marie unplaited her hair and let it fall in a curtain to her waist. Daphne, perched on the edge of the desk, reached out a hand to stroke the silk strands, letting them trickle through her fingers. Marie's hair was cool to the touch and filled the air with the scent of lavender and patchouli. It was a pleasant change from the smell of dusty volumes and old leather.

"It's the colour of amber, your hair," she murmured.

"So why did you choose to open a shop here of all places?" Marie said. "It's always so dark. It must put a lot of people off."

"Those who search for knowledge are never put off by darkness. You aren't, are you?" Daphne replied. "Besides, it suits me here. It's private. No one interferes with me. Come here and let me do it. You're not having much success, are you?"

Silence fell as Daphne took the brush and began to gently untangle the knots in Marie's hair.

Although her first venture into Harrogate unaccompanied had been disapproved of by the Mintons, Marie had managed to persuade them to let her repeat it by pointing out that there was no real alternative. She couldn't remain shut away in her room and they were too busy to spare her any time. They agreed reluctantly, but insisted that she must return well before dark. Revelling in her newfound freedom, she'd become a regular visitor at Daphne's bookshop, calling in at least three or four times a week. She decided against telling the Mintons about her new friend because she sensed they wouldn't approve.

Daphne inhabited such a different world. It was full of challenging ideas she'd never thought of before, and Daphne spoke about them with such passion that they caught fire in Marie's imagination. She always left the shop with arms piled high with pamphlets about the conditions of the working class, or women's right to vote, or articles protesting against women's economic dependence, and she read every one of them avidly.

Mr John Pickard had called on her that morning to inform her that he'd arranged a small dinner party in her honour, which would be held that evening at Devonshire Place. The dinner was to be hosted by Isabelle and Geoffrey Minton, and attending would be a few of their friends and neighbours. The idea was to widen Marie's circle of acquaintances. She had very little choice but to accept graciously, although she would far rather remain in her room reading Daphne's pamphlets.

Daphne now broke the silence that had fallen between them. "By the way, did you read the leaflet I gave you last week – about Bridgewater?"

"Yes, I did."

She'd been deeply moved by it. Daphne was its author, and it was inspired by an article published three years ago by a woman called Annie Besant, which had attacked the working conditions of the match girls in London. The dyes used at Bridgewater were destroying the health of the factory women in the same way, and Daphne had quoted some distressing examples.

"Are you thinking about taking the same action that Annie Besant took with the match girls?" Marie asked. She'd read that Besant had led a successful march through London. "I mean the circumstances are very much the same, aren't they? I think it's very courageous of you to take a stand."

Daphne's reply was, as usual, sharp and to the point. "My courage doesn't enter into it; it's my judgment that counts. I need to be careful how I advise the women. It's true that the poison is slowly destroying them. It's also true that when they die or they're too ill to work, no one will care. Someone else will step forward and take their place, and the wheels of industry will just grind on. Still, any wrong move on my part and they could suffer even more."

"But you *are* thinking about marching against the factory?" Marie had already pictured herself by Daphne's side, marching through the crowd-lined streets of Harrogate with everyone cheering them on.

"I hope we can avoid it. I hope that reason will win." Marie tried not to show her disappointment, but Daphne knew her well enough to be aware of it. "You have no idea what trouble a march might bring down on the heads of the women, Marie. Harrogate isn't London. The wrong action could hurt them far more than it helps them. Confrontation is the last thing these women need. Besides, I've not yet exhausted all other avenues. I'm writing to the other factory owners, asking them to bring pressure to bear."

Marie thought of the stand she'd made at the convent when Reverend Mother had tried to force her down a path that would surely destroy her. It was actions not words that had prevented it from happening. "Will letters change their mind?"

With a sigh, Daphne handed the hairbrush back to her. "I don't know. There's no easy answer. But I don't intend to involve the women directly unless I really have to." She returned to the task of sorting out orders, thereby putting an end to the discussion.

As Marie pinned up her hair, she heard Daphne mutter

one of her expletives. "Damn. Dr Stillwood's cancelled his order for the medical almanac. He's found a copy somewhere else. It's already arrived, hasn't it? Can you check that pile of books on the floor near the door? They're the new deliveries."

Marie spotted a heavy volume that was bound in red leather. With an effort, she extracted it from the pile. "*Farnsworth's Medical Dictionary*? Yes, it's here."

"I'll have to send it back to the publisher. That's the second time that man has cancelled an order at the last moment."

Curious, Marie started leafing through the book. It contained details of various remedies for a multitude of illnesses. There were some words she didn't understand, but, thanks to Sister Grace's training, she could make sense of most of it. She became aware that Daphne was watching her.

"You have an interest in medicine?" she asked.

"In the convent, Sister Grace let me help her in the infirmary. She used natural remedies, though, so nothing as complicated as these. She wasn't schooled, but she taught me how to make syrup from coltsfoot to cure a cough, and how to create a tincture from arnica to calm a bruise. She gave me her notebook full of remedies, jars of herbs and a Bunsen burner to heat up the mixtures. I brought them with me from France. I'm not sure what I'll do with them."

"Perhaps it's a skill you should cultivate."

"I'm not certain it's a skill I have. Reverend Mother certainly didn't think so."

Daphne set down her pen. "So, what happened to you at this convent of yours? You never talk about it." Daphne saw Marie's hesitation and made a move to pick up her pen again. "Of course, if you'd rather not tell me I completely understand."

"No, it's all right." They so rarely talked about personal things – perhaps this was the moment to remedy that. "It's just that it wasn't a very nice place. There was a lot of cruelty

– punishment rather than prayers. I didn't fit in there, I didn't need Reverend Mother to point that out me, but she made it clear from the beginning it was her opinion. The problem was, she needed the money that was paying for my education, but she resented having to take it. She must have had mixed feelings when that source of income came to an end."

"Was that when you came to England?"

"Not straightaway. I had no choice but to stay there; I had nowhere else to go – no family or home. I was willing to work for my keep. Sister Grace would have been happy for me to go on helping her in the infirmary, but that wouldn't do for Reverend Mother. Working on the farm and in the kitchens, I was told, was to be my future. There were two girls already working there. One of them was simple in the head; the other one had grown sick working from dawn until dusk without a break. She'd tried to run away but had nowhere else to go either. When she was returned by the authorities, no one in the convent felt any pity for her or gave her any help – and that, I'm ashamed to say, included me. It wasn't until I was threatened with the same fate that I felt any sympathy at all. You must think me very selfish."

"No." Daphne reached out and squeezed her hand reassuringly. "Who am I to judge? I still don't understand how you arrived in England, though."

"Neither do I really."

"But you didn't end up working in the kitchens."

"If I'd allowed that to happen, I knew I would become invisible to everyone. I would cease to exist, just like the two girls. It would be my life until the day I died. There had to be some other way, so I refused to eat and then became sick. Sister Grace convinced Revered Mother it would damage the good name of the convent if anything happened to me."

"Making a stand on your own – now, that *did* take courage," Daphne said, quoting Marie's words back to her.

"It was desperation. I have Sister Grace to thank for saving me. She must have had money somewhere, even though it should have belonged to the convent. I think she got in touch with Mr Pickard and arranged for me to be sent to England, and she's paying an allowance for me until my future here is settled. I owe her everything."

"She sounds too good to be true," said Daphne, dryly. "And who will help the other two girls?"

Marie flushed. "You see how selfish I am? I didn't even think about them. No one will help them, probably. They were unmarried mothers whose families had abandoned them. Their babies had been taken away from them and Reverend Mother said they were doing penance for their sins."

"And what was your sin?"

"I don't know. Being born, perhaps."

"I've never had to struggle. I've led a privileged life. My father's a mathematician – he teaches at Oxford. He made sure I had a good education, so he sent me to Girton." She realised Marie had never heard of it. "A ladies' college. I was an exemplary student and a great deal was expected of me. Many of the girls from Girton went into teaching, you know. One of them is now headmistress of Hull Ladies' College. My father would have been proud of me if I'd done that."

"Isn't he proud of you now?"

"No, I shamed him. I followed my heart, not my head." Daphne paused and Marie sensed the memory was still painful to her. "I followed Dora. I left home because of her. My father didn't approve of our friendship. He wanted to separate us, but nobody could do that – except, as it turned out, Dora herself."

The shadows in the backroom were lengthening and the sun was beginning to set. Silence fell and Marie didn't move, not wanting to break the intimacy of the moment.

"Dora was my closest friend at Girton and when we left we set up house together. My father made life hell for us both, so she took a job here in Harrogate. She said she didn't want me to suffer for our relationship, but I followed her and took the flat above this shop. When the shop came up for sale, I bought it using the allowance my father grudgingly gave me. I insisted that Dora move in with me. I wasn't ashamed of our friendship."

"Was *she* ashamed?" Marie asked.

"She must have been. She took up a teaching post in India a year ago, and I realised she was using India as a means of escaping from me. She couldn't bear the disapproval that surrounded us – disapproval of a friendship that must never be acknowledged. So, she ran away from it all and I stayed here. After that I became involved with the women at the factory and suddenly my own future didn't seem so important."

The shop doorbell rang and the intimacy of the mood was broken. "Well, there's a reprieve for you from all this maudlin sentimentality."

Daphne went through to serve her customer while Marie remained where she was. She felt better having shared everything with Daphne. Perhaps the pull of the confessional would always remain with her.

The voices from the shop now caught her attention. They became shriller. It was a man's voice: "If you try a trick like that again, I'll have the police on to you or worse." Daphne's voice, firm but angry, replied: "What he's doing is illegal. He's paying those women a pittance to work in appalling conditions. I intend to go on making a nuisance of myself until people start to take notice."

The man then said something in a low voice that Marie couldn't hear. The shop bell jangled as he left and then there was silence.

Marie tentatively pulled aside the curtain that separated the backroom from the shop. "Is everything all right?" Daphne, looking pale and shaken, pushed past her and leant against the desk. Marie pulled forward the chair. "Sit down," she ordered and, for once, Daphne obeyed. Marie always carried a small phial of Sal Volatile in her pocket. "Here. Inhale." She waved it under Daphne's nose. "Is that better?"

"Yes, yes, yes." Daphne pushed aside the phial tetchily. "I'm all right. It's not the first time something like this has happened. I don't suppose it will be the last. It's worth it," she said, fiercely. "It's all worth it. I know it is."

Marie had never seen Daphne so shaken. She always seemed to be in control. "Was that man from the factory?" Daphne nodded. "Was he threatening you?" Daphne nodded again, and for the first time it struck Marie how dangerous it might be to stand up to Bridgewater Dyes.

After a moment, Daphne pulled herself to her feet. Her mouth was set in a thin line of determination.

"That decides it. We will march. We have no choice. Reasoning with them is obviously not going to work."

It was relief to see the return of the old Daphne. "Then I want to march with you. I want to be a part of it, too." As Daphne opened her mouth to refuse, Marie quickly added, "After all, you keep making me read all these pamphlets. We can't let it go to waste."

It made Daphne smile. "Very well, Marie Montrecourt. Can you call by the shop tomorrow? We need to start on the banners."

"I will be there," Marie promised. "I won't let you down."

*

That evening, she stood outside the door of the dining room at Devonshire Place, listening to the rise and fall of voices, and wished herself anywhere but there. She felt no more like exchanging small talk with a group of people she didn't know than she felt like jumping over the moon. She wondered how they would react if she told them about the march, but Daphne had made it clear to tell no one. To be effective, it needed the element of surprise.

As she entered the conversation stopped and Isabelle moved towards her, drawing her further inside. Introductions were made to Alice and George Smith, who were neighbours of the Mintons. Marie thought they seemed an ill-matched couple. He had the round-eyed, permanently surprised look of an owl and his wife had the pointed features of a ferret. Martin Godson was introduced next. He was a pleasant, fresh-faced young man who worked for Geoffrey's brother, Stanley. His wife, Jenny, seemed equally pleasant. She was then finally introduced to Stanley himself, Geoffrey's elder brother. He stood up awkwardly to shake her by the hand.

"Good to see you again, Miss Montrecourt."

She couldn't recall ever having met him before, but then she remembered the man she'd passed in the hall after her first visit to the bookshop. "Yes, of course," she murmured, politely.

She took her place at the table and the conversation revived, allowing her mind to drift back to the march.

"And all the ingredients for this dinner have been provided by Stanley."

Marie realised that Isabelle was addressing her. "I'm sorry?"

"Stanley owns The Emporium in Prospect Crescent."

Geoffrey joined in. "It has a reputation for being Harrogate's highest of high-class grocers. You should visit it sometime, Miss Montrecourt. Very grand; very fashionable!"

"I should like to." Marie glanced at Stanley, but his eyes slid shyly away from her. He struck her as rather a sombre man, a man who had forgotten how to smile. His moustache drooped sadly over his small, pink mouth and his sandy-coloured hair sat sparsely on his head. She guessed his age to be about forty.

"I believe you're French, aren't you, Miss Montrecourt?"

She realised that Alice Smith was regarding her with bright, beady eyes.

"Yes, I am."

"You speak very good English – for a foreigner. I'd never have known it."

"Ah, but there is something different about her."

She was aware that George Smith hadn't taken his eyes from her since she'd joined them, but she'd been trying to ignore it.

"Very charming," he added.

His wife frowned, while Marie blushed and looked down at her plate. She was wearing the blue, silk chiffon gown that Isabelle had chosen for her on their visit to the department store, and the gas lamp behind her had turned her hair into a halo of red and gold. She realised that Stanley Minton was now staring at her. He became nervous when he saw she was aware of it, and patted his mouth with his napkin.

"I'm sorry. The colour… of your dress… it reminds me of the Blue Morpho." Marie had no idea what he was talking about, and Geoffrey groaned as his brother continued. "Morpho Peleides, it's a rare butterfly. I bought one from a collector many years ago. The wings are exactly that shade of blue. Sometimes I remove the pin that anchors it to its velvet pad and I hold it up to the light. Then the wings become opalescent."

Marie had no idea how to respond, so she simply smiled politely.

"Stanley, not everyone shares your obsession with dead insects," said Geoffrey.

"No, I'm sorry. Forgive me."

Stanley flushed and patted his mouth again, and Marie felt sorry for him. She helped herself to some of the poached salmon that was laid out on the silver platter in the centre of the table. It was garnished with cucumber and watercress. She declined Geoffrey's offer of wine.

"Do you like animals, Miss Montrecourt?"

Stanley's second attempt at conversation struck her as equally odd. "Er… yes. Yes, I do."

"Stanley does," Geoffrey interrupted. "My brother breeds St Bernard dogs, you see, Miss Montrecourt. He shows them, too. He won a prize for one of his dogs once, didn't you, Stanley? He's more obsessed by them than he is by The Emporium and butterflies, and that's saying something." As the housekeeper came in to clear the dinner plates, he noticed his brother had barely touched his food. "You're not eating much, Stanley. Not like you."

"No. Well, I still have this ache in my gums. Toothache," he explained to Marie. "It makes eating difficult."

"Oh, I have the perfect cure for that, Mr Minton," she said. "It's a tincture of cloves. I brought it from France with me. I made it myself."

"I should think the patented cures will do him just as well, my dear," said Alice, quickly.

"Really, you made it yourself?" Stanley almost smiled. "Then I should very much like to try it. Thank you."

"You made it yourself, Miss Montrecourt?" Alice's husband leant towards her. "How very clever of you."

"I'm sure Miss Montrecourt means well," Alice interrupted, "but I wouldn't take the risk of trying it if I were you, Stanley. Heaven knows what it might contain."

Marie chose to ignore the comment. "I will make sure you have a jar before you leave, Mr Minton."

★

The next day Marie arrived at the bookshop, eager to start work on the banners. The bell jangled as she went through the door.

"Daphne?"

Hearing a noise from the backroom, she pushed through the curtain.

The stench made her realise that Daphne was not alone. She saw a woman sitting in the cane chair just under the cracked mirror. It was hard to tell her age. She was wearing a shawl over a thin calico dress that seemed to be held together by patches. Her hair was covered by a bonnet and her boots were bound by rags. The factory women were well dressed in comparison. She seemed unable to sit still because she was forever scratching. Marie saw that her arms were covered with sores and bites. On the floor by the side of her was a blacking box filled with cottons and tapes and stay laces.

"This is Sal," said Daphne. "She sometimes calls in to see me when she's in the area – to get warm and have a cup of tea."

This was obviously one of Daphne's good causes. "I'll pour it," Marie said, eager to help.

"Life hasn't been kind to her," Daphne continued, always keen to point out the harsh realities of life. "You don't mind me talking about it?" Sal shook her head as she gratefully accepted the tea from Marie. "She lost her job as a seamstress a year ago. Soon after, her father died and her mother couldn't afford to keep her. There were six younger children to provide for, so Sal left home. However, she couldn't find any work. She's been hawking wares around the streets of Harrogate ever since."

"That must be hard."

The girl's face was pale and she seemed very weak.

"If she's lucky," said Daphne, "and she's made some sales, then she can afford to pay for the share of a bed in a lodging house – which probably has room for two families but houses ten. If she's unlucky, then she applies for a chit to stay in the workhouse at Knaresborough."

"I don't like the workhouse." Sal spoke for the first time and Marie was surprised by her voice. It was pleasant and low, with only a hint of a local accent. "You have to pick oakum."

Marie looked at Daphne enquiringly. "It's rope that has to be unpicked inch by inch, but as it's tarred and knotted it rips the fingers to pieces."

Marie glanced at Sal's hands, but they were so dirty it was difficult to see what its effect had been.

Aware of her glance, the girl said, "It's impossible to keep neat and clean when there's nowhere to wash and no money for clothes. It was different when I was working. I used to work at Leyland's, the department store. I was one of their best seamstresses."

Marie was too astonished to speak for a moment. She remembered the young women who had served her in the store when she'd visited with Isabelle Minton. "Why did you leave?"

Sal looked away, so Daphne answered for her. "The owner's son made advances that Sal rejected. Her work soon began to be criticised and she was eventually asked to leave. There was no appeal."

For the first time, Marie noticed that Sal was extremely pretty. All she had initially registered was the sorry figure. "That's dreadful."

"A young woman on her own is seen as fair game," Sal murmured.

"Wasn't there anyone you could turn to?" Marie asked.

"No."

"No other work?"

"The choice is limited without any references – and, anyway, how do you live while you look?" Her eyes were a deep blue, Marie noticed. "A few weeks, even a few days, living in a workhouse turns you into scum and then no one sees any good in you. All they see is the dirt and the rags."

Marie flushed, remembering the two girls at the convent. She'd been guilty of that. She'd paid them no attention and given no thought to their feelings, until she was threatened with the same fate.

Daphne turned to her. "You see, that's what could happen to the factory women if the march fails and they lose their jobs. They're decent, respectable women whose families can't support them. If they fall, who is going to catch them?"

"I don't know," Marie murmured. She'd been lucky – she had had Sister Grace to catch her.

"Thanks for the tea," Sal said. "I'd better get on."

Marie murmured a goodbye and her thoughts turned to her own future. She hadn't heard anything further from Mr Pickard.

When Daphne returned from seeing her visitor out, Marie could see she was angry. "And she's just one of the many, Marie, who struggle just to survive. Heaven help anyone who makes a mistake, because this world is an unforgiving place. No one gives any thought to those who fall on hard times. It's a thin line that divides those who fall and those who don't – anyone of us can fall foul of it."

"Yes." Marie understood that only too well.

"Let's leave the banners for today, shall we?" Daphne pushed aside the paint. "I don't feel like doing it, do you?"

Marie shook her head. "Not really."

"I don't know if I'm helping or harming the women by organising this march. I only know things can't be left as they are."

They sat side by side in the backroom of the shop, staring bleakly into space. Neither of them were sure of the answer.

*

When Marie arrived back at Devonshire Place in the afternoon, she was still lost in thought and almost bumped into the housekeeper in the hallway.

"Mr Pickard, miss. He's in the front parlour with Mr Geoffrey. He told me to tell you to go straight in."

Marie could hear Geoffrey's voice through the closed door. "So what do I gain from it?" he was saying. "You're expecting a lot from me."

She couldn't hear Mr Pickard's reply. She knocked.

"Yes?" Geoffrey called out.

"It's Marie," she called back. "Mr Pickard asked to see me."

There was a pause and then Geoffrey came out. He nodded towards the room. "He's in there," he said, pushing past her.

She could see the solicitor standing with one foot on the fireplace, his round, pink face was a deep shade of puce. Had he discovered about the march? Was he angry? He attempted a smile when she entered and his tone became avuncular.

"Miss Montrecourt, sit down. I need to speak to you."

She sat on the edge of the chair, facing him. He cleared his throat. "I believe you've made a friend of a woman called Daphne Senior. It concerns me."

She was astonished. How had he learnt about that?

"Harrogate is quite a small place. Nothing goes unnoticed, and people like Daphne Senior make themselves very conspicuous."

"I'm not sure why my friendship with Daphne would give you so much concern." There had been no mention of the march, so it couldn't be because of that.

"I appreciate you've been left alone a great deal since you arrived in Harrogate and I am intending to remedy that by introducing you to suitable people. I know of Miss Senior and she isn't a suitable companion for a young woman with no experience of the world."

Marie's first instinct was to fly to the defence of her friend, but she waited to see if he had anything further to say.

"Also, you should not be going out alone."

"But times are changing, Mr Pickard. The world is changing."

"Not here, not in Harrogate."

"Even here." She was going to add that Daphne was proof of it, but Mr Pickard didn't give her the chance.

"Miss Montrecourt, you have no experience of the world, so whether or not it is changing is something you're not able to judge. I have asked Mr and Mrs Minton to arrange some outings for you, but they must be accompanied. Stanley Minton has agreed to escort you. He's a very busy man, so it is kind that he has agreed to do so."

She was taken aback at this and was not sure how to feel. Why on earth would Stanley Minton agree to be her escort? Whatever the reason, however, her main concern now was Mr Pickard's opinion of her friend. "I'm grateful, but I still don't understand why I can't see Daphne."

"You recall our agreement when you accepted the terms of the allowance? I'm asking you not to see Miss Senior. It is for the sake of your own reputation. I'm afraid I must insist on it. You know the alternative?"

To be sent back to the convent. After a moment she gave a brief nod of acceptance, crossing her fingers behind her back as she did so. The girls at the convent always said that God knew you didn't mean to keep your promise if you crossed your fingers behind your back when making it. Nothing would prevent her from seeing Daphne again, and after the march she was certain that everyone would admire her friend's courage and integrity as much as she did.

CHAPTER FOUR

Evelyn stood on the steps of St Paul's Cathedral between his mother and Lord Renfrew, his father's oldest friend, and bowed his head as a frail Queen Victoria was helped into her carriage by the Prince of Wales. There were a few cheers from the huge crowd as she raised a hand to wave, but most stood in respectful silence. They were aware that they had come to mourn the passing of the Hero of Majuba, not to cheer their queen. Not since Lord Nelson had a man achieved such adulation from the people and now Evelyn faced the daunting prospect of stepping into his shoes. Whether he liked it or not, he had become head of one of the most prominent families in the country. And whether he wanted them or not, he now had responsibilities. He could already feel them settling heavily on his shoulders. During all the pomp, all the ceremony of today, one question was uppermost in his mind: was he capable?

Reading all the tributes to his father had only increased his feelings of inadequacy. *The London Chronicle* had written:

There is to be a memorial service to celebrate the life of Sir Gordon Harringdon, known as the Hero of Majuba. He gave this country back its pride during the British Army's terrible defeat at Majuba Hill in 1881 – the first war against the Boers. It is difficult now to separate fact from fiction, but what cannot be disputed is that during the battle for Majuba, he single-handedly charged at the enemy line and broke through. A lone Englishman in enemy territory, he evaded capture and survived for six months before rejoining his regiment in Pretoria. When the queen awarded him the Victoria Cross, she spoke for the nation when she said: 'Deeds such as his are at the heart of the British Empire. Our spirit will never be defeated.' Sir Gordon has been an inspiration to the nation ever since.

The Illustrated News was quick to draw a parallel between the past and the present.

Nineteen years after Majuba, as we fight once again our old enemy, the Boer, we remember Sir Gordon, whose spirit still inspires our fighting men who will, we know, avenge the defeat at Majuba and give the Boer the bloody nose they deserve.

Evelyn bowed his head again as the queen's carriage pulled away. If his mother had had her way, there would have been no memorial service. Without consulting him, she had planned to have his father laid to rest with no pomp or ceremony – just a simple service and a few close friends to witness his internment in the Mausoleum at Ardington. Evelyn had insisted that the nation would feel cheated if there was no ceremony and, fortunately, the queen had agreed with him.

"Your arm, Evie, please."

He gave his mother the support of his arm and helped her into the carriage, taking his seat beside her. Lord Renfrew took the seat opposite. His sister, Harriet, and her husband, the Duke of Beddington, settled themselves into the carriage behind.

He glanced at his mother. She hadn't looked at him once during the service. In fact, they'd barely exchanged a word since his father's death. It would probably be easier to prove himself to his peers than to persuade his mother to take him seriously. She insisted on leaving London for Ardington immediately after the service, so he returned to his father's apartment at Carlton Terrace alone.

He stood now at the apartment's study window, twirling

the whisky in his glass and watching a detachment of The Blues clatter down the Mall towards Buckingham Palace. At one time his father had wanted him to join that regiment. Evelyn had infuriated him by declining, saying he preferred a life of pleasure to one of regulation. Now he acknowledged the real reason for his refusal. He feared comparison to the Hero of Majuba, as he would surely be found lacking.

He turned and looked around the room. Everything was in its place, in meticulous order, exactly as it had been while his father was alive. He could visualise Sir Gordon sitting at the walnut writing desk in the centre of the room, or smoking a cigar in one of the green leather armchairs set either side of the marble fireplace. He could imagine him straightening the regimented rows of books on the shelves that lined the walls. All were bound in green leather; their spines gleamed with gold lettering and the crest of the Harringdons was embossed on every cover.

Not that Evelyn had been a frequent visitor here. He glanced into the large square mirror over the fireplace and ran a hand through his hair, which was long and unruly – so unlike his father's. He had his mother's eyes, but he had inherited the square jaw of his father. He was grateful he hadn't also inherited his father's patrician nose. It had given Sir Gordon the supercilious look of a man who disapproved of everything he saw.

He studied the portrait of his father that was hung over the fireplace. It had been painted after the Battle of Majuba on his return from Africa. The newly won Victoria Cross was prominently displayed on his chest. His father had nearly died fighting the Boers and what had been gained from it? Nineteen years later, the country was fighting the same war all over again.

"What a waste of lives, eh, father?"

The eyes in the portrait stared coldly back at him. It was

a perfect example of art mirroring life. There was a discreet knock at the door and Wilson, the butler, entered.

"Excuse me, Sir Evelyn, the Honourable Mr Austin Frobisher has called."

The arrival of his best friend was just what he needed to lift his spirits. "Show him in, Wilson. Show him in."

Austin Frobisher, called Siggy for no reason that anyone could convincingly explain, entered in a billow of scarves and overcoat tails, brushing aside Wilson's attempt to alleviate him of them. "Not staying long enough." Wilson obediently backed out and closed the door. "So, it's over, Evie. All went smoothly I hear. Must be a relief?"

"It is." Evelyn poured himself a whisky and raised the decanter to Siggy, who shook his head.

"Mama not here?"

"Mother decided to return to Ardington. Probably happy to get away from me. I'm glad you've turned up. I was beginning to feel rather low."

"Because of your father's death? You didn't seem to have much time for him while he was alive."

Evelyn stared moodily into his drink. "Perhaps I should have made more of an effort."

Siggy decided to change his mind and join his friend for a drink, helping himself from the decanter. "Typhoid, eh? A bit ironic, isn't it? To be one of the few who survived Majuba, only to succumb in later life to an insanitary water pipe while inspecting the slums of Islington."

Evelyn drank his whisky in one. "Things are going to change for me, Siggy, and I'm not sure I'm ready for it."

"It's a simple choice. Either adopt the mantle of Papa and prove you're worthy of it or continue indulging with me in the finer things of life to which your rank entitles you."

Evelyn poured himself another whisky. Siggy's insouciance was usually catching. Today, however, it failed to distract him. “It’s surprising how ingrained a sense of duty is,” he murmured. “I never thought I would be plagued by it.”

“Centuries of breeding,” Siggy said, sadly, “but some of us have managed to bat it away.”

“I’ve been thinking that I would have liked to know him better – my father. When I was finally allowed into his bedroom, it was so dark I could barely see him. He was already dead. He died a stranger to me.” Evelyn crossed over to the fire and kicked the logs back into life, creating a shower of sparks. “Dr Oliver told me that father had been in pain ever since Majuba. I never knew that. From a wound in his back that had never really healed. He was on morphine. I suppose that explains his moods.”

“He was never an easy man. Great men never are.”

Silence fell for a moment, broken by Siggy putting his empty glass on the walnut desk.

“Well, much as I love you, I do have to go. I’m due at Romano’s for dinner. You’re much missed there, you know. Soon as decency allows, I hope to see you back in the fold. We’ll all miss you if you choose duty over pleasure. Are you staying on here or joining Mama at Ardington?”

“I’m leaving for Ardington the day after tomorrow. There’s estate business to sort out and papers to sign.”

Siggy grimaced. “Do you know, you’re already beginning to sound uncomfortably like your father? Be very careful, my friend, I don’t think I could handle that.”

*

Wilson had travelled by train from London to Ardington the day before, so he could be there to greet his master on arrival. As Evelyn pulled up in the Renault, he was waiting at the top of the steps.

“Good journey, sir?” He signalled for a servant to take Evelyn’s luggage.

"Yes, but I'm in great need of a bath, Wilson," said Evelyn, entering the hall. He handed his coat and goggles to the butler, who was following behind.

"And a whisky, Sir Evelyn?"

"You read my mind. Where's mother?"

"Resting in her room, sir. Please excuse the disorder." He indicated the huge glass chandelier in the hall that had been lowered to be cleaned and polished. "Lady Harringdon was hoping to have everything finished before you returned."

"Yes, I left earlier than I expected. I'll be in the library. Let me know when my bath is ready."

"Yes, sir."

*

As Evelyn soaked in the warm water, he found himself dwelling on a matter that he could no longer ignore. He would have to take his father's seat in the Lords.

He'd always avoided politics. His father had been such a dominant figure in the Tory Party and in government. He was known for his ability to silence all opposition with a cutting phrase delivered in a voice of steel. Evelyn slid down in the bath, submerging his face. Still, what had it achieved but temporary glory? On his deathbed he was just a lonely old man and the commanding voice had been reduced to a painful whisper. Evelyn sat up, wiping his eyes free of water. The action reawakened the memory of his father's last words, and the letter by his bedside that had quickly been removed. Wrapped in his bathrobe, Evelyn rang for the butler.

"I'll dine in my room this evening, Wilson. Apologise to mother will you, but I'm very tired."

"Of course, sir."

"Oh, and Wilson..." Evelyn hesitated. "Did my father

know anyone called Montrecourt?" He was just curious, that was all.

"Not to my knowledge, sir. Would you like me to make some enquiries?"

Evelyn shook his head. "No, it's not important. Thank you, Wilson."

The butler withdrew and Evelyn threw himself back against the bed, closing his eyes.

*

Breakfast with his mother the next morning was, as expected, something of an ordeal. Apart from acknowledging one another, they said very little. He decided it would be a kindness to put her mind at rest about Ardington.

"Mama," he said, helping himself to kedgeree and coffee, "I intend to spend a good deal of my time in town rather than in the country, as father did. I'm assuming you'll be willing to continue to handle the estate business, as you did while father was alive."

There was a visible relaxing of his mother's shoulders, but she simply nodded. "If that's what you would like me to do, Evelyn, then of course I will."

"Good." He picked up *The Times*. There was nothing of much interest in it – just an article about the memorial service, which was written in the tone of adulation he would have expected. "By the way, I believe Wilson has put some of father's belongings in the attic. I thought I'd look through them, if you have no objection." Did he imagine it or did his mother's shoulders grow tense again?

"No. I have no objection."

*

There were crates and boxes all over the floor of the attic and Evelyn, his hands on his hips, wondered where to begin. It was obvious that some of them hadn't been disturbed for years, while others had obviously been placed there within the last few days. He casually opened one or two of them. One was stuffed with papers pertaining to the house. He saw some account books and flicked through one of them. It noted a series of payments to someone with the initials JP, which meant little to him.

In the other crate were clothes he'd never seen his father wear, as well as snuffboxes, cigar cases and reading glasses he'd never seen his father use. It all seemed strangely impersonal. He looked around; two chests that were set apart from the others caught his attention. They were thick with dust, but the dust had recently been disturbed. It was curiosity that made him open them.

The first one contained nothing but bills, deeds and plans for the house, which went back years. He was about to close the lid again when he realised that there were piles of notebooks underneath, neatly tied together in bundles. He untied them and recognised his father's precise, neat writing. They were journals. His father had obviously kept one for every year since 1874, the year Evelyn had been born. They finished in 1899, just before his final illness.

Evelyn opened the journal dated 1874 and flicked through it until he came to the date of August 3rd. His father had written: *Sarah has given birth to a son. I have an heir at last.* That was all, just two sentences – no indication as to whether he was proud of the event.

He glanced through the other journals. There was nothing personal in them; they consisted of punctilious and detailed notes on his public life, his speeches, the minutes of the meetings he'd addressed, his political philosophy – all obviously recorded for posterity and meant for publication.

Despite his father's continual denial, it seemed the opinion of posterity did matter to him.

Evelyn began to bundle them up again and then stopped. He'd assumed they ran chronologically and they did, except that there was a year missing. The journal covering the year 1881 – the year his father had fought in Africa – wasn't there.

He turned to the other chest. There were no more journals, just a carefully folded uniform – his father's regimental uniform. There was a button missing from the sleeve, but otherwise it was in perfect condition. Underneath, he found piles of newspaper clippings, which were all from the year 1881.

England's shame screamed one of the headlines. *Britain's Army defeated by a handful of Boer farmers at Majuba Hill. Our troops have been demoralised and defeated, led by Sir George Colley on a pointless mission to retake a position on Majuba Hill that we did not need to hold. His folly led him to his death and resulted in the death of many others.* His father's name was mentioned as being among those missing, presumed dead.

There were also cuttings in the chest that covered the period six months later, when his father had re-emerged alive and unscathed from the veldt. The tone was altogether different.

> *Sir Gordon Harringdon is safe. Hero survives alone in enemy territory.*
>
> *Despite a shaming defeat, Sir Gordon's survival represents the spirit of England that will never die.*
>
> *Sir Gordon is the hero of Majuba. He charged Boer guns alone, sword in hand. For six months he survived unaided in enemy territory. His intrepid spirit triumphed despite our defeat at the hands of those monsters. Let it be a warning to those who say that England's spirit has been broken.*

The strange thing about the last cutting was that someone, presumably his father, had scored it out in black ink. It had been done with some force, because the rest of the article was unreadable and the paper was torn. Why?

Evelyn put everything back in the chest and made his way down to the green drawing room. His mother had settled in a chair by the window with her embroidery. He poured himself a whisky and picked up the latest copy of *Punch*, seating himself opposite her.

"I've just been in the attic looking through a few things."

"Yes, so I see," she said, indicating that his trouser leg was covered in dust.

"Sorry," he brushed it clean. "I'm curious. Did father ever talk to you about his time Africa?"

"No, he never did."

"Isn't that strange?"

"I don't think so. There were many things we didn't talk about."

"It's just that I found his journals in the attic. They were in one of the chests. He kept detailed notes on everything, did you know? Nothing of a personal nature; they were more a record of his beliefs and his political life."

"I see."

"He enjoyed being called the scourge of the Liberals. He noted it down in his journals quite often." His mother smiled politely and concentrated on the stitching of a rose. "I think he intended them to be published after his death. Would you approve of that?"

"Yes. Certainly."

"With a little judicious editing, of course." He turned a page of his magazine. There were questions he wanted to ask her, but he didn't know how to begin. "I noticed there was one journal missing, for the year 1881. The year he served in Africa. Do you know where that might be?" He saw his mother flush slightly.

"Perhaps it wasn't possible to keep a journal at such a time."

"Yes, of course. You're probably right." His question had made her uneasy, which was confirmed by her next words.

"Evie, if you want to ask me something, then ask directly. Don't play games with me."

"I'm sorry. I'm certainly not playing games."

"I can feel your hostility, and if it's because I didn't write and let you know of your father's illness, well, I'm sorry, but all I could think about was the fact that he was dying. I admit it: I didn't even consider you. I hope you will soon be able to forgive me."

"Perhaps I was piqued at the time not to have been told of his illness, but I'm over that. I would resent it, though, if I felt things were being kept from me now." She didn't respond, so he decided to ask her directly. "Do you know someone called Montrecourt? I'm sure I saw a letter…"

She snapped shut the lid of her sewing basket and stood up. "Stop this nonsense." Her outburst was unexpected and he was too surprised to speak. "Keep out of things that do not concern you, Evie. That is my advice to you."

She swept out with a rustle of black satin, slamming the door behind her. He was astonished. Something was obviously troubling her and she wasn't willing to share it with him. After a moment, he rang for Wilson.

"Have them saddle Saracen, will you?" He needed air.

★

By the time he returned, he was feeling guilty and contrite about the way he'd cross-questioned his mother. The poor woman had her grief to deal with without also having to cope with her son's insensitivity. He should apologise. He saw that the door to his mother's writing room was slightly ajar. He pushed it open and was about to speak when he saw that she was on her knees in front of the fireplace. She was so intent on hurling papers into the fire that she hadn't heard him enter.

It was obvious that a great deal of paper had already been burnt because there was a huge mound of soot spilling over the fender. As the last of the papers were ripped in two and thrown into the flames, she sank back onto her heels and pushed her hair back with her hand, leaving a black streak of soot against the grey. He must have made some sound, because she turned and saw him. Her expression was one of guilt, but she quickly recovered her composure.

"What are you burning, mother?" he quietly asked.

She rose to her feet. "Only things that should have been thrown away years ago. Things of no importance."

"You should have let me see them first."

"Why? You said you intended to leave estate business to me. Well, this was estate business." He remained where he was, in the doorway. Realising she had offended him, she went over and laid a hand on his arm. "It was old estate business, Evie, no longer relevant. Believe me."

He waited until the sound of her footsteps had disappeared, before crossing swiftly over to the fireplace. He picked up the poker and prodded the smouldering embers, uncovering the charred remains of what appeared to be the front cover of a notebook. It was just like those his father had used for his journals. He could see a page in his father's handwriting. Was that the word Montrecourt he could see? He eagerly reached forward to salvage it, only to find that his movement accidently rekindled a flame. He had to stand back and watch as the page was slowly reduced to ashes.

CHAPTER FIVE

Marie felt guilty sitting here with the Mintons, enjoying herself in Standing's Oriental Café, while Daphne was slaving away at the shop, putting the final touches to the banners for the march. A date had been set. It was to be three weeks from now; every time she thought about it, Marie suffered a thrill of expectation. It was frustrating that she couldn't go *too* regularly to the bookshop. She'd explained to Daphne how John Pickard had forbidden it, and Daphne had urged her to be cautious – not only for her own sake, but to prevent drawing attention to the march.

Marie's guardian, meanwhile, had kept his word and arranged for her to go on various outings with Isabelle and Geoffrey Minton, and Geoffrey's brother Stanley.

Standing's was a much grander place than she'd expected it to be. Stained glass windows, tall bamboos and painted paper lanterns added a touch of the exotic to the luxury of the velvet and gilt decor. Waiters flitted through palm trees with trays piled high with food and there was a constant buzz of conversation.

The Mintons had suggested that it was acceptable for them to use first names as they were now well acquainted. However, Marie felt awkward using such familiarity towards the two men, whose personalities couldn't have been more different. Geoffrey was loud and bombastic, while Stanley was quiet and subdued. It was usually Geoffrey who dominated the conversation and today was no exception. Marie was quite content to let him as it enabled her to enjoy the mock turtle soup, the lamb cutlets and the strawberry tartlet without having to make any effort to reply.

*

The next day, to her surprise, Stanley presented himself at Devonshire Place. He was accompanied by two huge St Bernard dogs. He wondered, he said, if she would like to accompany him on a walk to Harlow Moor? The tails of the dogs wagged slowly from side to side as they gazed up at her appealingly.

She couldn't hide her surprise. "Just the two of us?"

"If you have no objection. I have spoken to Isabelle and Geoffrey, and to John Pickard, and they're all perfectly agreeable."

It was a beautiful day – too beautiful to stay inside – and another visit to the bookshop so soon after her previous one wouldn't be wise.

"Yes. I'd like that," she said. She changed quickly into her walking dress, before joining Stanley and the dogs in the hallway.

It was a pleasant spring day and Harlow Moor was packed with children playing with hoops and mothers pushing prams. Marie and Stanley walked a little stiffly side by side. She'd never been on her own in male company before and she had no idea what to say. Damson and Major, the two dogs, helped to dispel some of the awkwardness. They made a great fuss of her, lumbering at her feet, tails wagging vigorously, vying for her attention. When they stood on their hind legs with their large front paws on her shoulders, they were taller than she was. They tried to lick her face but she pushed them away, laughing.

She realised that Stanley was suggesting they might sit on a bench for a while to listen to the local brass band, which was playing in the bandstand. She said she thought that would be a lovely idea. Silence fell again.

She remembered the toothache he'd been suffering from when they first met at Isabelle's dinner party. She'd given him a jar of ointment, but had forgotten about it until now. She asked if it had cured the pain and he quickly assured her that it had. She asked how long he'd suffered with toothache and what he'd done to try and cure it before, and Stanley was able to outline with some enthusiasm every twinge he'd ever felt. After that little flurry of conversation, silence fell again.

Marie searched desperately for something else to say. "Do you like poetry?" she asked at last.

"No… I'm sorry… I don't read very much of anything. Just *The Grocer* – it's a weekly magazine. No time for anything else, you see. The Emporium takes all my attention. You must come and visit."

"But you do like music or you wouldn't have suggested listening to the band. I was allowed to play the piano at the convent sometimes."

"I don't know very much about music either, sorry. It was Geoffrey's idea to come here," he said awkwardly.

Perhaps it would be better to let *him* choose the topic of conversation. "Tell me what you do like then? Apart from work," she quickly added.

She could see him searching desperately for something to share with her. "I have the dogs, of course. " She nodded encouragingly. "And butterflies. I collect butterflies. I've always liked butterflies, ever since I was a small boy. I used to cup them in my hands and look at them through my laced fingers. I could feel them fluttering. Then they would escape and I would be left with nothing. It wasn't until I read in some newspaper about a man and his butterfly collection that I realised there was a way to keep them with me always. Now, I collect butterflies for a hobby. I bought my first case when The

Emporium opened. I've added a case to my collection every year since."

It was the longest speech she'd ever heard Stanley make. "And what do you do with them?"

He seemed surprised by her question. "I look at them. I like to look at them."

"But aren't they dead?"

"Yes, but their beauty is preserved forever."

It seemed so cruel to Marie, to kill something just to have the pleasure of looking at it. She didn't know how to respond. The subject was dropped. Luckily, they both became distracted by the antics of a tiny mongrel dog that was obviously determined to challenge the St Bernards to a fight. She laughed as the mongrel's owner struggled to drag his dog away, while Damson and Major stared after it in amazement. Even Stanley managed a smile.

★

It was the day of the march at last. Marie woke early, with excitement fluttering around her stomach. She'd been unable to sleep all night and she was pretty certain that Daphne wouldn't have slept either. She knew her friend was anxious because word about the march had begun to spread through Harrogate, and she was concerned about the possibility of adverse reaction.

Marie was able to slip out of the house unnoticed by the Mintons and make her way to the Majestic Hotel, outside of which the marchers were gathering. Apart from Daphne and Marie there were a dozen or so factory girls taking part in the protest, and their numbers were swollen by a handful of society women sympathetic to the cause – not as many as Daphne would have liked, however, but more than she had expected. There was a carnival atmosphere among the women. Clogs and shawls darted in and out between fashionable dresses and plumed hats. There was laughter and chatter that was full of nervous anticipation. It was a perfect June day with only the slightest breeze to stir the banners the women were carrying.

Silence fell as Daphne blew her whistle to attract everyone's attention. "Welcome ladies and thank you all for your support. We will march to the end of the street and turn right; then at the edge of town, turn left and stop outside the gates of the factory. This is a peaceful demonstration, but we must expect some animosity from passers-by – women as well as men, I'm afraid. Do not respond to it. We shall stand outside the factory for an hour and then disperse, leaving a small group behind to keep vigil. Any questions?"

None being asked, Daphne instructed the group to form into a double line. Still chattering and laughing they obeyed, with Daphne and Marie in the lead, carrying their banner high. It was painted with the words: *FAIR TREATMENT FOR WOMEN.*

After a while, the laughter and the chatter began to fade as it became clear that the march was not popular with the people of the town. There was thinly disguised hatred on their faces as the women marched past.

"Shame on you," someone shouted. "Get back home where you belong," was one of the least crude suggestions. Someone else shouted: "Whores".

Marie glanced behind her at the others. The factory girls were looking grim but determined. On the faces of the society ladies, however, she could read shock. It was a relief to reach the edge of town where there were less passers-by. Spirits began to revive even more as the women saw their goal ahead: the wrought iron gates dominated by the sign that read BRIDGEWATER DYES.

Suddenly, the double line of women faltered and then stopped. Uncertain glances were exchanged. "What is it?"

someone called from the back. "Why are we stopping?" In reply came the echoing clip-clop of horses' hooves from the side streets.

"What's happening?" someone called.

It soon became obvious what was happening as mounted police slowly rode into view. They took up a position facing the line of women, forming a barrier between them and the factory, batons in hands.

Daphne was the first to recover. "Don't worry, ladies. Nothing will happen," she shouted cheerfully. "We are doing nothing wrong. If we keep walking, they will give way."

Following her lead, Marie and the group started to walk forward. However, so did the police, their horses progressing effortlessly from a walk to a trot. As they gathered speed, the line of women hesitated. Then, after a second, realising the police were not going to stop, the line wavered. The horses were almost on top of them now, muscles straining, charging straight at them. There were screams as the marchers struggled to get out of the way of the pounding hooves and the raised batons. Marie threw the banner aside and hurled herself towards the wall, feeling the heat from one of the horses as it brushed past her body. Daphne was beside her and pushed her into a doorway.

"When I shout go, run for the gate across the road," she yelled. "It leads to fields that will get you back to the Stray."

"What will you do?"

"I won't be far behind you. Now, go!" As the last horse charged past, she pushed Marie towards the road. The police were reforming and getting ready to charge again. "Now!" Daphne shouted.

Marie did as she was told, skirts held high, feet pounding against the earth. To either side of her, other women were also running. Daphne remained where she was, heading them off from danger and pushing them towards safety. A few women lay in the road; their silk dresses torn and muddied, and their shawls and clogs covered in blood from wounds. Driven by panic, Marie kept running. She clawed her way over the gate and raced across the fields, not daring to look back.

It wasn't until she reached the safety of The Stray that she slowed down. She pushed a shaking hand through her hair, trying to tidy it. She glanced behind her. No one was following. Having regained her breath a little, she walked swiftly across The Stray to Devonshire Place. The housekeeper let her in. She ran up the stairs to the safety of her room. It was only then that her legs turned to jelly and she collapsed on the bed.

Panic turned swiftly to guilt. She should have stayed with Daphne to help the wounded. She splashed her face with cold water from the jug. Should she go to the shop and make sure that Daphne was safe? She was too afraid to do so. Suppose the police saw her and arrested her? She sat on the edge of her bed all night imagining the worst things that might happen, so that by the morning she was in a dreadful state with dark rings under her eyes from lack of sleep. She knew she had to see Daphne and make sure she was unhurt.

"I'm just going to walk on The Stray," she told Isabelle, who was too preoccupied with baby Jonathan to take much notice. It was obvious she hadn't heard about the march. Isabelle merely nodded an acknowledgement. Once out of sight of the house, Marie quickened her pace and headed for the bookshop.

It was as dark as ever in Market Alley, but there wasn't the usual light on in the shop. The door was ajar, though, which was odd. Marie pushed it open further, making the bell ring.

"Daphne?" There was no reply. She entered, closing the door behind her. "Daphne?" She heard a noise from behind the curtained partition. "Daphne?"

There was still no answer. She made her way to the small room at the back. As she reached the alcove, the curtain was suddenly thrust aside and the figure of a man hurtled towards her. He pushed her savagely in the chest and she screamed as she fell, striking her head against a corner of one of the shelves.

"Keep your nose out, bitch." She could feel the heat from his breath as he bent close. Then the figure rapidly disappeared through the door and was lost in the gloom of Market Alley. Marie lay winded for a moment, too shocked to move. She heard a groan and managed to struggle to her feet.

"Daphne?"

Her head was throbbing as she hung on to a bookcase for support. Through the open curtain, she could see wreckage. Books were scattered everywhere, shelves were overturned and, in the middle of the debris, a figure lay huddled on the floor.

"Daphne!"

Marie stumbled over to her friend as Daphne rolled onto her back. She'd been savagely beaten about the head and her face was barely recognisable. It was a mess of blood and broken bone. Marie pushed her fist into her mouth to stop herself from crying out.

Daphne tried to speak but her mouth was so swollen that she could barely form the words. A paraffin lamp had been knocked over and a small tongue of flame had caught at some torn paper. The flame was growing stronger as it fed on the dry parchment, but Marie was too intent on helping Daphne to notice.

"Who did this?" She was struggling to find the Sal Volatile that she always carried with her. "Who was it? Was it a thief?"

Daphne's attempt at a reply ended in a grimace, but she managed to shake her head. It was the crackle of the flames that made Marie look behind her. The backroom was filling with smoke. With a sudden whoosh, the flames shot high into the air.

Marie screamed. "We have to get out! Daphne, we have to get out of here!" But all her friend could do was lie still; she was too damaged to move. Marie attempted to pull Daphne towards the curtain, but she couldn't shift her. She was too small and not strong enough.

"Stand up. Please, Daphne," she begged. "Please stand up. We have got to get out of here."

With an effort, Daphne managed to drag herself upright. She was soon on her knees again, but Marie quickly caught her and started to pull her to the front of the shop.

"Go. Leave me. Look after yourself," Daphne managed to say.

"No." She wouldn't abandon Daphne, not a second time. "Come on. Keep going. Keep going."

A flicker of flame caught at Marie's dress. With a whimper of fear, she let her friend go, frantically beating the fire out with her hands. Daphne attempted to crawl along the floor by herself, but her face creased with pain. The flames had crept into the front of the shop now, leaping in an arc towards the ceiling. Marie was quickly beside Daphne again, urging her on.

"Nearly there. We're nearly there. Come on, Daphne. Please, please keep moving."

Her words ended in a cough as the acrid smoke entered her lungs. The heat was intolerable and her eyes were stinging. Then, a cold rush of air hit her. They were outside. They'd made it; they'd reached the safety of the alleyway.

A crowd had begun to gather. Someone had sent for the fire brigade, but Marie was only hazily aware of what was happening. A man was bending over the inert form of Daphne.

"He's a doctor," someone said.

The fire brigade arrived but the alley was too narrow for them to get close enough, and the crowd was in their way. Everybody was hustled out onto the main street. Daphne was carried off by the doctor. He placed her into a hansom cab and climbed on board with her.

A woman asked Marie if she was all right. She didn't reply. She had to stay with Daphne and go with her to wherever she was being taken. Just as she reached the cab, however, it drove off. The doctor hadn't seen her.

"Daphne." She tried to run after the hansom but she was too weak. She stumbled. Someone tried to help her but she brushed them aside. She didn't hear the policeman demanding her name and address. A man said, "She's from the Minton's lodging house in Devonshire Place."

That was it; she must get back to Devonshire Place. The Mintons would be able to find out where Daphne had been taken. She started to run across Long Street, down Stirling Avenue. She wasn't aware that she was crying. She wasn't aware that passers-by were turning to look after her – this wild woman, her hair awry and her face covered in grime. She hurled herself against the door of the house and pushed past the startled housekeeper, before rushing up the stairs, bursting into her room and throwing herself onto the bed in a state of collapse.

She had no idea how long she was lying there before Isabelle came in. It felt like it was hours, but it was only a few minutes. Isabelle was shocked at the sight of Marie's gaunt face, which was covered in soot. Her clothes were torn and smelt of smoke, and her hands were blistered and raw.

"What on earth has happened?"

It was a rhetorical question because Marie was in no state to reply. Calm and practical, Isabelle opened the door and ordered the housekeeper, who was hovering on the landing outside, to heat water and bring it up to the room. Marie was sobbing now, deep rasping sobs that tore her apart. Isabelle eased off her dress. The material was badly singed.

"Daphne's shop. It's burnt down." Marie shuddered

and clutched Isabelle. "Daphne's hurt. She's been taken somewhere. I don't know where. We have to find out where."

"All right. We will, we will," Isabelle said soothingly and Marie calmed down a little.

Hot water was brought in. Isabelle took it and waved the housekeeper away. She started to wipe Marie's face. There was bad bruising on her forehead and a trickle of blood near her mouth. Marie winced as Isabelle bathed it.

"Tell me what happened," Isabelle urged.

It was an effort for Marie to speak. "There was a man in the shop. He must have attacked Daphne. He pushed me and I fell."

"Who was it?"

"I didn't see him clearly." All she could think of was Daphne. Was she suffering? Had they saved her? "You will find out where Daphne is? You will, won't you?"

"Of course we will. Of course."

Reassured, Marie allowed Isabelle to undress her and put her to bed. Even so, she couldn't sleep. She wouldn't be able to do that until she'd found out where Daphne had been taken.

⋆

For three days after the fire, Marie was barely conscious of her surroundings or of the fuss that was going on around her. She sometimes thought she was back in the convent, and other times she imagined she was on a train. The steam from its wheels scalded her and the furnace that was being stoked consumed her. She was burning.

"She's crying. Why is she crying?"

It was Isabelle's voice she could hear. Marie tried to lift herself up in bed and managed to say: "I'm frightened."

"No, lie back. You're all right."

There were more whispered conversations in her room.

Isabelle's voice came through again: "She's still crying. I don't know what else to do for her."

★

For another three days, Marie slipped between reality and nightmare. Finally, on the third morning, she opened her eyes and saw the room clearly. Isabelle was sitting by her bed.

"Isabelle, where's Daphne?

Her voice was weak but Isabelle was instantly on her feet. "Are you all right?" She nodded and Isabelle leant against the bedpost in relief. "I've been so worried. We all have."

Nothing mattered to Marie except news of her friend. "Have you found out where Daphne is?"

"No, not yet." She saw the expression on Marie's face. "We are trying, I promise. Geoffrey's brother, Stanley, has called to ask after you several times."

"That's very kind of him," Marie murmured, but it meant little to her.

★

Over the next few days, thanks to Isabelle's care, Marie grew stronger. When the doctor saw her again, he agreed she was now strong enough to be helped downstairs. There was a parcel waiting for her in the parlour.

"It arrived two days ago," Isabelle said.

There was an envelope attached. Inside was a card. It read: *All that is left of the fire. It seemed to interest you, Daphne.*

As Isabelle went out to answer a knock at the front door, Marie opened the parcel. It contained *Farnsworth's Medical Dictionary*. She smiled – so Daphne had never got round to returning it to the publisher then. She looked back at the card. At least she was well enough to write.

Isabelle entered with Mr Pickard and Marie immediately assumed that he had come to give her news of Daphne. "Have you found out where she is? Can I see her?"

John Pickard was very angry. "She's at St Martin's Hospital being well looked after. My main concern is you."

"I'm well enough," she said.

"I warned you against seeing Daphne Senior and this is the result. You will never communicate with that woman again, do you understand? If you do, the consequence will be an immediate return to the convent."

"I will see her," she said to Isabelle when they were alone. "She mustn't think I don't care."

★

For another two days the Mintons and John Pickard refused her request, but the anxiety about her friend was threatening to make Marie ill again. So, Pickard reluctantly gave his permission for them to meet one last time. It was agreed that Isabelle would accompany her to the ward, while Geoffrey waited outside the entrance in a hansom.

St Martin's Hospital for Women was not a very prepossessing place. It was small and cramped and not very clean. There were eleven beds crammed into each of the eight wards. There were three wards on the ground and first floor, and two wards on the second. A small group of grim-faced women in starched white caps and aprons attempted to keep the place clean – obviously not very successfully, though, because the smell of urine and vomit was overpowering.

Daphne was on the second floor of the soulless building, and Marie and Isabelle climbed the bleached stone staircase to reach it. When they arrived, Marie saw a figure at the far end of the ward putting on her coat. She moved forward quickly.

"Daphne?"

As her friend turned, Marie was distressed to see that her face was still badly lacerated and swollen. One eye was severely bruised and her upper lip was split. Daphne's attempt at a smile ended in a grimace.

"Look at me. It's a good thing I was no picture to begin with, isn't it? I knew you'd come. They told me you weren't hurt." Daphne put an arm around her friend and hugged her. Isabelle turned away, evidently finding the familiarity embarrassing.

Marie dropped her voice so that Isabelle wouldn't hear. "Daphne, I'm sorry. I'm so sorry I ran away after the march. I was such a coward."

Daphne smiled grimly. "My best advice to you is to keep on running. Get as far away from me as you can. I've ruined enough lives already. The women will be sacked from their jobs. They'll be destitute. I've let them down. I've failed in everything I've tried to do. I'm not sure things will ever change. Maybe I was wrong to even try."

Marie hadn't expected Daphne to sound so defeated. She tried to think of something encouraging to say. "You did what you thought was right." It wasn't quite the inspiring turn of phrase she'd intended.

"Come along, Miss Senior." The matron had arrived. "We haven't all day to stand around waiting while you two gossip." She clapped her hands briskly.

"Will I hear from you?" said Marie, as she followed Daphne towards the door. Isabelle trailed a few feet behind.

Daphne kept on walking. "Best not, I think. I've caused enough trouble for you as it is. Did you get the book?"

"Oh, my goodness, yes. I wanted to thank you."

"Don't thank me. You might as well have it."

Outside the entrance, Geoffrey was pacing up and down. He was relieved to see his wife and Marie emerge at last, and he opened the door of the carriage for them. Isabelle climbed in, but Marie lingered for a moment longer on the pavement. There was a cab parked a little further down. She caught a glimpse of its occupant. His complexion was pale, and his hair was long, fair and wispy. He glanced towards Marie with piercing blue eyes – Daphne's eyes. He was then hidden from sight as he sat back to let his daughter enter. As they disappeared around the corner, Marie climbed into her own carriage to sit beside Isabelle and an impatient Geoffrey ordered the man to drive on.

CHAPTER SIX

The war was over at last. The Boers had been soundly beaten and the old humiliation of Majuba had been avenged. Evelyn joined in the national celebrations with Siggy. As soon as the celebrations were over, however, the recriminations had begun. There were rumours in the country that the government had not been open in its dealings with the people, that there had been corruption in the handling of the war. Spread by the government's opponents, it was having the desired effect of undermining confidence.

When the first war against the Boers had ended, Evelyn had only been four years old. He wondered if the same kind of rumours had been circulating then? Had his mother destroyed his father's journal because it revealed some official scandal involving this man Montrecourt? It was just a thought.

Relations between Evelyn and his mother were still strained so it was impossible to ask her. Though, if he was going to take his father's place in the political arena, he felt he had the right to know. Lord Renfrew, his father's closest friend, might be willing to discuss it with him, but he was an extremely busy man and was currently travelling around Europe on government business. Instead, Evelyn approached another acquaintance of his father: Marcus White. They arranged to meet at The Athenaeum Club in Pall Mall.

It was a club not entirely to Evelyn's taste. He agreed with Siggy that it was too stuffy and too formal. He preferred Whites, where William Arden, Second Baron Alvanley, had once laid a bet with a friend as to which of two raindrops would be the first to reach the bottom of its famous bow window.

The desire to bet on anything and everything was still alive and well at Whites. Evelyn couldn't imagine any such thing happening here among the Doric columns of the Athenaeum.

Evelyn stood up when he saw Marcus approaching. He was one of the City's most successful investors, but it was hard to believe that he was also one of the richest men in England by looking at him. It seemed that money alone could not buy style. Evelyn had long thought the man must be the despair of his tailor, as he always seemed to be on the point of bursting out of his waistcoat and trousers.

"It was good of you to find the time to see me," Evelyn said.

"Not at all." Marcus beckoned a waiter, and a whisky and a brandy were ordered. The two men settled back against the leather of their winged armchairs.

"Congratulations on your maiden speech in the Lords, by the way," Marcus said.

Evelyn knew it had lacked the power of his father's oratory, but it had been adequate. "Thank you."

"So, what can I do for you?"

Evelyn hadn't actually thought of a way to broach the matter that had brought him here. He didn't know how well acquainted Marcus was with the inside workings of the government. He decided to tread carefully.

"My father's death was so sudden that it was a shock to me. And all these celebrations have made me realise just how little I knew about his time in Africa. He would never discuss it."

"He was a very modest man, and it was in all the newspapers anyway."

"Yes, but I'd like to know more than just the facts that the newspapers published. I thought, perhaps, he might have discussed things with you."

"Lady Sarah can tell you more than I can."

"His death is still difficult for her to accept. Talking about him is too painful for her."

"Yes, of course. I presume it's Majuba you're asking about. We all felt it was a dreadful waste of lives. Colley took the hill in the night, against all advice. It had no strategic value. Having taken it, he was negligent in guarding it, and the Boers easily retook it. Colley was shot in the head. Your father was second in command and he took over. He charged the Boers alone, while his men were cut down around him. He was wounded but he escaped and survived, alone in enemy territory, until he rejoined what was left of his regiment six months after its defeat at Majuba. I think that sums it up."

There had to be something else. Colley's criminal negligence was common knowledge – no one had been able to cover that up. "That's what it says in the newspapers. I was hoping to learn more."

"I'm not sure I know more. Your father hated discussing it. All the adulation that greeted him when he returned to England would have turned the head of most men – not your father. If anything, it made him withdraw even more into himself." Marcus took a cigar from his pocket and offered one to Evelyn, who shook his head. After lighting it, Marcus studied it for a moment before continuing. "To be honest, he did discuss it a little with me. Not in any great detail, you understand, but perhaps I can fill in a few of the gaps if you're really curious."

Evelyn nodded eagerly. "Thank you. I am."

Marcus ordered two more drinks. He waited until they'd been served before continuing. "It must have been a terrifying experience for him. As he charged through the enemy lines, he was hit in the back by rifle fire. He clung onto his horse but he was finally unseated."

"He was thrown from his horse?" That wasn't in any of the newspapers.

"After some miles, yes. He told me he lay there for days,

bleeding profusely, without food, without water, in dreadful heat. He became feverish. By rights, he should have died. He thought he would die, but he stubbornly clung on to life."

"Yes, my father was a very stubborn man," Evelyn wryly agreed.

"His body was wedged between boulders and that's where he was found by a young French woman. Her husband, also French, was a local farmer. He had no love for the English, but luckily no love for the Boers either. The woman persuaded him to help the wounded soldier. Who knows why he agreed to it – some whim? They put him on the back of a cart and took him to their farmhouse where the woman nursed him back to health. Just as he was growing stronger, the farm was attacked by a group of Boers who'd heard a rumour that he was in there. The woman hid him. The husband fought them off but he was killed in the process. After their attackers had gone, and being afraid to stay at the farm alone, she led your father across country until he remade contact again with his regiment."

"But there's no mention of a woman helping my father in any of the newspaper accounts I've read. No woman has ever been mentioned."

Marcus shrugged. "It makes the story stronger without her, doesn't it? It was the image of your father's lone survival that caught the public imagination. The heroic survival of one man against all odds. It loses some of its power if he has to thank a woman for his escape – and a Frenchwoman at that."

"You mean, without her it made better propaganda."

Marcus inhaled on his cigar and let the smoke trickle out through his nostrils as he studied Evelyn. "Don't judge your father, Evelyn. Things are very rarely black and white."

"My father always insisted that they were. Something was either right or wrong, and there was no middle ground."

"Different times give rise to different values. My

understanding is that your father assessed the benefit to the country of propaganda as opposed to truth, and propaganda won – so the image of the lone survivor was born. What harm did it do?" He inhaled the smoke from his cigar. "I'd let things rest, Evelyn. We're heading for a general election and there are enough people trying to stir up trouble for us. Your father's story is as potent as it ever was, so let's not water it down with the truth. For the country's sake, for the Party's, don't pick the scabs off old wounds. You never know what you might uncover."

So that was the secret his mother had wanted to conceal: the existence of the Frenchwoman. She had wanted to protect the image of the lone hero. Evelyn wondered if his father had ever regretted his decision to bend the truth and had used his journal to ease his conscience by confessing it.

Marcus leant forward and lowered his voice. "Evelyn, the Liberals are looking for any stick to beat us with. Don't give them one by raising questions about Majuba. No matter how small it might seem to you, they will turn it into something big, I assure you. Will you drop the matter and let sleeping dogs lie?"

Evelyn finished his whisky. "What was the name of the farmer who helped my father?"

"Montrecourt, I think," replied Marcus. ""His wife was called Hortense."

Evelyn frowned. Montrecourt – that name again. It was becoming as troubling to him as it had so evidently been to his father.

*

Evelyn crumpled the pamphlet in his fist and hurled it to the floor. It had been stuffed through the letterbox of the front door at Carlton Terrace. Normally, Wilson would have found it first and destroyed it without bothering his master, but this morning Evelyn was too early for him.

The pamphlet was an abusive attack on the Tories written by some member of the gutter press, who was too cowardly to sign his name on it. The electorate had just voted to return the government – by a much reduced majority, it was true, but they were still in power. It was frustrating to read rubbish from people who refused to accept that fact. He bent down and picked up the pamphlet again. He'd taken his seat in the Lords now, so it was his duty to denounce such attacks. He smoothed out the creases so that he could read it properly. Someone with the initials J.H wrote it. He read:

> *My friends, Victoria is dead and we have a new monarch on the throne, but nothing else has changed. The election that our 'esteemed' Tory government hoisted upon us was a sham. Even though they lost votes, even though they barely have a majority left, they still control our lives. So-called great families like the Harringdons still grow rich by sacrificing the British soldier to their self-interested, expansionist ideals.*

Evelyn gave an exclamation of disgust. The man should not be allowed to get away with such a blatant lie. He should be taken to court – not ignored as the elders of the Party had advised.

> *Our politicians appeal to our nationalism; they talk glibly about the war; they try to persuade us that Great Britain had to avenge past insults and assert the rights of its British citizens in the Boer-controlled region of Transvaal. People, do not be fooled.*
>
> *This government's desire for war was being driven by nothing more than greed. That is what our men fought and died for. To secure the gold fields of South Africa for a group*

of adventurers and financiers, who have no allegiance except to profit, and no patriotism – merely a commitment to the marketplace.

Who are these politicians? Unelected peers of the land who need new injections of gold from the Transvaal to uphold their hereditary position. You were, and still are, being used, my friends, and we are still failing to challenge them.

At the bottom, in small print, was the address of the printer: Wickam's of Chain Alley. Evelyn rang for Wilson.

"My coat."

"Your breakfast, sir?"

"No time for breakfast," Evelyn said grimly. "I'm going hunting."

Chain Alley was off Fleet Street, he discovered. The printers were housed in a suitably grubby little office in the basement of a four-storey building that housed a number of other dubious-looking businesses. The man running the press was tall and lanky, and he'd long ago outgrown his suit. He had a permanent sniff.

Over the noise of the machinery, he didn't hear his visitor enter. Evelyn had to tap him on the shoulder to make his presence known. The man leapt in the air and then stared uneasily at the gentleman facing him.

"Yes, sir?"

"Are you Wickam?"

"Yes, sir."

Evelyn pulled the pamphlet from his inner pocket. "I want to know the name and whereabouts of the author of this." He waved the paper in front of the man's nose.

Wickam shifted uneasily. "I honestly couldn't say, sir. I just do the printing see."

Evelyn moved closer. "I think you will remember. Or I'll have you closed down. What you have printed in this pamphlet is scurrilous." He saw that the man looked puzzled. "Have you any idea what scurrilous means?"

"No, sir."

"All you need to understand is that it will land you in serious trouble. I want the name and address of the author of this garbage. If you make me leave without it, I will return with the law and have you put out of business."

"I just print what I'm given," the man protested. He saw the set of Evelyn's jaw and quickly added: "His name's Joshua Harlik, but I don't know where he lives. We do business at the Lamb and Flag down Wiltshore Street. That's the only place I've ever met him. He just sends word and I meet him there at the table by the window nearest the door. He's usually in there every morning about ten."

Evelyn nodded. "There, that wasn't too difficult, was it?" Pleased with himself, he headed for the Lamb and Flag.

It was a narrow building, squashed between two warehouses. It consisted of one dark, smoke-filled room that smelt of rancid fat and stale beer. He headed straight for the table nearest the door. Joshua Harlik didn't look like a rat or a weasel, as Evelyn had supposed he would. He was a smartly dressed young man, with a waistcoat and jacket of good quality. He looked like an educated man. He glanced up as Evelyn stopped by his table.

"Ah, Sir Evelyn, I presume. Good morning. I was told that you were looking for me."

"News travels fast," Evelyn muttered. He took the leaflet out of his pocket and flung it on the table. "Are you the author of this trash?"

"I am, although I would disagree with your description of it."

Evelyn sat down on the bench that was facing Harlik, itching to knock the smug expression off his face. "By what right do you accuse the government of leading this country into war for profit?"

"The right of a free man."

"The men you attack have dedicated their lives to this country."

"Men like your father, you mean?"

"Yes." Evelyn knew he must keep calm. He mustn't lose his temper because that was precisely what a man like Harlik would want him to do. What he *was* going to do, he wasn't sure. Reason with the man, perhaps? "My father fought beside his men. He was wounded in battle. He didn't cower behind a desk wielding a pen. He wielded a sword."

"The pen can be more effective at getting to the truth."

The man was obviously trying to bate him. Perhaps it had been a mistake to confront him, but he couldn't just walk away now. "Or it can be used to spread lies and rumours."

"Lies and rumours?" Harlik's laugh was derisory. "And this from a government who has turned the spreading of lies and rumours into an art form. Let's talk about your father, shall we? There is much I could tell you, my friend, about the Hero of Majuba, if you would like me to. Things that could seriously damage the legend."

Evelyn felt on much firmer ground now. The legend had never been stronger. "Tell me your lies, by all means," he said.

"My revelations," corrected Harlik. "Did you realise that your father was not alone when he crossed the veldt and made it safely back to camp?"

If that was the worst the man could do, then there was little to fear. Evelyn leant back in his chair, arms folded, and waited for Harlik to continue.

"All this lone hero stuff is rubbish, and if he lied about that, what else did he lie about?"

Evelyn shrugged. "I would suggest nothing."

"He was helped to escape by the wife of the man who'd sheltered him from the Boers. The man's name was Henri Montrecourt, a Frenchman."

His meeting with Marcus White had prepared him for this. He doubted such information would make much of a dent in his father's reputation – his mother had been foolish to worry about it. He started to rise. "If that's all..."

"No, it isn't," Harlik said, quickly. "I met Montrecourt a year before the first war against the Boers began." Harlik leant forward to make sure Evelyn was listening. "It was 1879 and I was in Africa doing an article about the diamond mines around Kimberley for *The Enquirer*."

At the naming of a left-wing rag that had since been closed down, Evelyn's lip curled.

"Hear me out," Harlik said. "I know your opinions, but hear me out. While I was there, I met Montrecourt in a bar in Pretoria. He was a pretty unpleasant individual even then. A Frenchman who loved his drink. He was boasting that he'd laid claim to a gold strike not far from Pretoria – somewhere called Witwatersrand. He didn't know if it was a good claim. Said he was meeting someone who could tell him. Ever heard of the River Valley Mining Company?"

"Yes." Evelyn knew of it. It was one of the biggest exporters of gold in Africa.

"Yes, well, in 1879 nobody had. Montrecourt said it was a representative of that company who was going to test the gold from his claim. I didn't think anymore about it, just another broken drunk dreaming about growing rich. Africa was full of them."

Evelyn shrugged. "My father wasn't in Africa until 1881 so I don't see how this can have anything to do with him."

Harlik ignored the interruption. "I saw Montrecourt again after he'd met with the representative. River Valley had produced a report on the sample. It was fool's gold, the report said. Rock that glitters like gold, but is worthless. At first Montrecourt didn't believe him, but they shared a few drinks and the Englishman said he might still be able to make money out of his claim anyway. The company needed to test machinery for a rich strike they'd made some miles away and he was willing to pay Montrecourt a reasonable sum for his worthless claim, as it would be useful to them for testing new equipment. By now Montrecourt was blind drunk and signed away the claim without argument, pocketing a fist full of notes. He was a rich man by his standards. The money didn't last him long, of course, and he was soon penniless again. On the other hand, the River Valley was declared one of the most successful mining companies in the area because of its discovery of a rich vein of gold at Witwatersrand."

"I repeat this has nothing to do with my father," Evelyn said impatiently.

"Hear me out. The war broke out at the end of the next year, 1880, and I had to return to England. Out of curiosity I did some digging when I got back, into the formation of the River Valley Mining Company, and found that your father was on the board. So were Marcus White and Lord Renfrew – both friends of your father, I believe?"

For a moment, Evelyn was thrown. But then he laughed at the ludicrous suggestion that his father and Lord Renfrew would be involved in the tawdry world of business. They were gentlemen.

"If you're claiming that my father was associated with this company and with cheating Montrecourt, then you're an idiot." His father, above all people, could never be accused of corruption. "I assure you business held no interest for him and, I repeat, he wasn't in Africa till 1881."

"No, but when he *was* there, the year of Majuba, it was Montrecourt's wife who found your father after the battle. Isn't that curious?"

The man was fishing for information, that was all, trying to forge links where none existed. "As my father was never involved with this River Valley business, then I can't see anything curious in it at all. You're desperately trying to make up a story that doesn't exist."

"A few months after Majuba, when the war was over, I went back to Pretoria."

"To dig out any dirt you could find?"

"I knew Montrecourt's farm was at Virkskruge, so I returned to the area to see what I could discover. The farm was deserted. I was told the official version – that Montrecourt and his wife had sheltered an Englishman. A Boer raiding party had arrived at the farm and Montrecourt had been shot. The woman and the Englishman escaped. A neighbour told me the unofficial version. That he had, in fact, seen the wounded Englishman leaving the farm with the woman, but an attack by the Boers never happened."

"So how did Montrecourt die?"

"A good question. I began to search around the farm and I found a grave. I opened it up. There wasn't a great deal left of him but it was Montrecourt all right, and I found a bullet in his ribs."

"So he *was* killed by the Boers."

"An English bullet."

Evelyn could see what Harlik was implying. It was ridiculous. "Weapons are captured by both sides in war."

"My friend, if there was no Boer attack on the farm and no other bullets were lying around for me to find, what does that suggest to you?"

"That you have a vivid imagination." Evelyn was furious at the man for making such an outrageous suggestion.

"I tell you what I believe. Your father was on the Board of the River Valley Mining Company that cheated Montrecourt out of his claim. It was your father's misfortune that it was Montrecourt who found him when he was wounded. Then, when Montrecourt discovered the connection between your father and the River Valley, he threatened to reveal your father's involvement in the deceit. Perhaps, finally, he'd found proof of it. After all, your father was wounded and he probably had a fever – who knows what he might have admitted under those circumstances? Whatever it was, I believe your father killed Montrecourt to protect his reputation. It wouldn't do for an English gentleman to be accused of fraud."

Evelyn was struggling not to hit the man. By coming here, he had given Harlik the opportunity to voice his poisonous lies. The Party had been right: ignore him and let him rot. However, Harlik hadn't finished with him yet.

"There was a great deal of money involved, and money can corrupt even the purest of us. Besides, the government were, and still are, anxious to hide the fact that they've made huge profits out of these wars. I believe that underneath the veneer of all that breeding, men like your father are venal and greedy, and they are guilty of having led this country into two wars simply to protect their own investments. If I keep digging, I will eventually prove it."

Evelyn regarded him with contempt. "Coincidence and conjecture, that's all this is. There are a great many words like *might have* and *perhaps* in your story. It's a ridiculous idea and you know it."

"I don't think so. I might not have got the story right yet, but there is a secret to uncover. Something happened after Majuba – something that's been hidden. Believe me, I can smell a scandal from a mile away."

Evelyn thought of something that Harlik had conveniently chosen to ignore. "Would Montrecourt's wife have helped my father escape if he had killed her husband? Had that entered your head?"

"Maybe she had no choice."

"Then all you need to do is produce her and your story is proven." He saw uncertainty flit across Harlik's face and knew that he had scored a point.

"Sadly, I have no idea where Hortense Montrecourt is. Once your father had reached the safety of the camp, I presume he abandoned her in the Transvaal."

"So, you have no proof at all then. Well, I suggest you drop this fantasy of yours, Harlik, unless you want to make yourself look ridiculous – or worse, you want to be hauled into court to face a libel charge." Evelyn screwed the pamphlet up and dropped it on the table before leaving.

Outside, a thick fog had descended since his arrival at the inn. He drew the collar of his coat up around his ears against the cold. His footsteps echoed through the empty streets. A hansom clattered past but Evelyn didn't hail it. He needed to walk.

It was obvious, of course, that everything the man had said was a lie or just conjecture. However, it wasn't only the name Montrecourt he'd heard his father say as he died; he had also used the word 'bury'. Had he said 'bury' or 'bury him deep'?

He strode on, the fog growing denser around him as he struggled to make sense of it all.

CHAPTER SEVEN

Marie missed Daphne; she missed the stimulus of her conversation and the thrill of playing even a small part in her world of ideas and ideals. Daphne hadn't written since leaving the hospital. Marie would at least have liked to know that her friend was well. She couldn't help feeling a little abandoned.

It was with difficulty that she settled back into the dull routine of how life had been prior to the march. The Mintons did their best to relieve the boredom and spent as much time with her as they could, and she walked out with Stanley every Sunday. It was kind of him, but they had little in common and barely exchanged a word. She was grateful for the presence of the dogs, which provided a topic of conversation.

Now, at last, John Pickard sent for her – "to discuss your future", his note had said. She'd been on the point of writing to him, because she had some ideas of her own that she wanted to discuss. She soon found herself sitting in his office, nervously facing him across the desk, while he leaned back in his chair and viewed her silently. This silence unnerved her and she decided to take the initiative.

"I'm sorry I've been such a trouble to you, Mr Pickard. If you could make Sister Grace see that we never meant any harm when we planned the march."

"You are answerable only to me, Miss Montrecourt."

This surely meant he hadn't told Sister Grace and she was grateful for it. "Then let me apologise to *you*."

"I did warn you not to become involved in Miss Senior's

circle," he continued. "She's ruined the lives of the women at the factory, and she very nearly ruined yours too."

"I know." Geoffrey had made plain to her what the consequences might have been. She could have been injured or ostracised – he said he wasn't sure which was worse. "And I'm grateful to you for persuading the police not to take action against me."

"I did nothing. It's Stanley Minton that you have to thank for that."

Marie was surprised. "He never mentioned it to me. That was very kind of him."

"He felt strongly that the matter should be dropped, as there is no danger of you repeating the offence. There isn't, is there?"

She shook her head. There would be no danger of that. "No. I'll write to him and thank him."

"You can do more than that, Miss Montrecourt."

"Oh, of course."

"The… er… allowance that's been made on your behalf – I told you it would be paid until your future was settled, but we can't wait indefinitely for that. Recent events have made me realise that it needs to be settled sooner rather than later."

Of course, Sister Grace couldn't go on supporting her forever – that she had managed to do so at all still seemed a miracle. "I have given that some thought, Mr Pickard. I decided I should look for some kind of work." What it would be and how she would set about it she had no idea, but it was the only solution. She caught sight of Mr Pickard's face. It had turned bright red.

"Work? Certainly not. I wouldn't allow it, Miss Montrecourt. I would be neglecting my role as guardian if I encouraged you to think I would. If Miss Senior has put that notion in your head, then put it straight out again."

She hadn't expected such a strong reaction from him. "I realise it won't be easy."

"For any young woman the workplace is full of dangers, but for someone with no experience of the world, or of life, the dangers are even stronger. You've led a sheltered life, Miss Montrecourt, and it is a harsh world out there. I don't think you're aware of it."

He was wrong. Working with Daphne had *made* her aware of it. She opened her mouth to say so, but Mr Pickard hadn't finished with his objections yet.

"Do you really think you'll find work with no references and no experience? Certainly not of the kind that any decent woman would find acceptable," he said. "If you persist with this, then I will have to wash my hands of you. The financial support you receive will end immediately. How do you propose to live while you look for this work?"

"I thought I could use the money from Sister to support myself while I looked. If you ask her…"

"I keep telling you, Miss Montrecourt, this matter concerns only me. I am your guardian and I'm entrusted to act in your best interests. I have a free hand to do that, and it is what I intend to do. If I withdraw my support, you may find you can no longer legally stay in this country, and there'd be no alternative for you but to return to the convent."

She could never face that. She tried to control the tremble in her voice. "Then what do I do?"

John Pickard leant back in his chair and cleared his throat. "There is an alternative. Let me put it to you. I have been approached by someone who is a great admirer of yours, someone who is willing to give you his support and protection. Quite rightly, he wouldn't approach you directly without my approval, but I would have no hesitation in giving him that approval if you were interested."

She wasn't sure she had understood his meaning. "I'm sorry?"

"Do you have an objection to marriage?"

She looked at him in astonishment. It had never entered her head. "I… No, certainly not. I'm just…" she broke off in confusion. "But I don't know anyone."

"I've been approached by Stanley Minton."

She was so astonished that she couldn't speak. He'd never given any indication that he was interested in her. She could feel her face turning pink. Was that what the outings had been about? "I never knew. I never suspected…"

John Pickard was watching her closely. "Yes, I can see it's come as a surprise to you, but it would be the perfect solution. At the moment, he's expressed an interest only and he obviously needs to be sure that it would be agreeable to you before proceeding."

She had no idea what to say. Silence was her refuge.

Mr Pickard took her silence for modesty. "Of course, you're flattered by his interest. I can understand that. Let me assure you that he is a decent man. He lives with his mother and father in Ilkley, a town just a few miles from here. He's supported them all his working life. He's a respected member of the business community in Harrogate. There's nothing about Stanley to offend anyone and, as your guardian, I would be happy to encourage his interest in you if you have no objection to it."

Did she object? The truth was that she had no idea. She'd never viewed him as a potential husband. She realised that John Pickard was waiting for her answer. She cast around for something to say. "I know so little about him. He seems a great deal older than me."

"Stanley is in his forties, which is a good age in a husband. You are very young and he has the experience to guide and protect you."

"But he's never indicated any feelings towards me."

"And nor should he have done, until he spoke to me."

"He wants to marry me?" she said, as if saying it aloud might help her to believe it. John Pickard nodded his confirmation.

"I won't fill your head with romantic nonsense, Miss Montrecourt – you wouldn't expect me to. For Stanley, I think he's of an age when his thoughts have turned to settling down and perhaps starting a family." He placed his fingertips together. "I know he respects and likes you. He sees in you a vulnerable young woman who needs his protection and, gallantly, he's willing to offer it. On your part, you will have a position of some standing as the wife of a prominent businessman. You will have security for the rest of your life and a home of your own. Weigh that against the alternative."

She needed more time to think. "The Mintons are Chapel and I was brought up a Catholic, wouldn't that prove difficult?"

"I've thought of that. Geoffrey tells me you never go to mass. I assume, therefore, you have no great commitment to the faith you were brought up in. I assume, under the circumstances, you will be happy to adopt your husband's faith."

Did Sister Grace approve of that? Or would she ever even know? John Pickard had made it clear that he was acting on his own initiative and, anyway, she could hardly write to her and ask. The decision was hers and hers alone.

"Think about it, Miss Montrecourt," said John Pickard, sensitive to the delicacy of the situation, "but I will need to know within the week."

She returned to Devonshire Place with her thoughts in turmoil and went straight to her room. She didn't want to see anyone, least of all the Mintons. Did they know about Stanley's intentions? They'd never given her any indication. She slept very little that night. How did she feel about Stanley Minton? Did she feel anything? How did she feel about the alternative? The convent wasn't an option, but neither was work if she had no means to support herself while she looked for it.

"He admires you and he wants to protect you" – that's what Mr Pickard had said. She remembered Sal and the factory women. Was marriage really such a bad prospect compared to theirs? She remembered the two girls at the convent. A marriage to Stanley would make sure that didn't happen to her. After a sleepless night, she had made up her mind. She sat down and wrote a note to Mr Pickard. It simply said:

I will be happy to accept Stanley Minton's attentions. Marie Montrecourt.

*

Having prepared herself for whatever might happen next, she found to her frustration that nothing did. Neither Geoffrey nor Isabelle gave her any indication that they knew about Stanley's intentions. Nor, over the days that followed, did she hear anything from Stanley. She was beginning to wonder if she'd imagined the whole thing.

Then, a few weeks later, she was invited to join the Mintons at the Harrogate Dog Show where Stanley was showing Damson in Best of Breed. They met him at the showground, but he was too preoccupied with parading Damson to do anything more than nod in her direction. When Damson won, Stanley's face burst into a smile. It was the first time Marie had ever seen him do so.

When they finally got the chance to talk, he addressed her directly. "Should we visit the funfair?" he asked. "Would you like that?"

Relieved that he'd finally done more than just acknowledge her presence, she agreed enthusiastically. "Yes, that would be lovely." Geoffrey and Isabelle agreed.

They all headed for the funfair – along with, it seemed, everyone else in Harrogate. The grounds were teeming with so many people that it wasn't easy to forge a way through but Stanley and Damson cleared the way, with Stanley self-consciously clutching the trophy under his arm.

As they approached the merry-go-round, the steam engine that drove it hissed out a great globule of steam. Even though she was some feet away, Marie could feel its heat on her cheek. Garishly painted horses bobbed up and down as mechanised musicians played pretend instruments – while the cylinder that actually provided the music laboured away hidden in its wooden box.

"Want a ride?" Geoffrey asked his wife, shouting above the noise. Isabelle hastily shook her head in reply.

"Do *you* want a ride?" Stanley asked Marie.

She was surprised. It didn't seem the sort of thing that would appeal to him at all. She realised he was trying to please her.

"Yes. I would like that," she said quickly, and Stanley handed Damson's lead to Geoffrey.

When the merry-go-round stopped, Stanley helped her onto the deck. He had to lift her onto the back of one of the horses because she was too tiny to reach its stirrup. She sat side saddle, clutching the long twisted barley-sugar pole to which the horse was attached. Stanley sat astride the horse next to hers, still clutching the trophy under his arm. The music started to play, the machinery whirred and the horses began to rise and fall as the merry-go-round turned. It began to gather speed, whirling faster and faster, and round and round. The music was deafening. Marie threw back her head and laughed, swept along by the excitement of it all. She became aware that Stanley was trying to say something to her. He leaned perilously towards her but his voice was drowned out by the music. She saw that he was struggling to free a blue velvet ring box from his pocket. This was the moment from which there would be no going back.

"Will you marry me, Marie?" He had to bellow the words to be heard.

Her hair had escaped its restraining pins, her cheeks were flushed with the excitement of the ride, and as the painted horse rose to its full height she could see across the whole fairground to the moors. She was flying through the air. This was freedom; everything was possible.

"Yes," she shouted back.

"What?"

"Yes, I will marry you."

He didn't say anything further, but as the merry-go-round began to slow down, and when the rise and fall of the horses came to a halt, he was able to lean towards her and slip the ring over her finger. She gazed down at the small circle of cut diamonds surrounding the blue sapphire. Her finger was so small, though, that the ring was in danger of slipping off again and she had to close her hand into a fist to keep it in place.

"I'll have it made to fit," he said.

As he helped her off the ride, she had to lean against him for a moment to steady herself because she felt quite giddy. She wanted to say something meaningful to mark the importance of the occasion, but she couldn't think of anything suitable to say. It was Stanley who spoke.

"We should inform Isabelle and Geoffrey that we are to be married."

He made it all sound so matter-of-fact. She looked down at the ring on her finger to prove to herself that it really had happened. She turned impetuously to Stanley, but he'd already left her side and was talking to Isabelle and Geoffrey. Isabelle gave an exclamation of delight and rushed over to her.

"Stanley's just told us. I am so pleased for you."

She hugged her and Marie clung on to her tightly, as if for support.

*

"How do you do, Mrs Minton, Mr Minton. I am so pleased to meet you both." The prospect of meeting Stanley's parents had worried her for days. Isabelle had done her best to reassure her but Stanley was equally on edge, which didn't help.

Everything was moving at such a pace. They were to be married a few weeks from now. A client of Mr Pickard's was making her wedding dress, the chapel had been booked, and now she was in the parlour of The Laurels in Ilkley facing Edith and Edwin Minton.

Edith, her squat figure emphasised by a shapeless black dress, smiled briefly as she shook Marie limply by the hand. Marie turned to Stanley's father. He was positioned stiffly in front of the fireplace, his ruddy complexion and bristling moustache giving him the appearance of a sergeant major in the British Army. He appeared to have been crammed into his best suit, which was obviously too tight for him. He didn't offer to shake her hand but nodded a welcome, the starched collar allowing little room for movement.

At Stanley's invitation, Marie perched uncomfortably on the edge of one of the brown leather armchairs. It was stuffed with horse hair and was extremely uncomfortable. Gladys, the daily maid, served ginger cake and tea. Marie's gaze settled on a glass dome on the mahogany sideboard. It contained a stuffed bird of prey with its claws wrapped around a dried twig, its wings frozen in flight. "That's very…" she struggled to find a suitable word, "unusual."

Edith nodded, accepting it as a compliment, while Stanley's father was too busy concentrating on chasing crumbs around his plate, before dabbing at them with his one remaining piece of cake, to say anything.

Stanley had told her that this was where they would be living when they married. Surreptitiously, she tried to take in her surroundings. From the little she could see, she found the rooms dark and oppressive. The curtains in the front parlour were closed against the sun and the air was permeated by the smell of stale cabbage. Perhaps she would be allowed to make some small changes?

It was a short visit, filled with pauses and slightly stilted conversation. She sensed their disapproval of her and mentioned it to Stanley. He waved aside her concern.

"You're imagining it," he said. "They're just not used to entertaining visitors."

*

John Pickard hammered on the door of her room. "Are you ready yet?"

"Nearly."

Marie leant forward to rearrange the circle of forget-me-nots that held her veil in place. There was a hammering at the door again.

"Miss Montrecourt, we are already late. I must insist we leave now."

"I'm coming."

It was the last time she would look into a mirror and see Marie Montrecourt. In future, it would be Marie Minton who would be staring back at her.

Despite a heavy downpour, a few curious passers-by lingered for a moment outside the chapel in Ilkley as the bride's carriage drew to a halt. Pickard, resplendent in a canary yellow waistcoat, helped Marie to alight. The pavements were running with water and she held up the skirt to prevent it discolouring her wedding dress, which was *peau de crepe* trimmed with small silver crosses.

The little Wesleyan chapel was dark and uncluttered by ornaments. There was nothing here to remind her of the rich hangings and jewelled crosses of the past – and for that she was grateful. She was too nervous to look at the small congregation gathered to witness the marriage and was only aware of the back of Stanley's head and the folds of pink flesh that rested on his collar. As she arrived beside him, the Reverend Jackson stepped forward and the service began.

It all happened so quickly; strange hymns, people standing, people sitting. She vaguely heard Stanley mumbling his vows and she tried to control the tremble in her own voice as she repeated the same words. Her hand shook as Stanley held it to place the plain gold band on her finger, then she realised that his hand was shaking too. It gave her some comfort.

The Reverend Jackson said something and Stanley carefully lifted Marie's veil. It caught on one of the flowers of the circlet holding it in place and she had to help him to release it. He kissed her briefly on the cheek, then placed her hand on his arm and they walked towards the door side by side. The small congregation fell into step behind them. She was Mrs Minton, now and forever.

It had been left to Isabelle and Gladys, the Minton's daily maid, to arrange the reception at Marie's new home. They'd decorated the front parlour with white ribbons, tying them to whatever a ribbon could be tied to, and had carefully placed vases of white carnations and roses throughout the house. The curtains were fully drawn back and one window was thrown wide open, but Marie was still aware of the smell of stale cabbage.

As the front parlour filled with people, Marie, still wearing her wedding dress, received warm congratulations from Jenny Godson and a sour smile from Alice Smith. She didn't hear or see either, however, as she was too busy watching Stanley lead his mother to an armchair. Her mother-in-law had said very little to her all day and she wondered if she had done anything to displease her.

"Can I get you something to eat, Ma?" she could hear Stanley asking.

She saw Edith wince painfully as she sat. "No. I'm not hungry. Don't you worry about me." As Stanley was about to take her at her word, she quickly added: "Well, perhaps a cup of tea then. I might manage a sip of tea. Just a small one, and very weak."

Marie watched Stanley trot obediently into the kitchen in search of the housekeeper. She glanced around and saw Edwin, Stanley's father, sitting near the window. She contemplated going over to talk to him, but she wasn't quite sure what she would say.

"You look very beautiful, Mrs Minton."

Startled by the whisper so close to her ear, Marie swung around and was surprised to find herself face-to-face with a young man. A shock of blond hair flopped over his forehead. His face seemed familiar, but she couldn't think where they might have met.

"Did I frighten you? I don't usually have that effect on the ladies. I'm Peter Minton, Stanley's younger brother. Welcome to the family. Welcome to Ilkley. Not sure it can measure up to Paris, though. Isn't that where you're from?" His smile was so infectious that Marie found herself smiling back.

"No. I've never been to Paris," she said.

"Doesn't matter, neither have I. That's better," he added, as she smiled again. "You are French, though?" She nodded. "Thought so, there's a tantalising hint of an accent. You looked like a frightened little mouse during the ceremony. You still do."

"I'm sorry. I'm so… it's all so strange. I'm pleased to meet you. I didn't realise that Stanley had another brother besides Geoffrey." She extended her hand.

"That's a little formal, isn't it? We're family now." He bent down and kissed her lightly on the lips. Startled, Marie recoiled. "It's all right, it's all right, it's permitted. It's an English custom to kiss the bride, but only family members.

Don't let old George Smith try it." The thought of George Smith even attempting it while his wife was around made her laugh. "Where on earth did Stanley find you?" he asked, softly.

Isabelle's arrival was a great relief to her, as she had no idea how to answer the question.

"Bring Marie outside will you, Peter? Stanley wants a photograph now that the rain's stopped."

As he led her out of the room, Peter said, "I've been studying you and, you know, I'm certain we've met before."

"I have that feeling too."

"I never forget a pretty face. It was outside Ogden's. It was snowing heavily. You ran away from me, down some alley."

She remembered now. It was the day she'd first met Daphne. "You were following me," she said, accusingly.

"I obviously made an impression." He grinned.

It was decided it would be better to have the grey stone house as the background of the photograph rather than the pen that the dogs occupied, so the photographer asked everyone to shuffle around. Damson and Major, excited by all the activity, were pacing up and down inside their cage, emitting the occasional bark for attention. The photographer was something of a martinet, however, and no one dared to move.

As he fussed one last time with the composition, Marie stole a curious glance at Peter who was chatting to Isabelle. It was impossible to believe that he was a Minton. He caught her looking at him and winked, and she quickly busied herself with arranging the skirt of her dress. The photographer clapped his hands to gain everyone's attention. "Now, please, no one must move until I say so." As they all obediently froze, the photographer uncovered the negative. Startled by the flash that followed, a blackbird took flight.

As the group broke up, Marie heard Alice Smith say to

Stanley's mother: "Are you all right, Edith? You look like you're at a funeral, not a wedding."

And Edith's curt reply: "As all right as can be expected."

★

The guests had left and Marie sat alone in the front parlour, surveying the debris left over from the celebration. Antimacassars lay crumpled on the seats of the horse hair armchair and sofa, and the glass dome over the tableau of the dead bird had been covered by a napkin. She'd seen Peter do that. He had been aware that she was watching him and he'd done it to make her smile. She looked up to see her husband observing her silently from the doorway. When he realised she'd seen him, he rubbed his hands together as if to warm them.

"Well, Peter's always the last one to go."

"Has he gone? He didn't say goodbye to me."

"That's Peter, I'm afraid. Not one to stand on ceremony." Another awkward pause followed as they both searched for something else to say. "He's gone back to Bradford. Ma's gone up to her room. Oh, she said to excuse her as she's very tired. Pa's gone upstairs too. It's been a bit of a strain for them both."

Marie glanced at the marble clock on the mantle. It was just seven o'clock. If she were in Devonshire Place now, she'd be dining with the other lodgers. If she were in the convent, she would be at prayer. "I should unpack, I suppose."

"No need. Gladys has done that for you," Stanley said. "You can rearrange everything to your liking tomorrow. I expect you're tired."

"Yes." She was grateful for his consideration, but she was longing for some small sign of affection. He'd been correct and formal all day, except when his hand had trembled as he slipped the ring on her finger. Impulsively, she stood on tiptoe and kissed him on the cheek. "Stanley, I do so want to make you happy."

Immediately, she knew she'd done the wrong thing because he became even more awkward. "Of course," he said, "I'm sure." He cleared his throat uneasily, then picked up one of the oil lamps that Gladys had lit before leaving, indicating for her to follow him up the stairs.

She had some idea of what would happen next. She'd listened to her fellow pupils gossiping in the dormitory, but they had never been explicit. She remembered hearing them say: "The man will know what to do."

They reached the first landing and Stanley obviously felt he should make some effort at conversation. "That's Ma and Pa's room," he whispered, pointing to a closed door. "And that's Peter's." He indicated another closed door next to his parent's room. "It's always kept ready for him. Ma believes he'll come back home to live here some day, but I don't think so. Trouble is Ma doesn't like to lose her sons."

There was another door next to Peter's room that was slightly ajar. Through the gap Marie could see an ornate stand made of wood and wrought iron, which supported a small sink. One of the new water closets stood beside it, decorated with a brown ivy design. Stanley saw Marie looking at it.

"That's Ma's pride and joy. It flushes when you pull the chain. But she insists we still use the privy outside in the yard. This one is only for show."

"What's in that room?" She pointed to a closed door opposite Peter's.

"It contains all Ma's 'collectables', as she calls them. Well – it's stuff we don't use any more really. And up here…" he continued on up a narrow staircase, "is my room. And the one opposite is yours."

"Oh."

She was thrown. She'd assumed they were to share a

bedroom, like Geoffrey and Isabelle, and Stanley's Ma and Pa. Why was it to be different for them? Not sure how she felt about it, she glanced inside. It was a small, neat box room, which smelt strongly of fresh paint and wallpaper paste. It had a window overlooking the back. The wallpaper was dark blue and patterned with large red flowers, and the curtains were of matching blue linen fringed with red. The dark colours made the room feel stifling.

"Ma got it redecorated for you." Stanley became aware of her lack of enthusiasm and added, "I hope you find it acceptable."

So was this to be her future? A marriage lacking in warmth and affection – and, yet, he had wanted to marry her. Had he since discovered something disagreeable in her, but gone through with the marriage anyway? She felt unwelcome and unwanted on what should have been a day full of hope.

"Is it acceptable?" he asked again.

She kept her voice strong when she replied. "Yes, perfectly acceptable, of course."

She entered the room and closed the door behind her.

CHAPTER EIGHT

No matter how hard he tried, Evelyn could not forget the meeting he'd had with Harlik. He was angry with himself for allowing it to trouble him. The suspicion that his father would stoop low enough to participate in fraud was unthinkable, and even more obscene was the suggestion that he would kill a man to protect his reputation. However, those last words of his father kept crawling out of the back of his mind to plague him: "Bury him".

The problem was he didn't have enough to do, which meant he had too much time to think. He was making little impression in the Lords and he was beginning to believe he never would. "Bury him" – there they were again, those words. They continually wormed their way to the front of his mind and he couldn't stop them. In an effort to stop torturing himself about it, he returned to the old ways – drinking too much, dining at the club, playing at the gaming tables – but none of it gave him pleasure any more. His participation was intense rather than joyous, and Siggy noticed.

One night Siggy took him aside and asked quietly: "What's going on, Evie?" At first Evelyn tried to shrug off the question, but Siggy persisted: "I know you too well, my friend. Something is troubling you."

Although Siggy had a reputation in society as an empty-headed, good-time playboy, Evelyn knew better. He was an intelligent, loyal and discreet friend, and after a few more protests Evelyn found it a relief to confide in him.

Siggy listened quietly as Evelyn told him about his father's missing journal and how he had found his mother burning it, and his meeting with Harlik and the accusation he had made about the gold claim. He didn't mention the other accusation – the killing of Montrecourt – that was too ludicrous.

"He implied that my father had profited by being on the Board of the River Valley Mining Company when they cheated Montrecourt."

"Oh, come on. That's absurd. Apart from anything else, business was a dirty word to your father. The man is obviously lying."

It was exactly the reassurance Evelyn needed to hear. "Yes, but why?"

"Oh, come on, Evelyn. To ruin the Party, attack the government – a million reasons." Siggy shook his head. "You had a complicated relationship with your father, Evie. And that you can even doubt him proves that it's still there. Love and hate, admiration and envy, they're very close together."

"But why did mother burn the journal? Why did my father say the name Montrecourt when he was dying if he didn't feel guilty about him?"

Siggy ordered them both another brandy. "I don't really understand these things, old fellow, but my advice – for what it's worth – is to stop all this nonsense about your father. You have to look to the future. Make your mark in the Lords." Evelyn was about to say he couldn't hope to do that, but Siggy interrupted him. "No, you are not your father, and if what you say is even half true then you're the better for it." He saw that Evelyn was still troubled. "Listen, search through all the papers at Ardington and look for this supposed link with the River Valley Mining Company. If it exists, you'll surely find it. If it isn't there, then in my opinion it *doesn't*. Now, drink up. There's another brandy waiting to be ordered."

★

Evelyn decided to take Siggy's advice. His mother was in Derbyshire visiting Harriet for a few weeks, so he was able to shut himself away in the attic without arousing her curiosity. After two days he had found nothing to link his father to the Mining Company, although he did discover one thing that surprised him: a series of letters and bills that revealed that his grandfather, Theodore Harringdon, had been a serious gambler. It was a trait he feared he might have inherited.

It seemed that the man had lost the family a fortune by betting on anything and everything that had an element of chance attached to it. He sold most of the contents of the house, and every painting he could lay his hands on, to fund his addiction. When he died, Evelyn's father had inherited nothing but debt, and by the 1870s Ardington was facing financial ruin. No wonder his father had been so fierce in his opposition to his son's gambling. He feared history repeating itself.

Evelyn searched further through the papers. There were letters from his father to some of his creditors asking if he could delay payment of his debts. His pride must have made those letters difficult to write. In them, he explained that there'd been a run of bad winters, which had driven workers off the land and into the cities where industry promised more secure employment. Farms had been abandoned and left to fall into ruin. It was clear that his father was faced with the very real possibility of having to sell off Ardington and everything he owned.

It took Evelyn another two weeks of searching through documents to find the outcome of that crisis. By 1880, miraculously, the debts had all been paid. The house and the lands were saved, and the estate was in profit again. Evelyn could see no reference as to how that had been achieved. What had occurred between Ardington's threatened demise and its salvation a few years later? It could be explained away if his father *had* been on the Board of the River Valley Mining Company and shared in the profits from Witwatersrand. That would certainly explain how Ardington had been rescued.

*

"*I don't mind boys staring hard, if it satisfies their desires…*"

The audience in the Waterloo Empire whistled appreciatively as Marie Lloyd swung her skirts high, letting the words of the song roll off her tongue with all her usual innuendo.

"More champagne down this end, Evie. Don't hog it all to yourself." Siggy, leaning on the bar at the back of the stalls, had to shout above Marie's singing. The rest of the group bellowed their agreement. "Come on, old man. Share it out."

Evelyn slid the bottle down to them. It was supposed to be a celebration of Siggy's birthday, but it was mostly just an excuse to get drunk.

"*Do you think my dress is a little bit…?*"

The audience roared as Marie Lloyd pulled her skirts a little higher.

"*Just a little bit. Not too much of it.* "

Shouts of encouragement came from the audience.

"Wouldn't have thought music hall was Renfrew's kind of bash at all. Eh, Evelyn?"

One of the group nodded to the opposite side of the bar where Lord Renfrew was in deep conversation with a young man. Evelyn glanced over to him. He'd begun to wonder how deeply Renfrew was involved in his father's affairs. Harlik had said he was on the Board of the River Valley Mining Company, too.

Renfrew spotted Evelyn and raised a hand in acknowledgement. After a moment, he took leave of his companion and crossed over to join the group. He placed a friendly hand on Evelyn's shoulder.

"Drop by to see me in the Commons tomorrow at three, will you, young fellow? Need to talk." He nodded to the others and headed for the exit.

"Thought he wouldn't be staying long." Siggy indicated for the barman to open another bottle of Moet Chandon. "Smile, for God's sake, Evelyn. We're celebrating."

★

The next day Evelyn woke with a terrible headache from the night before, the result of mixing too much champagne with too many glasses of Miss Lloyd's cheap whisky in her dressing room afterwards. He groaned. His meeting with Lord Renfrew was at three o'clock and he would be late. If only he could stop his head throbbing.

When he was shown in, Renfrew waved aside his apologies. "No matter. No matter. Thank you for calling by."

For a little while they exchanged pleasantries until, at last, his lordship got to the point of the meeting. "So, Evelyn, I believe you had a tête-à-tête with an enemy of ours – the so-called journalist, Joshua Harlik?"

Evelyn wondered how on earth he knew about that. "A little while ago, yes. He wrote a pamphlet and I wanted to challenge him on it. That's all."

"He is not a good individual, as I'm sure you realise." Evelyn nodded and Renfrew continued. "He's going around saying you sought him out, tried to persuade him to suppress some scandal involving your father?"

Evelyn flushed angrily. "That is absolutely untrue. I did seek him out, but only to tell him to stop printing lies in his pamphlets."

"Not a wise move, Evelyn. I should think he took full

advantage of the meeting and spewed out a few more lies to you."

"Yes." Why was it that every time he thought he'd managed to push his father's past out of his mind, it kept returning to plague him?

"So, what juicy scandal did he try to sell to you?"

Evelyn took a deep breath. He would never have a better opportunity to lay his doubts to rest than the moment just presented to him. "He said there was a link between my father and the River Valley Mining Company. Do you know if that's true?"

"And have you found one?"

Answering a question with another question was a technique Renfrew used to great effect in the House of Commons. "No. None."

"Good."

Evelyn hesitated, aware that his next question could sound like an accusation. "Were you yourself on the board of the company in '79, sir?"

"Harlik tell you that?" Evelyn nodded and Renfrew's face expressed his contempt. "That man has his nose in everything. Well, that one is true. I'm afraid war does create strange bedfellows."

"I'm sure there was a good reason for it, sir," Evelyn said, waiting to be convinced.

"There was. It was in this country's interest that I accepted a place on the board. It enabled me to influence the drawing up of a contract between the British government and The River Valley Mining Company that was very beneficial to us both. The government promised to fund them, and in return they promised us a large percentage of any profits they made, which we used to help pay for the war. Taxes alone couldn't cover it. As I said, that contract was in this country's best interests. I hope you can understand that?"

Evelyn nodded. In truth he understood very little, except that the ways of politics were extremely tortuous.

"I have told you this in the strictest confidence," continued Renfrew. "Very few people were party to this agreement and it has to remain that way. It would be very easy to misrepresent the government's intentions. No private person gained any profits from it, I assure you. You must take my word for that." Renfrew sat back in his chair. "Did Harlik mention that contract?"

"No. He might suspect something, but he can't have proof – otherwise, I'm sure, he would have already used it to discredit the government."

Renfrew smiled. "You learn fast. It would not be helpful for any of us if details of that contract were to become known prematurely; which is why knowledge of it was limited to a very few. In time, the facts will be made public, but until then I would ask you to keep it to yourself."

"I understand the need for discretion." Evelyn couldn't help but feel affronted.

Renfrew settled back, reassured. "Of course."

Evelyn wondered if he was being dismissed, but here was an opportunity that might not present itself again. "Can I ask you something of a more personal nature, Lord Renfrew? Did you know of a man called Montrecourt?"

After only the slightest hesitation, Renfrew replied, "I believe I have heard that name, yes."

"Was Montrecourt cheated out of his claim by the River Valley Mining Company? Forgive me, I'm not suggesting you had any part in it," he added hastily.

"Evelyn, Evelyn," Renfrew shook his head reproachfully. "I hear the voice of Harlik again. The extremes to which that man will go to discredit us never ceases to amaze me."

"It's just that Montrecourt told everyone that the River Valley had cheated him out of his claim and Harlik told me that my father was on the board at the time."

"Montrecourt was a deluded man and Harlik is a liar. Your father was never on the board of any company."

Evelyn felt the need to press him further. "Just before my father died, the last word he tried to say was Montrecourt. I heard him myself."

Renfrew seemed genuinely surprised. "Really? He said Montrecourt?" He regarded him in silence for a moment. "Evelyn, you say you want the truth. Very well, here it is. It's true that Montrecourt went around Pretoria accusing people of cheating him, but he had no proof. If there had been proof, others would have listened to him."

"But why did my father say his name with his last breath?"

"Reliving the moment after Majuba when he nearly died? When he was rescued by the man, perhaps? I believe Marcus White told you the story of his survival and how Montrecourt and his wife saved him? If your father had cheated him, would the man have helped him?"

"I suppose not." Evelyn hadn't thought of that.

"You realise that it's in Harlik's interest to believe what the Frenchman said, don't you, because he wants to destroy this government and the men who represent it? Don't let him succeed. If he can make you, Sir Gordon's son, harbour doubts about his own father, then think what mischief he can make among our enemies."

"I never really doubted my father," Evelyn said, with more fervour than was necessary.

"I should hope not. He served his country loyally." Evelyn nodded. "In fact, your family has always served this country well, which is the reason I asked to see you today." He paused for a moment. "As you know, there've been one or two unfortunate by-elections recently, which have resulted in our losing some valuable members of the cabinet. It's meant a re-ordering of responsibilities. The result is that there's a position to be filled in government. An unofficial position for the moment, but you'd be working to me, and it's a step up in your political career. I know your father would be pleased. Your mother certainly is."

Evelyn was surprised that he'd discussed it with his mother before mentioning it to him, but he was flattered. So he *had* begun to make an impression on his peers.

"I'd like to offer it to you. How would that sit with you?"

"It would sit very well with me, Lord Renfrew."

"Excellent. I'm delighted to hear it. I'm afraid I shall keep you busy, though. Very busy. It will leave you very little time for gallivanting off to the Waterloo Empire to see Marie Lloyd. Call into my office tomorrow. We'll have luncheon and take it further." He stood up, indicating that the meeting was over.

An excited Evelyn called into Whites on the way home, where, as expected, he found Siggy. They celebrated his appointment with two bottles of best Burgundy, although Siggy had mixed feelings about the news.

"I'm glad if you're glad, but does that mean we won't be seeing as much of you around the old haunts?"

"Afraid so, but it's what I need, Siggy. Stop me succumbing to a life of vice."

"I'll just have to succumb on my own then," Siggy said, with a grin. "More importantly, though, it'll stop this obsession you've developed with delving into the past."

"Let's hope so," Evelyn replied.

When he finally got back to Carlton Terrace, he was feeling distinctly the worse for wear. There was a letter waiting for him on the hall table. It seemed to have been delivered by hand. He opened it. It read: *Thought you might find this of interest. I got it from a reliable source.* It was signed J. Harlik. Inside that was a letter to the River Valley Mining Company, bearing his father's signature, asking them to accept his resignation from the board. It was dated just after his father's return from Africa.

Immediately sobered, Evelyn carried both documents through to his study. He lit a cigarette and inhaled deeply as he studied his father's letter to the mining company. There was no doubt that it was his handwriting. Lord Renfrew had lied to him – or was this another of Harlik's little tricks?

"Why the hell can't the man just leave me alone?" he muttered. He threw both letters into the fire and watched them burn.

CHAPTER NINE

She wanted to please Stanley – she wanted to please everyone at The Laurels – but perhaps she was trying too hard because it was having the opposite effect. Any offer of help around the house was rejected; any suggestion for changing the decor was dismissed. Stanley remained a stranger to her and his parents remained distant. Isabelle was the only Minton who seemed willing to accept her as one of the family, and she rarely visited The Laurels. It was on one of those occasions that Marie felt tempted to share her concern.

"I see so little of him. When I do, I try to please him, Isabelle, but he barely seems to notice me."

Isabelle patted her hand comfortingly. "You're very young, Marie, and you must learn to be patient. These things take time. Truthfully, the Mintons aren't the easiest family to get on with."

"No." She could agree with that wholeheartedly. "And Stanley doesn't discuss his work, and that's where he spends most of his time. His mother knows more about The Emporium than I do."

"Edith's always played a large part in Stanley's life," Isabelle said. "I'm afraid that will never change."

"Yes, but I thought there would be moments – when we were alone in our room together – when we could talk. We've never yet lain together as husband and wife. Our relationship is in name only and I don't know what to do." She broke off, aware that Isabelle was looking uncomfortable, obviously embarrassed by such intimate revelations.

"Goodness, is that the time?" her sister-in-law stood up hastily. "You must forgive me, Marie, but I really must return home. Geoffrey is expecting me." She turned at the door and smiled reassuringly. "Don't worry, everything will work out. I'm certain it will."

With that platitude she was gone, and Marie was left to face the realisation that there was no one she could turn to for help. There was no one in whom she could confide, except the dogs. She wandered across to the window, which looked out over the back garden. Damson and Major were pacing up and down in their pens. Stanley was neglecting *them,* too.

She went outside to join them and was rewarded by the warmth of their reception. "Well," she said, ruffling Major's fur, "I can either allow myself to dwindle into a nonexistent being or I can set about making a life of my own. Do you agree?"

Damson pushed a damp nose against her free hand. "You're right," she said, addressing the other dog, "I didn't make a stand at the convent to allow that to happen." Major barked in obvious agreement.

"So, what do we do?" The dogs sank down on their haunches, as if considering the problem, and she sank down on the grass beside them. "I can't get involved in chapel." That's where Edith ruled supreme and where she herself was viewed as a curiosity. She was the foreigner; the child bride whom Stanley had incomprehensibly married. "I could join the lending library and I could try to persuade Stanley to pay for piano lessons." Damson wagged her tail encouragingly. "And we three will all go for long walks together." Both dogs obviously understood the word walks because they stood up immediately and barked. "And I can treat any illnesses you have with remedies from Sister Grace's notebook. There, that should keep me busy."

By the time she left the dogs, her world had become full

of endless possibilities. She still hadn't turned her back on improving relations with her husband, though.

*

She called at The Emporium a few days later with Isabelle, hoping that a show of interest in Stanley's work might bring them closer together. She was greatly surprised by what she saw. The interior was unexpectedly elegant, with etched glass and polished wooden floors, all lit by crystal chandeliers. The shelves were piled high with boxes of herbs and spices, their exotic perfumes mingling with the rich aroma of roasted coffee beans. Lacquered canisters of tea and jars of candied fruit spilled out onto the counter. On closer inspection, she realised that the grandeur was beginning to fade. The chandeliers had crystals missing and the walls showed signs of damp, while the wooden floor was badly stained in places.

It seemed that Stanley was adding a tea room to the shop, having purchased Appleyards next door. He was in the process of having the adjoining wall knocked down, so there was a layer of dust everywhere. She was surprised to discover that Isabelle knew all about it and that Edith had helped Stanley to plan it. Only she, it seemed, had been kept in ignorance. Although Stanley seemed pleased by her visit, it didn't succeed in drawing them any closer together.

Apart from the dogs, Marie had made one other friend at The Laurels. It was Gladys, the Minton's daily maid. She was a hard-working woman with a family of five boys, and a husband who was unemployed. When Edith was out of the house and Edwin had gone fishing with his friend and Stanley was at work, Marie was always sure of a warm welcome in the kitchen. Luckily, she was there when Gladys scalded her arm badly on a boiler containing hot water, and she made up a cream for her to calm the burn and prevent scarring. To Gladys's astonishment, it worked. After that, there was always a special treat waiting for her when she visited the kitchen – a tray of her favourite biscuits or a slice of Madeira cake fresh out of the oven. It was an unspoken agreement between them that they would keep their friendship a secret from the Mintons. They both knew it wouldn't be approved of.

One day, Gladys came to work with a badly bruised face and Marie was shocked to discover the cause. Gladys had been beaten by her husband.

"Can't you do something about it? Tell someone?" Marie said angrily, immediately treating the bruising with arnica.

"No. No one wants to know what happens between a husband and a wife when the front door closes. It's just the way things are. You know, Mrs Minton, you could earn a bit of money for yourself out of these remedies by treating me and my neighbours. You could charge a half penny for it, Mrs Minton. It's cheaper than them going to a doctor. It would give you a bit of money of your own an' all."

"Stanley wouldn't allow it." Marie was as resigned to the inevitable as Gladys.

"Well, he doesn't have to know, does he? I'm not suggesting you tell any lies, but he's not often here, is he? What the eye don't see and all that? Be less to ask him for if you have a bit of money of your own."

Marie was surprised at how much Gladys noticed. "I'll think about it." she said, and over the next few days she did. Gradually, it began to seem a possibility. If she limited herself to only one or two remedies a week, the Mintons wouldn't notice. Perhaps, one day, when they were more comfortable with one another, she could tell Stanley and he might even be proud of her. She told Gladys she would do it. "Our secret," she said, and Gladys nodded.

*

She was upstairs putting the finishing touches to a cure for someone's bad chest when Gladys called up to her. "Mrs Godson is here, Mrs Minton."

There had been another change to her life just recently. Jenny Godson, the wife of Martin, Stanley's assistant, had taken to calling on her every Thursday to accompany her on a walk with Damson and Major. She was grateful to have the company of someone her own age for a change, although they had little in common. Jenny's interests ranged from her new curtains in the parlour, to Martin's sudden liking for her homemade rhubarb jam, and – most importantly – the joys of being a mother. It was a joy that Marie was beginning to believe she would never experience.

"Tell her I'm coming. I'll just collect the dogs," she called back. Carefully covering over the fever cure, she turned off the Bunsen burner.

The weather was cold today and the moors were covered in snow, but the two women kept to their usual route – up Spring Bridge Road and onto the moors when the road ended. They circled the Tarn, then walked along the rock-strewn ledge that ended back at Spring Bridge Road again.

Jenny dominated the conversation as usual, chattering on without seeming to take a breath. Today, it was mostly about the baby. Ralph was their first child and to the despair of his parents he'd been born with a club foot. They were too ashamed to admit it to their respective families. They were hoping some miracle cure could be found for him before it became too obvious to others. Marie was the only person in whom Jenny had confided. Marie realised it was the reason she'd sought out her company in the first place. She had a need to share her fears with someone. Marie understood that need only too well.

"I hope you don't mind my confiding in you like this?" Jenny asked suddenly.

"Of course not," Marie assured her.

"It's such a comfort being able to talk to you about him, Marie. I am trying not to worry, like you say. He is the perfect baby in every other way." She glanced at her companion, seeking permission to continue. Marie nodded encouragement. "Martin gets really upset if I bring the subject up with him and we're too ashamed to let anyone else know. We wanted him to be so perfect."

Sometimes Marie felt like shaking Jenny. "You shouldn't be ashamed of him, Jenny. At least you have a healthy child in every other respect."

"I know. I know. But when you have a baby, you'll understand how I feel," Jenny rattled on, blissfully unaware of the impact of the comment on her companion.

Marie allowed her thoughts to drift. Why had Stanley married her? From what she could gather, her husband had had little previous experience with women. Work had been his full-time occupation. She was beginning to wonder if his lack of experience was creating the gulf between them.

During her exploration of Ilkley, she'd discovered a second-hand bookshop. The sale of her remedies had allowed her to make the occasional, small purchase without having to ask Stanley's permission. The shop wasn't to the standard of Daphne's but it was cheap, and there were a few books on the shelves that she found interesting. There was the odd medical book for sale and she'd discovered one called *Esoteric Anthropology*. It had a chapter on conception, written clinically and concisely. There were diagrams, too. She'd bought it, ignoring the leer from shopkeeper. She wondered if she would ever find the courage to show it to Stanley.

"Shall I give you the recipe for the rhubarb jam, Marie? Marie?"

She realised that Jenny was asking her a question. "Oh yes, yes, that would be very nice," she murmured in reply.

Back at the house, she put the dogs in their pen and was crossing the hallway when she heard raised voices from the kitchen. It was Gladys's day off and no one else was usually home at this time. Glancing through the door she saw Edith sitting at the kitchen table, her face buried in her apron, obviously in tears. Stanley was standing beside her, looking shocked.

"Is something wrong?" she asked.

She glanced past her husband and saw Peter, Stanley's brother, facing them. He raised a limp hand in greeting. She looked back at Stanley.

"No, nothing's wrong. Just something that needs sorting out," Stanley said, "a family matter." He strode over to the door and slammed it shut.

"Then it's obviously nothing to do with me, is it?" she muttered under her breath.

As she walked up the stairs to her room, she could hear voices being raised again, but they weren't distinct enough for her to hear what was being said.

★

The next morning, Marie, her coat covered by a large linen apron, went about her early morning task of grooming the dogs. They made their usual fuss of her.

"Come on, boy," she patted her knees and Major ambled over, tail wagging. She took the brush and started to do battle with the tangles in his fur. She was so engrossed that she wasn't aware of Peter's approach until a snow ball hit the wire of the dog cage and showered her with snow.

"So this is how you pass your time, is it? I saw you through the window," he said.

She brushed the snow off her coat as Peter pushed his fingers through the wire pen to rub Major's nose.

"Am I distracting you?" he asked.

"No, of course not."

"Good. Oh, you did remember to walk backwards downstairs this morning, didn't you?"

She stopped brushing the dog. "Why on earth should I do that?"

"It's the first of the month today, didn't you know that? Brings you good luck if you walk backwards down the stairs on the first day of the month. It's a well-known fact." She laughed. "Ah, a smile at last."

She was curious. She couldn't help wondering what all the fuss had been about yesterday. No one had told her. "How long are you staying? I thought your work was in Bradford?" He shrugged noncommittally. "What was all the shouting about yesterday? Dinner was grim. Hardly anyone spoke."

"Stanley's in a foul mood. Apparently they've found subsidence under Appleyards and all work has had to be stopped until it's sorted out. It seems the place is haemorrhaging money, which is why Stanley needs to get it up and running as quickly as possible."

"Oh?" She viewed him quizzically. "Stanley said it was a family matter – that sounds more like a business matter to me."

Peter shrugged again and changed the subject. "Gladys tells me you haven't had breakfast yet?"

"I have it when I've finished grooming the dogs. I prefer to eat later."

"You mean alone – after Ma has headed out to clean the

chapel, Stanley has gone to work and Pa has disappeared to wherever it is he goes?"

She smiled but decided not to reply. She didn't want to get drawn into a discussion about her life at The Laurels. He didn't take the hint.

"So, you're an old married woman now. How does being a wife suit you?"

"I have no complaints." She moved around to the other side of the dog.

"Ilkley must be a strange place to find yourself in. Nothing like France, I shouldn't think? When did you leave France? Your English is very good – just a faint hint of something in there. Very mysterious."

"So many questions? Am I under arrest?" She said it lightly, but he was beginning to irritate her.

"Sorry. Sorry. Nothing better to do with my time than to be nosy."

She faced him, hands on hips. "Then I'll use the same excuse. I thought you lived in Bradford? Why have you come home?"

He held his hands up in surrender. "You're right, no more questions."

She nodded and returned to grooming the dog.

After a moment, he asked: "Do you walk these monsters?"

"After breakfast. It's my routine."

"Even in the snow?"

"Even in the snow."

"Feel like having company today?" She glanced at him uncertainly, so he added by way of explanation: "I need to get out of this house before it suffocates me."

She could certainly sympathise with that. "As long as there are no more questions."

He mockingly made the sign of the cross against his heart. "I'll be in my room. Shout when you're ready to go."

She watched him make his way back to the house, hands in trouser pockets, kicking up the snow as he walked.

★

Peter became a regular companion on her walks and Marie soon found herself relaxing in his company. He was pleasant to be with and, although his humour was sometimes very childish, he made her laugh. It was hard to believe he was a Minton. She never thought to ask Jenny Godson if she minded his joining them, because she seemed to accept his presence quite happily. So it was a surprise when, after a few weeks, Jenny arrived earlier than usual for their walk.

"Is something wrong?" Marie asked, taking her up to the small box room. She could see that Jenny was perturbed.

"Well, I just wanted to talk to you. Alone. With Peter always there, it's become difficult to discuss things like we used to do."

"Oh. You mean about Ralph?" Marie had forgotten Jenny's need to unburden herself.

"I can't really talk about him like I used to with Peter there."

"I'm sorry. I didn't think. Has something happened?" She indicated for Jenny to sit down beside her on the bed.

"Yes. Martin saw the doctor today. He said Ralph's foot isn't getting any better. If anything, it seems even more deformed and it's going to become obvious to everybody soon. We don't know what to do, Marie – the shame of it. Everybody will know."

That seemed a strange remark to Marie. Surely shame didn't enter into it, as helping Ralph was all that mattered. "There is something." Marie pulled a case out from underneath the bed. "I'm convinced that the only way to cure Ralph is to let him have surgery."

"An operation?"

"It would cost money but… here, look. Let me show you what I mean. I have an illustration somewhere of how the foot is formed."

She opened the case and Jenny saw that it was packed with books. On top was one called *Esoteric Anthropology*.

"No, not this one." Marie tossed it on the bed beside Jenny. "Maybe it's in Anne Robin's book."

Esoteric Anthropology fell open at a page containing a detailed drawing of the male nude body, the genitals prominently on show. Jenny stared down at it in mortification. She'd never seen the male body so openly displayed before. When she and Martin made love, it was in the dark and under the covers. She sat rooted to the spot, staring at the drawing. Marie leant towards her with another book and Jenny saw, with growing alarm, that it was called *Exploring the Human Form*.

"No." She shot to her feet and turned her back on the offending pictures. "I – er – what I came to say was that I can't walk out with you today. In fact, Ralph's taking up more and more of my time and I'll probably not be able to walk out again. Ever. I'm sorry."

Marie watched with some astonishment as Jenny headed towards the door. "You came all the way out here just to tell me that?" she called after her.

"I'll see myself out. I'm sorry to have troubled you."

Marie heard her footsteps rushing down the stairs. She then heard Edith, who had just returned from chapel, call out: "Is everything all right, Mrs Godson?" And Jenny's mumbled reply, "I've got to get back for the baby." Then the front door slammed shut. Marie looked at the book lying open on the bed. If that was the effect it had on Jenny, she couldn't imagine what it would do to Stanley if she ever found the courage to show him.

★

Although Marie missed Jenny, Peter more than compensated for her absence. He was always such an easygoing companion – except for today. They'd barely exchanged a word since they'd left The Laurels and he had a permanent scowl on his face. He picked up a branch and threw it for the dogs. Both of them bounded away in pursuit, legs flying in all directions, slithering past the stick and then running back to retrieve it. They snapped playfully at each other over who'd be the one to return it to the thrower.

"God! Sometimes I think I'd rather be dead than stuck in this place," he said eventually.

Marie was surprised by his vehemence. "Why did you come back then if you feel like that?"

"Why don't you mind your own business?" She was offended and he was immediately contrite. "Sorry. I shouldn't take it out on you." They continued walking in silence for a moment. "Trouble is, I get so restless staying in one place for too long. Always have. And Stanley's starting to insist I look for another job. As if they can be picked up that easily."

Peter had told her a few days ago that he'd lost his job and that was why he'd returned to Ilkley. She was surprised Stanley hadn't urged him to find work before. Perhaps that was Edith's influence. She was just happy to have her youngest back at home.

"What did you do in Bradford?" She'd often been curious about it.

"I was a clerk in an office at a saw mill."

"A clerk?" She was surprised; it sounded so dull. She'd imagined his world to be much more glamorous. He obviously read her mind.

"Beggars can't be choosers."

"Why did you leave?"

"I'm not sure I can trust you with that information." The frown went and he grinned at her. "It might turn you against me. Do you think it will?"

She couldn't help smiling, relieved to see Peter restored to good humour. "I won't know until you tell me, will I?"

"Will you keep it a secret? Do you swear?" He circled around her playfully as they walked.

She was happy to join in the game. "If you don't think you can trust me, then don't tell me."

"Will you swear?"

"All right, I'll swear."

"Fact is – I've done something a bit stupid, even for me." He pushed a stray lock of hair out of his eyes. "I… er… borrowed some money from the office at the mill. From the safe."

Shocked, she stopped walking. "You stole money?"

"I was obviously going to put it back again; I wasn't stealing it. I mean, the night before the cards were falling my way like magic. I couldn't put a foot wrong. Honestly, Marie, there's never been anything like it. I was on a winning streak and I knew it. I couldn't turn my back on it, could I? It was my chance to clean my life up, to make good. I wanted it so badly and the only thing that was stopping me was lack of money. I had the keys to the safe, and I just borrowed what I needed. The next night, luck deserted me and the sky fell in. I lost everything. Wham!"

She was still trying to take it in. "You stole money?"

"Borrowed it. I borrowed it. Stealing means you have no intention of paying it back. There is a difference."

"Not a difference anyone else will see." Was that the cause of the raised voices she'd heard on the day Peter had returned?

"Problem is the firm missed it before I could return it. If everything had gone as planned, it would have been back in the safe first thing the next morning. They would never have known anything about it, I'd be filthy rich and everyone'd be congratulating me."

"It is stealing."

"How can it be stealing when I intended to pay it back?"

"If the story's true." There was always the possibility with Peter that it wasn't. "If it's true, why haven't the police arrested you?"

"My boss said that if the money was paid back by the end of the next day, they wouldn't take any further action than sacking me on the spot and," he added lamely, "not giving me any references. And so it was paid back, by Stanley – and I was sacked and I didn't get a reference. You try getting work without a reference."

"Stanley paid it back?" Now she knew he wasn't telling the truth. Stanley was hard to separate from his money and Peter had told her the new tea room was taking every penny he had. "How much did you steal?"

"Borrow. I borrowed fifty guineas." He saw her look of horror. "I stood to make three times that amount if I'd won."

"Stanley could pay back fifty guineas? Just like that?"

"Well, thanks to you, yes."

"Me?"

"Ma told him to pay for it using the money you brought with you when you married him. So, thank you, Madame. I am very grateful."

Marie stared at him in astonishment. "What money? I don't know what you're talking about. I didn't bring any money with me."

He laughed. "Oh, come on. What do you think is paying for Appleyards?"

"I didn't… I don't have any money." She felt the need to sit down. She sank onto the grass, her skirts billowing out around her. Peter squatted down beside her.

"I mean the eight hundred pounds, you ninny."

She stared at him. This must surely be some of his nonsense.

He saw her look of disbelief. "You didn't know about it, did you?"

She shook her head, still trying to comprehend it. "Eight hundred pounds is a fortune. How could I provide such money?" There was no way that Sister Grace could have found such a huge sum either.

"I gather John Pickard, your guardian, paid it to him."

Thoughts whirled and twisted through Marie's mind. John Pickard had hidden the existence of such a sum from her? She had been lied to. Stanley hadn't wanted a wife nor had he wanted to offer her his protection; he needed her money for his business. If she had been told such a sum existed, how different her choice of future might have been. Whose money was it? Who had decreed how it should be used? Who had instructed John Pickard? She stood up and began to run down the hill.

"Where are you going? Marie?" Peter set off in pursuit, the dogs bounding after him. He caught up with her and grabbed her by the arm. "Where are you going?"

"To see Stanley and demand to be told what he knows."

"No, Marie." She'd never seen Peter look frightened before. "Don't say anything to Stanley or Ma. Don't tell them I told you. I shouldn't have said anything. And I might have got it wrong. I just overheard them talking one day. I've probably got it wrong."

She didn't think so. It would explain so much. She shook herself free. "Somebody needs to tell me what's happening."

"If you stir everything up, there'll be the devil to pay, Marie. Stanley will chuck me out in an instant if he thinks I've caused trouble, and I've nowhere else to go. You've got to leave things as they are. If they haven't told you it's for a reason. Please, Marie, stop and think – what good will it do to challenge him? How will it change anything? Promise me you won't say anything. It could make things difficult for *you,* too."

She turned away and continued down the hill, with Peter trailing miserably after her. She went straight up to her room and shut the door, leaving him to put the dogs in their pen. Stanley was out at work as usual and Edith was at chapel. She had no idea where Edwin was. She sat on her bed and stared at the wall. After what seemed like an age, she began to think through her confusion. Perhaps Peter was right. To confront Stanley would make her position at The Laurels even worse. She needed to know more before she took that risk, and the one person who could tell her was the man who had obviously lied to her from the beginning.

★

She wasted no time. She didn't write for an appointment and caught the train to Harrogate the next day, where John Pickard had his office. She walked straight past the clerk, who was too surprised to stop her, and confronted the startled solicitor across his desk. She came straight to the point.

"Did you pay Stanley eight hundred pounds to marry me?"

John Pickard looked shocked. He saw his clerk hovering anxiously in the doorway and waved him away. "Close the door," he ordered and turned to face her. "Sit down, Mrs Minton. Please, compose yourself. Shall I get you a glass of water?"

"No, thank you. I just need to know the truth," she answered not caring if he found her manner rude.

"What's given rise to all of this?"

"Peter told me he'd overheard a conversation. Is it true?"

After a moment, and with obvious reluctance, the solicitor answered, "Yes, it's true."

She expelled the breath she'd been holding and, totally bewildered, sank onto the chair opposite him. "But where did so much money come from? It can't have been from Sister Grace. It can't have been." None of this made any sense.

"Perhaps Sister wasn't responsible for any of this happening." She could see from the solicitor's face that this was the truth. "Why have you lied to me?"

"I never said it was the nun," he said awkwardly. "That's a conclusion you jumped to yourself."

"You never said I was wrong." He must have thought her such a fool. "You let me go on believing it."

"If it made things easier for you, I could see no harm in it. There is nothing more I can tell you."

Marie looked at him incredulously. "There is everything to tell me. Who has been providing for me while I've been in England? Who provided the money for me to be married?"

"My instruction, when you insisted on leaving the convent so precipitously, was to settle your future. I have done that to the best of my ability. By whom I was instructed, or why, I'm in no position to discuss with you. I am legally bound to respect my client's demand for privacy." He softened his tone a little. "You must see that for a young woman on her own, marriage was the only possibility."

"But I was given no choice in the matter." It was obvious he had nothing more to say. "Does Stanley know where the money came from?"

"He has no idea. I explained to him that I was restricted in what I could tell him. He accepted my word that it was all perfectly proper," Pickard assured her. "He agreed to the marriage because The Emporium was close to bankruptcy. And he accepted my terms, which were to make no enquiries about the source of the money and to make no mention of it to you. He signed a legal contract to that effect. In exchange, he agreed to give you the protection of his name and promised to provide for you for the rest of your life."

Stanley's coldness towards her made so much more sense now. Their marriage had been nothing more than a business arrangement to him. She was surprised by how much that hurt her. "Why did you tell me that Stanley wanted to marry me because he liked me?"

"Perhaps I was wrong to do that, but as a young and naive girl I believed you would find that a more comfortable reason for accepting his proposal. Stanley agreed to play his part."

For a moment, her anger flared. "And if I choose to end it now?"

"That isn't possible. Your husband will not agree to a separation, as the document he signed states that he forfeits the money if he does. Besides, you are dependent on him for support."

It seems she was trapped. Both she and Stanley were trapped in a marriage that neither of them wanted. "There must be something dreadful in my past for someone to want to be rid of me so cruelly," she said in a small voice.

"Now, now, Mrs Minton," he couldn't help speaking to her as if she were a child. "Everything has been done with the best of intentions and in your own interest."

She did not believe him. "Does Stanley's mother know about this agreement he signed?"

Pickard hesitated for a moment. "Yes, otherwise she wouldn't have accepted the marriage and that could have been awkward for all of us. But she only knows as much as Stanley and no more. Both of them have been told that he will lose the money if the existence of the agreement becomes public knowledge. Not even Stanley's father knows of it – of that, I'm certain. As for Peter learning of it – well, that's something I wasn't expecting."

"Don't worry," Marie's voice became hard, "Peter won't say anything. He's a Minton. He won't want to risk losing the money either."

CHAPTER TEN

Evelyn stared at the letter that was nestling among the rest of the mail. He'd barely glanced at the envelopes before picking them up, only noticing now that this one was addressed to his father. The postal stamp read "Pretoria". News obviously travelled very slowly in Africa – his father's death was evidently still unknown there. He threw the letter to one side, as he had a strong feeling he would regret reading it. After a moment, however, curiosity won and he picked it up and tore it open.

Inside was another sealed envelope without a name or address. Wrapped around it was the letter to his father. It was dated six months ago and the address was St Alphonsus Monastery, Pretoria. The writing was difficult to read and the sentences had a tendency to ramble, but he persevered.

Sir Gordon, please forgive me for writing to you so unexpectedly. You may remember our acquaintance in The Transvaal? I would not trouble you, but my cousin, Sister Grace, died over a year ago, in the Convent of Our Lady at Chartres. I was visiting Chartres and was fortuitously by her side at the moment she left this life. Her dying wish was that her letter of blessing should be passed on to her close friend, the daughter of Hortense Montrecourt. It is the sealed letter that I enclose with mine.

"Montrecourt," muttered Evelyn – that damned name again; the name that wouldn't go away.

Because I am now an old man, the letter continued, *it has taken me this long to write to you asking you to inform the girl of my cousin's passing. I only know that Marie is in England. No one at the convent could tell me where. I would not trouble you if there were any other way for me to make contact with her, but I can think of none. I believe you are the only person who knows of her present whereabouts; otherwise I would not trouble you. Could you place the enclosed letter in her hands?* There was a Latin phrase, too ill-written for Evelyn to even guess at, but it looked like a benediction. The letter was signed *Your humble servant, Father Dominic Connor.*

Evelyn was tempted to tear up both letters and throw them into the fire, as he had with Harlik's, but one of those letters belonged to the daughter of Hortense Montrecourt. Why had Harlik never mentioned to him that Montrecourt had a daughter? Perhaps it hadn't been in his interest to reveal it, because she might be able to disprove Harlik's version of events at Montrecourt's farm – otherwise the man would surely have produced her to corroborate his story. With this information, he could challenge Harlik and make him confess to lying.

★

The next morning, he visited The Lamb and Flag. The printer had told him Harlik was there every day at ten o'clock. Not today, apparently. The table between the door and the window remained empty. He ordered a beer and sat down to wait, aware that he was the centre of much curiosity. After half an hour, he crossed to the bar and beckoned the landlord.

"I'm waiting for Joshua Harlik," he said. "Isn't he usually here around ten?"

"Not for a while, sir."

"Do you know where I can reach him?"

The landlord shook his head. "Sorry, sir. No idea."

Evelyn didn't believe him, but there was not much he could do. "Would this help your memory?" He proffered a guinea, which the landlord, after a moment's hesitation, took from him.

"Well, he does write for that paper *Clarion Call*, so I'm told. I think they're somewhere in Titchborne Street, just round the corner."

All eyes watched as Evelyn pushed his way out of the inn.

The office of the Clarion, or what passed as an office, was closed and to Evelyn's irritation it meant he would have to return the next morning. It was a miserable day, more like winter than autumn, and as he hurried down Hampshire Street he heard his name being called. He stopped but couldn't see anyone.

"Sir Evelyn."

The call came again. In a narrow gap between two buildings, just wide enough for a man to slide down, he saw a figure beckoning him. He crossed over warily. It was Harlik. He looked unkempt; much rougher than when Evelyn had met him in the Lamb and Flag.

"I believe you've been asking for me," he said. "Are you alone?" Evelyn nodded. "Then follow me."

Evelyn hesitated. The narrow alleyway was dark and stank of urine, but Evelyn had no choice but to follow if he wanted a confrontation. At the other end of the alley, Harlik unlocked a door into one of the houses. Evelyn followed him into a small room that was lit by a shaft of light falling through the broken shutters. The room contained a mattress on the floor and not much else. Evelyn didn't attempt to hide his look of distaste as he took in his surroundings.

"Beggars can't be choosers," Harlik said wryly. "I'm a bit

limited to where I can go thanks to your friends. They'd like to hound me into prison if they could."

"Don't expect my sympathy," Evelyn said sharply.

"I don't. So what do you want with me?"

Evelyn handed Harlik the letter that was addressed to his father. The man read it and handed it back. "I'd heard that Hortense Montrecourt was carrying a child when she helped your father, but I dismissed it because I couldn't find any proof. How did she get to France?"

"The question I was going to ask you. Where is this daughter now?"

"I've no idea, obviously here in England. She might have a story to tell, mightn't she, this daughter? Lead us to Hortense even?"

Either the man was a brilliant liar or he genuinely didn't know where she was.

"Where's the letter that was enclosed with this one?" Harlik asked. "Does that give a clue as to where she is? What does it say?"

"I wouldn't know," Evelyn said coldly. "It isn't addressed to me."

"That wouldn't stop me opening it, but I can see that you're a man of principle," Harlik mocked. "So what are you going to do? How are you going to track the girl down?"

"I don't know," Evelyn admitted.

Harlik grew thoughtful for a moment. "I might be able to point you to someone who could help. If you can trace him."

Why was the man being so helpful? Unless he thought that the daughter would help prove his story. In which case, it would be better to walk away from the situation before he discovered things he would rather not know. "I won't bargain with you. If she proves you a liar, I'll make sure everyone knows."

"It's a risk I'm willing to take. Are you?" Harlik challenged.

"Yes." Evelyn responded curtly, after a brief pause.

"Well, I'm not sure there's a connection, but there's a man called John Pickard – something to do with the law. I don't know where he works, but I do know he's had dealings with your father – and there was some link to the Transvaal."

"How do you know that?"

"I once took up residence outside your father's apartment some years ago. I saw this man going in and out quite regularly. I noticed him because he always glanced around him first to make sure he wasn't seen entering or leaving. Very secretive. One day, I caught sight of some papers he was carrying. They were legal papers of some sort and I spotted the word 'Pretoria'. Couldn't see anything else and I could never find out what business your father had with him."

Something was beginning to stir in the back of Evelyn's mind. On the day he'd found the journals in the attic at Ardington, he'd discovered an account book detailing regular payments to someone with the initials JP. Was that John Pickard? Harlik was watching him speculatively.

"How did you know the name of this man, and why should his business involve Montrecourt's daughter?"

"I made friends with one of the maids who worked for your father. She told me his name. She couldn't tell me much more, except that she was sure she'd heard them talking about someone called Montrecourt. As to any involvement with the daughter, I don't know if there *is* one. Maybe he can tell you where the girl is; maybe even where Hortense is now. If you're really sure you want to find them?"

There was a mocking smile on the journalist's face. He was enjoying testing Evelyn's faith in his father.

"Thank you. I will track him down. I won't stop until I find the truth." Evelyn said firmly. He had kept his nerve and had the satisfaction of seeing Harlik's mockery falter as a result. He turned on his heel and walked away.

"Don't suppose you'd care to let me in on it, when you've found out what you want to know?" Harlik shouted after Evelyn's departing back. Evelyn ignored him, heading down the alley. The words "You can't stir up a hornet's nest without someone getting stung" drifted after him.

He needed to find this John Pickard.

CHAPTER ELEVEN

Marie had quickly realised that John Pickard was right. There was nothing to be gained by confronting Stanley with what she'd learnt from the solicitor. It would only sour their relationship more and gain her nothing. As for the money – wherever it came from, the building of the tea room had probably taken care of most of it. To Peter's relief, she made it clear that she did not intend to use his indiscretion against him, but it obviously didn't ease his fear that she might do so one day.

"I'm going to stay with friends in Bradford and I'm going to start looking for work," he announced unexpectedly at the dinner table, soon after her visit to John Pickard.

Stanley grunted his approval, Edith said she'd miss him, and Marie gave no indication that she'd even heard him. However, in his absence, life at The Laurels became duller. She kept herself occupied by making cures for Gladys's friends and taking the dogs for even longer walks.

A few weeks later, Stanley came home bursting with the news that the tea room was at last ready to be launched. Marie was astonished to be invited to the opening day. She accepted gratefully, ignoring the sourness of his mother's expression.

When it came to the day itself, Edith suddenly declared herself unwell and not strong enough to attend. Marie wondered if it was because she resented her daughter-in-law's inclusion. Edith had always made it clear that she considered The Emporium territory to be shared exclusively between herself and Stanley – not even Edwin was included in that. He hadn't even been invited to the opening.

The banner above the door of the new tea room, which announced the grand opening, flapped briskly in the chill wind. It read: *COME AND HELP US CELEBRATE*. One of the ropes holding it in place had worked loose on one side and the banner had folded back on itself, so all that could be seen was *HELP US*, but no one had noticed yet.

If she was honest, Marie found it rather a clinical place compared to the opulence of the Orient. The huge potted palms framing the doorway outside made it look like the entrance to the pump room. Inside, the décor was too cold, too silver and lilac, and too formal, with wrought iron grilles in the latest geometric design separating the tables. It needed a softer touch, a splash of luxury. Banquettes covered in soft velvet and in warm colours, like peach or russet. That's what she would have advised him, but, of course, she was never consulted.

Geoffrey arrived at Stanley's side. He nodded briefly to Marie. "Where's Ma, Stanley? Not like her to miss an occasion like this."

"She wasn't well enough to come."

"Did you send for the doctor?"

"No, she won't have him. Just a touch of indigestion, she says. She doesn't want a fuss making."

The bell on the tea room door rang and Marie turned to see who else had accepted Stanley's invitation. Harrogate town centre must surely be deserted. She saw that it was Peter, bowler hat pushed back on his head, hands characteristically thrust into the pockets of his overcoat. He spotted Geoffrey and Marie and headed towards them, picking his way adroitly through the crowd.

"Well, this is looking... rather jolly." He arrived by her side, picking up one of the silver-and-lilac menu cards from a nearby table. "Very smart! Has anybody noticed that the banner is falling down outside?"

"Tea or coffee, sir?" One of the waitresses had spotted the new arrival.

"Let it be tea, why not." When the waitress and Geoffrey had moved away he positioned himself behind Marie while ostentatiously studying the menu card.

"Had a very interesting time in Bradford," he whispered.

"Have you been drinking?" She could smell it on his breath.

"A bit. I might have something to celebrate today. It's a secret, but I'll tell you about it when we get back to The Laurels. Stanley says he'll be working late tonight, so I'll escort you home. Missed you," he whispered.

"Missed you, too," she acknowledged. There was no one who could make her smile the way Peter could.

As the afternoon drew to a close, Marie, exhausted from holding conversations with people she had never met before and probably would never meet again, suggested to Peter that they might leave. He was only too happy to agree. She asked him on the journey home about his secret but he insisted on being mysterious.

"Wait till we're home," was all he'd say.

By the time they arrived at The Laurels, Gladys had left and Edith was still nursing her illness in bed. Edwin was out with friends.

"Better keep our voices down," Peter whispered. "Otherwise Ma will be down demanding to know how it all went and that'll be the end of our little tête-à-tête."

He manoeuvred her into the front parlour, which was the room furthest away from the staircase. The curtains were closed and the piano covered. He took a hip flask out of his jacket pocket and held it out to her. "Whisky?"

She shook her head. He took a long drink and pushed the flask back into his pocket again.

"What's all this secrecy about?" She was beginning to

feel impatient. It was obviously something that pleased him.

"Well, I'd been wandering around Bradford for weeks trying to find a job and there was nothing. Not without any references. I was feeling low, really low."

An unwelcome thought struck her. "You haven't started gambling again?"

"No. There was no gambling involved. I did bump into an old friend, though. He lives in America now, manages a millinery factory in New York. He was home on a visit, just to tie up a few loose ends before settling over there permanently. Anyway, he says they need a foreman and he's offered me the job. I was telling him there was nothing happening for me in England. It's a good job, too, and pays well. The streets really are paved with gold out there he says."

"Peter, I really am glad for you." She was genuinely delighted, although she doubted it would be as easy as Peter seemed to believe it would be.

He took out the flask again and raised it in a toast. "To New York," he said.

Marie laughed. "To New York," she repeated. How would Edith feel about that?

"All I have to do now," he said, "is to find the money to pay for my passage to America."

"Could your friend not advance it to you?"

"I don't want him to know how low funds are. He might start having second thoughts and start asking for references." He sank down onto the sofa and she sat beside him. "I've spent the last few days trailing from friend to friend trying to raise enough, but no one is willing to back me." She opened her mouth to suggest he ask Geoffrey or Stanley, but he headed her off. "No, it's no good asking the family for help, Marie, if that's what you're going to suggest. Geoffrey won't part with a farthing that he doesn't have to. Work for it, is all he'll say.

And Stanley, well, he's still waiting for me to pay him back the fifty guineas I borrowed to resolve my little problem at the mill." He smiled. "And then I remembered the eight hundred pounds you'd brought with you to the marriage and that started me thinking."

"Oh?" She was puzzled. "I don't follow."

"You must be able to get your hands on more. Ask Pickard; he must know how to get it."

She began to laugh and then realised that he was serious. "That's silly, Peter."

"Think about it; we could both have a new start. You could come with me to New York."

She stood up. "Don't be ridiculous. You're not making any sense. You've had too much to drink."

He also stood up. "You have no marriage at all here, we both know that. Who in New York will even be aware of it? I know you like me; we could set up house together."

He caught hold of her by the shoulders and drew her close. His intensity was beginning to frighten her now.

"Peter. Please, you're hurting me." She tried to push him away, but he wouldn't let go. He tried to kiss her; they stumbled back against the fireplace and the bodice of her dress was ripped open. It was then that she saw, over Peter's shoulder, the figure of Edith silhouetted in the doorway with a look of horror on her face.

She realised how it must seem: her son with his arms around his brother's wife, and the front of her dress hanging open. Edith tried to speak, but her face turned purple with the effort. She clutched at her chest, then slowly – oh, so slowly – she slid to the floor, her mouth hanging open, her eyes glazed.

Peter turned, following Marie's gaze. He was horrified by what he saw. "Ma!"

He pushed Marie aside and she fell awkwardly against the piano, bruising her arm. She watched Peter trying to loosen the neck of his mother's nightgown. He slapped her cheeks to revive her.

"For God's sake, get water, get water," he called over his shoulder.

Badly shaken, Marie ran into the kitchen and returned with some water in a cup. Peter snatched it from her, he was trying to force the liquid between his mother's lips. It dribbled out of her mouth and ran down her chin. Marie stood helplessly by as he dropped the cup and clutched his mother to him, rocking her backwards and forwards.

"Ma! Ma!" He turned to Marie again. "McCullough. Get McCullough. Victoria Street, number nine. Tell him it's urgent."

At last, she regained control. "Take your mother upstairs," she ordered. "Make her as comfortable as you can."

But she feared, as did Peter, that Edith had already stopped breathing.

*

After the funeral, a mixed group gathered at The Laurels to mourn Edith's passing. Geoffrey and Isabelle were doing what they could to give support to Stanley and Peter. There were others from the family, like Edith's cousins from Sheffield and her sister from Edinburgh, whom no one had heard from in years. Then there were those who were present simply to pick up all the gossip they could, such as the ladies from the chapel, Betsy Capes and her friends, who had never been allowed across the threshold of The Laurels while Edith was alive.

Alice and George Smith were there, and the Godsons. Reverend Jackson, who had conducted the service, was there out of duty, flitting through the room proffering words of sympathy to anyone who would listen, while Dr McCullough was there for the free food and drink.

Marie was seated alone in a corner of the room. She was feeling the strain of the past week and hoped to avoid the necessity of conversation, but most of all she wanted to avoid Peter. The moment the doctor had declared Edith dead, he'd started to lie his way out of the situation. Marie had been playing the piano in the parlour, he said, and he was turning the pages of the music for her. Edith had been disturbed by the noise and had come downstairs, and in her weakened state the effort had proved too much. He wanted to get his version in first, before Marie had a chance to denounce him. Marie struggled to know what to do. If she told the truth, would anyone believe her? The family were suffering enough without her adding to their problems. Peter's explanation had been accepted, so she decided to allow the lie to remain unchallenged.

"Marie, is there more tea?" She realised Isabelle was trying to attract her attention. "Marie, Alice would like some more tea, dear." Marie stared back at her sister-in-law dumbly and Isabelle said, "I'll see to it. You stay there."

Marie watched Stanley cross over to Edwin. Father and son had taken Edith's death badly. She heard Stanley say, "Can I get you anything, Pa?" His father shook his head and tried to struggle to his feet. "No, you stay here," Stanley said. "I'll get you whatever it is you want."

"I don't want anything; I just want everybody to go away. I can't go on without her, Stanley."

He pawed at his son's hand and Stanley patted his shoulder awkwardly. Expression of any emotion never came easily to the Mintons.

"I shouldn't have left your Ma alone that day." Edwin wiped his eye with the back of his hand. "But she was always taking to her bed and nothing serious had ever happened before. How could I have known? But they were here, Peter and that woman. Why didn't they realise how ill she was?"

Marie had noticed that since Edith's death, Edwin had begun to refer to her as "that woman". Geoffrey now joined them.

"Pa's tired," said Stanley. "I think we need to get him upstairs, Geoffrey. Help me up with him."

Marie watched as the two brothers hauled an unresisting Edwin to his feet. Between them, they half led, half carried him through the door and up to his room.

*

It was some hours later and Marie was longing for everyone to go. She was tired and her head ached. She wandered into the deserted kitchen and glanced out of the window. Peter was in the garden and so was Geoffrey. They were in deep conversation. Suddenly, Geoffrey pushed his brother violently up against the wall. Marie gasped as he raised his fist.

"Mrs Minton."

"Yes?" She whirled around to find Betsy Capes hovering at her shoulder. Marie swiftly blocked the view from her.

"Is there any more tea?" Betsy tried to peer over Marie's shoulder.

Marie swiftly thrust a plate of sandwiches into Betsy's hands. "Perhaps you could take these into the parlour for me? I'll bring the tea through to you."

Unable to refuse, Betsy reluctantly did as requested. Marie waited until she was out of sight before turning to look outside again. The garden was empty.

*

The mourners had gone at last and Marie was alone in the parlour. She started to pile up the dirty plates. She felt drained of all energy. Stanley entered the room.

"Leave everything," he said, his voice flat and dull. "Gladys is coming in early to do that." He sank into the nearest chair. "This has been a dreadful day."

"Terrible," she said with feeling.

Ever since she'd seen Geoffrey threatening Peter in the garden, she'd been on edge. What had caused the assault? Had Peter confessed? Geoffrey came in and she glanced up quickly, trying to gauge his reaction to her. He didn't look in her direction.

"You should get to bed," he said to Stanley. "You look ill."

"You don't look so good yourself. Where's Peter?"

"Gone," Geoffrey said, and Marie didn't know whether to feel glad or angry. "Come on, get yourself to bed. Then I'll go, too." Stanley allowed his brother to help him to the stairs.

Alone again in the front parlour, Marie sank onto the chair that Stanley had just vacated. She heard her husband's bedroom door close with a dull thud. She then heard the creak of Geoffrey's footsteps returning down the stairs. She watched him close the door of the parlour quietly behind him.

He looked at her for a moment without speaking, then said: "Our Stanley's been badly shaken up by Ma's death."

"I know." She looked down at the pile of dirty plates in front of her. "Stanley said Gladys would clear all this away tomorrow, but I think I should make a start."

"So you and Peter were in the front parlour because you wanted to practice the piano and he was turning the pages for you. And Ma came down because the noise had woken her."

She fiddled with the dirty plates. "As Peter told you, yes."

"Only, you see, when I took Pa upstairs earlier, he said nobody had played the piano because the cover was still on it."

Marie felt a sinking feeling in the pit of her stomach. "Then maybe I covered up the piano after I knew your mother was dead? I don't remember."

"For pity's sake, woman, do you even know what honesty is?"

His words were expressed with such force that they shocked her into silence for a moment. Then, she felt a flood of relief. "Has Peter told you the truth? I thank God for that."

"He told me and it disgusts me." Why was Geoffrey's anger being levelled at her? "You couldn't keep away from him, could you? Peter's always had a weakness for women and you played on that. Keeping company with him every day, throwing yourself at him. That's what Ma saw when she walked into the parlour that day. You, half naked, throwing yourself at him – the shock of it killed her. "

"What?" She felt sick. "Is that what Peter told you? Is that what he said?"

"It's what he confessed. I'm not saying Peter is blameless – he's weak and he's a fool – but you led him on. You are his brother's wife."

"No. It's not true," she protested.

"Was the story about playing the piano true?"

"No." She knew that would condemn her, but she wanted to blow away the lies. "Bring him here, now. Ask Peter to confess. He attempted to make love to me and I tried to stop him. Let him come here and deny it in front of me."

Geoffrey viewed her with disgust. "Peter is well out of your reach by now. I've sent him away. The story I'll tell everyone is that mother was disturbed by the piano, as Peter said, and that he was so overcome with grief by her death that he didn't want to stay in the country."

"He's gone abroad?"

"He was offered a job in New York. All he needed was the money for a passage. Well, now he's got it. I gave it to him, on condition that he never comes back and never communicates with you again. He'll be half way to Liverpool by now, and in a few hours time he'll be on board ship."

"You paid for him to go to New York?" The irony of the situation overcame all other emotions. He'd got what he wanted after all. She began to shake and then she began to laugh, and she couldn't control either the shaking or the laughter.

Geoffrey was looking at her as though she was mad. "If it wasn't that my family's suffered enough," he said angrily, "I would tell them the truth about how Ma died. Stanley would have you out on the street where you belong and everyone would know you for what you are, but I'll spare our Stanley that humiliation by keeping quiet." He leant forward and she could feel his breath on her cheek. "Do you understand me? You will keep quiet, too. Do you realise what the alternative would mean?"

She felt numb. She nodded. She understood.

*

She had no idea how long she'd been sitting after Geoffrey left, but a faint light had begun to filter through the curtains in the parlour so it must almost be dawn.

Wearily, she dragged herself up the stairs to bed. She was about to enter her room when she heard a noise from Stanley's. He was still awake then? There it was again – the noise. She knocked on the door and, not waiting for his response, she turned the handle and entered. The paraffin lamp was lit and, by its light, she saw Stanley, seated on the edge of his bed in his night shirt, tears running down his cheeks. She felt nothing but compassion. He looked so lost.

"Oh, Stanley." She moved over to the bed and sat beside him, putting an arm around his shoulders. "I am so sorry."

He tried to brush the tears away but he couldn't control his shaking. "I miss her, Marie. She's always been there for me."

"I know." She understood such loneliness. "You have me, Stanley. I know I can't take her place, but I can try to be a wife to you if you'll let me." She gently eased him back against the pillows. "Perhaps you might want your wife beside you tonight; if not, turn me away. I'll understand." He looked up at her, his mouth hanging open, tears streaking his face. His breath smelt rancid. "Do you want me to go? Tell me if you'd rather I went. "

"No." He clutched at her. "I… no… don't go away. Stay."

She lay down beside him and could feel his heart beating rapidly. She held him as she would a baby.

"I feel so alone without Ma," he whispered.

"I know. I know."

Awkwardly, she started to stroke his head. She saw the moon reflected in the glass cases that lined all the walls. The wings of the butterflies pinned to the velvet were opalescent. She looked away from them.

"I think we're both feeling alone just now," she murmured, "but we have each other, don't we?"

That seemed to calm him. After a moment, he murmured: "Marie… if I haven't been all a husband should be, I'm sorry."

"It's all right. That's all right. Everything will be all right now. You'll see."

As he rolled on top of her, she closed her eyes. Perhaps this was the real beginning of a new life.

*

Marie delivered Damson and Major back to their pens. The dogs were tired. They were getting older, while Marie's walks were getting longer. She patted them absentmindedly and closed the gate.

Since his mother's death, she'd continued to sleep in Stanley's bed. He seemed to find some comfort in that and she was grateful to be wanted. Occasionally, they made love. It was always brief, never satisfying – although it seemed to satisfy Stanley well enough. They were actually growing a little closer. He even, occasionally, tried to talk to her about his business. She learnt that trade was not good at The Emporium and that the tea room wasn't providing the solution he'd expected.

Would he be happy or unhappy about the news she had to tell him? For some weeks she'd kept it to herself, wanting to be certain of her facts before she mentioned it, but today she was sure. Today, he had to be told. She hadn't wanted to tell him before he left for work so she'd stayed out, waiting for him to leave.

She was thrown, however, to find that he was still at home. Usually, he was on the train to Harrogate by seven o'clock. She glanced at the clock on the mantle. It was now ten o'clock. He saw her glance.

"I had a bad night. Thought I'd go in later. Martin will open The Emporium."

She knew he'd spent a bad night because his restlessness had kept her awake for most of it.

Stanley was rubbing his jaw. "It's this wretched toothache. It's been a week now since I had a decent night's sleep."

She knew that, too, having suffered the same fate by his side. He did look dreadful. "You should see a dentist. I have told you that."

"I know. I know. I mean to, but then I remember the pain a dentist inflicted on me years ago and I can't face it. Even the memory of it makes me break into a sweat."

"Well, you can't go on as you are." The practical side of Marie took over. "Which is worse? The pain you've got now or the pain from the dentist, which will be over in a matter of days? Things have changed. They're using different methods now. There's a man in Leeds who uses chloroform. I saw an advertisement for him in *The Mercury*. His name is Mongreve, I think. It sends you to sleep. You don't feel a thing."

Stanley rubbed at his jaw again, trying to ease the pain. "That's what McCullough said when I went to see him. I asked if there was anything he could give me to help it and he told me to see a dentist. He said my teeth were poisoning me."

"He's right. Your gums are blistered and some of your teeth have rotted. You'll lose all of them if you're not careful. You must go to the dentist." She searched through the newspapers on the chair beside her. "Look." She passed the copy of *The Mercury* over to him. "You'll find his name in there. It says he uses chloroform and it puts you to sleep and when you wake up it's all over."

Stanley grunted. "Seems too good to be true to me" – but she saw that he had noted the name and address.

She hesitated – perhaps this wasn't the best moment to break her news to him, but then he had to be told sometime. "Stanley, I've something to tell to you." There was no other way than to say it directly. "I'm having a baby."

He stared at her. "What?" After a moment he stood up, then he sat down again. "A baby?"

"Yes." She was nervous, but it was the baby that mattered now. She had to make Stanley see what a blessing this was.

"When…? How long have you known? When did you see Dr McCullough?"

"I haven't seen Dr McCullough yet. I know enough about things to know when I'm having a baby." She didn't like McCullough. He'd heard about the remedies she supplied to Gladys and her friends, and he'd made it plain to her that he didn't approve.

Stanley was obviously struggling with his feelings. "I'm sorry. I don't know what to do… what to say."

"Stanley, just say it pleases you."

"Pleases me?" He began to laugh. His reaction was so

surprising that Marie was thrown for a moment. He shook his head as if in disbelief. "Yes… it pleases me. It pleases me." He continued to shake his head in amazement. "A son?"

Marie didn't care which gender the baby would be; only that Stanley was pleased. For the moment, that was all that mattered. He shook his head in amazement again.

"A son!" He struck the table with his fist, making her jump. "I'll make sure he has something to inherit. I'll make sure of that."

"Of course you will," she said encouragingly. "And the baby will be loved and cared for like no other that's ever been born."

He began pacing. "People want to take all this away from me." He indicated the room with his arm. "Everything I've worked for. There have been problems ever since I opened that damned tea room. People only too eager to tell me I've over reached myself. Banks putting pressure on me for repayments. I'll show them, Marie. They can't write me off that easily."

"No, of course not." She suddenly felt drained of energy. Her lack of sleep plus the tension of telling Stanley were having their effect. "I'm sorry, Stanley. I need to lie down."

He looked concerned. "Are you ill?"

"No, just tired"

She'd been sick that morning. Gladys had been there and Marie was sure she'd guessed the reason for it, but Gladys knew Stanley hadn't been told yet and had made no comment. Marie had made herself an infusion of horehound and that had eased the spasms that followed.

Stanley was still absorbing the news. "Where's Pa? I want to tell him."

"He's staying with Joe Bottomley until tomorrow. Do you mind, Stanley, if I go upstairs to rest?"

"No, no, you go," he said, still preoccupied with the news.

She hesitated. "And it might be better if I stay in my old

room until after the baby is born. Would you mind?" She needed to be able to sleep.

He waved a hand to show he had no objection. "I'll send a telegram to Geoffrey and Isabelle," he called after her.

She had just reached her bedroom when a sharp stab of pain caused her to collapse onto the bed. She curled up on the counterpane for comfort, drawing her knees up to her stomach. Whatever the pain, whatever the discomfort, she told herself fiercely, this was a child of hers and it was truly wanted.

CHAPTER TWELVE

In the months to come, Evelyn found he had very little time to spend on his search for the man called John Pickard. Renfrew kept him so busy that he was barely able to sleep. The country was unsettled, accusations of corruption and profiteering during the war were flung at the Tories, and Renfrew had him producing figures and statistics until he was sickened by them. At the moment, however, things seemed to have calmed down and he was at last able to return to Ardington to search for the account book he'd tossed aside so casually just after his father's death.

He found it and it made strange reading. Page after page contained the same entry in his father's neat and precise handwriting: "Paid to JP the sum of Twenty pounds" – a sizable sum. The money had been paid on the same day each month for eighteen years. Then, nothing. The first payment was dated 1882, which was the year after Majuba. Everything always came back to Majuba.

Surreptitiously, he began making enquiries around town about a solicitor or a lawyer called John Pickard, but to his frustration no one at the Inns of Court had heard of him. Perhaps Harlik had been wrong; perhaps this man Pickard didn't work in the law at all. He was seriously tempted to confront his mother with the account book and ask her if she knew this John Pickard, but she was still frail after a minor stroke and he knew it would distress her to discover that he was still delving into affairs she had told him to forget.

As always when he was at a loss what to do with himself, he joined Siggy for an evening's drinking at White's. He found his friend in a good humour and full of plans for his coming trip to the hot springs of Baden-Baden, which was as well because Evelyn was proving a silent companion.

"All right," Siggy said, holding his hands up in surrender. "I give in. What's troubling you? Because something is."

"Sorry," Evelyn downed his brandy and signalled to the waiter for a refill. "I just… it's this Montrecourt business."

"Good God! Not that again? Thought you'd dropped it long ago."

"I've never quite shaken it off." Evelyn wearily ran a hand through his hair. "I might be able to if I can find some mysterious legal gentleman called John Pickard, who doesn't seem to exist."

Siggy frowned. "Where have you been looking? I know the name. He's a solicitor. I think he practices in the north of England. Harrogate, I think. I'm sure your man Renfrew used him to handle some business to do with his estates near York."

Evelyn was frustrated to discover that the information had been so close at hand all this time. "You're sure of this?"

"Pretty sure, but ask Renfrew. I'm sure you'll be seeing him in the next few days." It was said wryly. Evelyn seemed to spend his life at the beck and call of his lordship. "You're like a dog with a bone over this Montrecourt nonsense, Evie. Going to tell me why?"

"Someday, maybe, when I have all the answers," Evelyn replied.

*

The first thing he did when he returned to the Lords was to approach Renfrew. He wasted no time and asked him directly about John Pickard. Did he know him?

"Haven't you two met?" Renfrew looked surprised. "Yes, I've used him. John has acted for me on Radlett business and was very efficient. I recommended him to your father, too. He has offices in Harrogate. I'm quite happy to commend him to you, Evelyn. Now, if you'll excuse me. I have a busy morning."

"I'd be grateful to have his address," Evelyn pressed.

"Of course."

Renfrew was true to his word and the next morning Evelyn found a note of it on his desk. With more time on his hands, he saw no reason to delay following up the lead. He would drive to Harrogate first thing in the morning.

*

He discovered that John Pickard's office was on the first floor of a building that formed a half crescent. It was flanked on one side by the busy Leeds Road and on the other by the quieter Fellows Street. Evelyn climbed the stairs and walked straight into the inner sanctum. A surprised John Pickard half rose from behind his desk.

"I do apologise for turning up at your office unannounced like this, Mr Pickard." Evelyn's manner was polite but firm. "I took advantage of the fact that I was in the North to call on you on Lord Renfrew's recommendation. I believe you knew my father, Sir Gordon Harringdon?" Evelyn paused. He'd seen this man before – a child's representation of a man, with a round head on a round body? Then, he remembered. He'd been at Ardington on the day his father died.

"Yes, indeed. How good to meet you." The solicitor shook Evelyn by the hand, indicating the paper-strewn desk. "Excuse the mess, but, as you say, I wasn't expecting you." He held up a decanter of brandy. "May I pour you one?"

"No, thank you – a little early for me. Don't let me stop you, though. I had business in the North," he said, settling himself on the chair facing the solicitor, "and there's a letter I need to deliver – and I think you can help me. It's to a lady I think you know. Marie Montrecourt – daughter of Hortense Montrecourt?" He noticed the solicitor add a little more brandy to the glass. "You do know who I mean?"

"Yes. Yes, indeed I do."

At last, he sensed he was close to the heart of the matter.

"Although Miss Montrecourt is Mrs Minton now," said Pickard. "You have a letter for her, you say?"

"It was enclosed in a letter that arrived recently addressed to my father – from someone called Father Connor. Do you know him, too?"

"I'm afraid not, no." Pickard looked suitably regretful. "The writer didn't realise your father had passed away?"

"The priest had known him in Africa, apparently. He asked for a letter to be forwarded to Miss Mont… I'm sorry, Mrs Minton."

"Oh, if that's all, I'll certainly do that for you." The solicitor held out his hand to take the letter.

"I'd rather deliver it myself," Evelyn said pleasantly. "There's a great deal I'd like to ask her."

The hand dropped. "I really don't think it would be wise to call on Mrs Minton at the moment, Sir Evelyn. She is apparently expecting her first child. She would probably prefer not to receive visitors at the moment."

"Perhaps I won't need to trouble her if you can introduce me to the mother, Hortense."

"Sadly she died some time ago."

That was a blow. "How long ago?"

"A long time ago. Is it something I can help you with?"

Perhaps you could, thought Evelyn. "In my father's accounts, he noted a series of payments to you – the same sum at the same time every month for eighteen years. Can you tell me what those payments were for?"

John Pickard carefully straightened some papers on his

desk. "I'm afraid I can't discuss a client's business dealings with anyone."

"Not even his son?" Pickard looked even more regretful. "Not even when the client is now dead?"

"Forgive me, but if your father wanted his business to remain private, even from his family, then I can't ignore those instructions. Please be aware that I am merely a solicitor, Sir Evelyn. I simply do what I'm told and nobody tells me anything I don't need to know, and I prefer it that way."

Evelyn made no effort to hide his irritation. "I won't let the matter rest, Mr Pickard. If you can't help me, then I suggest you give me Mrs Marie Minton's address."

"I promise you, she knows nothing, Sir Evelyn. It would be so much better if you'd just let matters rest."

"That's what everyone keeps telling me, but they can never tell me why. Her address please," Evelyn said, with quiet determination. Determination won.

"Very well. It's out of my hands now," the solicitor muttered as he wrote down the address.

The address for Marie Minton was in Ilkley, which was a blow because he had business in London later that afternoon and he didn't have time to make a detour. It was frustrating to be so close to a resolution and yet be unable to conclude it. Or was he really looking for an excuse to delay the meeting, for fear of what he might discover? A little longer wouldn't make much difference, he told himself.

CHAPTER THIRTEEN

A terrible scream in the middle of the night shattered the peace of The Laurels. It was wrenched out of her body as she writhed in agony. Her sheets were covered in blood; her face was contorted with pain. The next scream turned into a long, low moan. Stanley rushed through the door in a panic.

"What is it, Marie? What's happened?" He stood there, horrified by the sight that met him, not knowing what to do.

Edwin peered around the door of the bedroom, his eyes still thick with sleep. "What's the row?"

"Get McCullough! Now!" Stanley shouted at his father. "For God's sake, don't just stand there, Pa. Get round there now." The old man disappeared. As Marie started to whimper, Stanley looked on helplessly. "What shall I do? What do I do, Marie?"

"Get some sheets, towels, anything," she managed to gasp in between moans.

He did as she asked. She pushed them between her legs, trying to staunch the flow of blood. That's how McCullough found her when he arrived.

"What's this? What's happened?" The doctor took off his jacket. In his haste to respond to the emergency he'd paid little attention to what he was wearing. His shirt hung loose outside his trousers, his braces were twisted, his shoes didn't match.

"Is the baby safe?" Stanley asked.

"Leave the room, Mr Minton," McCullough replied roughly. As the old man joined them, he added: "Both of you. Let me do my job as I see fit or I won't be answerable for the consequences."

Stanley, his clothes smeared with Marie's blood, nodded but didn't move.

McCullough called to Edwin. "Make some sweet tea for your son, Mr Minton. Get him out of here."

Edwin nodded and led a dazed Stanley out of the room. Through her pain, Marie heard Edwin say: "She's lost the baby then, has she?"

She clenched her fists and turned her face to the wall. She would not look. She couldn't make herself look at the deformed pile of flesh that McCullough was wrapping up in the bloodied sheets. For months, she'd carried that thing inside her. She leant over the side of the bed and wretched into the bucket the doctor had placed beside it. Her mouth tasted foul and the blood was still flowing between her legs. Why did it have to end like this?

"Why?" The word emerged as a long drawn-out sigh that McCullough barely caught.

"Mrs Minton, you may want to arrange a funeral."

"Go away," she whispered.

"It sometimes helps the grieving." The tears flowed down her cheeks. "Very well. Take this." He handed her a small phial. "It will help."

She knew what it was. Laudanum to keep her quiet. She obediently swallowed it. What did it matter?

Stanley entered the room and saw the bloody bundle that McCullough was carrying. Marie watched him turn away.

"Oh, God, is that it?" he muttered.

She felt no connection with the events that were being acted out in front of her. The laudanum was beginning to work. She felt herself drifting away. "What happens to it now?" she heard Stanley ask. The voices were getting fainter and more distant.

"I asked Mrs Minton if she wanted to arrange a funeral. She isn't in a fit state to decide."

"Arrange a funeral. I'll pay whatever it takes."

"I'll make sure the boy receives a Christian burial."

She saw Stanley lean against the wall and heard McCullough say: "I'm sorry, Mr Minton. The baby was lying in the wrong position. I did what I could. If your wife had come to me earlier, rather than relying on those concoctions she insists on making, then the matter might have turned out differently."

Was he saying it was her fault? She tried to grasp what was being said. Did he mean it was her fault the baby had died?

"As for your wife..." Marie realised Stanley hadn't asked about her. It didn't matter. Nothing mattered anymore. "To be truthful," McCullough continued, "she's in the hands of God, not in mine. She's still losing blood and she's too weak to lose much more. I'll call round to see her tomorrow."

*

Marie stirred in the early hours of the morning. There was a dull ache in her stomach, as if she'd been severely kicked. Her mouth tasted foul. She groped on the bedside table looking for the hand mirror. Was this her face, hollow-eyed and drained of blood? Strands of hair were plastered against her forehead. She dropped the mirror onto the bed and looked down at the sheets. There was blood on them. The blood was still draining out of her. Is this how it was going to end? "Noooo!" Her mouth opened wide in a scream of protest but no sound emerged. She turned on her side and closed her eyes.

When she opened them again, it was to find Isabelle sitting on the bed beside her.

"Isabelle?" Marie's voice was little more than a croak. "You shouldn't have come all this way." She saw her sister-in-law looking at the pile of bloodstained sheets in the corner of the room. "Gladys is coming back up for those."

"I was so sorry about your news, Marie." Isabelle leant towards her. "Let me stay with you for a few days. You need a woman beside you."

"I have Gladys."

"Gladys isn't family." She saw tears welling up in Marie's eyes and she took her sister-in-law in her arms. It was like holding nothing, like holding bones. She wiped the beads of perspiration from Marie's forehead. "I know we aren't always the easiest of families, but when something like this happens... well... it should bring us together, don't you think? Now, come on. You must eat."

Marie began to shake her head, but Isabelle ignored her and picked up the bowl of soup that Gladys had brought in a few moments before.

"I insist. This soup is very light. Come on, Marie, just a spoonful. Come on." Like a child, Marie obediently opened her mouth. "That's good. Now, another one. That's good."

When the soup was finished, Isabelle continued to sit with her, holding her hand, until the sun set, until the shadows began to fall, and Marie finally fell into a deep sleep.

*

It was because of Gladys that Marie eventually made the effort to get out of bed. As far as she was aware, Stanley hadn't been near her since she'd lost the baby. He'd taken the death very badly, Gladys said.

"Come on now," Gladys steadied Marie as she rolled out of the bed. "I'll help you downstairs."

Marie leant heavily against her, still feeling extremely weak. "Has Stanley left for The Emporium?"

"I think he's gone to that dentist of his again. It seems to be helping him. He keeps going back there."

"Well, at least that's something."

They reached the parlour and Marie sank back against the cushions of the armchair.

"You rest there and I'll make you a cup of tea," Gladys said. She hesitated for a moment. "I don't know if I should mention this, but…"

"Yes?" Marie prompted.

"Well, yesterday, I bumped into Dr McCullough in the town. He said things."

"Like what?"

"Things like: Mrs Minton dabbles with matters she knows nothing about. He said you made up all sorts of concoctions. He said: Lord knows what's in them. It's a wonder she didn't kill *herself,* let alone the baby."

Marie was horrified. "He said that? He accused me of hurting the baby?"

"It's what he meant. It wasn't my place to disagree with him, but I did say that I'm sure you know what you're doing. And if you ask me, Mrs Minton, it was his fault. He should have known the baby wasn't lying right. He's hiding the fact that it's his fault by blaming you."

Marie tried to control a growing panic. Had he said that to Stanley? Was that why he was avoiding her? Did he blame her for the baby's death? She had to make him see it wasn't her fault or else how could they ever face each other again?

When he got home from work that evening, Stanley was startled to find her sitting in the parlour. "Sorry," he mumbled, turning to leave. "Don't mean to disturb you."

"No, don't go," Marie said quickly, before he could close the door. "We need to talk." Reluctantly, he came back into the room. "Has Dr McCullough talked about the baby? About why he…" She couldn't bring herself to say "died", but she didn't need to finish the sentence. Stanley knew exactly what she meant. He didn't reply, but simply nodded. "Does he blame me?" she asked. "Did he say it was my fault?" He nodded again. Her stomach churned. "And do you believe him?"

"You were taking something. Pa saw you. It was something you'd made out of those herbs of yours."

"Horehound, an infusion of horehound – it's harmless. And if your father had asked me about it instead of running off to you or Dr McCullough, I could have explained that to him."

"You didn't go to see McCullough straightaway because you thought you knew better. But all I know is that my son is dead," he said with bitterness.

"I lost him, too." She gripped the arms of her chair and struggled to her feet. "I lost my baby, Stanley, and you have to believe me – it wasn't anything to do with herbs. The baby was lying wrongly."

"What do you know about anything?" he said, viciously. "You're just an ignorant woman who's spent all her life in a convent." He was whipping himself up into a rage. It had been building up since the baby's death. "Pa told me something else today as well. He said he'd heard you've been going around making these so-called 'concoctions' for other people. You've been charging money for it."

Marie closed her eyes. She wasn't ready for this confrontation – not yet.

"Grubbing around for a half penny here and a half penny there like some kind of fairground fraudster? What do you think it makes me look like, eh? Like a man who can't support his wife. Like someone making his wife earn because he can't pay his way."

"Taking money from me didn't worry you when you married me, did it?" The words were out before she realised. "But, of course, it wasn't a half penny I brought you then was it? It was eight hundred pounds and you snatched at it!"

Stanley's mouth fell open in astonishment and Marie sank

back into the armchair, exhausted by her outburst, immediately regretting having revealed what she knew.

Stanley replied slowly: "How long have you known about that? Did Pickard tell you?" Then, his anger flared up again. "That man made me swear I wouldn't say anything to you about it. You've both made a fool of me. You knew that damned agreement tied me to you forever."

She couldn't let him think she'd had anything to do with that. "No, I didn't know anything about it at the time, I swear. It was Peter who told me about the money. He overheard you and your mother talking about it. Then I went to see John Pickard and I demanded to be told the truth. Like you, he told me nothing about where it came from. But if the eight hundred pounds had been given to me instead of you, neither of us would be trapped in this nightmare. Instead, it's been frittered away on a tea room that no one wants to visit."

She was breathing heavily now, and Stanley's face was turning a bright red. He leant over her and she cowered back in the chair, uncertain as to what he would do next.

"That eight hundred pounds bought you a roof over your head, woman, and if I could tear up that agreement now I would, but Pickard will refuse it – because then he'd have you back on his hands and that's the last thing he wants."

Marie's heart was beating fast, but she was determined not to show fear. "None of this is of my making."

"Did my son have to die so you could get your own back? Is that it? Because you *did* kill my son – you and your concoctions – and that *is* of your making. Well, I can at least put an end to that."

He strode out into the hall and she saw him take a walking stick from the stand. She struggled to her feet. "Stanley!" She followed him, trying to run up the stairs after him, but she tripped over her skirts and fell heavily, so he reached her room before she could stop him. She saw him raise the stick.

"No, Stanley, don't," she shouted.

He smashed it down on the shelves where she stored everything for her remedies. Bottles were shattered; glass and liquid flew through the air; rare herbs and oils spilled everywhere. The precious ingredients that Sister Grace had collected over many years were ruined. He tore the Bunsen burner from the gas tap, the thin rubber tube still attached to it.

She crawled the rest of the way up the stairs, but by then his work was done. Without a word he threw the stick aside and clutching the Bunsen burner like a trophy he strode to his room, locking the door behind him.

She sat on the floor in the middle of the mess and hugged her knees to her chest, rocking backwards and forwards as her tears flowed unchecked. She had wanted this baby so desperately; how could anyone believe she would have hurt it? She would never have harmed it. It was wicked and evil to say so and Stanley was wrong to even think it, and so was Dr McCullough. She would never destroy anything that was so precious to her.

She stayed there throughout the night and it was where she woke up the next morning. She was stiff and in pain, but she wearily began to clear up the mess. She would tell Gladys there had been an accident. It would only worry her if she knew the truth.

CHAPTER FOURTEEN

As Evelyn's motor car crawled along The Grove in Ilkley, it emitted a huge cloud of blue smoke followed by a loud bang. It startled two passers-by and a horse pulling a milk cart was panicked into galloping down the high street.

He hardly noticed, he was too preoccupied. Over the last few weeks, he'd struggled with the question of whether or not he should call on Marie Minton. What would he do if she proved beyond any reasonable doubt that his father had cheated Montrecourt out of his claim, and then killed him in cold blood in order to conceal it? But then the uncertainty of not knowing would be worse, he had finally concluded.

He turned his motor car left into Pewter Street and pulled up outside a grey stone terraced house that identified itself as The Laurels. He became aware that curtains were twitching in the houses nearby and a group of small boys were heading towards his motor car with open mouths. He jumped down and peeled off his gauntlets, removing his cap and goggles. He hesitated for a moment in front of the painted red door with its brass knocker. It opened just as he raised his hand to knock.

"Yes?" The woman who answered it was staring in wonder over his shoulder at the bright blue motor car behind him. "Yes, sir?" she repeated.

"I've called to see Mrs Minton? I believe she lives here?" The woman nodded, still staring past him. "Would you tell her I have a letter for her?"

"A letter?" Then, obviously remembering her manners, she added: "I'm sorry, sir. Come in. Just wait here in the hall a moment."

She disappeared up the stairs and Evelyn heard the murmur of voices. He glanced around him at his surroundings. Not to his taste, but comfortable enough.

The woman returned. "Mrs Minton says will you wait in the front parlour, sir? She won't be long."

"Yes, thank you." He followed her into a room to the right of the front door.

"Let me take your coat and things, sir."

He handed her his gloves and hat, and unbuckled his leather coat. The parlour was rather dull and the decoration was unimaginative. His attention was caught by a glass case containing a stuffed bird on a twig – not a thing of beauty to his mind.

"I'm sorry to keep you waiting."

The voice was low and musical, with the faintest trace of an accent. He swung around to face her and stared in astonishment at the young woman who had entered. He wasn't sure what he'd expected of Montrecourt's daughter, but he had never expected her to look like this. This young woman could have stepped out of a painting by one of the Pre-Raphaelites. She seemed so young – little more than a child. Her hair, the colour of amber and hung loose, formed a halo around her face, which was very pale. Her eyes were a deep brown and seemed full of sadness. She wore a white lace waistcoat over a white dress, and a black shawl embroidered with roses was thrown around her shoulders. He found his voice at last.

"Mrs Minton?"

"Yes."

Marie had been resting on her bed when Gladys had come upstairs to say she had a visitor. She was still weak after the miscarriage and, assuming the caller was a neighbour who had yet to learn she was no longer making the cures and remedies, she hadn't bothered to change. She was embarrassed to find that her visitor was actually an elegant young man who was staring at her in astonishment, presumably unaccustomed to being received by a young woman in a state of *déshabillé*. Gladys should have warned her.

Her visitor quickly bowed his head in a polite greeting. "I'm sorry; I've obviously disturbed you, Mrs Minton."

"I'm sorry to greet you so informally, but I wasn't expecting anyone and I've been resting. I haven't been well recently."

He had kind eyes – she noticed that. Blue eyes, which expressed concern when she mentioned that she hadn't been well.

"Then you must sit down," he said, as though he was the host and she the visitor. He was obviously used to being obeyed and, a little flustered, she sat down as instructed. He took the armchair facing her. "And I should be apologising to you for turning up on your doorstep unannounced. I should have sent my card first."

He was a man of some substance, she could see that. She wasn't sure what she should do next, but he took charge of the situation.

"Forgive me. Let me introduce myself, Mrs Minton. I'm Evelyn Harringdon."

He seemed to be waiting for her to react to the name, but it meant nothing to her. After a moment, all she could think of to say was: "Gladys said you have a letter for me?"

"Yes, that's right. I'm afraid it's taken an awfully long time to reach you. The circumstances surrounding its arrival were… quite strange." She saw him take two envelopes out of his inner pocket. He held one of them up. "Some months ago, this letter was delivered to my father. I should explain that he has been dead for some time, so it was obviously a surprise to me. Inside it was contained this sealed letter for you." He held up the other envelope. "But I had no idea who you were or how to reach you, until I accidentally met Mr John Pickard."

"Mr Pickard?" She remembered all too well *her* last meeting with the solicitor.

He handed her the letters. "I suggest you read the one addressed to my father first. It's from a priest, Father Connor." He seemed to be waiting for her to react again, but she shook her head to show the name was unknown to her. He looked disappointed. "Well, it will explain why your letter was enclosed inside mine."

She took both the letters and stared in astonishment at the name on the first envelope. "Sir Gordon Harringdon?"

She could scarcely believe it. Sir Gordon was famously known as the hero of Majuba, and this gentleman standing in her front parlour was his son. She wished fervently that she could disappear into the ground. To have greeted him dressed so casually was shameful. He was indicating for her to read, but she became puzzled after the first sentence.

"The Transvaal?"

"In Africa. My father served there, in the first war against the Boers in 1881."

"I don't understand."

"Read on," he urged, and moved away to allow her to continue.

The next sentence caused her to exclaim aloud. "Sister Grace is dead. I didn't even know that she was ill. She was a good friend to me."

He turned and his face expressed concern. "I am so sorry. I hadn't realised the news would come as such a shock to you. It was very insensitive of me."

She looked at the other envelope. It was Sister's letter. She couldn't bear to open that one – not yet.

The young man knelt down beside her. "Does nothing in Father Connor's letter mean anything to you?"

She could see that he wanted her to say yes. She read it again and then shook her head. "No, I'm sorry."

He stood up, deeply disappointed. "I had hoped. I believe your father was in Africa at the same time as mine. I had hoped you could tell me something about him. But now I've met you, I can see you're too young to have known him. Did your mother ever mention anything about him?"

"No. I was born in a convent just outside Chartres – not in Africa."

"But your mother is Hortense Montrecourt?"

"She was. She died at the convent giving birth to me. I never met my father. No one has ever been able to tell me anything about him until now." Her unexpected visitor had revived hopes she had long ago abandoned. "I don't even know my father's first name. Can you tell me what it is?"

For a moment, he seemed reluctant to answer. "I believe your father's name was Henri."

"Henri," she repeated the name quietly to herself. "Can you tell me anything else?"

He turned away. "No, not really. I've been told that your mother helped my father escape the Boers after his regiment had been defeated at the Battle of Majuba. And that your father died – was killed – when the Boers attacked his farm where he'd given shelter to my father. You can't tell me anything more?"

She shook her head. This was astonishing news to her. It was difficult to take in. "My father died protecting Sir Gordon Harringdon? Why did no one ever tell me?"

"No one knows," her visitor said. "It was never mentioned."

She stared at him as one thought rapidly spiraled into another. She found herself making connections, jumping to conclusions. Things that had made no sense to her before were now beginning to fall into place.

"It can't be," she murmured, "but it must be." She saw his lack of comprehension. "Your father must have been my benefactor." In her excitement, she caught hold of Evelyn's arm. "Don't you see – if my parents helped your father escape he would be grateful, wouldn't he? John Pickard would never tell me who had paid for my keep at the convent, but it must have been your father. I had thought it was Sister Grace, but it wasn't."

"Your keep?" He was as astonished as she was.

"Didn't you know?" she asked incredulously. "Did he keep it a secret even from his son?"

"Yes, even his son didn't know." Evelyn murmured. "He was a very private man. Didn't like to take credit for his actions. I didn't know of your existence until I received this letter."

"He must also have provided the dowry for me to marry. To show his gratitude for what my parents had done to help him. It has to be." She was excited and astonished. "But why was John Pickard instructed never to mention his name? I don't understand why." Her visitor said nothing. "It was him, wasn't it? He did want to show his gratitude, didn't he?"

"Yes, it must have been like that." She waited for him to explain further, but he didn't. "Did your mother leave you nothing that would tell us more about what happened at the farm on the day the Boers attacked?"

She shook her head. "No. I only have some small mementoes, but nothing that means very much." She crossed to a sideboard drawer and withdrew the battered tin box. She opened it and took out a small lump of rock. "I always pretended, when I was a child, that this was precious. I've no idea where it came from, but it belonged to my mother."

He slowly took the rock from her. It was fool's gold.

"And I have this, too," she said.

She was holding up a tarnished regimental button. He took it over to the window to study it better. She was smoothing out a torn piece of paper as he murmured: "My father's regiment."

"And these are the last words my mother wrote. I've never understood them." She began to read them aloud, translating them from the French: *I cannot forget what I have done, what I have been made to do. May God forgive me, and forgive him too for making me do it. Protect my child.* Are you ill?" she asked in concern, noticing he'd grown very pale.

"No. I had a late night yesterday and I'm just a little tired." He turned abruptly towards the door. "I must go."

Surprised by the suddenness of his decision, she followed him into the hallway. "Did those words mean something to you?"

"No, I'm afraid not." He attempted a smile. "I'm so sorry. You must think me very rude." He took his coat and hat from the hall stand where Gladys had left them.

She thought she could guess at the cause of his sudden change of mood. "I'm sure that our talk must have awakened sad memories of your father," she said, gently.

"Yes, that's right. Things I hoped I could forget." There was a hint of something she couldn't define, but then his manner changed again and he became businesslike. "My father obviously expressed a strong wish for confidentiality in the matter of the money he provided, for reasons we've discussed. I would ask you to continue to honour that wish. In fact, I would ask you to not discuss his involvement with your family at all – not even with your husband. It would be the right way to repay his kindness."

John Pickard had made exactly those conditions, so she wasn't surprised. "Of course I won't discuss it. May I keep Father Connor's letter, though?" Otherwise, after her visitor had gone, she would think she had dreamt these extraordinary events.

He seemed about to refuse, but then thought better of it. He nodded. "If you promise not to show it to anyone."

"I will show it to no one," she said. "I promise."

He took her hand in his and bowed over it. Then he was gone and she was left alone. She heard Gladys approaching from the kitchen. She would have to give her some explanation for the man's visit. She would say that he had had business in the area and had been asked to deliver a letter to her from one of the sisters in the convent where she was born. It was as close to the truth as she could make it.

*

Evelyn drove down The Grove little caring where he was heading. He was now certain that his father had killed Montrecourt. It was Hortense's note that had finally convinced him: *I cannot forget what I have done, what I have been made to do. May God forgive me, and forgive him too for making me do it.* It wasn't gratitude that had inspired his father to help the girl – it was guilt.

He couldn't even begin to imagine what had happened on that day at the farm. Hortense must have been there when his father killed Montrecourt. "Bury him" – the words made sense now. Perhaps he had forced her to help him get rid of the body. The only redeeming feature in the whole sordid business was that his father must have finally suffered remorse. He'd resigned from the Mining Company and had used some of the money to support the girl. It was surely self interest that had made him provide for her marriage, though. The name of Montrecourt would disappear forever once she became Marie Minton and there would be no remaining link to the past.

Evelyn struck the steering wheel with his fist in anger – damn his father! Not only had he robbed the girl of her family, he'd cheated her out of her inheritance. Blood money might ease his father's conscience, but it didn't ease Evelyn's. Just what he could do about the girl he had no idea, but he would keep in touch with her just in case.

CHAPTER FIFTEEN

Marie stood nervously outside the Kursaal Tea Room, which sat between the magnificent Spa Rooms and the Kursaal Theatre. Strains of music drifted across from the spa as the resident orchestra played a selection of melodies from Edward German's "Merrie England".

She was clutching the letter she'd received a week ago from Sir Evelyn Harringdon. This was the second letter he'd written to her since his visit. The first had been to apologise for having called on her so unexpectedly, and to assure her that he would always be as concerned for her future wellbeing as his father had been. She had replied immediately to say it had been a great pleasure to meet him and that everything he had told her about her parents had been precious to her and would remain secret.

The second letter, some weeks later, enquired after her health and mentioned that he would be in the area again, and it would be delightful if they could meet. He was happy to call on her at The Laurels or, if she preferred, they could meet at the Kursaal in Harrogate for afternoon tea, if she thought her husband would have no objection.

Again, she had replied immediately and said it would make her very happy to meet with him, and that the Kursaal sounded very nice. She didn't show either of his letters to Stanley. To do so would have meant an explanation about the role Sir Gordon had played in her life. Instead, she hid them in her mother's tin box with the priest's letter. After Evelyn's visit, she'd been unable to resist writing to Father Connor in Pretoria to ask him if he could tell her anything further about her parents. She decided there was no need to mention this to Evelyn, as the priest would probably never receive her letter anyway.

She peered through the glass door of the Kursaal. She'd never been inside. Round tables were scattered under a vaulted glass roof and elegant palms flanked the arches. It was quiet at the moment because there was a matinee playing in the theatre, but once the performance was over she was sure the place would be full of people. She caught sight of Evelyn seated at one of the tables in the corner, with his legs stretched out and a silver-topped cane leaning against his chair. He looked up and saw her, and raised a hand in acknowledgement. Taking a deep breath, she pushed open the door and entered.

He stood up to greet her. "Mrs Minton, I'm relieved to see you looking so well."

She'd dressed with care for their meeting this time. She'd chosen her favourite gown of rose silk voile, with its dropped sleeves trimmed with black taffeta. The Eton jacket was trimmed with tabs of the same black taffeta and the wide-brimmed hat, set slightly to the side of her head, was rimmed with pink roses that exactly matched the colour of her dress.

"Thank you," she said as he took her jacket and held the chair for her to sit. "I was surprised to hear that you were here in the North again so soon."

"I've allowed myself to be persuaded to stand in a by-election – to represent Fallsworth."

"How exciting. Fallsworth is near York, isn't it?"

He placed her jacket on the back of her chair. "I would have preferred another constituency – this one is under the patronage of Lord Renfrew, so I don't think there's much doubt I'll get in. I would have liked to prove myself capable of it without his help."

"But you *are* in the House of Lords. I read about you in the newspaper."

"It's in the Commons that we need to increase our influence. Anyway, it does mean that I'll be in the area quite frequently over the next few months." He sat down facing her. "And as I had some time on my hands today, I thought it would be extremely pleasant to look you up again. After all, I feel responsible for you."

"Responsible?"

"I inherited my father's estate and with it, I inherited his responsibility for you."

"No, you mustn't feel that," she protested. "It's very kind of you, but you have far more important things to worry about."

As the waiter approached, Evelyn said with a charming smile: "Maybe we should order?"

They studied the menu, heads close together and decided, to Marie's delight, on a champagne afternoon tea: orange pekoe served with a glass of champagne and small squares of smoked salmon sandwiches, followed by iced cakes. The order was given and Evelyn settled back. She saw that he was observing her closely and wondered if her hat was awry.

"Do you lead a very busy life?" he asked suddenly. "I'd like to hear about it – your life. Your husband has a business here in Harrogate, I believe."

"Yes, The Emporium, and a tea room, though I know very little about them. Stanley doesn't like me to get involved. He works very hard."

"So, no outings to the Kursaal for the two of you, then?"

"No outings at all." Did he think she was complaining? She mustn't give him that impression. After all, it was his father's money that had provided this life for her. She quickly added: "But things aren't dull. I take piano lessons and visit the lending library, and then there are the dogs to care for. They're St Bernards – Stanley used to show them, but he doesn't have much time for that anymore. So I take care of them. I've grown to love them. Of course, compared to becoming an MP, Sir Evelyn, it must seem very dull."

"Evelyn. Just call me Evelyn," he said, pleasantly. "And I shall call you Marie, if I may?" He sat back as the waiter approached. "Ah, here's tea. Shall you pour or shall I?"

He found it difficult not to watch Marie. She took such delight in everything around her. It was refreshing to see the world through her eyes. So different from the bored young women to whom his mother kept introducing him.

Siggy had asked him the other day if he'd managed to track down Montrecourt's daughter. He'd lied and said no – he didn't really know why. Perhaps he wanted to keep the knowledge of her existence to himself, because Siggy would demand to be told the reason for his continued interest in her and advise against it. He didn't want to have to justify his actions to his friend – nor to himself either.

*

Marie placed yet another of Evelyn's letters in the tin box under the bed. She'd recently removed it from the drawer of the sideboard in the parlour, having discovered her father-in-law about to open it. He protested that he'd taken it out of the drawer by mistake, but she didn't believe him. He'd taken to watching her. When she challenged him, he said it was because he wanted to make sure she wasn't making any more of those foul concoctions.

Evelyn had written to her every week since their meeting in the Kursaal. Wonderful, lighthearted letters that were full of gossip about the by-election, with descriptions of some of the constituents that made her laugh out loud. Gladys always collected the post from the hall before Stanley and his father were up. If she was curious as to why so many letters arrived addressed for Marie only and in the same handwriting, she never commented on it.

Marie always replied instantly, trying to think up amusing anecdotes in reply to his, although there was little amusement to be had at The Laurels these days. Stanley was barely ever home and when he *was*, he locked himself in his bedroom. It was a relief to her, as his mood swung between elation and depression with increasing rapidity. He complained about everything. This week, it was about the weather.

Indeed, today had been unbearably hot, and Marie was sitting near an open window reading, trying to take advantage of what little breeze there was. Her dress was open at the neck and drops of perspiration were forming at her throat. They glistened in the sun like bright beads. She heard the front door close. Stanley was home early. To her surprise, he came into the parlour instead of going straight upstairs as usual. He took off his jacket and flung it onto one of the chairs.

"Travelling by train isn't fit for a dog," he muttered. She saw that his shirt was damp with sweat. He looked around. "Where's Pa?"

She turned her attention back to her book. "He's gone to the Red Lion with Joe Bottomley."

"He's drinking too much – ever since Ma died. He's becoming impossible to live with."

She didn't disagree. Edwin had become extremely petulant just recently, finding fault with everything she did.

Stanley took out a handkerchief and wiped his forehead. "Martin Godson gave in his notice today."

She looked up in surprise. "Martin? He's worked with you for years."

"Wants more money – says he can get better wages elsewhere. I said to him: if you think you can do better somewhere else, then go on, clear out. I don't want you. He wasn't so cocky when he left." He winced and rubbed his stomach. He saw her watching him. "I have this ulcer – McCullough says so."

There was a time when she would have offered to make him a remedy that would relieve the pain, but Stanley had put an end to all of that. He was particularly on edge tonight. He kept walking around the room, repositioning ornaments on the mantelpiece, straightening cushions, staring out of the window. His restlessness was making her uneasy.

"I need to talk to you," he said abruptly.

"Oh?" Had he finally noticed the letters she'd been receiving? Or, more likely, had his father noticed and said something?

He cleared his throat. "We're both going to have to accept a few changes around here. Big changes." He walked about the room again. There was sweat on his upper lip and on his forehead. "For a start, I'm selling the dogs."

She stared at him for a moment, not taking it in at first. "The dogs?" She rose to her feet, her book falling unnoticed to the floor. "You can't do that."

"I can't afford not to. I never see them these days, anyway. I don't show them anymore. Work is taking up all my time, so what's the point of them?"

Her anger flared. "They're not some commodity you sell in the shop; they're a part of the family. I love them. They love me. You can't mean you're going to sell them." Tears were very close. She brushed them aside.

"They're animals, for heaven's sake, Marie – just animals. Don't let's get sentimental."

"They're my companions. This house is where they belong. You can't get rid of them."

"Well, this house is going too. There'll be no room for them where we'll move to."

She stared at him. "Move?"

"I'm selling The Emporium and the tea room. I intend to start up a new business in a new town. The Laurels will go on the market. I intend to make a fresh start. Make a new life."

He'd given her no indication that he was contemplating such a thing. "Why? What's the reason for all this?"

"Don't worry. You'll still have a roof over your head – that's all that bothers you, isn't it?"

She stared at him, utterly bewildered. "You can't just walk in here and tell me our lives are changing so completely. You can't sell our home just like that. Have you told your father?"

"No, not yet."

She knew for certain that Edwin wouldn't stand quietly by while he sold The Laurels. "You can't turn all our lives inside out like this with no warning." He must surely have a fever or something. His face looked flushed and his eyes were red-rimmed. Was he ill? Had she been so preoccupied with thoughts of Evelyn that she hadn't noticed?

"You'd better accept it," he said brusquely. "There's no other way out of the mess – and it is a mess." He threw himself into one of the chairs by the table and ran a shaky hand through thinning hair. "Let a man make one mistake and he's never forgiven, that's the truth. I opened the tea room too soon, that's what all the banks are saying. But it could have worked – the war was over and people had money to spend again. It was the right time to expand the business. I was just unlucky that's all. That damned tea room has drained me of every penny. The banks are calling in their loans."

She tried to sound calm. "Is it really that bad?"

"Yes, but then the answer came to me. Build a new Emporium. Start again. This morning I accepted an offer on the shop and the tea room. I'm losing money on the deal, but it'll clear the debts and pay the damned banks off. I'll make money out of selling The Laurels – enough to rent somewhere and start a business again."

"You should have talked to me about it first, and your father." She meant he shouldn't have carried the burden alone, but he misunderstood her and took it as a criticism. He turned on her angrily and for a moment she thought he was going to strike her.

"And what good would telling you do, eh? You'd save us, would you, with your ha'penny quackery?"

She was still struggling to make sense of it all. "Has all the money I brought with me gone?"

That incensed him. He grabbed her by the arm and thrust his face close to hers. "I was paid to give you a roof over your head and that's what I've done, isn't it? And that's what I'll go on doing because I don't have any choice, do I?"

She was frightened, but it was important not to show it. "Let go of my arm, Stanley," she said quietly.

He glared at her without moving. They heard the front door open. Edwin was back. Stanley let her go.

"You'd better not say anything to Pa about this," he warned. "I'll tell him in my own time." He strode out of the room.

Shaken, she sank down onto the window seat. She heard Edwin cross the hall and managed to compose herself just as he entered the room. He was looking over his shoulder after his son.

"Everything all right?" he asked.

"Everything's perfectly all right," she said with a tight smile.

*

Marie had known that Stanley's father would not take his son's news well, and he didn't. Though she shut herself in her room, she could still hear their raised voices. When she saw Edwin later, he glared at her as if it were all her fault. Meanwhile, Stanley was doing his best to avoid both of them. He spent most of his time travelling to nearby Leeds where he was looking for premises that might be suitable for a reborn Emporium.

It was a grim atmosphere that settled on The Laurels. The dogs were sold and Marie felt as if her heart had been wrenched out of her. She went for a walk when the new owners came to collect them. She would be losing Gladys, too. There was no way *she* could travel to Leeds, which she hated anyway. "Great, dirty place it is," she said.

"What will you do, Gladys?" Marie knew she earned barely enough to feed her family as it was.

"There'll be other work," she replied stoically, but they both knew that their lives would be the poorer in every way.

The only solace Marie found now was in Evelyn's letters. Through them, she could escape into a different world and forget the chaos of her own. When he wrote to say he had won the by-election, she wrote back immediately to congratulate him and to say how proud she was to know someone of such importance. With the modesty she had come to expect from him, he dismissed his achievement as the triumph of influence over talent. He suggested that they might meet somewhere to celebrate his success. She suggested a small tea room in the nearby market town of Otley.

*

A railway connected the two towns and it was only a short walk from the station to the tea room. When she arrived, it was to discover that Evelyn wasn't there. For a moment, she panicked. Had she got the wrong date or the wrong time? As if on cue, he entered full of effusive apologies. Constituency business had kept him longer than he'd expected.

"I've only just arrived myself," she reassured him. "Please don't worry. I know how busy you are."

They ordered tea and cakes and then fell into easy conversation – as old friends should.

"You don't mind me writing to you so often, do you?" he asked eventually, as Marie poured them a second cup of tea.

"No. Oh, no."

"I was surrounded by petty bureaucracy every day. Sometimes it drove me to distraction. I needed to unburden myself to someone and I hoped it might make you smile."

"It did." She was flattered that he'd thought of her at all. "Tell me about election day."

She listened intently as he gave her a blow-by-blow account, making her laugh at his description of some of the voters. She listened in admiration as he quoted extracts from his acceptance speech.

"I could never speak in public like you," she said in admiration.

"If you had to, you would," he assured her.

She smiled and shook her head, then glanced at the clock behind the counter. She couldn't believe how quickly time had passed since her arrival. She should be going. She'd been able to slip out of the house unnoticed because both Stanley and Edwin were absent, but Edwin would return soon and she didn't want to have to explain where she'd been. She was pleased to see that Evelyn was genuinely disappointed when she told him she had to go.

"I haven't asked anything about you?" he said, full of remorse. "All I've talked about is myself."

"But that's much more interesting." She meant it. She realised, of course, that now he was a Member of Parliament, he would be far too busy to keep in touch with her. She would miss him. "I expect you'll find yourself extremely busy from now on," she said, holding out her hand. "I just want to thank you again for all your family's kindness to me."

He surprised her by taking the proffered hand and kissing its palm. Then he folded her fingers over it. "Hold on to that until we meet again, and we will. I have more reason than ever to be in the north now I'm elected. I intend to be zealous in my attention to my constituents, but I'm sure that will leave me time to call on you. If you don't think your husband would object," he added as an afterthought.

Marie flushed, but her honesty made her say: "I haven't discussed our meetings with Stanley. He's so busy, you see. Besides, I would have to explain to him how and why we met, and that could prove difficult considering your father's request to remain anonymous."

To her relief, he seemed to accept that completely. "Of course, your decision is absolutely correct. My father's wishes must be paramount."

CHAPTER SIXTEEN

The train from Ilkley was ten minutes late and Evelyn was impatiently pacing up and down outside the station at Harrogate waiting for Marie. He'd planned a surprise outing for her, and now he was nervous in case it didn't please her. At least the weather was on his side. It was a beautiful day with a cloudless sky.

He'd managed to see Marie three times since the by-election and they exchanged weekly letters – neither of them giving a thought to how Stanley would feel about it if he knew. After all, there was no harm in it. He was an old family friend.

At last he saw her hurrying out of the station towards him. "I'm so sorry," she said.

She had obviously been running because she was breathless and a lock of hair had fallen loose. He smiled reassuringly. "You're here now and that's all that matters."

He caught her by the hand and hurried her over to his motor car, and began to drive with his usual speed through the deserted countryside. He glanced at her. She'd looked a little pale when she'd arrived, but the drive was bringing the colour back to her cheeks.

"Where are we going?" she asked.

"Wait and see," he teased.

Finally, he pulled up by the side of a small inn nestling on the bank of a river. There was a rowing boat tied up to the capstan nearby and he gestured towards it. He enjoyed the changing expressions that crossed her face as she looked around her: curiosity, surprise, anticipation.

"Climb on board, Madame, and wait. I will answer all your questions on my return," he said.

He headed for the nearby inn where he'd arranged for a picnic hamper to be prepared. He placed it in the boat beside her and laughed as she tried to peek inside. "Patience," he said, with mock reproof.

He rowed them out to a small island in the middle of the river, skilfully manoeuvring the boat until they came to a stop among reeds.

"How on earth did you manage to organise all this when you're so busy?" Marie asked, as he helped her onto the bank.

They headed for the shade provided by a nearby sycamore tree and with a flourish Evelyn produced a rug from the hamper. "In case the grass is too damp for Madame." He started to unpack the picnic. "To be honest, it wasn't very difficult to organise. I've always kept in touch with Gerrard. He used to work at Ardington, on the estate, but now he owns the inn over there." He nodded to the far bank. "I wrote and told him I wanted a picnic, and said when I would need it and voila! He owns this island and the rowing boat. So you see, I can't take much credit for anything."

"You must take all the credit for finding such a perfect spot."

As they feasted on chicken, salad and freshly baked bread, Evelyn chattered on about anything he thought might amuse her. Eventually, she leant back against the trunk of the sycamore tree with a sigh of contentment. The only sounds to disturb the silence surrounding them were the gentle lapping of water and the songs of birds.

"I couldn't eat another thing. Mr Gerrard's been more than generous." She wiped her hands on a napkin to get rid of the grease. "This has been the most wonderful day, Evelyn. Thank you. I'll never forget it."

He thought how lovely she looked, the sun throwing

patterns of light and shade across her face as the wind gently stirred the leaves above her. A shaft of sunlight caught her hair and for a moment turned the burnished copper into blood-red. A hint of sadness crossed her face. He wanted to reach out and brush it away – which was stupid, he told himself sharply. To even think like that was stupid. He realised that his longing to be alone with her had been a mistake. They'd only ever met in public before, with other people around them. Marie was a married woman and he reminded himself that his intention was simply to offer her protection if she needed it – nothing more.

"We ought to move," he said abruptly. "I'll pack all this away."

She was surprised by his change of mood, but she immediately agreed. "Of course, I've taken up too much of your time."

He wanted to deny it and say he could think of no better way to spend his time than to be with her, but he didn't.

"I'll take you back to the station." He tried to keep his tone light. He didn't want to spoil the day for her. His weakness was not her fault.

On the drive back, a companionable silence fell between them. At the station it was hard for him to say goodbye to her, but it was even harder to watch her disappear as the train pulled away. The emptiness she left behind was profound.

*

It was some weeks since their picnic and Marie hadn't heard anything further from Evelyn. She understood – in fact, she'd even half expected it. Political life was bound to start taking up more and more of his time.

She *had* received a letter this morning, though, and it was an unexpected one. It was from Pretoria, from the Abbot of St

Alphonsus Monastery, in response to the letter she'd written to Father Connor after her first meeting with Evelyn. In it, she'd asked the priest for any information he could give her about her parents. She'd heard nothing and had assumed her letter had never arrived, but it obviously had. The Abbot was apologising for the delay in replying. He wrote that Father Connor had left for France some time ago, to end his days at the Abbey of Saint Foy in Conques. "Whether he will survive the journey," the Abbot had written, "is in God's hands. I am sorry I am not able to help you further."

She folded the letter and placed it in the tin box under her bed. She felt a little guilty that she'd written to Father Connor and not told Evelyn, so it was almost a relief that this was the end of the matter.

★

The next day, she returned from the lending library clutching a novel. She hoped that *The Mill on the Floss* and George Eliot would succeed in distracting her from thoughts of Evelyn. She entered the living room and saw that Stanley was waiting for her. For once, he was looking pleased with himself.

"Well, I've done it. I've bought a new business," he announced. "It's in the centre of Leeds. The premises used to belong to an ironmonger, but I'll convert it into a grocers. And I've found somewhere for us to live, close to the new shop."

"Oh," was all she could think of to say. She'd managed to convince herself that his plans had been set aside.

"Is that all you can say?"

She made an effort to show interest. "I'd like to see where we're going to live."

"It's all arranged. I've already paid the first month's rent."

"If I'm going to live there, surely I should see it before we move in?"

He glowered at her and then shrugged. "See it if you must, but it's all I can afford." As he turned to go, he added: "By the way, don't say anything to Pa about any of this."

As Edwin barely exchanged a civil word with her these days, there was very little chance of her telling him anything.

⋆

They caught the tram from outside Leeds railway station. It had a single deck and was a clanging, rattling contraption, above which sparks spat from the electric cable to which it was attached. It swayed and spat its way down the Headrow. As it passed the Town Hall, Marie caught a glimpse of a group of women brandishing placards. There was a crowd watching as three or four policemen wrestled them to the ground, tearing the placards out of their hands. Marie could just make out the lettering on one of them. It read: *Votes For Women*. She saw a figure she thought she recognised. It was Daphne; surely it was Daphne. She stood up excitedly. "That's Daphne Senior, I'm sure of it. I thought she was in London."

She made a move, as if intending to get off the tram, but Stanley grabbed hold of her arm and dragged her roughly back onto the seat.

"Sit down and keep quiet," he hissed, aware that other people on the tram had turned to look at them curiously.

Marie shook her arm free. It was too late to do anything about it now, anyway. The tram had moved on and the group of women was lost from sight.

Stanley finally got up. "We're here," he said brusquely. Marie, clutching onto the backs of the seats for support, followed him off the tram. "This is Briggate. The shop's down that alleyway over there." He indicated an opening between the three story buildings. "The place I've found for us to live is just five minutes' walk away in Garibaldi Street, number fourteen."

He set off at a pace and she almost had to run to keep up with him. That was how he was these days, either bursting with energy or overwhelmed by lethargy, and she never knew which one to expect.

*

The rooms were unfurnished. The owners of the house, a Mr and Mrs Gilpin, had the basement and ground floor, while the rooms of the apartment that Stanley had rented were spread over the first and second floors. Both parties shared the same door into the street, but a flight of stairs led up to the apartment's front door from the communal hall. Once inside, there was a small landing from which a few more steps led up to a scullery, a kitchen and a parlour. More steps led up to the second floor, where there were two large bedrooms.

Marie slowly paced around the empty room. She crossed to the window to peer out, the heels of her shoes clicking against bare wooden floorboards. She stared into the house opposite. It was so close that if she wanted to she could lean out and touch its window. She turned away and observed the pale green distemper on the walls around her. It was clean and it wasn't a hovel. She should be grateful for that.

"It's all I can afford." Her silence was beginning to irritate him. "We won't be here for long anyway – just until the shop starts making money. Then I'll buy a house."

"It's very pleasant," she said, trying to sound positive.

She'd noticed one thing immediately. There were only two bedrooms. Since the baby had died Stanley had shown no inclination to restart marital relations, and she had no desire for that either. The fear of becoming pregnant again burned fiercely inside her. She'd also heard Dr McCullough say to Stanley that she might not be strong enough to survive another miscarriage.

"There are only two bedrooms," she murmured.

"Yes, well, as you can see, there'll be no room for Pa here."

She looked at him in astonishment. Stanley had always provided Edwin with a home.

"I've been supporting him for years. It's about time our Geoffrey helped out. The old man's getting worse – nattering at me all the time and poking his nose into things that don't concern him."

Marie knew he would be devastated by the news. "It will be a shock to him."

"He'll be alright at Geoffrey's. It's not as if I'm sending him to the poor house."

She held her silence. It was up to Edwin to fight his own battles and it was better than her having to share a bed with Stanley. "When will you tell him?"

"After I've spoken to Geoffrey."

"When will that be?"

"In my own time, when I'm good and ready. Until then, I'll thank you to keep quiet about it."

Marie nodded and fell silent.

Some days later, while she was in the parlour idly running her fingertips across the keys of the piano, the door burst open and Edwin stormed in. He strode over to the piano and shut the lid with a bang, nearly trapping her fingers.

"Couldn't wait to get rid of me, could you?"

Marie looked up at him in astonishment. "I'm sorry?"

"Couldn't wait to get rid of me," he repeated. "How did you persuade him to turn me out? He's a fool, our Stanley, to believe anything you say. "

"Are you talking about you moving in with Geoffrey? It wasn't me who suggested that."

"Stanley said you'd say that. It's the only way she'll agree to the move, he said, if she can still have a room of her own and

I can't afford anything bigger. I told him to kick *you* out then, not me."

"Mr Minton, I had no say in this move." Like Peter before him, Stanley had twisted the truth and put her in the wrong. It was a skill the Mintons shared.

"Didn't you go with him to Leeds to see it?" Edwin demanded.

"Yes."

"And did you tell Stanley that I should be there with you both?"

She couldn't say that she'd been strong in her protest. The truth was she had been relieved. Her silence was enough to confirm Edwin's suspicions.

"You're crowing now that you've got rid of me, but the minute he moves to a bigger place I'll be moving back in – and you'll be sorry for it. I'm not got rid of that easily and I never forgive."

He slammed the door after him as he left.

CHAPTER SEVENTEEN

Geoffrey called to collect Edwin the day before the move to Garibaldi Street. He was furious at having his father 'foisted on him' as he put it and Edwin refused to speak to either Stanley or Marie, so it was a huge relief to Marie when they finally left.

By contrast, it had been greatly distressing to say goodbye to Gladys. She promised to call on her whenever she could, but Gladys said she better not. She said her husband was a difficult man and didn't like visitors. On the morning she and Stanley left, Marie hugged her tightly, unwilling to let her go. They were both tearful. Finally, Marie walked away and didn't look back.

The landlady at Garibaldi Street had been out on the front doorstep all morning watching the removal men do their work. Marie was doing her best to ignore her.

"Don't scratch that paint," Mrs Gilpin shouted after them as they staggered up the stairs with yet another crate. "All damages will have to be paid for, Mrs Minton. What's in them boxes anyway?"

The crates were numbered and Marie was crossing them off her list as they were taken into the house. "In the first six crates? They're mostly books."

"Books?" Mrs Gilpin pursed her lips. "Well, I hope the floor will stand their weight. I hope you're not planning to run a lending library up there, because no business can be carried out on these premises."

"No, they all belong to me." Marie crossed off yet another crate.

"It doesn't seem natural to have that many books," she heard the landlady mutter. Then, to her obvious horror, she saw the piano. "Great, noisy thing, that is," she complained. "Gilpin needs his sleep. He doesn't want disturbing by some piano pounding out through the house every hour of the day and night"

Marie tried not to show her irritation."I'm sure I can practice at a time that will suit us all."

"So, your husband's bought the old ironmonger's shop in Briggate, has he?" Mrs Gilpin followed her into the house, wanting to gossip. "Turning it into a grocers? Needs a lot of work doing to it, if he's going to do that. Is that where he is now?"

"Yes. If you'll excuse me, I have a great deal to see to as well," Marie said, following the removal men up the stairs to the apartment. "I mustn't keep you," she called over her shoulder, leaving Mrs Gilpin with no option but to end the conversation.

When the removal men had gone, Marie wandered into her bedroom. It was much bigger than the box room she'd had at The Laurels. There was plenty of space for the large wardrobe and the chest of drawers that she'd salvaged from Peter's room. Unfortunately, her window looked straight into the window of the house opposite, but she would make lace curtains to give her some privacy. She ought to start unpacking. She wouldn't touch Stanley's things. He'd made it clear he wanted the crates containing his belongings left in his room unopened.

The first thing she unpacked was the tin box containing her few treasures. She sat on the bed and took out the last letter Evelyn had sent her some months ago – the one inviting her to the picnic. He hadn't written since and she missed not hearing from him. He was thinking about her, of that she was certain. She would write to him tomorrow. She had a good excuse now. She had to tell him about the move and give him her new address. She knew he would want to know. She put his letter back and placed the box in a drawer at the bottom of the wardrobe.

She returned to her unpacking. She emptied three crates containing her clothes and then turned to the crates of books. There were no shelves yet for them, so she began piling them up on the floor of her room. She came across *Farnsworth's Medical Dictionary* – the book that Daphne had sent her after the fire. She idly turned the pages and memories of their time together came flooding back.

It *was* Daphne she'd seen from the tram that day. She'd read about the demonstration in the Yorkshire Clarion. *Women like Daphne Senior, banned from demonstrating in London, come up here to create their mischief instead,* the reporter had written. *It was a cheering sight to see that woman and her cronies marched onto the London train by our fine police officers. Let their husbands and fathers keep them out of our way, locked up at home where they belong.* Did Daphne still live with her father, she wondered? She must hate that.

She put the book aside and took the Bunsen burner and Sister Grace's notes out of the crate. The only two things left to remind her of her time in the convent. They were of little use now. She sighed wearily. There was one crate of her clothes left to unpack, but she was tired. She would leave that until tomorrow.

★

When Stanley returned from the ironmongers that evening, she immediately knew he was in one of his darker moods. His face looked drawn and he said he wanted nothing to eat. He'd been on his hands and knees scrubbing the floor all day, he said, because the woman he'd hired to do it hadn't turned up.

"The place is filthy – a pigsty."

Was he beginning to regret the move? Well, there was no going back now. The Laurels had been sold. For a moment, she felt sorry for him. "Do you want me to unpack your things for you tomorrow?" If he was tired, then unpacking was probably the last thing he wanted to do.

"No." She was surprised by his vehemence. "Keep your nose out of my things. I'll do it tonight if it bothers you."

She was going to say that she was only trying to help, but he'd disappeared into his room before she could. Soon after, she retired to hers. She lay awake for the rest of the night listening to him moving around – presumably unpacking. It wasn't until dawn was breaking that the house fell silent. She suspected that she would be receiving a complaint from Mrs Gilpin the next morning.

After Stanley had left for work, Marie sat down and wrote to Evelyn. It was a difficult letter to write. She didn't want it to sound as though she were asking for a reply, so she tried to keep it businesslike.

> *Dear Evelyn, I hope you are well and not working too hard,* she began. After thinking for a moment, she added: *I am very well and I am simply writing to tell you that Stanley and I have moved to Leeds, to the address at the top of this letter. Stanley decided to sell The Emporium and The Laurels and make a new start, which is very exciting for us. I am only troubling you with this as I feel I should keep you informed. Please do not worry about replying. Yours, Marie.*

She re-read it three times before sealing it. She put on a coat and opened the door of the apartment just as Mrs Gilpin was raising her hand to knock on it. The landlady peered over her lodger's shoulder. "I see you've unpacked. No doubt that's what kept me awake all night? Backwards and forwards, tap, tap, tapping – all night long."

"I'm sorry it disturbed you. It won't happen again." She saw Mrs Gilpin eyeing the letter she was carrying and slipped it into her pocket before the landlady could read the name on it.

"I can post that letter for you, if you like," Mrs Gilpin volunteered.

"No, thank you." Marie smiled politely. "There's no need. I want to take the air." She made an attempt to push past the landlady, who didn't move.

"Oh, and something I should mention," Mrs Gilpin added. "If you need any cleaning, or any laundry doing, just let me know. It's in the rent." Marie still made no move. "So, do you need anything doing now or not?"

"No, thank you." She'd rather have her tongue torn out before she called on Mrs Gilpin for help.

The landlady grudgingly accepted defeat. "Right, well, I'll be off then. Gilpin's due back from work soon and he always likes his meal on the table waiting for him. Knock on my door if you want anything. I'm usually in. Let's hope tonight's a bit more peaceful, shall we?"

Once outside, Marie set off at a brisk pace down Garibaldi Street and found a pillar box three streets away. Her letter safely posted, she decided to explore a little further. She continued past the Theatre Royal and crossed Leeds Bridge. She stopped for a moment to stare down at the muddy waters of the River Aire. A branch of a tree was trapped in a grey circle created by an unseen current. It tugged at the branch from below, trying to drag it under.

She walked on. A tram rattled past on silver rails, blue sparks spitting above it, and an omnibus, full of laughing, chattering people, rushed past pulled by four horses. It swayed unsteadily as it bounced across the rails. A motor car exhaust exploded making the horses jump, and the omnibus swayed even more violently. Gladys was right; it was a noisy, dirty city.

On her return to the house, she stood in the middle of her bedroom and surveyed the last crate to be unpacked. It contained clothes and some of her piano music. Gladys had packed this one for her. She could tell because it was much neater than the crates she'd packed herself.

She was removing the last few dresses when she discovered that Gladys must have mistakenly packed some of Stanley's clothes with hers. There were three jackets and a pair of tweed trousers. She carried them into his room and laid them on a chair. He could put them away himself later.

She hadn't been in Stanley's room since that first visit to Garibaldi Street. It was a larger room than hers and cheerless, with brown-and-white striped wallpaper and a dark oak wooden floor. His bed was in the centre and he'd put his desk along one wall, his wardrobe along another and a bookcase just beside it. The cases of dead butterflies were already hung on the walls. That must have been the tap, tap, tapping Mrs Gilmour had heard during the night. Just looking at them made her feel sad.

As she turned to go, she accidentally kicked something lying on the floor near the bed. She bent down and picked it up. It was a bottle; a small, blue bottle, a medicine bottle. It was labelled *Chloroform – Poison*. Puzzled, Marie stared at it. It must contain at least five or six ounces. Had Stanley's teeth been troubling him again? He hadn't mentioned it. But no dentist would have sanctioned him to administer it to himself, as it was far too dangerous. Perhaps the pain from the ulcer he'd mentioned was worse than he'd admitted? But, then again, no doctor would prescribe his patient such a dangerous substance either.

She dropped the bottle back onto the floor where she'd found it, staring at it for a moment before hurrying back to her room. She found *Farnsworth's Medical Dictionary* and quickly turned to the section covering chloroform. She stood a bottle of witch hazel on the page to keep it flat as she read.

> *Chloroform is very similar to ether in its effect and, like ether, it can become addictive if misused. It is a colourless or water white liquid with a sweet, non-irritating odour. Its effect when used as an anaesthetic is beneficial if administered by a trained practitioner, but skill is needed to prevent it proving lethal. It can be used in industry in various solvents such as cleaning agents, but great care should be taken when handling it. Signs of inhalation are continual sickness, bursts of irrational anger, and a haggard and worn look. A mere teaspoon, if ingested, can kill even a strong man.*

Marie fell back on her heels, knocking over the bottle of witch hazel as she did so. The stopper was loose and the liquid stained the page, but she didn't notice. Was Stanley inhaling chloroform? She'd read about such things. It would explain his changing moods and the time he spent in his room with the door locked. It would explain everything. Marie remembered an article she'd read about it. The reporter had published a letter left by a man to his family:

> *I cannot abstain from the folly of chloroform, though I have tried,* he wrote. *I know the danger of the wine cup is nothing to that of the chloroform bottle. It has ruined me but still I cannot turn my back on it.*

The room began to spin and she had to lean against the bed to steady herself.

*

Two days passed and still Marie hadn't confronted Stanley with her discovery. She didn't know how to begin. It began to dawn on her that it might be the reason he hadn't wanted his father around. He was afraid the old man might nose out his secret.

The Mintons would surely disown him if it became known. Marie had no doubt about that. For a moment, she wondered if she should turn to John Pickard for advice, but he would say Stanley had committed a crime and might feel it his duty to denounce him. Having Stanley in prison wouldn't resolve anything.

The one person she didn't even consider turning to was Evelyn. He must never learn the sordid truth about her marriage. He mustn't become involved. His good name must be protected.

She was making herself sick with worry. She couldn't sleep, and it was during one of those long, endless nights that she heard Stanley scream. She leapt out of bed and was in the middle of throwing on her robe when she heard a crash. She ran down the corridor and into his bedroom. She stumbled over his body on the floor. She saw a flicker of movement; there was a groan and then Stanley began to haul himself slowly to his feet using the bedpost for support.

"I'm sorry." His body was trembling – the fall had obviously shaken him badly. "Stomach pain. Nothing to worry about." He wiped the back of his hand across his mouth. She realised he must have caught himself as he fell because she could see blood. "I'm all right, it's the ulcer," he insisted.

She saw the bottle of chloroform at the foot of the bed and picked it up. It was empty. "Oh, God. No."

"Medicine for my stomach," he said quickly.

She turned on him angrily. "I'm not a fool, Stanley. I know what it is and it will kill you if you keep using it."

Just then, there was a hammering at the front door. It was

Mrs Gilpin. "Everything all right up there, Mr Minton? Mrs Minton? I heard a crash."

Stanley, with unexpected strength, grabbed hold of Marie's arm. "It's my ulcer. Do you hear me? Tell her it's my ulcer or you'll ruin us both. Tell her that."

Marie shook herself free and ran swiftly down the stairs. She composed herself before opening the front door. "I'm sorry if we've disturbed you, Mrs Gilpin. Everything's perfectly all right. My husband was ill, that's all."

Mrs Gilpin's nightcap had slipped over one ear and her grey hair hung in thin strands around her face. "The crash woke Gilpin up as well." She was peering over Marie's shoulder and said, "Oh, my lor', don't you look dreadful?"

Marie turned quickly to find that Stanley had followed her down. He was leaning against the wall to steady himself. "I have a bad stomach, an ulcer. Sometimes it plays me up. I'm sorry. I passed out. That was the crash you heard. Sorry for the noise."

"It's more than playing you up by the looks of you. You'd better call in Dr Hornby first thing. He's new, just taken over the practice. Very young, a bit green, but he's better than nothing. I'll call in on him tomorrow for you, shall I? Get him to come around?"

"I'll see to it," Marie said quickly.

"He lives three streets away. Forty-nine, Wellington Road."

"Thank you." She closed the door in the landlady's face before she had finished her sentence. She heard the woman mutter "Ingratitude," then her footsteps clattered down the stairs to the hall and a distant door closed. Marie turned to face Stanley accusingly.

"It's like I said, just a bad stomach – an ulcer," he muttered, but he was unable to meet her eyes.

"I know the truth, Stanley." She could feel nothing but contempt for him. "I found the bottle days ago and it was nearly full – now it's empty." He started to protest but she spoke over him. "How long have you been using it? What in God's name drove you to use such foul stuff?"

He sank onto the stairs and put his head in his hands. "Mongreve gave me some once, to clean my suit."

"Mongreve? The dentist?" She was horrified. "You've been inhaling it all this time?"

"You don't understand. It helped me after the baby died. It helped me." She was shocked to see tears running down the cheeks of this unemotional man. "On one of my visits, he'd stained my suit. He gave me some chloroform to clean it with when I got home – he told me to destroy the rest. But I didn't. Don't look at me like that." He became angry. "I had to find some way to go on. Chloroform was a way out. It gave me sleep and peace. It killed the hurt of the baby's death. I didn't worry about money so much. Then things started to get worse with The Emporium and the tea room and I had to take more of the sweet liquid to cope. Last night, the peace left me and the nightmares began. Snakes were crushing Pa, squeezing him to death and he was crying out in agony. I couldn't reach him." He shuddered and beads of sweat broke out on his forehead.

It was painful to see him in such a state. "That's how it is, Stanley. It's a false friend. It will destroy you. You have to stop."

"No, I can't. All I have to do is inhale more."

She wanted to shake him. "It will kill you. That's what it does. It kills people."

"Some people maybe, but not me. I'm careful, you see. I know what I'm doing. I know just how much to take."

"No Stanley, you don't."

"I do, I have control. Each time I use it I gaze down into the valley of the shadow of death – each time I have pulled myself back from the edge. I know how to cheat death. The sweet liquid holds no terror for me, it gives me strength. As for these stomach pains, this sickness, the fainting – it's as likely to be caused by the ulcer as the liquid."

"Only a doctor can tell you that. Let me fetch Dr Hornby."

"No."

She was angry with him for risking both their futures. "It's a degrading, filthy, shameful habit, Stanley – and once it's taken hold of someone, they lose all reason and will do anything to satisfy their craving for it. Do you want that to happen to you?"

He was on his feet now, towering over her. "You know nothing. You are nothing."

"I'll go for the doctor."

"If you do, I'll make sure you pay for it. Do you know how? I will point to you and I will say you enticed me into it. And you did. You sent me to that dentist. What do you think would happen to you then? You'd be locked away. I'd make sure of it."

For a moment, she was too stunned to reply. Then she turned her back on him and ran up the stairs. "I won't stay here in this house."

He quickly caught up with her. Before she realised what he was doing, he hit her across the face and slammed her into the door. "You'll stay where I tell you to stay." She fell to the floor. She didn't cry and she didn't flinch; she was too astonished to feel pain. She just stared up at him stupidly.

"You will say what I tell you to say, woman. You're my wife." He grabbed her arm and hauled her to her feet, dragging her into his room.

Not knowing what he was going to do, she tried to hit out at him with her free hand. It incensed him even more. He tore at her clothes; she kicked and bit. He twisted her arms and punched her on the side of the face. There were flashes, like lights through her brain.

"No."

Her cry was cut short, choked in her throat as he pushed his hand over her mouth. No one must hear; no one must know what he was doing. The weight of him on top of her was crushing. She could hear him sobbing. Crying out and sobbing. She couldn't fight back. She hadn't the strength. He was pushing her onto the bed, forcing her head down into the pillows. She was suffocating.

He was pulling up his nightshirt. His body was flabby and white. He was pushing inside her, making her head bang, bang, bang against the iron bedpost. He was grunting like a pig, his mouth spewing out words she couldn't hear because her head was being crushed. He was fighting to reach a climax. Moaning: "I can't, I can't, I can't."

Blindly he hit out, his fist connecting with her shoulder. He hit out again, but this time he pounded the pillow by her head. He rolled off her with a groan, lying on his stomach. He pawed at the counterpane, pulling it over his head.

In the silence that followed, she lay beside him too frightened to move. His assault on her had been shocking, brutal and unexpected. After a while she slowly began to slide off the bed, but her legs wouldn't support her and she fell onto the floor. She looked up quickly. He hadn't moved. Terrified that every step she took might reignite his anger, she finally reached the door. She swiftly slipped through it and was down the corridor and into her own room in seconds. She locked the door behind her.

She made no noise and she didn't cry. She felt too numb for that. She poured water from the jug into the bowl, then took a cloth and, using it like a scrubbing brush between her legs, she washed the smell of him away.

CHAPTER EIGHTEEN

In the study at Carlton Terrace, Siggy leant back in his armchair and viewed his friend through half-closed eyes. "You know you're beginning to look distressingly like your father. Especially with the shorter hair. I rather liked the way it used to curl up against your collar. You're obviously taking your new status as MP for Fallsworth far too seriously."

"Stop it Siggy." Evelyn was in no mood for his friend's banter. "It's about time I took *something* seriously or accepted my responsibilities."

Responsibility – or duty, as his father would have called it – was pulling him apart. He hadn't written to Marie since their picnic together. It wasn't because he didn't want to, his need to see her was great, but because he was afraid he wouldn't be able to control his emotions. He hoped she would think that work was taking up more of his time. But today he'd received a letter from her that troubled him. She'd written that Stanley had sold everything and that they had moved to Leeds. It had taken him by surprise. It seemed so sudden. She'd given him no reason to believe that anything was wrong, but it worried him nevertheless.

"So, what's on the political agenda in the near future?" Siggy asked.

"Oh, Renfrew wants me to accompany him to France – some political shindig, rather big – about trade and manufacturing. Strengthening the Entente Cordial we put our names to last year. Very important, it seems, so I've said yes."

"Stop!" Siggy held up a hand in protest. "Enough. I'll hear no more."

He crossed over to the drinks cabinet to refill his glass and Evelyn smiled. He knew just how little Siggy could tolerate anything involving politics. His friend held up the decanter and Evelyn nodded. As Siggy poured him another brandy, he came to a decision. He would write to Marie and arrange to meet her, but this time he would make sure it was in a public place. He needed to reassure himself that all was well with her before he left for Paris.

*

Marie felt she was living in an unreal world, as though she were trembling on the brink of some high cliff, not knowing if she would fall into the chasm at her feet. Stanley made no mention of what had happened between them. If he felt any shame for what he had done, he gave no indication of it. On the days he felt strong enough he went to the new shop, and when he felt ill he locked himself in his room. She knew why. He was still inhaling, but she was too frightened of the consequences to confront him about it.

She saw that a letter had been pushed under the door of the apartment. Mrs Gilpin must have collected the post that morning. It was addressed to her. With a stab of pleasure, she recognised Evelyn's hand. Thankfully, Stanley was still locked in his room, so she carried the letter to hers and quickly opened it.

He began by thanking her for sending him her new address. Then:

I have to go to France soon on political business, but before I do I would very much like for us to meet again. In my capacity as guardian angel, you understand. I want to make sure all is still well with you after your move. If there is anything I can do, please let me know. I am in the north for the next few days. If it is convenient to you, perhaps we could meet outside the Town Hall in Leeds.

She scribbled an immediate reply.

I would so much like for us to meet, and outside the Town Hall sounds very suitable.

She stopped for a moment. Dare she risk seeing Evelyn? He knew her so well. Might he guess she was troubled? She had such a need to see him, though. She would just have to make sure he didn't suspect anything. Besides, he'd said he was going to France and there was a favour he might be able to do for her. She wouldn't mention that in her letter.

She continued writing:

My new home in Garibaldi Street is very pleasant. After a moment, she added: *And Stanley seems to have settled happily into his new business. All is well with us. Yours, as always, Marie.*

She heard the sound of vomiting coming from Stanley's room and wondered how long he could survive if he continued to abuse himself so.

*

"How's your husband this morning, Mrs Minton?" Mrs Gilpin had caught Marie on her way out to post her reply to Evelyn. "Your husband was sick again last night, wasn't he? I saw him go out to work earlier this morning and I thought he looked dreadful. Have you called in Dr Hornby to see to him yet?"

Mrs Gilpin was the last person with whom she wanted to

have this conversation. "No, there's no need," she replied. She hated finding herself in a position where she had to perpetuate Stanley's lie. "It's not serious. It's his ulcer. He has these bad attacks sometimes and then he's fine again."

"If your husband keeps being sick like this, then it is serious. Anyway, how can you be sure it's an ulcer? It might be something else, something catching. I can't be too careful with Gilpin's health. If you don't call the doctor in, then I will."

Marie nodded and shot out through the door before the landlady could press her for further information. When Stanley came home that afternoon, Marie was waiting for him.

"Stanley."

"What?" He didn't pause as he climbed the stairs to his room.

"I bumped into Mrs Gilpin this morning. She was asking questions."

Stanley stopped and turned. "What questions?"

She repeated their conversation, ending with the landlady's ultimatum. "If we don't call in Dr Hornby, she threatens to do it."

"That damned woman should mind her own business. I won't see any doctor."

They both knew that if his addiction was discovered, he would be in trouble with the law and his access to chloroform would end. He was sweating now, just at the thought of it.

"You don't have any choice." Marie was trying to sound reasonable. "Perhaps it will be the saving of you."

He ran down the stairs towards her and she backed away quickly until the wall prevented her from moving back any further. "You're the one who hasn't any choice, woman. Everybody knows you fancied yourself as some kind of quack. Pa knows it and McCullough – they know all about these so-called cures of yours. I'll tell them you tricked me into using it."

His words astonished her. “Nobody will believe you.”

“Dare you risk that?”

She tried to appeal to him. “Stanley, the matter’s out of my hands. It wasn’t my idea to call in Dr Hornby, but Mrs Gilpin will if we don’t.”

He looked at her slyly, out of the corner of his eye. “This doctor – Mrs Gilpin says he’s green.”

“Yes.”

“Well then, you’d better convince him it’s the ulcer. You’re supposed to know so much about these things. Convince him it’s the ulcer that’s making me ill.”

“How can I?”

“You’d better find a way because if they find out about the chloroform I’ll be ruined, and so will you. We’ll have no money. No home. Convince him or it’ll destroy us both.”

*

As she stood by the side of Dr Hornby, she noticed that his spectacles had a habit of continually sliding down his very thin nose. She was finding it difficult to control her nerves. Everything depended on his willingness to accept her interpretation of the symptoms.

“You say the pain is a dull, gnawing ache, Mrs Minton? In your husband’s side?”

“Yes,” she said, with a conviction she knew was a lie.

“Well, you’ve been very clear about the symptoms. Your husband is very lucky to have such a good nurse attending him. It certainly seems like an ulcer, as you suggested.” She ignored the look of triumph that Stanley shot at her. The doctor turned to Stanley. “And your previous doctor did mention the onset of an ulcer, you say?”

“McCullough? Yes, he did. He was in no doubt about it.” Stanley assured him.

Dr Hornby took Stanley's pulse again. "It is sluggish," he murmured. He pressed Stanley's stomach, which gurgled under the pressure of his fingers. "Here? Is the pain here?" Stanley winced and grunted a yes, beads of sweat breaking out on his forehead.

Marie frantically searched her mind for any other symptoms that might lead him to the diagnosis Stanley wanted. "Sometimes, he's been unable to work with the pain, which usually comes on about two or three hours after he's eaten."

"That is certainly symptomatic of an ulcer," he agreed. At last, to her relief, he appeared to be convinced. "Well, I think an application of leeches to the abdomen is the first step we should take, Mr Minton."

"I'll leave you then," Marie said, desperate to escape from the sick room.

She made her way to her bedroom, closing the door behind her, before collapsing onto the bed exhausted. Her head was throbbing. Didn't Stanley understand that all they were doing was putting off the moment of discovery?

There was a knock on her door. "Mrs Minton, have you a moment?"

At the sound of Dr Hornby's voice, Marie quickly arose. "Yes, of course." She opened the door and he hovered respectfully just inside the room.

"Well, I think I'm fairly certain it *is* an ulcer, but I'm afraid that it might not be possible to keep it under control. I'm thinking of surgery."

She hadn't planned for that. "Did you say that to Stanley?"

"Yes, and it seemed to upset him. He became quite aggressive about it, in fact."

She thought quickly. "You must forgive him. Stanley is very afraid of such things. Don't you think surgery might be a little too radical at this stage?"

She saw the seeds of doubt beginning to take hold. "Well, of course, I don't want to cause him unnecessary suffering. Perhaps there are one or two things we can try before that," he agreed. "I'll visit again in a few days' time. If the leeches haven't helped, then I would suggest a starvation diet for… let's say… seven days?" He scribbled out a prescription. "Now, have these pills made up, Mrs Minton. They'll hopefully calm the gut. Absolutely no alcohol. He must rest in bed as much as he can. And take care of yourself. You look worn out."

"I will. Thank you so much, Dr Hornby. You've been very kind." She just wanted him to go before he had second thoughts about surgery.

Obviously touched by her concern for her husband, he added: "And if his condition takes a turn for the worse, call me at once. Anytime. I'll see myself out."

After he'd gone, she looked blankly at the prescription, knowing it would not do any good. All she could do was continue with the lie, wherever it might take her.

*

Whether it *was* the tablets or the relief of not being found out, Stanley began to gain some strength over the next few days. He was able to go to the shop again and Mrs Gilpin, knowing the doctor had visited, seemed content to leave them alone.

Marie was thankful for her husband's absence because it made it easier for her to slip away to meet Evelyn. She saw with a burst of pleasure that he was waiting for her outside the Town Hall. He hadn't noticed *her* yet. He seemed changed. His hair was cut shorter and he'd grown a small moustache; he looked less boyish, more distinguished. He looked a little older and a little more serious.

Suddenly he saw her and waved, coming down the steps of the Town Hall to meet her. She found herself unexpectedly self-conscious as she held out her hand for him to shake. He hesitated, and then shook it with an equal formality. The awkwardness hovered in the air as he suggested they take the tram from outside the Town Hall to Roundhay Park where they could walk together. Marie agreed; just being in his company was enough for her. It didn't matter where they went.

Though cold it was a beautiful day and the park was filled with other couples strolling under the trees, their bare branches making stark patterns against the blue of the winter sky. The hem of Marie's walking skirt became flecked with mud, but the winter sun was unexpectedly bright and she was grateful she'd thought to bring a parasol with her.

They hadn't exchanged many words since meeting, but gradually the awkwardness thawed.

"You must tell me more about the work you do," she said, breaking the silence at last.

He was surprised. "Really? It wouldn't bore you?"

"No." She knew it wouldn't and it would also avoid having to talk about herself.

"I don't know, Marie," he said, after a moment's thought, "sometimes I wonder if I made the right decision when I became involved in the political world. Nothing is straightforward."

As he began to talk about what he wanted to achieve, she was reminded of Daphne. He had that same passion, that same desire to make a difference to the world. He said he was angry about those who were doing their best to destroy civilised society. People outside the House of Commons, and sometimes people inside it, too – people who used politics for their own ends. She didn't understand, but it didn't matter. She just liked listening to his voice.

"And the devil of it is, I can't do anything about it," he said, with a sharp laugh. "Not yet, anyway."

"Your work is very important to you, isn't it?"

He smiled wryly. "It's taken over my life. Who would have thought it? Certainly not my father."

"He would be proud of you," she said. "I'm glad my father saved his life. It makes me proud of *him*."

Evelyn was looking at her with an expression she couldn't quite decipher. Had she brought back sad memories of his father by mentioning the past? She didn't want to spoil today. Perhaps she shouldn't risk asking him for the favour she wanted. But then he smiled and she felt reassured.

"I can't believe it," he said, in mock horror. "Here I am in the company of a beautiful young woman and all I can do is drone on about politics, when I have much better things to tell you. Let me give you the latest escapade of mother's pet spaniel, Lady."

He always knew how to lift her spirits and as the anecdote unfolded, she found herself laughing out loud.

"Then Lady took hold of his trouser leg and wouldn't let go," he finished. "The man was running down the drive with Lady clinging on to him for dear life. She was certainly no lady that day."

"I'm not sure I quite believe that story." She wiped away a tear of laughter.

"Oh, do, please believe it," he beseeched.

She laughed again. "Tell me what you did last week. Apart from your work in the House of Commons, I mean. I'd like to know."

"Let me see. I went to the West End to some dreadful musical comedy. Shall I tell you about the show?" She nodded enthusiastically. "It was at the Gaiety. Absolutely awful. Won't run long. Gabriel Ray was the star."

They settled on a bench beside Waterloo Lake, built by soldiers returning from the Napoleonic Wars. It was used as a boating lake but as it was out of season, there was no sign of the launch that usually ploughed across the huge expanse of water. As Evelyn began to tell her the outlandish plot of the musical, Marie shut her parasol, resting it against the bench between them. When he reached the end of the tortuous plot, he waited for her to comment. She said nothing.

"Have I been talking too much? You look a little tired." He was regarding her with concern.

"No," she said quickly. "I love to listen to you. You lead such an interesting life in such a different world."

"Is everything all right with you? The move and selling the house – are there any problems?"

He was as perceptive as she'd feared. "No, of course not," she said lightly. "Stanley just wants to build up a new business, that's all."

She was relieved to see she'd managed to reassure him. They sat side by side on the bench, watching the ripples on the lake and the ducks foraging for food. She wondered if this was the moment to ask him for the favour? Would he be angry? Should she risk it? But if he *could* find Father Connor, discover something more about her past – anything, no matter how small – it might give her the strength to face whatever lay ahead of her.

"Evelyn, I have a favour to ask of you."

"Anything that it's within my power to do," he said instantly.

She took a deep breath. "When you wrote to me, your letter said you were going to France? Please don't be angry with me, but, after your first visit to The Laurels, when you left Father Connor's letter with me, I replied to it."

She couldn't tell from the expression on his face whether he was angry or not, but she'd gone too far to stop now.

"I only asked him if he could tell me anything at all about my mother and father. Time passed and I'd given up any hope of a reply, but then I received a letter from the Abbot in Pretoria. He said that Father Connor had left for France. He wanted to end his days in the Abbey of Saint Foy in Conques. I decided not to do anything further about it, but when you mentioned going to France… . I don't know if Father Connor is still alive, but when you're in France, and if you have the time, would you be able to make some enquiries for me? If he is alive, and you have a moment to visit him, you could ask him if he remembers anything else about my parents – anything at all. Would you do that? It would mean so much to me."

He was very quiet. The sun had gone in now and the day had grown suddenly cold. It was getting dark. "I shouldn't have asked you." She was annoyed with herself for troubling him. "It's getting late. I must go home."

She reached for her parasol, just as Evelyn reached out to pass it to her. Their hands touched and he enfolded her hand in his own. "I will make those enquiries for you, if I can."

"Thank you."

She barely noticed how close they were until he kissed her gently on the lips. She broke away in confusion and stood up.

"I'm sorry." Her face was flushed.

He was immediately on his feet beside her. "No, the fault was mine, Marie. My mistake, an error of judgement – it won't happen again."

"No, of course not." She took her lead from him. "As you say, an error of judgement. I should go home now."

"Yes, of course," he said, formally.

They began retracing their steps and conversation was nonexistent as they waited for the tram. They sat side by side like strangers as it rattled through the streets to the Town Hall. When they reached their stop, he helped her to alight and, in the shadow of the huge lions that guarded the Town Hall steps, she held out her hand to him.

"Thank you, Evelyn, but please don't worry about finding Father Connor. I shouldn't have troubled you."

He took her hand to shake it, but he didn't let it go. "A

promise is a promise. If I find him, I will talk to him. I will either write or visit you."

Slowly, she withdrew her hand. There was so much she couldn't say. "A letter will be enough, if you have the time. I have enjoyed today. I will always remember it."

"Do you forgive me?" he asked anxiously.

"There's nothing to forgive."

He watched her walk away from him, her skirts trailing in the dust of the pavement. He was furious with himself for losing control. He had ruined everything. It was just that she had seemed so terribly sad. It was why he'd agreed to find Father Connor for her if he could, although every instinct screamed out that he would be a fool to try. He doubted the priest could tell him anything he could share with her. Still, he had promised her now and he would call on him if he could. He would then decide what to do about Marie.

*

"Where have you been?"

Stanley's voice, coming out of the darkness of the parlour so unexpectedly, startled her. She had assumed he would be at work for at least another hour. She hoped the darkness hid the guilt he would read in her face.

"I didn't think you'd be home from the shop yet."

She took off her coat as Stanley lit the paraffin lamp on the table by his side. He held it up to look at her. "Where have you been?" he repeated.

"I went walking."

"You're looking very smart just to go for a walk. Where did you go?"

"I took the tram to Roundhay Park. I needed air."

He stood up. She saw with a sinking feeling that his face had a yellowish tinge and his pupils were dilated. He'd obviously been indulging in his habit. It would be sensible to get out of the room as soon as she could. He hadn't finished with her yet, though.

"You went out at noon. I know because I came home early and I saw you leaving Garibaldi Street. It's now six o'clock. You've been walking all this time?"

"Yes."

She turned to go again, but he placed himself between her and the door. "Look what I fell across."

He was brandishing a bundle of letters. She recognised them instantly. They were Evelyn's letters. For a moment, she couldn't speak. Then she found enough self-control to say: "Those are mine. How did you get them?"

"I discovered them."

"They were in my room. What were you doing in my room?"

He ignored her question. "So, who is he – this Evelyn?"

He had read the letters then. She tried to remember what Evelyn had written. She was certain they contained nothing that Stanley could use against her.

"Well?" he demanded.

"He's a family friend."

"You have no family except me."

She glanced away without replying, not wanting to antagonise him. She just wanted this to be over.

"You meet this 'family friend' in secret, do you? Without telling me anything about him?" He waved the letters in her face. "What kind of a 'friend' does that make him?"

"If you've read the letters, you'll know he called to thank me because my parents saved his father's life during the first war against the Boers. He'd only just found out about it and he was in the area..."

"But you've been meeting him ever since, behind my back. What do you think that would look like to people – a wife meeting another man in secret? And all these letters and all these meetings?"

"He's an honourable man, Stanley." She backed away as he made a move towards her. "He's Sir Evelyn Harringdon." She brandished his name like a shield for protection.

"I know who he is. I'm not such a fool as you think." She was flat against the wall now. "Sir Evelyn Harringdon, MP for Fallsworth – with a reputation and a career to lose if anyone finds out about these letters, along with a statement from the deceived husband."

Evelyn must not be dragged into a scandal. "Those letters contain nothing to my shame, nor to his. They're the kind any friend would write."

"The difference being that this 'friend' is a man and you kept meeting him in secret. Wouldn't people be interested to know that?"

"Give them to me." She tried to snatch the letters from him, but he hit her across the face with them, banging her head against the wall. "Please Stanley, give them back to me." She wasn't too proud to beg. Then, she remembered something he didn't know. It would mean breaking her word to Evelyn, but it was either that or staying silent and letting him be ruined. "You don't understand, Stanley – his father, Sir Gordon, was our benefactor. He provided the money when we married."

"What?"

The news threw him as she had hoped it would. "So you see, Stanley, we've had nothing but kindness from Sir Evelyn and his family. Now Sir Gordon is dead and his son simply wanted to tell me. To offer help if we should ever need it."

Instead of pacifying him, it infuriated him even more. "So why wasn't I told? Why didn't father and son make themselves known to me, eh?"

For a moment, she was thrown. She'd never questioned

Evelyn's explanation, but perhaps it did sound odd. "Sir Gordon didn't want thanks."

"Rubbish. If the father bought you a husband because your mother saved his life, then the debt was paid. What does the *son* think he's bought? What right does *he* claim? What money did he pay you?"

"Nothing." She had to stand up to him. "Until now, Stanley, I've done everything you've asked of me. I've told lies for you to Dr Hornby and I've concealed your use of chloroform from everybody – but even if it ruins us both, God help me, I will speak out if you try to use those letters against him."

He lunged forward and gathered the collar of her dress in his hands, twisting it tightly around her throat until the material bit into her flesh. He was choking her, she couldn't breathe.

"The workhouse, is that where you want to end up? Because that's what will follow if you tell anyone."

She was fast losing consciousness. Then, without warning, his mood suddenly changed. He let go of her dress, leaving her collapsed against the wall, gasping for air.

"Of course, I might be persuaded not to use them." She could smell the staleness on his breath as he leant over her. "The sweet liquid – I need more of it. The bottle is empty. I need it and I'm not strong enough to make the journey to my provider in Ilkley. Get it for me, go tomorrow, and I'll keep quiet about these letters."

She barely hesitated. If that's what it would take to protect Evelyn, it was a small price to pay. She held out her hand. "Very well, but give me the letters."

"They'll stay with me until you've done what I ask. Then, I'll destroy them."

She looked at him with contempt. "Where do I get this chloroform?"

He returned to his armchair, his energy suddenly spent.

"His name is Johnny Johnson; he's got a chemist shop in Ilkley. I'll give you the address and the directions."

She watched him slump back in his chair and wondered if anyone could despise a man as much as she despised her husband.

CHAPTER NINETEEN

Evelyn could think of nothing worse than to be in Paris on a bright winter's day and have to spend it sitting in an over-decorated room on the Quai d'Orsay discussing international trade. He felt he had little to contribute to the proceedings and he was finding it increasingly difficult to concentrate. He had promised Marie that he would try to contact the priest. He would keep his promise, but the more he thought about it, the more he regretted it. The Montrecourt business kept dragging him back to a past from which he wanted to walk away.

He became aware that Lord Renfrew was holding out his hand for something and was regarding him with a quizzical expression. "Do we inhabit the same world, Evelyn? The document please, for the third time of asking."

"I'm sorry." Evelyn swiftly searched through the papers in front of him until he found the relevant document. As the voices droned on again, Evelyn's mind drifted back to his last meeting with Marie. He was convinced something was wrong with her.

"Well, that closes the business for today." Renfrew was addressing him again. "As I told you, Evelyn, I have no need of your services for a few days. The time is yours to do with what you will."

"Thank you." It was his intention to use the time to visit the Abbey of Saint Foy.

At dinner that evening, in Bertrand's Restaurant in the Rue de Rivoli, he asked his friends for the best route to Conques from

Paris. Comte Antoine de Figeac immediately offered to drive him there himself. His family had a chateau nearby.

He waved aside Evelyn's protests. "It's no trouble. I have family business to see to, anyway. And I'll drive you back again the following day."

The next morning they set off early. The journey was a pleasant one and Antoine dropped Evelyn in the centre of town. "Meet you here later this evening," he said. "Around six?" He drove off, leaving behind a cloud of exhaust smoke.

Conques was a medieval walled village on the wooded slopes of a steep gorge that rose from the Dourdou, a tributary of the River Lot. It was a major staging post for pilgrims en route to Santiago de Compostela and Evelyn could see that their feet had worn smooth the narrow, cobbled streets and stairways over the centuries.

The gothic Abbey of Saint Foy dominated the village. It was packed with the faithful, but thanks to the liberal use of Antoine's name, he was not kept waiting. Almost immediately, he was ushered through the crowds into the presence of one of the Premonstratensian monks who lived there.

"How can I help you?" Although the man's voice was quiet, it resonated around the domed chamber.

Evelyn's French was fluent and he had no difficulty in communicating the fact that he had travelled from England and was trying to trace a Father Connor who, he believed, might have taken up residence there.

"Yes," the monk replied. Evelyn had half hoped the answer would be no. "He's a very old man, but a visit with him is possible as long as you don't tire him. Follow me."

They walked through twisting corridors that seemed to go on forever, but at last the monk stopped and knocked on a door. When a frail voice called out in French to enter, he opened it and indicated for Evelyn to go in. There was a narrow window in the wall that let in a tiny shaft of light –

just enough for Evelyn to make out what looked like a white mound of sheets on a stone bench. The mound moved and he saw a face.

"A visitor for you, from England," the canon said, and left them together.

Evelyn wasn't sure how to begin. "I hope I don't disturb you?"

"Nothing disturbs me these days," the old man replied, wiping his eyes. They looked sore and were constantly watering.

The cell was freezing, the warmth of Evelyn's breath created a cloud as it struck the air. He was grateful for the thickness of his coat. "Father Connor, isn't it?" The old man nodded. "I am grateful to you for seeing me."

"English, in English." He was so frail that his voice was a mere whisper. "I don't get the chance to speak English so much these days."

"Of course." The old man's face was blue with cold and Evelyn wondered how he had managed to survive so long in such harsh conditions. "I came to see if you can help a friend of mine."

The old man indicated for Evelyn to sit on the stone bench beside him, which he did. "I've called to see you on behalf of a young woman, Marie Montrecourt." He paused, but there was no reaction from the priest. "Well, she's married now. Her name is Marie Minton, but I believe you knew her as Marie Montrecourt?"

"No. I never knew her," the old man said.

Evelyn wondered if the old man's memory was going. "But you sent a letter to her."

"Ah yes, but it's the girl's mother I knew. A sad little creature."

"Her name was Hortense, I believe?"

"You've come all this way to ask me the mother's name?"

"No. I'm trying to find out…" He didn't finish because the priest had started talking again, obviously unaware that Evelyn was in mid-sentence.

"Sad little creature," he repeated. "I met her when I was in the Transvaal during that terrible war. I remember the heat, the red dust, the flies. I worked out there as a missionary with the natives. Then, my superiors summoned me back to France. No reason given; no thanks for all the work I'd done; no suggestion of how I should get home, of course."

The memory seemed to amuse him because he smiled, then fell silent. The silence lasted so long that Evelyn wondered if the old man had fallen asleep. Perhaps his visit was proving too much for him.

"I found a way home, though, in the end." Evelyn realised the priest had simply lost himself in the past. "I heard there were some injured British troupers in a camp nearby. I forget its name now. They were being taken to a hospital in the Port of Durban. I found my way to their camp and I begged a lift. I hoped to find a ship to take me to France."

"Was it in Durban you met Hortense Montrecourt?"

"What?" Evelyn repeated his question slowly and loudly. "No, no. In the camp; she was flitting like a lost soul through the tents. She was carrying a child."

"She had her daughter with her?" The old man was surely growing confused. Marie had said she was born in France.

"No, she was *with* child. That was very plain to see. She seemed close to birth. It was the day Sir Gordon Harringdon stumbled into the camp looking like a dead man. After Majuba, everybody thought he *was* dead. They kept saying it was a miracle that he was alive." He shook his head. "That's a word cheapened by much over use. He walked into the camp leaning on the arm of a young woman. That was my first sight of Hortense. I heard them all saying they thought he'd been killed. When they saw he was still alive, rumours started –

people speculating what had happened to him after the battle. Some rumours said he'd been taken prisoner, escaped, and fought his way back through hostile territory – but the war had ended by then, so I don't know the truth of it. A proud example of the British spirit that will not acknowledge defeat, that's what they were all saying in the camp – officers and men alike."

"I can remember the crowds waiting to welcome him home," murmured Evelyn.

"What the British did over there was nothing to boast about. There's nothing to be proud of in thieves and murderers burning crops, destroying families and abusing women. Both sides were as bad as each other – Boer and British. It was the Africans who suffered, as always." The old man sank back into silence again.

He must get to the reason for his visit quickly or the old priest would be too exhausted to continue. "Can you tell me anything about the baby's mother? For example, what did she look like?" If he could tell Marie that, it would at least be something.

"I remember..." The old priest paused for a long time. "Sir Gordon said Hortense was married to a French prospector. Henri Montrecourt, I think his name was."

"Montrecourt was a prospector, yes." Evelyn didn't want to discuss Henri. "About Hortense – can you tell me anything?"

"The man was killed helping Sir Gordon escape a Boer patrol. Sir Gordon said he'd brought his wife back with him to the camp out of gratitude, because she wanted to go to France for the birth of her baby."

"Yes." He wanted to move the priest away from events at the farm. "Do you remember what Hortense looked like?" he repeated, but the priest was obviously determined to tell his story in his own way.

"The girl had no family left in Africa. No family in France

either, as it turned out, but maybe it seemed to her a safer place to be. She travelled to France in my company. I'm still amazed that she survived the journey as she was very sickly. I took her to the Convent of Our Lady – the English Convent. My cousin, Sister Grace, was one of the nuns there and that's where she had her child."

"The child that was Marie," prompted Evelyn.

"I prayed for the soul of Hortense who died giving birth to her, and I still pray for the soul of the little baby who came into this life so cursed."

"Cursed?" Evelyn was surpised by his choice of words. "Why was the child cursed?"

"Because her mother died of syphilis and the baby was tainted by it. It's a miracle it lived."

Evelyn's face slowly drained of colour. "Syphilis?"

Unaware of the shock he'd just delivered, the priest continued. "Hortense was so young when she died and she had so very little to show for her life. I remember," his face softened, "she had this lump of rock – just a lump of rock. She called it her gold and her treasure. She would hold it up to the light to see it glisten. Fool's gold, I assumed it was. And she had a button that she clutched tightly in her fist, like a talisman. They had to prise it out of her hand after she died."

Evelyn was still trying to absorb what he'd been told. "Hortense had syphilis? How can you be sure?"

"I'd been around enough army camps to recognise the disease. Poor Hortense had led a dissolute life. She was forced by the husband to sleep with anyone who would pay for her. She told me he was penniless and he used her to get money from the miners."

Evelyn couldn't remain seated. The old man put out a comforting hand.

"You mustn't let her fate disturb you. Hortense was not

alone when she died. I was with her. I took her final confession. I gave her absolution. I know the terrible things she did and I asked God to forgive her for them."

All Evelyn could think about was Marie. Thank God she knew nothing about the dreadful life her mother had led.

Father Connor leant towards Evelyn. "Tell Marie Montrecourt that her mother begged me to write to the father of her child and I did."

"But surely Montrecourt was already dead when Hortense was in France?" Perhaps the old man had become muddled? His memory had failed him? Perhaps none of this was true.

The priest ignored Evelyn. "I wrote to him in God's name, telling him about his daughter. Tell Marie he did not turn his back on her completely. It may give her some comfort. Tell her he gave her the only thing he was capable of giving – his money. Reverend Mother told me that it was he who paid for the child to be raised at the Convent of Our Lady; he supported her throughout her life."

Evelyn slowly sank down on the stone bench.

"Maybe he still does support her," continued the priest, remaining lost in his own world. "Although it's my belief the syphilis will have killed him too by now." Then he looked at Evelyn and registered for the first time the impact of his words. Assuming it was distress for his friend, he added comfortingly: "Tell Marie Montrecourt that in his own way, her father did care for her. I hope that will bring her peace."

"Her father… was it…" Evelyn's whisper was barely audible. "Was it Sir Gordon Harringdon? When she was dying, is that the name Hortense said to you?"

Father Connor crossed himself. "That must remain known only to God and her confessor," he said.

But Evelyn didn't need the priest to confirm what he already knew.

⋆

The night after agreeing to buy the chloroform for Stanley, Marie barely slept. A confusion of thoughts and fears swirled around in her head. When the chloroform *did* kill Stanley, then his addiction would surely become public knowledge. What would happen to her then? How would she live? Even if she pleaded ignorance about its use, she would still be ostracised by decent people. As the sun rose, she wearily climbed out of her bed. There was something else she had been thinking about. Evelyn was still vulnerable. He must never make contact with her again – not even by letter. He must not rush to help her. They must become strangers. She must not only close the door on their friendship, but lock it too – for Evelyn's sake. She took out paper, pen and ink and began to write.

Dear Evelyn, although it was a great pleasure to see you on your last visit, I fear you may have misconstrued our friendship, which I am willing to accept was probably my fault. I have too much respect for my husband to allow the mistake to go uncorrected. Therefore, I think it best to be plain and say that, although I am grateful for your kindness, my feelings go no further than that. I think it advisable, therefore, that we no longer meet nor communicate in any way. Out of respect for me and for my husband, I would ask you to agree with my request. Please do not reply to this letter, no matter what news you have for me from France. Your friend as always, Marie Minton.

She blotted it carefully and re-read it, then sealed it and placed it on her dressing table. She would post it on her way to Ilkley.

She glanced in the mirror. There was a livid wheal on her

neck left by Stanley's attack on her yesterday. She took a scarf from a drawer and wound it in such a way as to conceal it.

Stanley was sitting up in bed when she entered his room. He looked dreadful. "I need money for the chloroform," was all she said.

"Get me a bottle of brandy as well." He handed the money over. As she took it, he held on to her wrist. "No more protests about being innocent?" he mocked. "No more whining, 'Where are the letters, Stanley?'"

She shook herself free. She knew where they were – underneath Stanley's mattress.

As she went down the stairs to the hall, the Gilpin's door opened and Mrs Gilpin popped her head through.

"Going out, Mrs Minton? And that poor husband of yours still ill in bed?"

Marie managed to remain pleasant. "My husband is sleeping now, Mrs Gilpin, but he's asked for a small bottle of brandy. I'm just going out to buy it for him." Then, without really knowing why, she added: "Dr Hornby is insisting Stanley sees a surgeon. There's a danger the ulcer will burst very soon."

"Well, an ulcer's a very terrible thing, Mrs Minton. A serious matter if it bursts. It must be a worry for you."

"Yes, it is." Marie continued towards the door.

"Will he ever be well enough to turn that ironmongers into a grocers like he planned?" she called after Marie, but she was gone – avoiding the necessity of a reply.

*

Evelyn had no clear recollection of his return journey to Paris but somehow he got there, and when Renfrew saw him he realised at once that something was wrong.

"Are you ill?" he asked.

"I think I must be," Evelyn muttered.

"Then get yourself back to England and see a doctor about it," he was ordered.

On the voyage home, he tried to convince himself that the priest had been wrong. He was an old man with a faulty memory. He'd grown muddled and confused. Evelyn only needed to confirm that his father had died from typhoid fever to prove it. That was why he was at Harley Street now, demanding to see Dr Oliver.

"It's impossible to see the doctor without an appointment, I'm afraid, sir. There's no point in waiting," the receptionist said.

Evelyn ignored the man's protests. "He will see me and I will wait, and I don't care how long it takes."

Dr Oliver, hearing raised voices, came out of his room to find out what was the cause of the disturbance. He was surprised to see that it was Evelyn. They hadn't met since Sir Gordon's funeral.

"Evelyn, how very good to see you. Is there a problem?"

"I was trying to explain to this gentleman that without an appointment—" the receptionist began.

"It's about my father. I need to talk with you."

"I see. Well, tomorrow—"

"Now, I need to talk to you now. It's about the cause of his death and I need to discuss it with you urgently, and I'd rather do so in private if you don't mind."

"Ah. Yes, of course. Yes." Oliver took out his pocket watch and consulted it. Evelyn was aware that the receptionist was watching the scene curiously, but he didn't care. "I have ten minutes before my next patient. It's all right, Stephen," he said as the young man started to protest. "This won't take long." He held the door of the consulting room open for Evelyn and then closed it behind them. "Now, how can I help you? Please, sit down." Evelyn was too agitated to accept the invitation. "I heard you were in Paris with Lord Renfrew."

"I returned this morning." He knew Dr Oliver was watching him with some concern. "I've received information recently…" Evelyn broke off, for the moment too distressed to continue.

"Information that's disturbing to you. Yes, I can see that."

"This may seem a strange question to ask, Dr Oliver, and if so forgive me, but I mean to have an answer and I mean to have the truth." He took a deep breath. "My father's final illness, what was it? It's imperative you tell me." Dr Oliver was so thrown by the unexpectedness of the question that for a moment he didn't answer. "Why did you and mother prevent visitors?"

"It was typhoid. Your mother was concerned about the danger of infection, which is why she kept everyone away."

Evelyn saw that the doctor was uneasy. "Don't lie to me, Dr Oliver. It's too important."

After a moment, the doctor said quietly: "I can see that it is. Very well. It was syphilis. He caught it in '81, in Africa."

"Oh, God!" Evelyn's legs buckled and he sat down abruptly on a chair. "I thought syphilis either killed a man straightaway or it was cured."

"I treated your father with mercury when he returned from Africa. We thought it *was* cured. I was as shocked as you are now to discover that the man who'd been dubbed the moral conscience of the nation had caught such a disease. But then, after the heat of battle, with heightened emotions, values can become twisted. That's how I assumed it had been. Every camp has its followers of women who know how to pleasure for a price, and under pressure of war, why should your father be any better?"

"Because he pretended to be!" Evelyn spat out words.

"Try not to judge your father too harshly, Sir Evelyn. We've neither of us been tested in the way he was. As I said, I had assumed Sir Gordon was cured, but there is a new theory now, and your father's case was an example of it. The disease can occasionally lie dormant for a long time, then it can become active again. Fatally."

"So for all those years it had been festering inside him. How appropriate," Evelyn said bitterly.

At a loss what to do next, Oliver suggested Evelyn might like to talk to his mother about it. "Though be careful," he added, "she's become very frail."

"I haven't been home. I can't face her. I can't forgive her. She knew he had syphilis and said nothing."

"I think you're being a little hard on her. She did what she had to do to save the reputation of good man."

"A good man!" Evelyn repeated his words with contempt. "There's something else I need to know. If a woman is diseased with syphilis, and if that woman has a daughter, will that daughter carry the disease?" He was thinking of Marie.

Oliver pursed his lips in thought. "If the daughter does survive – and that is rare, although it does happen – then she would not necessarily have inherited the syphilis. She would not be strong, she would probably lose any baby she conceived before it was born, but she would not necessarily carry the disease."

He waited for further questions, but Evelyn's thoughts remained with Marie. He remembered she had once told him that she had miscarried a child. She would never know why because he could never tell her.

*

It was the afternoon. She'd returned from Ilkley and had been sitting in Stanley's room, watching him for what seemed like hours. Though his eyes were closed, she knew he wasn't really asleep.

How had it come to this – sitting by her husband's bedside waiting for him to die? It had never been a love match, but she had never expected it to end like this. In fact, after Edith's death, there had even been a moment when their marriage might have worked, but any chance of that happening ended when the baby died. She saw that Stanley's eyes were open now.

"Planning how to get your hands on those letters, were you?" He felt under the mattress to make sure they were still there.

She hadn't even attempted to take them from him. She wouldn't be able to move him. He was too heavy.

"Where's the chloroform?"

"There." She pointed to the blue, fluted bottle that was standing on the table beside his bed. "With the brandy. Now give me the letters. You promised you would if I got the chloroform."

"Well, I've changed my mind. You see, they're going to provide me with an income for as long as I need it. A little bit of money to give me comfort and paid to me on the first of every month. He won't miss it. While I have these letters, he'll have to go on paying me for my silence, won't he?"

She stared at him too shocked for a moment to speak. "You can't do that. I won't tell him that."

"You won't have to. I've got his address from the letters. I'll write tomorrow."

"I won't post it."

"That fool Hornby's calling some time tomorrow. I'll get *him* to post it for me."

"No. Stanley, please don't do this. Evelyn's a decent man. He doesn't deserve this." She could see her words were having no impact. "You mustn't drag him into this sordid mess."

"He dragged *himself* into it when he wrote the letters." He reached for the blue, fluted bottle and studied it. "This stuff isn't working so well. Next time make it a bigger bottle. I have to use more of it each time to have any effect. Tried swallowing it to see what that would do, but it just made me sick."

"It would have killed you otherwise," she muttered.

"Well then, wouldn't *you* have been happy? Go on, get out. And close the door behind you."

She reached the sanctuary of her room and leant back against the door. She was trembling. What would Evelyn think of her when he received Stanley's letter? She wanted to scream, to throw things. She needed to keep busy or she would go mad. She started to fold some of the newly washed clothes that lay on the chair nearby.

She opened a drawer and began to pile the clothes into it. Sometimes, in her darkest moments, she'd caught herself wondering what it would be like to hold a pad soaked in chloroform over Stanley's mouth while he slept, keeping it there until he stopped breathing and end it all. That she was even capable of such thoughts shocked her. She slammed the drawer shut and turned her attention to the bookshelves. They needed tidying. She started to pull the books out one by one, piling them on the bed.

She realised she was holding *Farnsworth's Medical Dictionary*. It fell open at the section dealing with chloroform:

If swallowed, a mere teaspoonful could kill a strong man.

She thrust the book aside. Tomorrow he was going to write to Evelyn. She had to try to change his mind. She had to try.

She returned to his room. He was drowsy but he was awake.

"What do *you* want now? Come to see if I'm still breathing? Well, I am."

Should she just demand Evelyn's letters outright or try again to reason with him.

"Oh, for God's sake, if you've got anything to say, say it. Otherwise, get out and leave me in peace."

"Stanley, listen to me. If you want me to go on collecting the chloroform for you, I will, but only if you give me those letters. Otherwise you can go hang. What will you do then?"

He studied her for a moment without saying anything. "Well, I have been giving it some thought," he said slowly.

She clung desperately to a faint hope. "Does that mean you will give them to me?"

"I'm certainly not going to write to him." He took the letters from underneath his pillow and studied them.

She almost fell on her knees beside the bed in gratitude. "Oh, thank you, Stanley. Thank you."

"Instead, I'm going to send some of them to a journalist I know on the *Evening Post*. When he's read them, he'll pay me a fortune to get his hands on the rest and I'll succeed in ruining your little friend at the same time. As for the chloroform, I'll have enough money to pay Johnson to deliver it here. So I don't need you."

If she had been strong enough, she would have flown at him, dragged him from the bed and torn the letters out of his hands. Even in his weakened state, however, she knew she was no match for him. She needed to get out of the room.

★

It was midnight. She'd been sitting on her bed for hours. A distant dog barked. Her room was lit by a cold, silver light as the moon reappeared from behind a cloud. She could hear herself breathing – short, sharp intakes of breath. She began pacing up and down in her room, up and down. Had he threatened to send Evelyn's letters to the journalist just to frighten her? If so, he'd succeeded.

Now she was outside the door of Stanley's room – she had no recollection of how she'd got there. She opened the door. Stanley was lying on his back with his mouth wide open. There was no sign of the letters. Her eyes went to the bedside table. The chloroform bottle was nearly empty. Not enough left to put on a pad and be sure of ending it all. The bottle of brandy stood beside a wine glass.

On the floor in a corner of the room was a pile of Stanley's clothes, lying where he'd thrown them. Underneath she could see the Bunsen burner he'd torn from the gas tap when he'd destroyed Sister's herbs. The thin rubber tube was still attached to it. She was beside it now, looking down at it. She had no recollection of picking it up. She was only aware that her hand was shaking uncontrollably. Stanley stirred, but his eyes remain closed, his mouth stayed open.

She looked to the table, at the bottle. Was it only a teaspoon left or was it a little more? She was pouring some brandy into the wine glass and then adding the remains of the chloroform to it. She was detaching the rubber tube from the Bunsen burner. It felt like a dream.

*

Gerry's Bar was in Soho. Part of a cellar, it was accessed from the street by a steep flight of stone steps. It was a place of cheap gilt chandeliers and worn red velvet, low lighting and dark shadows. It exactly suited Evelyn's mood. He could be alone here. The air was a fug of cigarette and cigar smoke, which had no way of escaping in that windowless room.

The barman greeted him warmly. "Sir Evelyn, good see you again. What would you like, sir?"

"Oblivion," Evelyn muttered, "but absinthe will have to do."

The barman poured him a glass of the green liquid, and

filtered iced water through a slatted spoon containing a sugar cube, turning the green liquid cloudy. Evelyn took his drink to one of the alcoves. "Bring me another," he called over his shoulder, "straightaway. And keep them coming."

He'd received a letter from Marie that morning. She had written that they mustn't meet anymore and he knew she was right. He should be grateful, because it spared him having to face her. He couldn't bear it, knowing her past as he did now.

He stared in surprise at all the glasses lined up in front of him, every one of them empty. Had he drunk so much? The glass he held in his hand was still full. Wormwood, it sounded evil and it was evil – the basis of absinthe. How many of these had he drunk? He had no idea. What was the time? He had no idea. What he did know was that the alcove in which he was sitting was spinning round and round and round. He tried to catch the barman's attention to tell him to send over a bottle, but he couldn't seem to lift his arm. He did manage to slide his watch out of his waistcoat pocket. What time was it? He peered hard, trying to make sense of the multiplicity of watch faces that floated in front of his eyes. It couldn't be two in the morning. He couldn't have been sitting here all that time.

"Evie?"

Evelyn tried to lift his head from where it had sunk onto the table. It didn't seem to want to move.

"It is you. My dear boy, I saw a heap in the corner and I thought I recognised the jacket. A group of us are just passing through after Buffy's party. Called in for one last drink. Evie, it's Siggy." Siggy surveyed his friend. He'd been sick down the front of his jacket. He called over to the barman. "How many of these has he had?"

"I lost count, sir."

"You are in a state, old boy," he said softly. "Come on, Evie, you're coming home with me." He signalled to one of his group to give him a hand to hoist Evelyn to his feet. "Call a cab," he ordered another.

"Well, I don't know what's caused this, old dear," he said, as Evelyn rolled backwards and forwards to the sway of the hansom as it galloped through the city's deserted streets, "but you're going to have one hell of a headache tomorrow."

*

How long had she been sitting here in her room, her hands gripping the arms of her chair? She looked down at her knuckles. They were white.

She was fighting to make her mind blank, but images managed to force their way through. The look in Stanley's eyes; her hand still shaking as she closed them. The way the rubber tube twisted and turned slowly in the air as it landed in the yard below. She couldn't recall taking Evelyn's letters, but she must have done because they were in the fire in front of her – nothing but a pile of ashes now.

Gradually, she began to be aware of the sounds of the outside world: the rumble of a milk cart, the clatter of horses' hooves, the chiming of a distant church clock. Life was going on and she had to go on too, somehow. She had chosen a path and she had to follow it. If she could make herself believe that Stanley had died of a burst ulcer, then others would believe it too. There need be no mention of chloroform, no scandal, and Evelyn need never know how close he came to ruin. The question was, could she live with the knowledge of what she had done?

*

"Mrs Gilpin. Mrs Gilpin." Marie hammered at the landlady's front door. She heard Mr Gilpin coughing.

"All right. All right, I'm coming." Footsteps shuffled to the door. "Do you know what time it is?" Mrs Gilpin grumbled. "It's six o'clock for heaven's sake." She broke off when she saw the state her lodger was in.

"My husband's had some kind of attack. I think he's dead," Marie said. Her distress was genuine. "Please, help me. I don't know what to do."

"Oh, my lor'!" Mrs Gilpin pulled her dressing gown around her and shuffled after her distraught lodger, up the stairs and into Stanley's bedroom. "Oh, my lor'!" she repeated. She crossed to the bed and peered down at Stanley. He was lying on his back. She touched him. "He's definitely dead. Did you close his eyes?"

"I came in just now to make sure he was all right and I found him like this..." Marie broke off. She had the strangest sensation that only one part of her was functioning, the part that was saying the words. The other parts were still numb and frozen. She sank into a nearby chair and covered her face with her hands. The functioning part of her spoke again.

"I should have sat up with him; I shouldn't have left his bedside. It must have happened while I was asleep. He made me leave him. It was about ten o'clock. He said I looked tired."

Marie heard a noise and glanced towards the door to see a cadaverous-looking man, also in a dressing gown, entering Stanley's bedroom.

"Gilpin, come and look at this. Poor Mr Minton, he's dead."

Marie had never met Mr Gilpin before; he'd only ever been a disembodied cough until now. She watched as he wandered around peering at everything, lifting up the wine glass, poking at the fire. Then for the first time, her eye was caught by the blue fluted bottle that was partly concealed on the mantelshelf by the clock. The chloroform. She'd left the bottle in full view. Mr Gilpin obviously hadn't seen it because he crossed over to

Stanley without a comment and leant over him, touching the pulse on his neck.

"Funny smell," he said as he bent closer to the body.

"Brandy." Marie's heart was still beating fast. "When I found him, I tried to give him brandy to revive him and I must have spilt some. He asked me to get him some, you remember, I told you." She turned to Mrs Gilpin. She wanted them to go now, before she lost her nerve – before they saw the bottle. "I must get dressed. I must fetch Dr Hornby. I must get the doctor."

"No point in rushing to do that," said Gilpin dryly. "The man's dead. There's nothing the doctor can do to help him now. It'll keep till a more civilised hour, when people are up and about."

Marie's knees went weak and she sank onto the chair behind her. Mrs Gilpin, moved by a rare moment of understanding, said: "Come on, Gilpin, better leave her to herself for a minute."

When they'd gone, Marie stared at the fireplace. She had no recollection of putting the bottle there. She knew she had to get rid of it and she had to stay calm.

*

By eight o'clock, she was dressed and pacing the room impatiently, waiting to set off for the surgery. Once Dr Hornby signed the death certificate stating that Stanley had died of a burst ulcer then this nightmare would be over. Mrs Gilpin appeared, as usual, the minute she heard Marie in the hallway.

"I'll come with you to the doctor's, shall I? You shouldn't be out on your own."

The small, blue bottle nestling in Marie's coat pocket suddenly felt extremely large. "No," she said quickly. "I'd rather go alone. It's not far." She shot out through the door before Mrs Gilpin could draw breath to protest.

She hurried past Wellington Road where Dr Hornby had his surgery, heading for the bridge over the River Aire. She had the presence of mind to take a quick look around her to make sure no one was watching, but she was quite safe as people were too busy rushing to work to have time for anything else. She slipped the bottle out of her pocket and leant over the parapet as if staring into the grey water. As a milk cart passed, she used the clatter of the horses' hooves to disguise the splash of the bottle as it hit the river. It wasn't sinking. It was bobbing jauntily in a circle, waltzing round and round on the surface of the water as if to taunt her. Then, at last, to her relief, it was caught by the current and was swept out of sight. She turned back towards Wellington Road and the surgery.

Dr Hornby lived above his work and he responded to the persistent hammering on his front door with some irritation. "Can't it wait another five minutes until surgery opens?" he shouted, until he saw it was Marie. "Great heavens, Mrs Minton, what on earth's the matter? Come in." He ushered her inside and quickly put out a hand to support her as she staggered.

"Stanley died in the night."

He was clearly shocked. "This is terrible news, terrible news."

"The ulcer must have burst. I was asleep in my room. I found him this morning. I didn't know what to do..."

"I knew I should have called in the surgeon," he muttered, then turned his attention to calming her. "Look, I know it's distressing, Mrs Minton, but you mustn't work yourself up like this. It won't help. Go back home and I'll follow shortly. Will you be all right to go on your own?" She nodded, but as she turned she stumbled again and he steadied her. It was obvious she was in no state to be by herself. "Wait here a moment; I'll come with you. You're still in shock. Let me get my bag."

★

It took a huge effort of will for Marie to stand beside the doctor gazing down at Stanley lying on his back on the bed. She realised that Dr Hornby's attention was caught by the wine glass. He had picked it up and was sniffing at it. "Brandy," she said. "I tried to revive him with brandy." She was shocked how easily the lie came to her.

Dr Hornby clicked his teeth with his tongue in disapproval. "Not the wisest thing to do."

"It *was* the ulcer, wasn't it? You said it might burst." She wanted Dr Hornby to sign the death certificate and sign it quickly, and then it would all be over, but Dr Hornby wouldn't be hurried. He deliberated over the body, checking and rechecking it. She watched, the strain beginning to build.

"It's the ulcer. It couldn't be anything else, could it?" she said again. "It must have burst. You said it might. Could I have done more to help him?"

He patted her hand sympathetically. "No, no one could have done more. You've worn yourself out looking after him." He bent over the body again. "Well, given his history it would seem to me that the obvious cause of death is indeed the ulcer." He glanced at her pale face. "I don't see any sense in prolonging your distress, Mrs Minton. Once I've signed the death certificate, you can lay your husband's body to rest."

She almost fainted with gratitude. "Thank you."

She was distracted by the distant sound of raised voices from the hallway downstairs. Footsteps ran up the stairs. There was a hammering on the Minton's front door. Startled, Marie muttered: "Excuse me." She hurried down from the bedroom and opened the door of the apartment to find herself, to her horror, face-to-face with Stanley's father.

"Where is he?" He glared at Marie, who seemed to be blocking the doorway. Angrily, he tried to push her aside. "I want to see my son."

Marie caught hold of him. "He's dead."

"I know he's dead." Edwin's voice quivered with emotion. "She told me when she let me in." He pointed behind him and Marie saw Mrs Gilpin standing in the hallway looking up. Her husband joined her.

"Let me pass. Let me see my son."

Dr Hornby came out to see what the commotion was about and Marie stepped aside to let Edwin through. He gazed down at his son's body, while the doctor remained respectfully near the door and Marie paced up and down the corridor outside the room. She wanted to express sympathy but feared facing him. She tried to find comfort in the fact that he need never know of Stanley's addiction, but it didn't help. She watched the old man gently bend down to kiss his son on the forehead. She had to turn away. She couldn't bear to watch.

She heard him say. "God bless you. I called to see how you were and I find you like this." He straightened up and looked at Dr Hornby. "I came here to patch things up between us. We'd not seen each other for months. We quarrelled when he came to live in Leeds; we'd never quarrelled before. He was a good son. I didn't even know he was ill." His voice broke. He couldn't continue.

"It was a perforated ulcer," Dr Hornby informed him. "I was treating him for an ulcer."

"I didn't even know he was ill," Edwin repeated. "Nobody told me."

Marie tried to control the tremble in her voice, but she knew she had to speak. She had chosen her path and she had to walk along it to the end. "We didn't want to worry you." She turned to the doctor. "As you know, my husband has suffered from an ulcer for a long time. Dr McCullough will confirm that." Both the Gilpins entered as Marie was speaking. She was thrown by their reappearance. "Stanley's always suffered that way."

"If he was so ill, why wasn't I told?" Edwin asked.

"You'd kept yourself apart from us since we moved from The Laurels, and – like I said – Stanley didn't want to worry you." She saw the Gilpins exchange a look. "Dr Hornby diagnosed an ulcer, didn't you, doctor? He was due to see a surgeon very soon if he didn't improve." She turned to Edwin. "I was going to tell you. I'm sorry. It's been a shock for you."

Nothing was going to stop Edwin now. He hadn't been there when his son died and he wanted to blame someone.

"If I'd been here, it wouldn't have happened. But I was thrown out by her." To Marie's horror, he pointed at her and turned to the Gilpins, sensing their sympathy. "She didn't want me near my own son."

An uncomfortable silence greeted the old man's outburst. Marie knew she should protest that it was Stanley who hadn't wanted him at Garibaldi Street, afraid he'd discover his use of chloroform, but she couldn't admit to that. Otherwise what had it all been for?

"It's not natural to separate a son from his father," Edwin continued, "and that's what she did." Marie looked towards Hornby for support. Edwin saw the look. He turned on the doctor. "You say he died from an ulcer; how do I know that's true? I want a second opinion."

"Mr Minton, I know you're upset," Dr Hornby said soothingly, "but it was an ulcer, I do assure you."

"It was not an ulcer. He was not ill with an ulcer. He would have told me. I demand a second opinion. There's something not right. Something's not right."

Marie felt the ground slipping away from under her feet. She tried to say: "That's just being foolish. You're upset", but she could barely form the words.

It was Mr Gilpin who put a stop to any further discussion. "I suggest we all keep calm. Dr Hornby, as you know, I'm the registrar for births, marriages and deaths in this area and Mr Minton has a right to demand a second opinion. I should mention that there was a faint smell of something on the body when I first leant over him. Not brandy," he said curtly, as Marie opened her mouth to speak, "something else. I didn't attach too much importance to it at the time, but now... well, if there's any concern about the cause of death then I won't register it, Dr Hornby, unless there's a post-mortem."

Marie was so astonished by Gilpin's revelation that she became rooted to the spot. Dr Hornby looked offended. "Of course we can do a post-mortem on the body, Mr Gilpin," he replied, "if you doubt my competence, but I have no doubt myself as to the cause of death. I was simply trying to save Mrs Minton further distress when I suggested I could sign the death certificate. Which was a perfectly correct suggestion as, in my opinion, he died from natural causes."

"This is all so unnecessary, surely?" Marie was struggling to remain calm. "I have no reason to question Dr Hornby's judgement."

"Well, I have," said Edwin emphatically, "and if this gentleman says there was a funny smell in the room, then we should find out what it was."

Dr Hornby glanced at Marie apologetically. "Mrs Minton?" What other choice did she have but to nod her head in agreement? "Very well," said Dr Hornby briskly. "I suggest I send a telegram to Dr Shelton, a very eminent pathologist at St Mary's Hospital, and ask him to perform the post-mortem here this afternoon. Will that satisfy you, Mr Minton?" Edwin nodded. "Mrs Minton?"

She realised that Dr Hornby was waiting for her answer. "Yes, I'm sorry. It's just that I'm finding all this so hard to take in." Everything was spiralling out of control.

"That's understandable," said the doctor, sympathetically, "but the sooner this matter is cleared up, the better for us all. It may be expensive, Mrs Minton. Dr Shelton is a very busy man and his services are not cheap."

"No matter what the cost, this needs to be settled," she managed to say.

"I want another doctor present as well," said Edwin stubbornly.

Dr Hornby did not hide his exasperation, but another name was mentioned, a Dr Morton, to assist in the post-mortem, and it was agreed that a telegram should be sent to him. The Gilpins, satisfied that everything was now in hand, returned downstairs to their rooms. Dr Hornby hovered at Marie's shoulder, hoping for a quiet word, but Edwin made it clear that he had no intention of leaving them alone together so the doctor said his goodbyes. He turned at the door.

"I'll contact the undertakers for you, if you would like me to, Mrs Minton? I'm sure this matter will be quickly settled."

Alone together in the bedroom, Marie faced Stanley's father across the bed on which Stanley lay. This was not how it was meant to be. "I am so sorry for the pain this has caused you," was all she could think of to say.

He glared at her fiercely. "You'll not put my son in a coffin until I say so."

"No, as you wish." A wave of nausea welled up inside her. She desperately needed to sit down.

"I'll wait outside in the street when the post-mortem happens, but I will be here. I will have the truth." With a final glare, he swept out of the room.

As the door slammed behind him, Marie felt the room begin to spin.

⋆

Dr Hornby was faithful to his word and later that morning a Mrs Wilkinson arrived at number fourteen Garibaldi Street.

She'd been sent by the undertakers to wash and lay out the body of Stanley. She passed on a message from the undertakers that the coffin shell was to be delivered the next day. She asked Mrs Minton if she would like to help her lay out the body, as she often found it aided the widow. It seemed to concentrate their minds and made it easier for them to accept what had happened. Marie declined. She needed to get out of the room as soon as she could.

As she was going, the woman told her that she was really a laundry woman who laid out the bodies of the dead to augment her income. "If you like, I can take the sheets and pillowcases from the bed, wash them and bring them back again. Would you like me to do that?"

Without thinking, Marie nodded. "Thank you, that's very kind of you." With one last glance at the body of Stanley, she fled from the room.

CHAPTER TWENTY

Dr Hornby was the first to arrive for the post-mortem and Dr Morton followed soon after. Marie went into the kitchen to make tea for them. She needed to keep herself busy to stop herself thinking too much. There was an air of unreality about everything that was happening to her. She shivered, aware of the macabre fact that the kitchen was the place where her husband's body was soon to be dissected. She hurriedly left and entered the parlour, handing the tea to the two doctors. It took every ounce of self-control to stop her hands from shaking.

From now on, Dr Hornby told her, she must remain out of the kitchen and out of the parlour too, so she went up to her bedroom and tried to rest on the bed. She heard a brougham draw to a halt and she leapt up, pulling back the lace curtain to look out. It must be Dr Shelton arriving. There was a knock at the door of her room. It was Mrs Gilpin.

"If you want to use our front parlour to wait in, Gilpin says you'd be welcome."

Marie refused. She was so on edge that she was afraid she would give herself away. She heard the body of Stanley being moved from his bedroom to the kitchen. This was unbearable. She looked out of the window again and was faced with the sight of Edwin pacing up and down on the pavement opposite. She looked down the street and saw Geoffrey hurrying towards him.

Mrs Gilpin had also seen the two men and she joined them outside. A few words were exchanged. The old man looked up towards Marie's window and saw her watching. He turned back to Mrs Gilpin and nodded, and all three entered the house together, obviously heading for the Gilpin's parlour. Marie dropped the curtain.

Now she could hear Geoffrey's voice. He must be just outside the kitchen where the body was laying. He was talking to Dr Hornby. "You must let me see him. I just want to see him, before..." She didn't hear the end of his sentence. There was a murmured agreement from Hornby and then silence. After a moment, she heard Geoffrey leave and return to the Gilpins. He'd made no effort to call on her. She hadn't expected him to. All she could do now was wait.

★

His head ached and his mouth tasted foul. Siggy had rescued him from Gerry's Bar, but it wasn't until the following afternoon that Evelyn realised he was in Siggy's apartment, sleeping on Siggy's sofa. He tried to stand up, and every time he fell down again. Siggy fed him his well-known hangover cure of eggs and Worcester sauce, and a host of other ingredients that Evelyn would rather not know about. It did the trick. In a few hours, he could walk without collapsing.

"Stay another night, old dear. You still look dreadful."

"No, I should go home. Wilson informed me that mother intends to visit Carlton Terrace today, God knows why. She'll probably be there already, demanding to know where I am." One of Siggy's finest qualities was knowing when not to ask questions, and he asked none now. "I appreciate you putting me up like this, Siggy, and at such short notice."

"You would have done the same for me. Do you want

me to call you a cab? I'm not sure you'll manage to walk very far."

"No. No, I need the air. I'll be all right."

*

He let himself into Carlton Terrace, hoping that perhaps his mother hadn't arrived yet.

"Evelyn." Hope promptly vanished as his mother's voice rang out. "Come in here, will you? We need to talk." She was silhouetted in the doorway of the study and it was obvious that she'd been waiting for him since the morning. "Close the door behind you."

He did as she instructed, keeping his back to her in the hope she wouldn't see the state he was in, but nothing escaped his mother's sharp eyes. "You look as if you've slept out in the park all night," was her scathing comment. "Dr Oliver telephoned me yesterday to see how you were. He was worried about you, said you were behaving strangely. You really do look ill. Are you going to tell me the cause?"

"If you spoke to Dr Oliver, I think you already know the cause. It's the past, Mama, the past – as always. Africa. Majuba." He saw her back stiffen, but the time for stepping around the truth was over. "Father killed a man called Henri Montrecourt – not, as I first thought, because he wanted to protect his own reputation, but because he was sleeping with Hortense, the man's wife. She wasn't just any wife, though. She was married to a man who regularly sold her for sex to anyone who was willing to pay her price. Well, father paid the price in more ways than one, didn't he? He caught syphilis."

His mother put a hand out to steady herself as she sank onto a chair, but her face remained expressionless.

"You knew all about it, Mama, which is why you lied to me and told me it was typhoid fever that killed father. Well,

I should tell you that what you said didn't satisfy me and I tracked down the daughter of Hortense Montrecourt – my father's daughter."

"You did what?" His mother was astounded. "You met her?"

"Despite father paying the convent to keep her shut away, yes, I met her – and she deserved a better life than the one father foisted on her."

Silence fell as Evelyn turned to pour himself a brandy. His mother broke the silence.

"Your father paid for Hortense's passage to France, but he did not pay for the child to live at the convent. I did."

Evelyn turned in astonishment. "You did?"

"I was with him when a letter arrived telling him that Hortense had died and had left a daughter. He destroyed it. He was a weak man, Evelyn, though the world never knew it. He wanted to forget what he had done, wipe it out of his mind, but I knew the existence of a daughter couldn't be so easily dismissed. Our family has powerful enemies, as you know. One hint of your father's… indiscretion… would have left us at their mercy. So I paid John Pickard to arrange for the girl to stay at the convent away from prying eyes. I hoped she would take her vows and stay there for the rest of her life and we would be able to forget about her, but, unfortunately, things didn't happen that way. When it became obvious she was to leave, I instructed John Pickard to collect her and arrange for her to be married into a decent family as far away from us as possible."

Evelyn couldn't contain his anger. "So she was just an inconvenience as far as you were concerned, was she?

"I don't apologise for what I did. I would do it again to protect what I think is important."

"And what about Marie? Did anyone think to ask what was important to her?"

"I'm not sure I understand the question. How could a girl like that matter? I made sure her future was secure – what more could she ask for?"

Words failed Evelyn, but his expression conveyed his answer.

*

The post-mortem, which had begun at eleven o'clock, ended at two o'clock in the afternoon. Marie knew it was over because she saw Dr Shelton and his assistant re-entering the brougham. As she went downstairs, she stared as if mesmerised at the closed kitchen door from behind which she could hear the murmur of voices. Had they discovered anything? What was their conclusion?

"What's happened?" Edwin was running up the stairs towards the open door of the apartment, followed by Geoffrey.

"I don't know. I haven't heard," she replied.

Mrs Gilpin came out into the hallway below and called up, "Gilpin says you should all stay down here. Let the doctors come here to talk to you."

Edwin and Geoffrey obediently returned. Marie took one last look at the closed kitchen door and reluctantly followed.

In the Gilpins' parlour, she sat, hands folded in her lap, staring intently into space. Edwin paced the room and Geoffrey drummed his fingers on the arm of his chair. Mrs Gilpin had made some sandwiches and tea, but no one was interested in eating. At last, the door opened and Dr Morton and Dr Hornby entered. Edwin and Geoffrey stood up, while Marie remained seated, not trusting her legs to support her. Dr Morton, his face grave, ignored Marie and crossed straight over to Stanley's father.

"Mr Minton, I should tell you that the contents of the

stomach are suspicious and are to be preserved for further examination."

Edwin gasped and fell back onto his chair. Geoffrey turned pale. For Marie, everything in the room seemed to slow down and stop. Time stopped. Her ability to breathe stopped. He hadn't said chloroform, she clung to that. He hadn't said they'd found any trace of chloroform.

Dr Morton now turned to the landlady. "Mrs Gilpin, the rooms above are to be locked and sealed and held under the jurisdiction of the District Coroner." He finally turned to Marie, whose face had drained of colour. "Nothing must be removed from those rooms, Mrs Minton. You must not enter them or pack anything, or take anything away."

What did that mean? Were they accusing her? Was she under suspicion? "But my clothes? Can't I take any of my clothes?" Bewildered, she glanced around as if looking for them.

"Only the clothes you stand up in," Dr Morton replied. "It is a normal precaution, Mrs Minton, under this kind of circumstance."

She felt a little reassured. "A coat. I need a coat."

Dr Hornby came forward with a solution. "If Mr Gilpin and I go together and take a coat, would that be all right?"

Dr Morton nodded. The men departed in silence and returned a few moments later carrying Marie's coat. Her hands were shaking so much that she almost dropped it. She must take control of herself – after all, nobody had accused her of anything. It then struck her that she was being turned out of the house.

"I don't know where to go. Where will I go?"

"Stay with friends, perhaps?" Dr Hornby suggested.

"I know no one." She looked at Geoffrey and Edwin, who turned away. "No, I have no one."

Mrs Gilpin spoke up. "I've got a sister who lives three

streets away, Tilly Crawford. She has a spare room. I'll talk to her. Will that suit?" Dr Morton nodded. Marie had never thought she would feel gratitude towards Mrs Gilpin.

"Your keys will be returned to you, Mrs Minton, as soon as the coroner's officer has finished with them," said Dr Morton.

"The funeral?" Geoffrey said. "When can we hold the funeral? I want him buried in Harrogate, where he was known and respected."

"The body will be taken to the mortuary and released once the coroner has signed the release form," replied Morton.

Marie couldn't let them ignore her. "I'd started to arrange things. Dr Hornby was arranging things for me."

"I'm aware of that," Geoffrey said curtly, "but Stanley always said he wanted to be buried in Harrogate. I can see no point in you troubling yourself with these arrangements, as you know no one there. Isabelle and I will keep you informed about matters." She wanted to protest, but, before she could, Geoffrey turned back to Dr Morton. "I'll arrange for Stanley's body to be collected as soon as the coroner allows."

"Then I'll bid you good day." Morton turned to the landlady. "A policeman will be calling soon, Mrs Gilpin – an officer of the coroner's court." To the others, he said: "You will be informed when the date for the inquest is set."

Marie turned to face Edwin and Geoffrey, but they refused to look at her.

"Come on, Pa, let's go. There's nothing more for us here. Thank you," Geoffrey said formally to Mrs Gilpin. "I'm sorry you had to be involved in this." Neither man said anything further to Marie.

Their departure left an awkward silence. "What is going to happen now?" Marie asked in a voice that could barely be heard.

"I would suggest you try and rest a little, Mrs Minton,"

said Dr Hornby. "Stretch out on the sofa here? If Mrs Gilpin will permit?"

"I'll get her a coverlet," the landlady said, and her husband followed her out of the room.

It left her alone with the doctor for the first time since the post-mortem had begun. She turned to him, unable to contain her anxiety any longer. "What does all this mean, Dr Hornby? I'm at a loss to know."

"It means that your husband's sudden death has given us all a great deal of concern," he replied. Before she could question him further, he added awkwardly: "I'm sorry, but I can't say anymore than that, Mrs Minton. Forgive me."

*

The inquest was held in Leeds, in the Old Court House in Turner Street, off the Headrow. It was a squat, square building, erected at the beginning of Victoria's reign, and overshadowed by the vast neo-classical grandeur of the newer Town Hall nearby. Marie found the room dark and oppressive; the windows being too high up and too narrow to let in much light, and a layer of dust covered everything.

She hadn't been sure what to expect from the proceedings, but it appeared that the only thing to happen on this first day was that the jury would be sworn in and then taken to view the body of Stanley Minton – which was lying in the mortuary. On the following day, she learnt, the hearing itself would begin.

To her relief, the inquest had caused very little interest and, consequently, there were still very few people in attendance on the second day. The coroner, Charles Wallington, entered. He was a long, thin man with an air of weariness about him. He nodded briefly at the jury of twelve men, who were settling down on the long wooden bench to his left. More benches faced the coroner and a chair had been placed to the right of his desk for those who were about to give their testimony.

Marie was already seated on one of the benches at the front of the hall, accompanied by Tilly, Mrs Gilpin's sister, who was thrilled to find herself thrust so unexpectedly into the heart of such drama. The key to the rooms in Garibaldi Street had been returned to Marie yesterday, but she had decided to stay on with Tilly until the inquest was over. She couldn't bear to go back to the apartment. She was afraid to stay there alone.

"You all right, Mrs Minton?" Tilly asked.

Marie nodded, distracted by the arrival of Edwin, Geoffrey and Isabelle. Isabelle gave her a brief smile, but the two men chose to ignore her completely. The Gilpins arrived with Dr Hornby and she was dismayed by the sight of Betsy Capes entering the court, two of her cronies trailing behind her. They sat in front of the only other person present, who was a young reporter from the *Leeds Mercury* – or so Tilly informed her in some excitement. He stretched his legs out along the empty wooden bench and yawned.

"Are you sure you're all right, Mrs Minton?" Tilly leant across and touched her hand. Marie nodded, forcing herself to concentrate on the proceedings. She could only pray that the whole thing would soon be over.

Mr Wallington, the coroner, addressed the jury in a bored voice that conveyed his familiarity with the procedures.

"As I told you yesterday, the purpose of this inquest is to establish by what means the deceased came to his death. I will call on anyone I believe can throw some light upon that matter. If something isn't clear to you," he peered at the jury over the pince-nez he'd just placed on his nose, "then ask. My intention today is only to confirm the identity of the deceased and the details of his life."

He called forward Edwin Minton, who swore on oath to tell the truth. The coroner began his questioning. "You identified the body of the deceased as that of your son Stanley James Minton?"

"Yes, I did."

"And he was how old?

"Fifty years old." Edwin's voice trembled a little, and he gripped his walking stick tightly until he regained control of himself.

"And the death, you say, was unexpected as far as you were concerned?"

"What father would expect his son to die before him? There was no reason for it. He had many years ahead of him. He'd just started up a new business."

Marie listened closely as Edwin gave a glowing summary of Stanley's past and present life, starting with the day he had bought the small grocers on Prospect Crescent. "He turned it into The Emporium, one of the most successful businesses in Harrogate. He did well. You ask anyone. All his customers respected and liked him. He supported me and his mother, God rest her soul, all his life. He was a good son."

Marie understood why he didn't want the stigma of failure to follow his son to the grave, but it was far from the truth.

"But he sold The Emporium," the coroner prompted.

"He wanted to better himself and move to Leeds."

"And you weren't with him at the end? You'd gone to live with your other son," Wallington checked his notes, "Geoffrey?"

"I'd been thrown out." Edwin glared at Marie. "By her."

Marie shook her head in denial, but Edwin was pointing an accusing finger at her. "She forced me to go. She threw me out. Why? Because she didn't want me to see what she was up to, that's why. Ask her what was in all those pills and potions she kept making. My wife, Edith, never trusted her."

"Pills and potions?" Wallington looked confused.

Marie was astonished. Did he mean the remedies she used to make? She hadn't expected that to be used against her.

"All I know is, our Stanley was a healthy man when I last saw him," Edwin continued doggedly, "before he moved to Leeds. He had no reason to die. That's what Dr Morton said to me at Garibaldi Street. She was already rushing that fool," he pointed at Hornby, "into signing a death certificate when I arrived. Why was that? Because she wanted him buried before any questions were asked." Marie saw Betsy Capes and her friends craning forward, to better hear the old man's words. "I put a stop to that. It was me who demanded a second opinion. That didn't please her."

"Had Mrs Minton objected to a post-mortem then?" the coroner asked.

Marie knew she hadn't and she was glad of it now. Reluctantly, Edwin had to take back his accusation.

"She said she wanted it settled. She said she'd pay whatever it cost. But why did she separate me from my son? Why did she get me out the way if she didn't have anything to hide?"

Because your son had something to hide, she wanted to say.

"Thank you, Mr Minton," the coroner said firmly. It was obvious that Edwin wanted to say much more, but one look from the coroner made it clear that that was all the time he was going to be allowed. "I can take evidence from you at a later stage, if necessary."

"Mrs Minton?"

She realised that the coroner was beckoning for her to come forward. It took an effort of will to make her way to the seat at the front, but, once there, she managed to keep her composure. It was just for a little longer, surely.

"Mrs Minton, you've heard what Mr Edwin Minton had to say? Do you confirm that your husband died between the evening of May 30th and the morning of May 31st at number fourteen Garibaldi Street?"

"Yes." Marie's voice was clipped and tense.

"We've heard that the deceased was normally in good health? Is that correct?"

"No," she said firmly. "Ask anyone. When I married Mr Minton, he already suffered from a severe stomach complaint and painful gum disorders. He later developed an ulcer. He might have been strong, but he certainly wasn't healthy."

She glanced towards the Mintons. Edwin was glaring at her; Geoffrey was observing her with open hostility. Only Isabelle seemed to have any sympathy for her, and even she looked away when she caught Marie's glance.

She knew she couldn't let Edwin's accusations remain unchallenged. "The pills and potions that my father-in-law mentioned were harmless. I learnt how to blend them at my convent in France. They contained natural herbs for curing simple ailments. My husband always said they helped him." At least she had nothing to hide there. "And I'm sorry to contradict my father-in-law, but I didn't throw him out of the house. It was my husband who insisted he should go."

Edwin shouted "Lies!" and Geoffrey tried to restrain him. Isabelle covered her face with her hands, embarrassed by his outburst.

The coroner frowned at Edwin. "I don't think this is a suitable moment to air family grievances, Mr Minton. The time will come for that. I am now adjourning the inquest until July 20th, by which time the pathologist will have submitted his analysis on the contents of the deceased's stomach." With those words, the coroner brought the proceedings to an end.

Marie was stunned. July 20th? She'd assumed it would all be over by the end of today. How could she bear to wait until then to discover what the pathologist's findings were?

"Mrs Minton?" She looked up, still stupefied by the news, to see that Dr Hornby was gazing down at her with concern. "You look very pale. Can I offer you my arm for support?"

"Dr Hornby, yes. I… thank you."

"You're under more of a strain than you realise," he murmured. "I'm sure anyone would be."

She gratefully took his arm as he led her from the hall.

CHAPTER TWENTY-ONE

It had been three weeks since the adjournment of the inquest and Marie had found it the longest three weeks of her life. It was a relief when she received a telegram from Geoffrey informing her curtly that the burial of Stanley could now take place, as the coroner had signed the release for the body. He was to be buried at the Telford Street Wesleyan Chapel in Harrogate. *Service begins at eleven a.m.,* was all the telegram said.

The train was late and she had difficulty finding the street on which the chapel was situated. When she eventually arrived, it was to find that the service had already begun and the doors were closed. She had to push hard against them to force them open. The rattle caused all heads to turn and the minister to halt his sermon. Flushed and out of breath, she closed the door behind her. It was only a small chapel, but it was crowded. Where had they all come from, these people? She recognised Betsy Capes, Geoffrey and Alice Smith, the Godwins and Gladys, but all the others were strangers to her.

The Minton family were seated on the front pew; Edwin next to the aisle, then Isabelle, then Geoffrey. To reach the only space left beside them, Marie realised she would have to push past them all. Their message was clear. She was not welcome to sit with them. For a second, she faltered. Then she gained courage and walked deliberately down the aisle, aware she was the focus of everyone's attention. The clatter of her feet on the flagstones sounded unbelievably loud.

Steeling herself for the ordeal, she walked up to Stanley's coffin and placed a hand on it, bowing her head in respect.

It was what she had to do. It was what was expected of the grieving widow.

The minister stayed silent as Marie, still the target of all eyes, turned and crossed to the front pew. At first, the Mintons made no attempt to make a space for her, but she didn't move. She remained where she was in the aisle, waiting for them to slide along the bench.

It was Isabelle who acted. She stood up and indicated for Geoffrey to move along the pew. She sat down beside him again and then Edwin slid towards her to close the gap. Marie took the vacant seat on the end. The tension in the chapel eased and heads were lowered to prayer books again. The minister continued with the service.

As the ceremony unfolded, Marie stood when everybody else stood and sat when everybody sat. She mouthed hymns she didn't know and bowed her head to prayers she didn't hear. There were times during the ceremony when it was almost unbearable, but she had travelled so far along the path there was no turning back.

When the service was over, she found herself at the head of the procession, immediately behind the coffin, as it was carried down the aisle and out to the cemetery. Despite the blue sky, it was cold and damp. The weathered gravestones were proof of their exposure to the elements. The minister had to raise his voice over the caw of the jackdaws disturbed by the crowd, who had gathered around the grave. Everyone shivered in the wind that seemed to have sprung up from nowhere.

As the vicar read from his Bible, Marie stared blindly down at the oak casket containing her husband's remains. As it was slowly lowered into the ground, she picked up a handful of earth. Her hands were so cold she could scarcely move them, but she managed to scatter the soil onto the polished wooden surface. She was aware of Isabelle sobbing and of Geoffrey placing a comforting arm around her. Both he and his father stood like ramrods as the minister read the final words.

Once it was over, the Mintons were immediately surrounded by a sympathetic crowd, but no one approached the widow to offer their condolences. No one except Gladys.

"I'm sorry, Mrs Minton. It must have been a dreadful shock for you," she said. Marie nodded, not trusting herself to speak. "We can go together to the wake at Devonshire Place, if you like."

Marie shook her head. "I haven't been invited." Gladys looked scandalised. "The Mintons blame me for every ill that's ever befallen them, Gladys. You go. Leave me here. I just need a moment alone."

Gladys squeezed her arm and moved away, and Marie turned to look down into the pit where Stanley's body had been laid to rest. Would he be relishing the fact that she'd condemned herself to everlasting purgatory? There was one thought that gave her comfort. He could no longer harm Evelyn.

⋆

He stared at the short paragraph in *The Times* that had made him abandon his breakfast and head for the privacy of his study:

> *The inquest into the death of northern businessman Stanley Minton, previously the owner of The Emporium, Harrogate, who died unexpectedly some weeks ago, is to re-open in Leeds tomorrow.*

Stanley Minton was the name of Marie's husband. The Emporium had been the name of Stanley's shop. What the devil had happened? She'd never indicated to him that her husband was ill.

Wilson knocked discreetly on the door. "The Honourable Mr Austin Frobisher has called to see you, sir."

"What?" Evelyn was still distracted by what he had just read. "Oh, show him through, Wilson." He folded the newspaper and put it to one side.

Siggy bounced into the room with his usual flurry of coat and scarves. "Called in because I'm off to America soon, Evie. New York, no less. I may be gone for a few months."

"Good." Evelyn's gaze returned to the newspaper.

Siggy was aware that he didn't have his friend's full attention. "Sorry, have I called at a bad time? Shall I go? Come back later?"

"No. No, of course not," Evelyn said apologetically. "Something's come up, that's all." He picked up the newspaper and handed it to Siggy, pointing at the relevant paragraph.

Siggy scanned it quickly as Evelyn began to pace around the room. "Well, I can see it's obviously disturbed you, but I'm not sure why."

"The dead man's wife was Marie Montrecourt. You remember, I told you about her. The daughter of Hortense Montrecourt?"

"Good God, Evie, that was moons ago. You said your interest in her had long since faded."

"Well, it hadn't. I saw her and wrote to her quite often. We grew close – too close. Then I discovered things about her – about her past. Things I can't discuss with anyone. Not even with you, Siggy. I can't even tell her."

"And was that the cause of your seeking oblivion in Gerry's Club?"

"Yes," Evelyn said.

His friend tossed the newspaper back onto the chair. "I have a bad feeling about all this, Evie. Don't get involved."

"I feel responsible for her, Siggy. I have reasons for feeling responsible."

His friend snorted derisively. "I assume she's pretty and is probably playing on your sympathy. I believe women are very good at that."

"Not Marie."

"Look, I won't pry into why you feel this responsibility." He held up a hand as Evelyn opened his mouth to speak. "You've obviously convinced yourself that your father cheated her out of a fortune, I know that. If you make contact with her now and it becomes known to the newspapers, how long will it take for them to sniff out the same thing?" Siggy asked.

Evelyn knew he was right, and there was even more for them to sniff out than Siggy suspected.

"Just a thought," Siggy continued, "is there no one who can keep in contact with her for you – let you know what's happening without you becoming directly involved. Someone who can be trusted to be discreet?"

Evelyn thought for a moment. "There's John Pickard, I suppose. He's the solicitor in Harrogate – he who obeys instructions and asks no questions."

"Perfect. He's your man. Telephone Pickard and instruct him to keep an eye on things for you."

"What? Now?"

"Now seems as good a time as any," Siggy replied.

The solicitor was just leaving his office when the telephone rang. "John Pickard speaking."

"Pickard? Sir Evelyn Harringdon here."

The solicitor sounded surprised. "How do you do, Sir Evelyn."

Evelyn glanced at Siggy, who nodded encouragingly. "I believe that Mrs Minton's husband has died recently? Am I correct?"

"Er, yes. Yes, that's right. There's an inquest in progress. I think it reconvenes very soon."

"How is Mrs Minton bearing up?"

Pickard appeared at a loss how to answer. "I'm sorry, Sir Evelyn, I'm no longer in touch with the family so I have no idea."

"It's just that, as you know, my father always felt an obligation towards her, and I wanted to ensure that she was coping with the strain. Why is there an inquest, by the way?"

"It seems there are a few complications about the death, Sir Evelyn. If you're really interested, there was a report in the *Leeds Mercury* about it. I could read it to you if you want me to?"

"Yes. Do that."

"I have it here somewhere." Evelyn could hear the rustling of paper. "Ah, yes, here it is. The headline in the *Mercury* is, *Mysterious Death of Stanley Minton.*"

Pickard then proceeded to read out the article. It was full of purple prose of the most lurid kind, praising the young widow's beauty, and the evident hostility of the husband's family, including their suspicion that Stanley's death was not a natural one.

"So what does all that mean?" Evelyn asked impatiently.

"I suppose it means that Stanley's family are accusing her of playing some part in it, although there appears to be no proof. No doubt it will be proven to be a ridiculous assumption when the inquest reopens."

"This *is* absurd." Evelyn said angrily. "To place the poor woman in such a dreadful situation is nothing short of vindictive." There was silence on the other end of the phone. "Right, Pickard, I want you sitting by her side every day at the inquest and I want you advising her, until this nonsense is settled."

"I hardly see how that will help," John Pickard protested.

"I will pay you well for any inconvenience, of course – and whatever fee you think fit."

The solicitor began to protest again. "Contracts, property and investment – that's all I know."

"Just advise her when to speak and what to say. Is that too

much to ask? I can't be seen to be involved and my father trusted in your discretion, I know."

The solicitor silently absorbed this. "Oh, I see. Yes, of course. You want to preserve your father's anonymity. Things could be said; things mentioned at the inquest in the heat of the moment, perhaps?"

"Yes, something like that." He longed to ask Pickard to pass a message on to Marie, but it would be better for them both if she knew nothing about his involvement. "Please don't mention our conversation to Mrs Minton, Pickard. Just keep reporting back to me."

"Very well, but what reason can I give for my renewed interest in her affairs?"

"Tell her it's because you were once her guardian and you still feel bound to offer her your help."

Evelyn replaced the telephone and turned to Siggy. "It's done," he said. "Let's hope this appalling situation will soon be over."

*

Marie was astonished when Tilly showed John Pickard into the parlour. He was a stranger to her now.

"Mr Pickard, how do you do?" She put aside the embroidery, which she was using as a distraction through the long days of waiting. She held out her hand by way of greeting. He took it and bent over it politely. "This is a surprise," she said, indicating for him to sit.

He remained standing, turning his hat in his hand. "Mrs Minton, I'm calling out of concern for the situation in which you find yourself."

She was immediately on edge. Had he heard something? Was there fresh news? She managed to sound calm. "What situation is that?"

"I don't know if you've read the *Mercury*?"

"No," she said.

He cleared his throat. "Well, there are rumours – and Stanley's family are encouraging them – that the forensic evidence uncovered by the autopsy has raised some difficult questions, which suggests this inquest is going to be anything but straightforward."

Marie could no longer hide her panic. "Why? What have they found?"

"I'm afraid I've failed to find that out. Nothing for you to worry about, I'm sure of that." He carefully placed his bowler hat on the table in front of him and sat down facing her. "But I do believe you're in need of advice. I see it as my task to provide it."

She gave a sharp laugh. "I have no money, Mr Pickard, to pay you with. I'm afraid I'm helpless in the face of such rumours."

"Not true. I see it as my duty to protect you from them. No money is needed."

She was astonished by his generosity. "I can't take up your time."

"I was once your guardian and I feel it my duty to help. I will sit by your side every day at the inquest. I will advise you when to speak and when to keep silent. I would ask you to accept my advice, no matter what the provocation. Will you do that?"

She wanted to throw her arms around his neck in gratitude, but she simply murmured: "Thank you. I no longer feel so alone."

*

Thursday 20th July turned out to be one of the hottest days of the year. Not that it made much of an impression inside the

Old Court House where the inquest had been reconvened. On one side of the courtroom, the windows overlooked a stone wall and on the other side a bare yard. Consequently, most daylight was excluded. It meant the gas lamps remained permanently lit, forming flickering pools of yellow light against the dark, panelled walls.

When Marie arrived with John Pickard by her side, she was surprised to find that, unlike the first two days, the courtroom was half full. It increased her nervousness considerably. Pickard increased it even more by pointing out that there were now three journalists in attendance.

"Damned reporters; they're like carrion crow," he growled. "That fellow over there is from *The Illustrated Penny News* and over there – he's from *The Daily Herald*. I see our friend from the *Mercury* is back again. Haven't they got anything better to do?"

Marie wished fervently that they had. "Why are they all here? What do they expect to hear?"

"They live in hope of learning something that will sell their newspapers. The words 'unexplained' and 'death' attracts them like a rotting carcase attracts flies," he muttered.

Marie turned to look at them and saw that the man from *The Illustrated Penny News* was sketching her. She immediately turned away from him only to see the Mintons, who were taking their seats, glaring at her. Isabelle kept her eyes lowered.

The Gilpins now entered, passing Betsy Capes, who had increased her circle of cronies to the extent that they now took up one whole bench between them. The rest of the faces in the courtroom were people Marie had never seen before. She recognised Dr Shelton, who was in deep conversation with a grey, dry-as-dust little man. Was he the pathologist? So much was resting on what he had to say.

"Mrs Minton?" The coroner was obviously aware of the increase in the ranks of the press and intended to show them an efficiently run inquest. "Mrs Minton, please." He waved for her to come forward.

John Pickard rose to his feet. "I'm sorry. I am John Pickard, Mrs Minton's solicitor, and under my instructions Mrs Minton will not speak at this moment."

Marie, in the process of standing, obediently sank back onto the bench again, not a little bewildered.

The coroner drummed his fingers impatiently on his desk. "Very well, if that is your wish, sir. Then let us proceed with Dr Shelton."

As the doctor made his way to the front, Marie whispered to Pickard: "Why not?"

"Because we need to hear what everyone else has to say first," he whispered back. "There must be no risk of a contradiction that could prove damaging to you."

She fell silent as the elegant Dr Shelton took his seat at the front of the court. He swore the oath to tell the truth, then began his testimony.

"I am Dr Howard Michael Wishart Shelton, physician at Leeds General Infirmary. I, along with my colleague Dr Morton, was called in by Dr Hornby on the afternoon of June 1st, to do a post-mortem on the body of Stanley Minton." He confirmed where the post-mortem had taken place and who else was present, then he laid the details of his findings succinctly before the jury, describing the dissecting of Stanley's organs in gruesome detail. With the instinct of a showman, he saved his most startling revelation until the end.

"When I opened the stomach and intestines," he said, "I was astonished to find that there was an overpowering smell of chloroform."

Aware that she was the focus of all eyes, Marie struggled to show no reaction. She glanced at John Pickard, who instantly said: "Say nothing. This is nothing against you."

Dr Shelton waited for the reaction to die down before

continuing: "The kidneys and the liver were damaged, but I don't believe they were the cause of death." He added that there was also a small ulcer in the intestines, but it had certainly not burst. "It would have caused the deceased minor pain and might, in time, have become a serious problem. No, the cause of death was, in my opinion, the fact that the deceased swallowed chloroform. The lining of the intestines was inflamed. I concluded that death was most likely due to the contents of the stomach. I suggested that they be sealed and the coroner be told."

"What time do you estimate death to have occurred?" Wallington asked.

"I can only suggest between the hours of eight o'clock at night and six o'clock in the morning when Mrs Minton found him."

"And the amount of chloroform in the stomach?"

"A few ounces, maybe. It's difficult to say. Certainly enough to kill him." Another murmur rippled through the hall.

Marie tried to stop her hands from shaking by folding them in her lap. With no further questions to be answered for the moment, Dr Shelton stepped down.

The pathologist was called next, the grey man sitting beside Dr Shelton. Eminent in his field, Dr Moore was an academic who appeared to have been shut away from the light of day for years. Everything about him was grey: his hair, his suit, his face. His voice was so small and high-pitched that everyone in the court had to lean forward in order to catch what he was saying.

He described himself to the jury as a specialist in forensic medicine and a senior analyst to the Home Office. The jars containing the contents of Stanley's stomach, plus other specimens, had been sent to him for examination. His job was to do a report on them for the Home Office and to pass on his findings to the inquest. Dr Moore then launched into a complex and, to most people in the room, incomprehensible summary of his findings. It seemed to last forever.

"So what are you saying?" The coroner, whom John Pickard had told Marie was a landlord by profession, with no knowledge of the medical profession, was obviously irritated. "Are you agreeing with Dr Shelton that chloroform was present in the stomach or not?"

"The stomach fluid was fairly acidic and contained some element of chloroform, so the conclusion has to be that there was an administration of a dose of chloroform."

"He swallowed it?" Wallington asked.

"One would assume so."

Marie sat forward on the bench, her body tense.

"May I ask a question?" the foreman of the jury interrupted, and Marie, along with everyone else in the room, turned to look at him. Wallington nodded. "Wouldn't this liquid be an unpleasant thing to swallow?"

"It has a hot and fiery taste. I suppose that might be lessened by mixing it with brandy. And brandy was also found in his stomach. If chloroform had been swallowed, however, I would have expected there to be signs of vomiting, but I believe there were no signs of vomiting at the scene and none in the windpipe."

Marie closed her eyes. *Thank God.*

Wallington took up the questioning again. "How much did you say the deceased swallowed?"

"I didn't specify. Unfortunately, I didn't receive the contents of the stomach until two weeks after the post-mortem. They stayed in the mortuary until they were sent to me and the jars in which the specimens were stored were very badly sealed, so it's difficult for me to be certain. Dr Shelton's assessment from the post-mortem was that he had swallowed about an ounce or two."

"And that would be enough to kill a man?" the coroner asked.

"I haven't been involved in such a case before, but I would assume so."

"In this case, I would think that's an acceptable conclusion," said Wallington.

"May I ask another question?" It was the foreman of the jury again. The coroner waved at him impatiently to get on with it, obviously with thoughts of luncheon on his mind. "Is chloroform something that can be used by one person against another?"

Marie knew why that question was being asked, and so did everyone else in the room.

"It could be. But there's an element of risk because there's no understanding about the size of dose that would prove fatal, and it is unpleasant to take. It also creates a painful burning sensation in the throat. And, in my opinion, it would be virtually impossible to swallow without some of it going into the windpipe as the deceased resisted it. It would also have caused a severe irritation both there and in the throat, but there was no sign of that at all."

She hadn't known how high the risk of failure was. If she had, she would never have dared to take it.

"And have there been cases before where chloroform has been used for homicidal purposes?" Wallington was asking.

"I must admit, throughout my career as an analyst, I've never been involved in a case where chloroform was used in that way."

There was a murmur of curiosity as this information was whispered from one person to another.

"I should point out again," continued Moore calmly, "that the deceased's kidneys were severely damaged and the liver enlarged. When the deceased's skull cap was removed and the brain most carefully examined, there was some abnormality in the ventricles of the brain. Although, as I said, the specimens were very badly preserved."

"And the significance of these things?" asked Wallington.

"With such damage to his major organs, the deceased

would not have lived much longer anyway. As for the ventricles of the brain, the abnormality was what I would expect to find in the brain of someone who has inhaled chloroform more than once. That would be an explanation for the condition of the kidneys and the liver, too."

"Meaning?" Wallington pressed him impatiently.

"I suspect there was a history of the deceased inhaling chloroform. Perhaps it was also inhaled before the fatal dose was taken, for whatever purpose."

Marie curled over on the bench and covered her face with her hands. So now it was all out in the open, every shameful fact about Stanley's addiction. It would be in all the newspapers tomorrow.

"But you still say that it was the amount in the stomach that was the cause of death?" Wallington asked.

"I would say so. If the deceased was a habitual user."

Geoffrey could contain himself no longer. He leapt to his feet. "This is preposterous! My brother was a clean-living, hard-working man. Whatever happened to him, she did it."

Marie started to rise too, but John Pickard grabbed hold of her arm and dragged her down again. All eyes were still on Stanley's brother, so the exchange between solicitor and client went unobserved by the jury.

"If you say anything now, you will do more harm to yourself than to them," Pickard muttered. "I warn you, don't say anything." After a moment's indecision, Marie bit her lip and sank back onto the bench.

Wallington was still trying to calm the irate Geoffrey. "Mr Minton, please sit down. You'll have your chance to speak later."

It seemed for a moment that Geoffrey would ignore the warning and the atmosphere in the court grew tense, but he reluctantly resumed his seat, shaking his head in disgust. Edwin wiped his eyes with the back of his hand. Isabelle muttered that she was too distraught to stay there any longer and hurried from the court. The disturbance over, Wallington turned again to the pathologist.

"You were saying, Dr Moore?"

"There might be the possibility that it was swallowed by him accidentally, I suppose. Or suicide?" Geoffrey restrained himself with difficulty as Dr Moore continued. "But again, I would expect there to be some vomiting, some scorching of the throat."

"And there was none?"

"No."

"So there is no clear indication of how he consumed it."

"Not at this stage. No."

"Thank you, Dr Moore. I may need to call on you later."

As Dr Moore stepped down, Wallington announced a break for luncheon and the hall was filled with voices as the pathologist's testimony was discussed and dissected. The artist from *The Illustrated Penny News* quickly sketched a portrait of the bereaved widow leaning on her solicitor's arm as she was led out of the courtroom, the target of all eyes.

On Pickard's insistence, and with the help of a liberal disbursement, he and Marie had been allowed a private room into which food had been brought from the local public house. Marie didn't even look at it and Pickard showed no inclination to eat either. She began pacing the floor agitatedly.

"I should speak now, shouldn't I? After everything that's been said. Stanley *did* use chloroform, though I prayed that the inquest would never need to know. I wanted to protect Stanley's good name."

Pickard held up his hand to stop her. "I don't see how anything you can say will alter their decision as to how he died. Now more than ever, it's imperative for you to remain silent. Just leave the court to draw their own conclusions. There is nothing that condemns you."

"They will print it in the newspapers though, won't they?" Evelyn would read about it. Would it shock him? Would he be disgusted? She was glad she'd forbidden him to contact her. He had to keep his distance or risk being drawn into a scandal.

When the inquest reconvened, the coroner turned first to Marie. "Mrs Minton, I would like to hear your account of what happened on the night of your husband's death."

John Pickard responded as before. "I am advising my client to remain silent for the moment."

Speculation as to the reason for this continued refusal to speak broke out among the courtroom. The reporters scribbled, while Wallington leant towards Pickard.

"If she doesn't speak, it may look bad for her."

"I won't take the responsibility of agreeing to her examination until we've heard all the evidence," insisted John Pickard, now convinced that this was the correct path to take. Marie's nerves threatened to make her an unstable witness. The less she said, the better.

"Mrs Minton?" Wallington leant towards her, peering over his spectacles, ignoring the solicitor. "Before it's too late?"

Marie stared down at the floor, unsure what to do. The solicitor fiddled uneasily with his papers. Why didn't she answer? There wasn't a sound in the courtroom. Finally, Marie said, in a voice that was barely audible, "I will take my solicitor's advice."

"Very well. I believe Mrs Minton gave Dr Hornby an account of the events leading up to the death of Stanley Minton. I shall call on him to pass it on to us, if Mrs Minton is willing?" Marie nodded.

Seated on the chair, Dr Hornby carefully unfolded his wad of notes and Wallington groaned. "Please, keep to the point, Dr Hornby. I believe Mrs Minton confided in you the events leading up to the discovery of her husband's body?"

"She did and I made careful notes after the post-mortem

in case the information would be useful. However, to start at the beginning…" He cleared his throat, determined not to be hurried as he gave a detailed account of his various visits to the house in Garibaldi Street. "I was called on by Mrs Minton to attend her husband just some weeks before his death."

He droned on, checking and re-checking his facts with his notebook, until finally, to Wallington's obvious relief, he reached the evening of Stanley Minton's death.

"Mrs Minton told me that she sat with her husband all that evening – his last evening. She gave him a little tea and that's all he had the whole day." He looked up. "I think Dr Morton, who is yet to give his evidence, will be able to confirm that." Hornby returned to his notes. "She poured him a little brandy and left it by his bedside. She returned to her room and tried to get some sleep."

"They have separate rooms?" the coroner queried.

"Yes." Hornby looked at the jury and waited to see if there were any further questions before continuing. "Mrs Minton spent a restless night full of anxiety for her husband. It was around six o'clock in the morning when she saw her husband next. She went into his room to see how he was and it was then that she discovered him…" he consulted his notes "laid out on the bed, were the words she used. She couldn't see any sign of life. She tried to force a little brandy through her husband's lips. I told her that this was not a wise thing to have done. Anyway, it was then she realised that he was dead." There was absolute silence in the hall as he turned the page over. "She called Mrs Gilpin into the room and later she called on me."

Wallington interrupted. "When you yourself saw the body of Stanley Minton, there was nothing untoward in his appearance?"

"No. Nothing."

"There's been a suggestion he may have habitually inhaled

chloroform," Wallington said. "You saw no sign of that? You were not aware of it when you were treating him for an ulcer?"

"I saw no signs and I was not aware of it. I had no reason to look for it. I've never come across such a case before. I only saw what I expected to see. He had an ulcer, I knew that. I'd been treating him for an ulcer. It was obvious to me that it had burst."

"But it hadn't?"

"At the time I believed it had. I had no reason *not* to believe it had."

"And Mrs Minton never mentioned to you that her husband used chloroform?"

"No."

"Did you see any sign of a bottle of chloroform in the room on the morning of his death?"

"I did not."

"Was there brandy in the glass still?"

"The glass was empty when I saw it. The bottle of brandy was still there."

"How did the deceased's wife react to her husband's death in your opinion?"

"She was distraught," Hornby said firmly.

"Thank you, Dr Hornby." Wallington dismissed him with a nod.

It was Mrs Gilpin who now faced the assembly, with pursed lips and folded arms. She'd bought a new bonnet for the occasion and new gloves. The coat, though, was an old one, but she'd only worn it the once, to her mother-in-law's funeral.

"You live at number fourteen Garibaldi Street?" the coroner asked. "You rented rooms to the deceased and his wife?"

"They came to look at the rooms over a year ago now. They liked them, so they took them."

"Would you say the deceased was a healthy man?"

"Well, not in my book – and he seemed to get worse. He began to look dreadful."

Marie glanced at the jury. That's what she had told them at the beginning of the inquest. Did they remember?

"And Mrs Minton was concerned for him, which is why she called in Dr Hornby?"

"Well, it was me who insisted the doctor be called in. She seemed very unwilling at first. Didn't seem to think it necessary. I wanted to know what this illness was. Well, you never know what people have picked up, do you? Besides, we couldn't get any sleep with him being sick every night."

"It was sickness he had?"

"He collapsed once."

"Collapsed?"

"I heard this thump one night, not long after they'd moved in. They both came to the door when I knocked. He looked dreadful. He told me he had stomach trouble. That's one thing that Gilpin hasn't suffered from. Nearly everything else, but not that."

"Yes, thank you, Mrs Gilpin," said Wallington. "Can we keep your husband out of this unless it's relevant? Let's just stay with what happened on the actual night he died?"

"The following morning, May 31st it was, I was in bed and there was an almighty banging at my door. Gilpin says – I have to mention him now," she said quickly, seeing that the coroner was about to interrupt her. "It's relevant." There was a ripple of amusement around the court, but the humour of it escaped Marie. "Gilpin asked who was at the door. Well, it obviously had to be her, didn't it?"

"What time would this have been?"

"About six o'clock, I think."

"Did you hear anything else during the night?"

"Not a thing."

"Go on."

"Mrs Minton was in a terrible state. She said her husband had suffered some kind of attack during the night. She didn't know what to do. Well, I followed her upstairs. Gilpin came too. Gilpin said—"

"Just concentrate on what you said and saw. You said that Mrs Minton was in a terrible state and you followed her into the deceased's room? What did you see there?"

"The deceased was lying on his back. He was definitely dead, stone cold."

Marie failed to suppress a shiver. It was a moment she would never forget.

"What did you see in the room, Mrs Gilpin? Apart from the deceased."

"There was a wine glass by the bed. It smelt of brandy. And there was a small bottle of brandy beside it. She'd brought it in with her the previous day. Said her husband had asked for it."

"And that's all you saw?"

"All that I can remember seeing."

"What happened then?"

"She," Mrs Gilpin pointed at Marie, "wanted to go for the doctor then and there, but Gilpin said that as Mr Minton was dead she should wait until a more civilised hour as nothing could be done for him now. She went to fetch the doctor about eight o'clock. I offered to go with her, but she ran off before I could."

"And she was by herself in the room with the deceased until she set off for the doctor?"

"Yes."

"Would you say Mrs Minton was distressed by her husband's death?"

"I suppose she was. She seemed to be, yes."

"Thank you, Mrs Gilpin."

As Mrs Gilpin passed Marie, she glared at her for bringing shame to a respectable house. Wallington looked at his pocket watch. It had been a long day and he, for one, had heard enough for the moment. He announced his intention to adjourn and said, "I will take further evidence tomorrow. Mrs Minton, you may want to reconsider your decision about remaining silent."

Marie turned to Pickard, but he shook his head, taking her arm to hurry her out of the courtroom.

"Surely I have to say something now?" She tried to shake herself free.

"Keep your voice down," he muttered. He continued to push her ahead of him towards the street. "You must say nothing until I tell you to speak."

They were now outside. They'd almost reached the carriage when suddenly Geoffrey appeared in front of them. He thrust out an arm to block their way, pushing his face close to hers.

"I will see you in hell for what you've done to our Stanley," he said in a low voice.

She opened her mouth to say something but she couldn't form any words.

Pickard was all too aware that the reporters were not very far away and a group of people loitering on the steps of the building were already beginning to take an interest in what was happening. "Geoffrey, this is not helping your brother." He put a calming hand on Geoffrey's arm, but Geoffrey angrily shook it off.

"Nothing can help my brother now, but I won't see his name dragged through the dirt by a woman like her." He turned on Marie. "I have lost two brothers because of you. One to America and one to the grave."

There was nothing she could say because he was right.

Geoffrey turned back to Pickard. "Whatever happened to Stanley, she did it and I'll make sure she damn well pays for it."

★

Unexplained Death Of Prominent Yorkshire Businessman read the headline of *The Illustrated News*, and underneath it: *The shocking facts behind the suspicious death of Stanley Minton.*

Evelyn read the article with growing alarm. Pickard had said he would keep him informed of events and he'd heard nothing. He picked up the telephone and dialled the solicitor's office. Before the man could say anything, Evelyn went straight into the attack.

"Why wasn't I told anything about the chloroform? Why did I have to read about it in the newspapers?"

Pickard excused himself by saying that events were moving so swiftly, he couldn't keep up with them.

"For God's sake man, what kind of a family did you marry her into?" Evelyn said accusingly.

"A respectable one, as far as I could see," the solicitor protested. "I am as shocked as you are about what has been revealed at the inquest." Evelyn's silence made Pickard anxious. "I'm worried about the fact that she kept quiet about Stanley's addiction. It doesn't show her in a good light."

Evelyn's voice was cold when he replied: "Shame and pride drove her not to discuss it, I would think. I presume you're not suggesting that Mrs Minton could have harmed her husband?"

"No. No, not at all," the solicitor hurriedly reassured him. "I think it more than likely that the unhappy man accidentally killed himself, as many of those addicted in this way often do." Evelyn grunted his agreement. "I hope you approve that I am advising Mrs Minton to say nothing for the moment. She is very highly strung and putting her through the ordeal of being questioned might be very distressing for her. Do you agree?"

"Of course I do, if it will spare her pain. You say the suspicion is that the husband killed himself?"

"Or that it was an accident, yes," Pickard assured him.

"Very well. I think the course you've chosen is probably the wisest."

Relieved to have Sir Evelyn's approval, Pickard rang off, and Evelyn proceeded to pour himself a larger than usual whisky. It wasn't his normal habit to take a drink so early in the day, but this morning he was in need of it.

CHAPTER TWENTY-TWO

The room was three quarters full when Betsy Capes and her friends arrived. There was still an hour to go before the inquest was due to start, but they managed to claim the few remaining seats near the front. They saw Geoffrey enter and take his usual place, but he was alone.

Marie's entrance with her solicitor caused a flurry of interest, but the coroner soon had everything under control. Mr Gilpin made his way to the front.

He mumbled his way through his testimony, regularly breaking off to cough. A glass of water was produced for him as he confirmed his wife's statement virtually word for word.

"I followed my wife into the deceased's bedroom," he said. "I leant over him to make sure he wasn't breathing. I smelt something and I told her – Mrs Minton – and she said it was brandy. It struck me at the time that it wasn't brandy I smelt. Now I realise it was chloroform." There was a murmur from the listeners as Mr Gilpin took a sip of water.

"I looked around the room and I saw the brandy bottle and a wine glass. The glass had the same sweet smell I'd noticed near the body."

"You've described seeing the brandy bottle and the wine glass. Did you see anything else?" the coroner asked.

"I noticed a bottle on the mantelshelf. A medicine bottle; it was blue and it was fluted, like a poison bottle."

Marie drew in her breath sharply. She could have sworn that Mr Gilpin hadn't seen the bottle. He'd given no indication.

"A medicine bottle?" Wallington repeated. "Containing what?"

"A medicine bottle. I don't know what it contained because when I came back into the room after the doctor had arrived, the bottle had gone."

"Gone?" the coroner repeated.

"Gone," confirmed Gilpin.

"Might it have contained chloroform?"

"It might have done."

"But when you returned to the room the bottle had been removed?"

"Yes," Gilpin said firmly.

Marie struggled to hide her dismay.

"I believe Mr Edwin Minton, the deceased's father, arrived soon after?"

"Just as Dr Hornby was about to sign the death certificate, yes."

"What was Mr Edwin Minton's reaction to this?"

"He was very angry. He said his son was a fit man and this should never have happened. He said that Mrs Minton had got between him and his son. She had thrown him out. She denied it. She also said that it was Dr Hornby's opinion that the deceased had died of natural causes. This upset the father. He said he didn't believe his son had died of natural causes. He said he wanted his death looked into. He was insistent that there was reason to doubt the cause of his son's death. Witnessing this and remembering the strange smell on the body, I said I'd refuse to register the death if the doctor signed the death certificate."

"Did Mrs Minton know you were the Registrar for Births, Marriages and Deaths?" Wallington asked.

"No, I don't believe she did. She seemed shocked," replied Gilpin. Another murmur rippled through the court.

The strain of continually being the target of all eyes was beginning to take its toll on Marie. She made a determined effort to focus her attention on a small mark on the wall just above the coroner's head. She stared at it until her eyes began to water, hoping she could block out the endless words.

"Ezekiel Jacobs," Wallington called.

Marie frowned. Who was Ezekiel Jacobs? It transpired that he ran a chemist shop not far from The Emporium, from whom Stanley had once bought a small amount of chloroform – ostensibly to remove some grease from drapes in The Emporium. For which act of kindness to a neighbour, he complained to the coroner, the police were now threatening to prosecute him. He'd volunteered this testimony in the hope of softening their hearts. Marie began to fidget.

"For heaven's sake," Pickard muttered, "sit still. You're as jumpy as a cat with fleas."

Another name was called: Matthew Flint. It appeared he was another chemist from whom Stanley had acquired a small amount of chloroform, long before he'd moved to Leeds. "He'd spilt grease on a suit," Flint said, "and as I knew him to be a respectable man, I could see no harm in it." He swore passionately that he'd never done anything of the kind before or since.

Matthew Flint stepped down. To her relief, neither man had been able to link the chloroform to her. Wallington now addressed the jury. "So, gentlemen, this leaves unanswered the question: if, as Dr Moore suggested, the deceased appears to have frequently inhaled chloroform, what was his source? We can be sure that neither Mr Jacobs, nor Mr Flint, were regular providers."

Marie was aware that the jury were looking at her, waiting for her to say something. She looked at John Pickard. He shook his head.

Mr Hart, the manager of the Harrogate and Bingley Bank, gave his testimony next. He contradicted Edwin's statement that Stanley's business was a great success, revealing, on the contrary, that Stanley was very close to bankruptcy. He was forced not only to sell the business in order to pay off his debts, but his house as well. A reluctant Martin Godson followed and confirmed the bank manager's statement.

"He was ill with worry," Martin said. "I hated to leave his employment, but I knew The Emporium was never going to recover and I had my family to consider."

"And you say you became concerned about the deceased's state of mind?"

"Yes, I did."

Dr Morton, who had been prevented from attending the inquest before because of ill health, was the next person to be called by the coroner. He confirmed Dr Sheldon's findings, disagreeing a little about the amount of chloroform found in the stomach. "But a goodly amount," he said.

"Any idea how it got there?" asked Wallington.

"Swallowed, but how? Without the resulting effects outlined by Dr Moore, I have no idea."

"Could he have taken it himself?"

"I suppose he could have done. But why no burning in the throat? Why no vomiting?"

It was a struggle for Marie to remain impassive. If she could pretend this was happening to someone else, she might get through the rest of this ordeal.

John Pickard leant towards her. "It looks as though the conclusion is that Mr Minton may have killed himself," he murmured. "In which case, you will have been spared the pain of having to speak."

Marie closed her eyes in relief. "For which I am grateful, and I thank you for your advice."

Inspector Fowler, the policeman acting for the coroner's court, was called next. He was the policeman who had inspected the Minton's rooms once the post-mortem had confirmed that Stanley had died in suspicious circumstances. The impression he gave to the jury was that of a methodical man committed to his profession, a man for whom accuracy was a religion. He confirmed that a bottle of brandy had been found on the table beside the bed, and a glass.

"And was there any sign of the blue bottle on the mantelshelf that Mr Gilpin saw?" asked Wallington.

"None."

"So between Mr Gilpin's sighting of it and Dr Hornby's arrival, the bottle disappeared. Removed from the scene completely, and it wasn't found anywhere else when you searched the rooms?"

"That is correct."

"Who could have removed it?"

"Only Mrs Minton."

Could she not tell them she'd got rid of the bottle to save Stanley's addiction becoming common knowledge? She looked at John Pickard, but he was listening intently to the evidence and didn't notice.

"If it wasn't in the rooms when you searched them, then where did it go?" the coroner was asking.

"It was quite a small bottle. It could have been concealed in a pocket. Mrs Minton went to fetch Dr Hornby. According to Mrs Gilpin she was anxious not to be accompanied."

"You're suggesting it could have been disposed of by Mrs Minton at that time?"

"It must have been. And something else in the lodgings caught my notice."

One of Inspector Fowler's men was moving forward with a book. Marie recognised it as her copy of *Farnsworth's Medical Dictionary*. What now? The policeman placed the heavy volume on the table in front of the coroner.

"That book belongs to Mrs Minton," Fowler said. "As you'll see, it has her name inscribed on the fly leaf. It's a medical book, an official list of drugs and directions for their preparation. As we've heard, Mrs Minton liked to dabble in such matters. Inside, there is a description of chloroform and the effect it has if inhaled or swallowed. The book fell open naturally at that page, which has a small stain on it." Wallington opened the book and nodded as he saw the stain the witchhazel had made. "This is a spillage that evidently made the page stick – you can see a small tear where it has been separated from the page opposite, so it's clear that this page was referred to frequently."

John Pickard glanced at Marie and saw that she was looking faint. He muttered: "Don't lose your nerve now. This proves nothing."

It was now Geoffrey's turn to be called and Marie's heart sank. If Edwin had tried to damage her, Geoffrey would surely succeed.

At first, it was evident he was finding it difficult to speak. As he swore his oath on the Bible, he could scarcely be heard. He cleared his throat a great deal and seemed uneasy, but gradually his voice gathered strength. He repeated what his father had told the inquest about how his brother had built up his business from nothing. He departed from his father's testimony by admitting that the business had been in trouble.

"My brother had been through a difficult time, it's true, and that is why he sold the shop and the house. But that gave him the money for a new start and he was looking forward to a new beginning, here in Leeds. He was excited, and there's no doubt in my mind that he would have been successful. The only problem he had was that woman. In my opinion, she didn't want him to succeed. She didn't want Pa to live with them. She made my brother's life a misery. If Stanley looked like a sick man to Martin Godson, it was because she was making him ill."

"I gather the family didn't welcome the marriage?" Wallington interrupted dryly.

"We believed she was using Stanley. She didn't love him.

She might try and fool everybody that she did, but she didn't love him at all." He looked at Marie, who stared defiantly back at him.

"In what way was she using him?" Wallington asked curiously.

"She brought a bit of money with her to the marriage. She was trying to buy respectability, but her behaviour made that impossible."

Marie exchanged an uneasy glance with John Pickard. The same thought had struck them both. The introduction of the money could threaten Sir Gordon's anonymity if it was pursued, but Geoffrey had *her* in his sights, not the money.

"She didn't just destroy Stanley. She ruined my other brother, too. She had an affair with him, after she was married. That's why he left home. I had to pay for him to go to America to get him away from her."

Heads craned to catch a glimpse of the widow. John Pickard studied his nails. Marie clutched her hands together. "It's not true, it's not true," she murmured. This was worse than anything she could have imagined.

"You are under oath..." Wallington reminded Geoffrey.

"I know. She lied about what happened on the night Ma died. She said they were playing the piano. The truth was she tried to seduce Peter, and Ma saw it and the shock killed her."

Marie was on her feet. "No, none of this is true."

The hall erupted into chaos, the press scribbled and John Pickard raised his voice above the babble. "This is a disgraceful accusation and my client is greatly distressed by it. Mrs Minton is unwell. She needs water. She needs air."

"Very well. We'll take a short break," Wallington conceded, to the disappointment of all those present.

In a state of collapse, Marie was helped out of the courtroom by Pickard. He took her to the small room put aside for their use. She immediately shook herself free and crossed to the window, pulling the sash down, leaning on the window ledge, closing her eyes, feeling the cold air on her burning cheeks. Pickard remained near the door, leaning with his back against it.

"Is it true?" he asked eventually. "About Peter Minton?"

"No!" She was close to tears.

Seeing her distress, Pickard made a decision – one he realised he should have taken days ago. "I'll ask for an adjournment and then, when you've had time to calm yourself, we'll hire you someone who can give you better legal advice than I can offer."

"No. I want this over with now." She couldn't face a prolonged ordeal. Outside, the wind was blowing an inn sign. Its creaking was jarring her nerves. "I am going to return to the inquest and speak out."

She gave him no chance to protest and strode back into the hall, leaving Pickard with no option but to follow.

She was fully aware of the crowd's excited anticipation as she took her seat. Wallington settled himself behind his desk. "Have you anything else to say, Mr Minton?" he asked of Geoffrey, who shook his head. He seemed to regret having said as much as he had, realising it didn't reflect well on the family.

Marie struggled to her feet. It was time for her to defend herself. However, the coroner wasn't looking in her direction and before she could gain his attention, he'd called for Detective Inspector Fowler. Her hesitation had lost her the chance to speak in her defence. "I believe you have some further information, Detective Inspector," said Wallington.

"Yes, sir."

The coroner nodded. "If Mr Johnson is here, then bring him forward."

Marie turned in horror to see the chemist, Johnny Johnson, jauntily enter the courtroom between two policemen. She gave John Pickard a look of despair and sank back onto the bench.

"Mr Johnson," Wallington said, "I believe you were apprehended by the police two days ago for trading illegal drugs on a regular basis."

"I was, sir. Yes, sir." For a man who'd just been arrested, Johnson seemed extremely chipper.

"Tell us your connection with the deceased, if you will."

"Well, I have – I should say, I had – a little chemist shop in Ilkley. Old Sutton Lane. I had a bit of a… sideline, I suppose you'd call it. I supplied a few regular clients with a little bit of extra stuff if they needed it. Mr Stanley Minton was one of them. His interest was chloroform, so I provided it."

"How much chloroform did you provide him with?"

"At least three or four ounces a week. Even after he moved to Leeds, he'd visit me. No questions asked, you see."

"And did you supply him with this quantity this year?"

"Yes, until the last time, when a lady came into the shop."

"When was that?"

"On May 30th, I think it was. She didn't give her name. She said she wanted five ounces of chloroform. I didn't ask any questions. I never do. It was when I saw the drawing of her in the newspaper I realised who she was."

"And who was she?"

"The lady sitting there. Mrs Minton." He pointed at Marie.

There was a gasp throughout the courtroom. John Pickard closed his eyes. Marie turned to him. "I can explain."

Detective Inspector Fowler was now conferring with the coroner as Marie struggled to her feet, but anything she had to say was drowned by the noise from the crowd. The jury didn't notice her either; they had their heads close together.

"What's happening?" Marie turned to Pickard again.

"To be blunt, Mrs Minton, if you speak out now you may well hang yourself."

What followed happened so quickly that Marie was bewildered. She heard the coroner asking the jury if there were any further questions. The foreman shook his head.

"We have heard all the testimonies now," the coroner said, "and it remains for me to start the difficult task of summing up the proceedings."

He was brief and to the point. "There appears to be no doubt as to the cause of death. Chloroform. But there are three possible ways it could have been administered: an accidental dose, a deliberate taking of it by the deceased himself, or by some other person."

He then outlined the facts that the court had heard during the inquest and concluded with the words: "So, gentlemen, accidental death, suicide or murder, which is it? You are not here to prove how it was done, just the circumstances in which, in your opinion, the fatal dose was administered. Do you need to retire to consider?"

The foreman leant across to the others and they conferred in whispers. The foreman stood up. "We have already reached a verdict."

Marie muttered, "Oh, my God," and John Pickard took out a handkerchief, which he used to mop his face.

"We believe that the deceased, Stanley James Minton, died from chloroform administered by his wife, Marie Minton, for the purpose of taking his life."

Geoffrey's triumphant cry of "Yes" rang out, echoing around the court. Marie slumped forward on the bench.

"This is a verdict of wilful murder against Mrs Marie Minton," Wallington said, looking towards the back of the hall where Detective Inspector Fowler was waiting. "I will ask to clear the room. Clear the room, please."

Still arguing over the decision, the crowd was herded

through the doors as Fowler moved forward to receive the coroner's warrant. He turned to Marie, who slowly rose.

"Marie Minton, I arrest you…"

She heard nothing, saw nothing. She felt numb.

★

Evelyn tossed the newspaper aside angrily. Even *The Times* had taken to calling it *The Garibaldi Street Poisoning Case*. It reported the result of the inquest and that the trial had been set for the first Monday in October.

He glared at his mother, who was sitting, ashen-faced, in the armchair facing him. "How could Pickard have allowed it to come to this?" he said furiously. "He was grovelling to me on the telephone this morning, saying he'd made a mistake – that he'd advised her badly. He's right; he should have let her speak out."

"I assume he was afraid she would condemn herself."

He should have known his mother would have no sympathy for Marie. "That's nonsense. Anyway, I'm going to see her. I can't let her face this alone."

His mother quickly rose to her feet in protest. "No, Evie. No, I won't let you. You'll destroy everything. Everything I've done to protect this family will have been futile." He made a gesture of dismissal and she caught hold of him by the shoulder. "Look at me – do you think it's been easy for me all these years? Nursing secrets, protecting your father, protecting you and the family? It's taken its toll; it's worn me out. And if you persist in getting involved in this mess, then it will finish me. Is that what you want?"

Alarmed by her agitation, he tried to calm her. "No, of course I don't want that. Here, sit down, Mama."

She refused, clutching hold of his hand. "Before you do anything else, talk to Lord Renfrew. Please."

"Renfrew?" The request took him by surprise. "Why involve him?"

"He's *already* involved. After your father returned from Africa and I learnt what he had done, I turned to Lord Renfrew for advice. He knows everything. Without his support, I wouldn't have been able to carry on. Talk to him; listen to what he has to say. This family's future is in your hands now."

★

Evelyn hovered in Lord Renfrew's outer office while his assistant announced him. He heard Renfrew say: "Ah, yes, I've been expecting him. Send him in."

He still had no idea why his mother had insisted he visit Renfrew. Whatever the man had to say, he was determined not to let Marie face this ordeal alone.

"I'll come straight to the point, Evelyn," Lord Renfrew said as he entered. "Your mother telephoned me. The Garibaldi Street case, involving this woman Marie Minton—"

Evelyn didn't let him finish. "She isn't *this woman*, Lord Renfrew. I think you know the truth about our relationship. She is family and I will stand by her."

"Very chivalrous," Renfrew said, and if sarcasm was intended Evelyn didn't care. He waited for Renfrew to continue which – after a moment – he did. "It might surprise you to know that I was present in the camp on the day that your father returned as if from the dead."

Evelyn *was* surprised. He wasn't aware that Renfrew had ever been to Africa.

"I was in the area on, shall we say, unofficial business and I was dining with the Colonel of the Regiment when Gordon, weak from malnutrition and suffering from fever, emerged from the veldt leaning on the shoulder of a young woman."

"I know this – it was Hortense Montrecourt." A look from Renfrew silenced Evelyn.

"The doctors gave Gordon morphine to help him fight the fever and I decided to sit by his bedside while he slept. I had nothing else to do with my time. As the fever became worse, your father became delirious. His words were jumbled and chaotic, but gradually I began to make sense of them. What he said was deeply disturbing to me. It seems that during the battle for the ridge on Majuba Hill, after General Colley had been shot, the men had looked to Gordon, as second in command, for orders. He panicked. This was his first battle. He gave no orders because he didn't know what orders to give. He abandoned his men and fled. He didn't charge the enemy heroically, he ran away and he was shot in the back for it. He told me this. He clung onto his horse as it carried him through their ranks and away from the battlefield. Some time later, the girl – Hortense – found him."

Evelyn listened to Renfrew's story with growing disbelief. He wouldn't stand by and let his father's reputation be destroyed. "He was a man in a fever. You can't believe what he said under those conditions."

"But by the next morning," Renfrew corrected him, "your father's temperature had dropped and the fever had passed, and he repeated the story to me. I was reeling from his revelations, just as you are. If the truth were discovered, then your father would have been shot as a deserter and the consequences for your family, for the Tory Party, for the whole government, would have been catastrophic. The country was already demoralised – if one of its leading figures were tried for cowardice..." Renfrew left the sentence hanging in the air.

"I'm sorry, I don't believe this." If he accepted it, then nothing would remain of the man he'd tried so hard to emulate.

Lord Renfrew was regarding him sympathetically. "I

wouldn't have told you any of this if I didn't feel I had to. To continue: I emerged from the hospital tent the next morning wondering how the devil I could salvage anything out of this disaster. Then I discovered that rumours had already begun to circulate about Gordon's miraculous survival. They were as far removed from the truth as they could be. Some of the few who had survived Majuba said that they'd witnessed their officer charging the Boers single-handedly, brandishing his sword. Someone else said that they'd actually seen him break clear through the enemy line as the bullets bounced off him. Ridiculous, of course, but that is what they said. Word began to spread that for six months he'd trekked through enemy territory alone, living off the land, fighting every step of the way. Who cared about truth when morale needed lifting? His exploits quickly became magnified in the telling, and throughout the camp soldiers' heads were lifted high again and shoulders squared again as a result. Glasses were raised and toasts drunk to Sir Gordon Harringdon, the man who had made a fool of the Boers. The wretched defeat at Majuba was no longer the humiliation it was first thought to be because of the spirit of one man and his will to survive."

Evelyn sat with his head bowed, no longer protesting his disbelief.

"I'm sorry, Evelyn. We did try to protect you from this – your mother and I. That afternoon, a newspaper reporter arrived in the camp. He wrote for *The Chronicle*. I hesitate to describe it as a newspaper, but it had a high circulation among the middle classes. It suited my purpose, perfectly. I told him that I'd heard the amazing story of his survival from Sir Gordon Harringdon himself. The exploits the men were boasting about were true, every one of them."

"So he was no more than a puppet, with you and mother pulling the strings," Evelyn said, bitterly.

"To be fair to your father, he was an unwilling accomplice

in the lie. It was a struggle to persuade him to go along with it at first. The poor wretch said he deserved to be punished, even shot. I told him to think it through. The public outcry would be devastating. It would be like losing the war all over again and the Harringdons would become a spent force in the political arena forever."

Renfrew poured Evelyn a whisky. He drank it straight down. "Did my father kill Montrecourt?"

"Yes, but it was in defence of Hortense. Your father had just learnt that she was having his baby. He knew it was his because she hadn't been with another man for months. She was loyal to your father, despite Montrecourt's beatings. I think she actually loved him. When Montrecourt found out about the baby, he wanted to get rid of it. Gordon saw him punching her in the stomach. He lashed out at him, but he was still weak. When Montrecourt attacked him, he took the rifle that Hortense thrust into his hands and shot him. They buried the body together. He paid for her passage to France where she had the baby."

"And mother saw to the rest," murmured Evelyn.

"They were strange times, Evelyn. Strange things happened."

"Yes, and Marie and I are still paying for them," Evelyn said quietly.

Renfrew offered Evelyn a cigarette, but his hand was shaking so much he could hardly hold it still enough for Renfrew to light.

"It's not a very edifying story, is it?" Renfrew took a cigarette, too. "If it becomes known that your family and the Montrecourts are linked, then curiosity will be aroused. Who knows what the gutter press will unearth? Even the smallest hint of what lies hidden will destroy your mother, your sister's family and you, and leave you in no position to help Marie Montrecourt. She will surely become the first casualty of any scandal."

"I can't just walk away from her," muttered Evelyn stubbornly.

"I'm not suggesting that you do. I have an idea. We can hire the best counsel in the country to defend her. You can pay for it by all means, but let me do the arranging. I presume the young woman knows nothing about her relationship to you?"

Evelyn shook his head. "It shames me to say it, but she still believes her parents saved my father's life and, out of gratitude, he paid for her education and arranged for her marriage."

"Let it stay that way. Distance yourself from this business."

"She will know that I'm paying for her defence. Who else would it be?"

"Will she talk about it?"

"No. She promised she would remain silent about my family's involvement with her and I know she will keep her word."

"Let's hope so. Evelyn, I know this will be hard for you, but you have to finally sever the ties between the Harringdons and the Montrecourts. Let the past be buried forever. It's in her best interests, too."

Too overcome to speak, Evelyn simply nodded.

CHAPTER TWENTY-THREE

Armley Gaol was a grim, grey stone building, whose crenellated walls could be seen for miles. Built in 1847, its four wings spread out like a cross from a central tower. This was Marie's home while the case against her was being prepared. Regular journeys to the police court in the Black Maria were her only escape; but now that the magistrate had concluded there was a *prima facie* case for her to answer, even that escape was closed to her.

Her cell was long and narrow, like a horse trough. The window was high up, set close to the ceiling, so that nothing was visible from it. There were no chairs, no tables, just a narrow bench and a small bed, and it was extremely cold. Marie pulled a blanket around her to try to keep herself warm.

She didn't know what to do. Like an animal caught in a trap, she waited for things to take their course. She didn't say she was guilty, but she didn't say she wasn't guilty either. She repeated she didn't know what had happened. Maybe it would all go away.

She'd been thinking a great deal about Evelyn during these last days. By now, he would know every detail of the squalid reality of her life with Stanley. The newspapers had made much of it. Would he be shocked? Would he despise her? Would he wish they'd never met?

"You've got a visitor."

A wardress had opened the door of her cell and Marie peered through the gloom. She could only vaguely make out the figure of a man. He towered over the wardress, who stood aside to let him pass. He took off his hat, bending almost double to enter. His mane of white hair ended just above the velvet collar of his grey suit. He wore a bright red waistcoat crisscrossed by a thin black trellis of lines.

"Thank you." He smiled charmingly at the wardress, who ignored him, clanged the door shut as she left and turned the key. He turned his attention to Marie. "Good morning. My name is Sir Herbert Manners and I may be about to act in your defence."

Startled, she said: "But I don't know you."

"I'll try not to let that statement offend me." He looked for somewhere to lay down his hat. He finally gave up the search and decided to keep it on his knee as he sat on the bench beside Marie. After studying her closely, he said, "You appear to have friends in high places."

She stared at him in astonishment. Surely there was only one person to whom that could refer to – Evelyn? It must mean he hadn't abandoned her. She leant forward eagerly. "Did *he* send you?"

"I'm sorry, my client doesn't wish to have their name revealed."

She sat back. She was being foolish. Of course, his name mustn't be mentioned. Everything she'd done had been to protect his name. He must remain removed from her. She wouldn't have it any other way. She became aware of Sir Herbert's scrutiny, to the point of feeling uncomfortable.

"Yes," he said, suddenly, "I'm sure we're going to get along just fine. Now, tell me, what happened on the night your husband died?"

It was the question she'd been dreading the most, though she knew she would have to face it at some point. She thought of Evelyn. He still believed in her and she mustn't let him down. "I think my husband must have killed himself. I don't know how."

Sir Herbert nodded encouragingly. "Just tell me what happened."

He listened with head bowed and eyes closed as she told him the story that Dr Hornby had repeated at the inquest. It was a story she had gone over and over again in her mind. She had sat with Stanley for part of the night, but then she had gone to bed. When she had called in to see him the next morning, he was dead.

He listened without saying a word. When she'd finished, he sat for at least another five minutes without speaking. Then he nodded, stood up and said pleasantly: "Thank you so much, Mrs Minton."

She watched in some confusion as he tapped on the door of the cell and left without a further word when it was opened. Was he going straight back to report to Evelyn? Had he believed her or not? Why hadn't he said anything?

Much later, when a meal of potatoes and gravy was brought to her, the wardress asked: "So is he taking your case, then? Sir Herbert Manners?"

"You know who he is?"

"I've heard of him. Who hasn't?"

"I haven't and I don't know what he's going to do." Marie pushed the food away, untouched.

"You'd better hope he is. He's the only chance you have of getting off."

*

Sir Herbert called on her the next day and the one after that, each time firing questions at her like bullets from a gun.

"What was your relationship with Peter Minton?"

"A friend and companion," she said.

"Nothing more?"

"Nothing more, I swear."

He questioned her about her life at The Laurels. She talked about the loneliness; how Stanley's behavior had changed after the death of their baby and how she realised now it was the effect of the chloroform on him. She talked of his violence towards her.

"Why didn't you tell anyone?" he asked.

"I was too ashamed."

And still the questions flowed, so that by the end of the third day she was becoming worn out by the constant bombardment. As he stood up to go, with his usual "Thank you, so much," she said in exasperation: "That's all you ever say. You have to tell me if you're going to take my case or not."

"Yes, of course I'm going to take your case." His tone reflected mild surprise. "I've always enjoyed a challenge."

*

Monday 2nd October was a bleak day. It was damp, with the promise of more rain to come, but still the crowds assembled outside the Crown Court. The Garibaldi Street Poisoning trial was about to begin and public interest in it was running high.

Sir Herbert Manners cut something of a flamboyant figure, with his white hair flowing from beneath a silk hat, as he climbed the stone steps to the line of classical columns fronting the baroque façade of the Town Hall.

Manners looked around him. He would have to force his way through the crowds who were waiting for the courtroom doors to open. He had known the case would create some interest, but he hadn't expected quite so many people to turn up. The whole of Fleet Street must be here.

The Town Hall's domed vestibule echoed with the footsteps of lawyers, solicitors and barristers scurrying like black beetles across the marble floor, piles of papers and law books clutched under their arms. Sir Herbert spotted one of his junior counsels.

"Mr Lawler." He crossed the floor to shake his hand. "Everything in order?"

"Indeed, Sir Herbert."

"Is Mrs Minton here?"

"In the Bridewell downstairs. She was brought in through a side entrance."

"Good, then let's go inside and face the opposition."

Lawler pushed open the double doors of the courtroom and Sir Herbert swept through them into his favourite arena.

*

In contrast to the activity above, the prison in the basement was silent. Marie sat alone in one of its holding cells. She was more frightened than she'd ever been in her life. She found it impossible to keep a limb still. She walked up and down incessantly – as the cell was very small, it didn't take many steps to cover it. The white flagged floors were damp and the whitewashed walls were icy cold. There was only a slit for a window, so there was very little daylight. Even her cell in Armley Gaol was more comfortable than this.

She stopped, listening to the footsteps echoing along the stone corridor. They were approaching her cell. It must be time. The key turned slowly in the lock. The door of the cell swung open. "You ready?" the wardress asked, her face expressionless. "Come on, they're waiting for you."

For a moment, Marie wondered what would happen if she refused to move, if she sat on the floor of the cell and refused to go with her, but she didn't. Instead, head bowed, she obediently followed her gaoler along the tiled corridor, through the spiked door and up the steps that lead to the dock. As she entered the wooden cubicle in which she would have to sit and listen to the evidence given against her, she caught her first glimpse of the courtroom and was overwhelmed by the huge number of faces, which were all turned towards her. Women stood up at the back of the court to get a better view.

She had dressed carefully, as instructed by Sir Herbert, and was wearing a simple dress of black silk. She looked, as he had hoped she would, too young to be a widow. Her hair was swept up into two wings and on top was perched a small hat. A feather curled over its short brim, but there was no veil.

"I want everyone to see your face," Sir Herbert had said. "Give no one the opportunity to say you have anything to hide."

The counsel for the prosecution was Mr Henry Redcar KC, a short, balding man. He had made it known that he believed the case would be over in a few days, as he was convinced there was little doubt as to the accused's guilt. He said he'd been astonished to learn that Sir Herbert Manners had agreed to act in her defence, but assumed it was the case's notoriety that had attracted him. It was well known that Sir Herbert would do anything, go anywhere, for publicity and he hoped the man wouldn't indulge in his usual long-winded rhetoric. Redcar had arranged to take his wife on holiday to Nice the following week. The arrangements had greatly preoccupied him during the run up to this case. It had meant leaving a great deal of the preparatory work to his junior counsel.

Mr Justice Pollard, resplendent in scarlet robes, was in charge of proceedings. He was a courteous man with a reputation for toughness. Once he had taken his seat, he wasted no time in signalling for the proceedings to commence.

The opening formalities were gone through, the jury chosen and Marie was asked to stand. As she rose, she stumbled a little. The wardress sitting beside her put out a hand to steady her. She was asked how she would plead. "Guilty or not guilty of the charge of murder?"

She tried to keep her voice firm as she replied: "Not Guilty."

A murmur of anticipation ran through the court.

The Prosecuting Counsel gave his long opening speech outlining the grounds for Marie's arrest. He touched upon the circumstances of her marriage and the events leading up to Stanley's death. He concluded by saying: "We are not here to discover the cause of death. There can be little doubt that the inquest proved that Stanley Minton died from the effects of chloroform in his stomach. What we are here to discover now is how that chloroform was administered and by whom."

"There are only three ways that could have been done," he said, facing the jury. "The deceased took it himself with a view to destroying his life. Why would he do that? You will hear that his difficulties were behind him; he was starting a new life. Why would he take such a painful way out? Swallowing chloroform, even when mixed with brandy, would be painful."

Marie looked down at the floor as she listened to his description of the events that would haunt her for the rest of her life.

"Was it then an accident? Again, for the reasons already stated, I will show that the chloroform could not have been swallowed accidentally. The only reasonable explanation for how the chloroform found its way into the deceased's stomach, therefore, is that it was administered by some other person. And we will prove that person was his wife."

Marie was aware that she was under intense scrutiny from everyone around her. Redcar then warned the jury to keep an open mind, to ignore what they may have read in the newspapers. They must judge the accused by the evidence given in the court alone. When he sat down, all attention swung to Sir Herbert.

"My Lord," Manners rose languidly to his feet. "I reserve the right to give my opening speech after I have heard the full case for the prosecution."

There was a murmur of surprise from the assembly and

Marie clasped her hands tightly in her lap. Was there to be a repetition of the inquest? After a moment, she asked the wardress for some paper and scribbled a note to Sir Herbert, which was passed down to him by his legal team who were sitting in front of the dock. He opened it and read: *I beg you, please do not abandon me*. To Marie's alarm, he folded it and pushed it into his waistcoat pocket without turning around.

The first witness called by the counsel for the prosecution was Edwin. Marie watched as he was helped into the witness box by one of the ushers, a chair was provided for him and a glass of water placed close to hand. He would spare her nothing, she knew that. He took the oath in a voice that could scarcely be heard.

Redcar rose to his feet. "Mr Minton, if you would be so kind, please inform the court how you first met the accused."

Edwin retold the story of Stanley's marriage and of the distrust that his dead wife had always felt towards the bride. He had a tendency to drift away from the point and it was obvious to everyone in the court that he had been affected greatly by the tragedy of his son's death. He rambled on at some length about Marie's "dabbling with unnatural remedies".

"Edith wouldn't touch the stuff," he said. "Who is that woman to tell people what's wrong with them? She's not a doctor."

Gently, Redcar guided Edwin back to the moment he'd discovered that his son was dead. As Edwin relived it, his voice broke and he paused while he wiped his eyes with his handkerchief. "She kept me away. She never told me he was ill. She tried to stop me seeing him even after he was dead. If I hadn't made a scene, she would have had my son buried without anyone being the wiser."

Marie saw a look of sympathy on the face of every juror and some angry glances were directed towards her from the galleries.

"Thank you, Mr Minton," said Redcar, resuming his seat.

Sir Herbert Manners rose. "No questions," he said.

There was a murmur of surprise in the court and Marie closed her eyes in despair. This was one of the most hostile witnesses and Sir Herbert hadn't challenged his testimony. She was unaware of his reason for it, which was that he believed putting the old man under pressure would strengthen the jury's sympathy for him and be of no benefit to her at all.

She knew that the next witness would be equally hostile. Geoffrey Minton swore the oath in a loud, clear voice. He was obviously in a belligerent mood and eager for the questioning to begin.

The counsel for the prosecution asked Geoffrey to tell the court how Marie Montrecourt, as she used to be called, came to be a member of the Minton family, and Geoffrey related how he had been approached by the solicitor, John Pickard, and asked to arrange a meeting between Marie and Stanley. It took place at a small dinner party held at Devonshire Place.

"It was the worst thing I ever did. As soon as she joined the family, she created trouble. She left a trail of destruction behind her." He warmed to his theme. "It was because of her that Ma died."

To Marie's relief, Sir Herbert was on his feet at last. "My Lord, I feel I really must object to that statement. Mrs Edith Minton's death is not in question. There were no suspicious circumstances surrounding it, as far as I can ascertain."

The judge turned to Geoffrey. "Are you suggesting there was something suspicious about the death of Edith Minton?"

"Well, no. Not really. Not as such."

"Then I would ask you to make your answers relevant to the questions asked and not to speculate," said Judge Pollard, firmly.

Redcar immediately switched tack. "Mrs Edith Minton died of a heart attack, I believe?"

"My Lord—" Sir Herbert hauled himself to his feet again.

Judge Pollard held up his hand to stop him. He turned to the Prosecuting Counsel. "Is there some relevance to this questioning, Mr Redcar?" he asked.

"Yes, my Lord. I intend to show that the accused is not as innocent as the defence counsel will try to prove, and the circumstances surrounding Edith Minton's death will make that clear."

Marie glanced nervously towards Sir Herbert. *Where was this leading?*

"Very well. I will allow it. You may answer," said Mr Justice Pollard, after a moment's consideration.

"Peter, my younger brother, spent a great deal of time with her… with the accused," Geoffrey said. "He was living at home at the time. They used to go out walking together while Stanley was at work. They went out on the moors. One day, when Ma was ill upstairs in bed, she came down and surprised the two of them. She found that woman and Peter…" he tailed off, not knowing how to put it, "in a compromising situation."

He was repeating Peter's version. She had warned Sir Herbert about Peter's lie, but she'd never thought Geoffrey would repeat it in public.

"And how do you know this?" Redcar asked.

"Peter told me."

"It was plain to your mother that they were in the middle of a physical act – that there was a carnal relationship between the accused and her husband's younger brother? Is that what you're saying?" Redcar asked.

"Yes, sir. It killed Ma when she saw them together."

There was a murmur of condemnation from the courtroom. The jurors looked at her with contempt. She could feel her cheeks flaming. Sir Herbert scowled, then shuffled his papers on the desk in front of him.

Geoffrey was aware of the stir his words had caused and

was eager to take advantage of it. "Peter told me he needed to leave for America to get away from her, because she wouldn't leave him alone."

Marie was desperate to protest. If Evelyn read this in tomorrow's newspapers, it would cause him great distress. To her relief, Sir Herbert rose to his feet.

"Forgive me, my Lord, but I want to enquire if we are to hear this testimony from Mr Peter Minton himself, or does this tarradiddle only exist in the imagination of the witness? One who has displayed nothing but antagonism towards my client?"

"I was about to challenge the evidence myself, Sir Herbert, if you will let me draw breath." The judge swung the question in the Prosecuting Counsel's direction. "Mr Redcar?"

It was Redcar's turn to shuffle his papers. He glanced at his junior, who shook his head. "We have tried to make contact with Mr Peter Minton, my Lord. He was in New York. It would appear that soon after receiving our telegram, Mr Peter Minton left that city. I believe he was heading west, but that is such a vast territory and communications there are so rudimentary that we've lost all trace of him."

Sir Herbert Manners smiled at Redcar, having already discovered that for himself.

Marie saw the smile. This was all just a game to them; to these men who held her future in their hands, it was just a case of scoring of points.

Mr Justice Pollard then said, firmly: "Without the witness, I suggest you abandon that line of questioning. And I advise the jury to ignore it."

A game, Marie repeated to herself. She knew there was no way the jury could forget what they had just heard.

Redcar turned back to Geoffrey. "Mr Minton, have you any other reason to think there was an affair between your younger brother and the accused?"

The judge opened his mouth in reproof, but Geoffrey swiftly replied: "Well, she admitted lying about what they were doing on the night Ma died. She said at first that they were playing the piano, then, after Ma died, she told me mother had seen them in a compromising situation."

Sir Herbert turned to look at his client and she knew such inconsistency must give credence to the lie. Why had she allowed Peter's first explanation to go unchallenged? She should have told the truth immediately. That Peter had tried to seduce *her*, not the other way around.

Redcar continued: "And did the deceased know of his wife's involvement with his brother? Did you tell Stanley?"

"No. I knew it would destroy him. He loved his wife."

Remembering Stanley's violence towards her, Marie reflected that it was a strange kind of love.

"And as far as you know, Stanley was never made aware of the circumstances?" continued Redcar.

"He would have thrown her out of the house if he'd known."

"And if he *had* known, might he have fallen into despair?"

"He wouldn't have killed himself, if that's what you mean."

"Very well. Were you aware that the deceased was in financial difficulty?"

"He was, in the past, which is why he sold The Emporium, but he'd just bought a new business. He was starting again. He was very excited about it."

"So you can see no reason why he should take his own life?"

"No. He had everything to live for."

"Were you aware he was inhaling chloroform?"

"He never did." He saw the judge was about to speak. "Well, I didn't witness it. If that happened, it happened when she was by herself with him – after they moved here to Leeds. Maybe that's why she wanted Pa out of the way. She fooled around with pills and potions, didn't she? Why not with chloroform?"

Sir Herbert was on his feet. "My Lord, this is too farfetched."

"Thank you, Mr Minton," Redcar said quickly. "That's all I have to ask. Sir Herbert may have one or two questions for you,"

Sir Herbert surveyed Geoffrey for a moment without speaking. The silence was intense and Marie, for one, found it unbearable.

"This is an extremely difficult time for you, Mr Minton, I appreciate that, and I offer you my sincere condolences." Geoffrey nodded, warily. "You are obviously of the opinion that Mrs Minton carries the responsibility for her husband's death?"

"I am," Geoffrey said, emphatically.

"But what would she have to gain from it?" Sir Herbert asked curiously.

"Well…" Geoffrey shrugged.

"Not money. There was very little of it to be had by all accounts and most of it was tied up in this new business venture. Why not wait until he'd built up the business again? Why take steps now when it would leave her penniless?" He turned to the jury. "The marriage between Stanley Minton and Marie Montrecourt was more of a business arrangement than a love match. I have here a copy of an agreement drawn up by Mr John Pickard and signed by Mr Stanley Minton." He held up a document. "It states that money will be paid into Mr Minton's business account when the marriage certificate is signed. It also insists that his wife should remain ignorant of the arrangement. She was a convent girl, unworldly. She was easily persuaded that he was marrying her for love."

Marie was horrified that the contract had been introduced into the case. She had never mentioned any such thing to Sir

Herbert. She prayed Evelyn would not suspect her of betraying his father's request for anonymity. Would Sir Gordon be mentioned by name?

Sir Herbert handed the document to the clerk of the court, who took it to the judge, who in turn passed it on to the jury.

"Mrs Minton certainly brought money with her into the marriage," Sir Herbert continued. "The sum of eight hundred pounds, in fact."

There was a gasp of surprise. Reporters exchanged looks with raised eyebrows. Marie leant forward. He mustn't name Evelyn's father. However, Sir Herbert had no interest in pursuing the source of the money – much to the reporters' frustration. He had a more pressing point to make.

"This eight hundred pounds was lost when her husband's business failed. And his business did fail, have no doubt about that, leaving him virtually penniless – leading to him having to sell The Emporium and his home. It surely had to be in his wife's interests to see the new business in Leeds flourish, as it was her only chance to recoup some of the money from her dowry." He turned to Geoffrey. "As a businessman yourself, you must agree that this was the only way she would receive any return on her money. Isn't that right, Mr Minton?"

"I suppose so."

"You arranged for Mrs Minton to meet Mr Stanley Minton, you say? Why did you agree to that?"

Geoffrey shifted uneasily and glanced towards the judge. "It was suggested to me by Mr Pickard, who was the girl's guardian."

"But why did you agree to it?" pressed Sir Herbert. Geoffrey shrugged. "Let me jog your memory. Was it, perhaps, because Mr Pickard agreed to your demand that you be paid ten per cent of the dowry if you arranged that meeting? Ten per cent of eight hundred pounds means you would receive eighty pounds if the marriage came about. Is that correct?"

"Yes."

The admission was reluctantly made and Marie wondered if Isabelle had been party to that agreement.

"But that was a suggestion made to me by Mr Pickard," Geoffrey added quickly – aware of the murmuring in the court. "It wasn't my idea."

"But you didn't refuse it, did you?"

"I only had Stanley's interest at heart. I knew he needed the money."

And who in his family had her interests at heart, Marie wondered, bitterly.

"Precisely, Stanley needed the money," continued Sir Herbert, "and no one would lend it to him because financially he was heading for bankruptcy. No one in the family told his future wife, though, did they?" He turned to the jury. "I would point out that this was a young girl of eighteen who had spent all her life in a convent. She had no living relatives to guide her. She was ignorant of the world and its ways. I would suggest that this innocence was something the Mintons found very useful."

Geoffrey leant over the edge of the witness box. "It's my opinion that she used her money to buy respectability."

"I'll come to the matter of respectability in a moment, Mr Minton. My client should have had every reason to believe that her money was going into a successful business, which would give her security. In other words, the family lied to her for their own gain. Far from *her* using *you*, I would suggest your family used *her*."

Geoffrey shook his head vehemently from side to side.

"I would suggest your family's dislike of her stemmed from the moment they took possession of her money. And far from Mrs Minton gaining from her marriage, I would suggest she lost everything she had. Therefore, the only future for her lay in her husband recouping his losses. It was not in her interest to cut his life short."

"What she got out of the marriage was my family's good name and support," Geoffrey shouted and Mr Justice Pollard banged his gavel on his desk.

"Please, Mr Minton. Please control yourself."

Geoffrey fell silent. It took a little longer for the commotion in the body of the court to subside. For the first time, Marie sensed a wave of sympathy.

Sir Herbert's tone became pleasantly conversational. "Let's look further into this respectability you say Mrs Minton was so desperate to acquire. I believe that Mr Peter Minton once worked for Harcrofts Mill in Bradford?"

Geoffrey looked warily at the Prosecuting Counsel, who looked equally baffled.

"Yes," he replied.

"Does this have relevance to the matter in hand?" the judge asked.

"It does, my Lord."

"Very well."

"I have here papers and statements," Sir Herbert held up the documents, "which I will pass to the bench, from Mr Harcroft. They confirm that Mr Peter Minton stole fifty guineas from the company safe in order to finance his gambling. I will call Mr Harcroft if necessary?"

Poor Peter, thought Marie, *his lies were finally catching up with him.*

Redcar was on his feet. "I must protest, my Lord, that this is irrelevant."

"My Lord, this is very relevant," Sir Herbert said, firmly. "Peter Minton's name has been introduced into this case by his brother Geoffrey to blacken my client's character. I intend to show that the reverse is true."

After a moment's thought, Mr Justice Pollard nodded. "Very well, but get to the point quickly, Sir Herbert."

"This young man, Peter Minton, had been in constant

trouble. The money was refunded to the mill and Mr Harcroft agreed not to prosecute, but he sacked him and gave him no references. This left the young man unable to find a job. He was offered one in New York, but he needed money to get there. I suggest, Mr Minton, that your brother lied to you about my client's attempted seduction in order to persuade you to pay for his passage – and that's what you did. Isn't that correct?"

Marie was on the edge of her seat, waiting for Geoffrey's reply. He surely had no choice but to admit it.

There was a long pause and then Geoffrey mumbled: "I gave him money for his passage, yes." Marie looked at the jury triumphantly, but their attention was still on Geoffrey, who immediately returned to the attack. "But they *were* having an affair. They weren't playing the piano the night Ma died, so what were they doing?"

"Were you shocked when Peter told you his final version of what had happened?" Sir Herbert asked. "That the accused had tried to seduce him?"

"I was disgusted."

"But his first story was that they were playing the piano. Why believe the one rather than the other? Because it suited you to believe the final version? You decided to keep quiet about it and not tell Stanley. Why?"

Geoffrey flushed. "I didn't think our Stanley could cope with the truth."

"Because he was already depressed about the death of his mother and the failure of his business," Sir Herbert suggested, and pressed on before Geoffrey could express an opinion. "Later on, there was the added stress of the death of the baby that his wife was carrying. That would be enough to drive anyone to despair." Geoffrey shook his head in denial, but Sir Herbert had no intention of letting him speak yet. "You've admitted to enticing an innocent and vulnerable young woman into a marriage with your brother so that you could profit from it. After taking her money, you, like the rest of your family, abandoned her to a husband who was killing himself with chloroform, who used violence against her, and to a brother-in-law who tried to take advantage of her innocence."

"She wasn't innocent. She's never been innocent." Geoffrey was incensed to find himself on trial like this. "Peter didn't have to force his attentions on her, did he? He told me so. And as for this miscarriage, I believe the baby wasn't Stanley's. I believe it was Peter's. And I believe she got rid of it."

Marie was so distressed by such a shocking accusation that she covered her face with her hands.

"You know that to be true?" Judge Pollard asked.

Geoffrey thumped the rail in front of him. "I suspect it."

"Did Peter ever admit to it?" Sir Herbert remained calm.

Geoffrey failed to reply. The judge turned to the jury. "No regard must be paid to this witness's last statement."

Marie gripped the rail in front of her as the courtroom echoed with the crowd's shocked reactions. One of the wardresses leant forward to ask her if she was all right. She nodded, struggling to sit upright. She had longed for that baby, more than she had longed for anything. How could anyone believe she would have harmed it?

Sir Herbert raised his voice over the noise in the courtroom. "My Lord, this is an abomination. I must insist that there is no foundation for such a statement. No proof. It's an attempt to blacken the character of this innocent young woman in the eyes of the jury. Every statement he's made has been designed to do that."

"I have said that I agree. I have asked that the jury will disregard it."

Marie sank back in her chair, her eyes closed. She wasn't sure she could take much more.

Excused from the witness box, and aware of the sorry

figure he'd cut, Geoffrey hurried from the court to take refuge in The George across the street from the Town Hall.

After the dramatic revelations made by Geoffrey, it was something of an anti-climax when Martin Godson was called to give evidence. He confirmed that Stanley had lost money on the tea room and The Emporium, but that he'd received an excited letter from Stanley a week before he'd died, detailing his future plans.

"Not the letter of a man about to commit suicide then?" Redcar said, with which Martin agreed wholeheartedly.

Sir Herbert rose to ask Martin why he had left Stanley's employ and Martin reluctantly admitted that Stanley had been getting difficult to work with.

"Didn't you say at the inquest that you were concerned about his state of mind?" Martin acknowledged that he had. "You asked for an increase in your wage, didn't you, and he refused? You thought he was going bankrupt, didn't you?"

"For a while, but I was proved wrong," he added quickly. "After he sold The Emporium, everything was all right."

"And how do you know that?"

"Because of the letter he sent me, like I said."

Sir Herbert addressed the jury, "We know that the deceased was under the influence of chloroform and that this can result in mood swings that range from the suicidal to the euphoric in the space of a few hours. The inability to face up to reality is also recognised behaviour of an addict."

Jenny Godson was called by Redcar and she described the walks she used to take with Marie. She admitted that once Peter joined them, she'd begun to feel excluded and had stopped accompanying them. "I felt awkward in their company."

"So after that, after your withdrawal from those long walks on the moors, taken on a regular basis, they were left with just each other for company. But there was another reason why you felt awkward in Mrs Minton's company, wasn't there,

Mrs Godson?" Jenny stared down at the floor. "Mrs Godson?" Redcar prompted.

"Yes. She… er… she has books. She showed me books that were not right for a lady to look at. I told my husband, Martin, and he said it wasn't right and that I shouldn't go back to the house."

Sir Herbert was on his feet. "My Lord, Mr Redcar is leading every witness into blackening Mrs Minton's character. He's leading the witnesses."

"I disagree, Sir Herbert," Judge Pollard said firmly. "If I think he is leading the witness, I will intervene."

"Thank you, my Lord," Redcar said. "My learned friend is intending to portray the accused as a naïve young convent girl, and it's my intention to prove that she is certainly no such thing." He turned back to address Jenny. "What was it about these books you found so shocking?"

"There were pictures and drawings of intimate parts of the body," Jenny mumbled, wishing she could disappear.

"Intimate drawings of the male body and the female body?"

"Yes," Jenny said faintly.

Marie remembered Jenny's reaction when she'd shown her the books. She had been trying to help her, not alarm her.

Taking pity on her obvious embarrassment, Redcar said: "I won't press you further, but these are the books, my Lord." He waved his junior counsel to hand them to the clerk. "Detective Inspector Fowler found them in Mrs Minton's bedroom. They are books of a sexually explicit nature. *Esoteric Anthropology* by T.J. Nicols has graphic descriptions and drawings of the naked body, and expresses a dubious morality. The other is *Exploring the Human Form* by Anne Robin, a most indecent book as you will see."

Some of the ladies present surreptitiously made a note of

their titles as Redcar stood down. Marie shook her head in amazement. The books were accepted medical texts, surely he understood that? Sir Herbert rose and pressed Jenny to describe to the jury any scandalous or suggestive incidents she'd observed between Peter Minton and his client on their walks.

Jenny thought deeply and then shook her head. "Nothing scandalous, no. They just seemed to laugh a great deal and I couldn't always follow what they were saying. As I said, I felt excluded."

"Before the arrival of Peter Minton, you used these walks to confide in Mrs Minton, didn't you?"

Jenny glanced sharply at Marie, who frowned at Sir Herbert. What had passed between her and Jenny was private and she had told Sir Herbert so. "If you are to survive, I need to know everything," he'd said to her. So Marie had disclosed how Jenny had expressed concern for baby Ralph. How worried she had been about his deformed foot.

After a pause, Jenny said: "Yes, I suppose I did confide in her."

"And that was harder for you to do with Mr Peter Minton around?" Jenny nodded. "So the point of these walks, as far as you were concerned, had ended. That was the reason you didn't go on them anymore, perhaps? For your own personal reasons; nothing to do with their behaviour?"

"I don't know what you mean?"

"Neither do I," the judge said, with some irritation.

"The books that Mrs Minton showed you. Why did she show them to you?" Jenny hesitated again. "Let me help you remember. Your child was born with a club foot, wasn't he?"

Marie looked at him in horror and Jenny began to show symptoms of distress.

"I told Mrs Minton that in confidence."

"And she told me in confidence," Sir Herbert said coolly, "and now I'm breaking that confidence, because Mrs Minton is on trial for her life."

Jenny brushed away a tear and her voice broke as she said: "He was, yes."

"These were medical books that Mrs Minton was showing you, weren't they? And she was trying to help you to understand why the foot was deformed, and trying to advise you on what a surgeon might do to cure it?"

"I don't know. I was so embarrassed by the books that I didn't listen. I made my excuses and left."

Marie sensed compassion in the courtroom for Jenny and became aware of a wave of animosity directed towards her. Sir Herbert had handled this witness badly and he knew it. "I have no more questions, my Lord."

After ascertaining that Redcar had no desire to recall the witness, the judge declared an end to that day's proceedings. The court emptied slowly as a heated discussion divided the departing crowd – some had sympathy for the accused, others angrily condemned her.

For Marie, the day had been one unbroken nightmare. She wasn't sure how many more days she could endure. She tried to stand, but fell back weakly. One of the wardresses, seeing her difficulty, took pity on her.

"Come on, Mrs Minton, lean on me," she said.

Gratefully, Marie took her arm.

*

Evelyn looked up as Wilson showed Renfrew into the library at Carlton Terrace. "I received your note, Lord Renfrew. You've been abroad?"

"Yes," Renfrew said. "Got back yesterday." He noted the signs of strain on Evelyn's face. His desk was covered with newspapers, and every one of them was opened on an account of the trial.

"Your note said you needed to see me urgently?" Evelyn said.

"Yes. It's about the..." Renfrew gestured towards the newspapers "court case."

"I can't even imagine what she must be going through." Evelyn had barely slept since the trial had begun. "My only comfort is that Sir Herbert appears to be doing a reasonable job, given the circumstances. I still feel I should be there."

"No, you should not," Renfrew said in alarm. "Now more than ever you need to remain distant and objective. The gutter press would pounce on the slightest hint of a connection between your family and hers. They're a pack of hyenas. God knows what they would make of it, but I'm certain they'd find some way of using it to destroy her, too."

"Men like Harlik would," Evelyn said angrily. "He's already sniffed out some of the dirt. He knows I was looking for Marie. I'm astonished he hasn't gone into print with that already."

"Don't worry about Harlik," Renfrew said grimly. "He's in the debtor's prison where he can do no harm."

Evelyn was about to question Renfrew further about that, but the look on his lordship's face suggested that a query wouldn't be welcome. There were more pressing problems to worry about.

"Everything seems to be under control," Evelyn said instead. "And I'm not ungrateful for your help, Lord Renfrew. You made a wise choice when you hired Sir Herbert Manners."

Renfrew cleared his throat, uneasily. "Yes – there's just one problem, Evelyn. Sir Herbert wasn't my choice. Before I went abroad, I approached Sir Russell Walters and asked *him* to take the case. I assumed, as I hadn't heard from him, that this was going ahead. I only discovered on my return that Sir Herbert Manners was acting for the girl instead."

It took a moment for Evelyn to take it in. "So who's paying for his services?"

"I don't know and I can't find out. More worrying still, Manners is a friend of Campbell-Bannerman and a passionate Whig supporter. So I ask myself: is this a political move? Has Sir Herbert discovered something about Majuba, about Hortense, about your father, which he intends to use against us at some stage?

Evelyn was unable to contain his disgust. "For God's sake, this is Marie's life we're talking about – not some political matter." He began to pace the room.

"Calm down, sir," Renfrew commanded and Evelyn attempted to obey. "At the moment, there's no indication that Manners is acting against her interests or ours. He knew about the marriage agreement between Stanley and Pickard, but he hasn't pursued it. I believe he knows nothing about your family's involvement. Pickard has continued to remain discreet. There may be no political agenda at all."

"But who is paying him, and why?"

Renfrew shrugged. "No idea, but at the moment not even Sir Russell Walters could serve us better."

CHAPTER TWENTY-FOUR

The trial was now in its third day and curious onlookers had gathered outside the Town Hall to gaze at the major players as they arrived. They had no tickets to get them into the courtroom itself. For those inside the court, there was the hope of more sensational revelations to come.

Mr Gilpin's testimony had already created a stir. In the view of the reporters, the disappearing chloroform bottle was damning evidence against Marie – followed as it was by the laundry woman's statement that, after she'd laid out Stanley's body, she had changed and washed the sheets on the deceased's bed. There was no doubt in their minds that Marie had something to hide.

"Was it your suggestion to Mrs Minton to clean the sheets?" Redcar had asked. The laundry woman replied that it was. "And did Mrs Minton accept the offer eagerly?" he asked.

"She seemed very pleased with the idea," agreed Mrs Wilkinson.

Marie couldn't understand why that was so important, until Sir Herbert took Redcar's place.

His only question was to ask the witness if there was any sign of vomit on the sheets, to which she replied: "Not that I noticed."

It was Detective Inspector Fowler's turn to give evidence today. He repeated the testimony he'd given at the inquest, telling how he had searched the Minton's rooms and found no trace of the blue bottle that Mr Gilpin swore he saw on the mantelpiece.

"The rooms were locked immediately after the post-mortem and a thorough search done. There was no glass bottle. So between six o'clock when Mr Gilpin saw it, and eight o'clock when Dr Hornby arrived, it was removed from the premises."

"Would the accused have had an opportunity to dispose of the bottle during that period?" Redcar asked.

"Yes, when she left the house to fetch the doctor," Fowler replied.

There was a murmur throughout the crowded gallery. Marie stared straight ahead, her face expressionless. The book, *Farnsworth's Medical Dictionary*, was now being passed to the clerk for the judge and jury to inspect.

"This book was found in Mrs Minton's room. As you will see, the page headed chloroform has obviously been read many times by the accused," Fowler said.

Marie closed her eyes in resignation. She'd explained to Sir Herbert that while she'd been looking up the effects of chloroform, she'd knocked over a bottle of witchhazel and it had made the page stick. The page had torn, and that had made it seem as if she had frequently consulted it.

"Was there anything else found in the bedroom of the accused that gave you cause for concern?" Redcar asked.

"There were several books of a nature I would not expect to find in anyone's bedroom, let alone the bedroom of a well-brought-up young lady."

"What were the books that you found, Detective Inspector?"

"Books of a sexually explicit nature, as has already been described. *Esoteric Anthropology* by T.J. Nicols, and *Exploring the Human Form* by Anne Robin – the latter of which was the subject of a court case for indecency some years ago."

Then it was Sir Herbert's turn to question the policeman. "Detective Inspector Fowler, *Esoteric Anthropology* is considered a serious medical work, is it not? Some people in the medical profession set great store by it."

"Some do, I suppose," Fowler admitted, reluctantly. "Doctors might."

"And as for *Exploring the Human Form* – although a charge of indecency was brought against it, the charge was dropped, was it not? It was accepted as a book that pushed back the boundaries of medicine, isn't that true?"

"It may have been, but I would still not expect to find such books in the bedroom of a young woman."

"Not even if she has an interest in medical matters, as appears to be the case with Mrs Minton?"

"It doesn't seem right to me, that a woman should take an interest in such matters."

There was a stir in the back of the gallery. A woman's voice cried out, "Shame!" Marie glanced up, surprised by this unexpected outburst.

"I will not have interruptions," growled Mr Justice Pollard.

"Thank heavens it isn't Florence Nightingale you have in your sights, Detective Inspector Fowler, or where would our poor soldiers in the Crimea have been?" Sir Herbert asked.

That comment was greeted by cheers and clapping from four women at the back of the gallery, to the annoyance of those around them. It appeared that Mrs Minton's case had caught the attention of the Women's Social and Political Union, and some of its members had managed to get hold of tickets. Mr Justice Pollard made it clear that he intended to make an example of those women if they became unruly.

Dr Hornby was the next to take the stand, and Marie couldn't help feeling sorry for him. He looked like a broken man. He'd shown her kindness and, as a result, he was being made to look like an incompetent fool. He was unhappy to find himself called as a witness for the prosecution and Redcar knew he would have to work hard to get him to admit that he'd been wrong about the ulcer, which was proving to be the case.

"You were so convinced that you were right in your diagnosis that it blinded you to the truth," Redcar accused, continuing his attack on the doctor's professional judgment. "You never suspected Stanley's Minton's use of chloroform, because you'd already made up your mind about the cause of his illness. Perhaps if you'd kept a more open mind, Stanley Minton would still be alive today."

When it was his turn to question the doctor, Sir Herbert had only one point he wanted to make. "How would you describe Mrs Minton's state of mind when her husband died?"

"She was greatly distressed," said Hornby, emphatically.

Of course I was, Marie wanted to shout out. Taking another person's life was repellant to her, but at that moment she'd seen no other way out. Trapped, at the end of a dark tunnel, she had had nowhere to turn. Stanley wouldn't have hesitated to destroy Evelyn, she was sure of that, and he was already killing himself. But how much harm would he inflict on an innocent man before he did?

It was Dr Shelton's turn to give his evidence next. He repeated what he had said at the inquest and in precisely the same order. His final statement, as it was at the inquest, being: "And the smell of chloroform was overpowering when we opened up the stomach."

"And this was the cause of death?" Redcar asked.

"Without a doubt."

"Death was not caused by the perforation of an ulcer as Dr Hornby assumed?"

"There was a small ulcer in the intestines, but it had certainly not burst and was not the cause of death."

Sir Herbert Manners took over the questioning. "Dr Shelton, you said when you opened up the body that you saw no signs of irritation or burning in the windpipe."

"None."

"Nor any signs of vomit?"

"None."

"Isn't that unusual? Wouldn't you expect to see such signs where the deceased had swallowed chloroform?"

"I have never met a case where somebody has swallowed chloroform, but I would expect there to be signs of vomiting, and a burning of the windpipe and mouth."

"Thank you."

It had been completely unplanned, the means she'd used to end her husband's life. It was seeing the Bunsen burner with its thin rubber tube still attached. She'd remembered seeing Sister Grace using a pipette in the infirmary to transfer liquid from one place to another. She would suck it up as if through a straw, put a finger over the top to stop it running out and carry it to its destination. Then she would remove the finger and release it. *A mere teaspoon, if ingested, can kill even a strong man*, Marie had recalled reading in *Farnsworth's Medical Dictionary*.

She dragged her attention back to the courtroom. Dr Moore had now taken the stand. He was describing the contents of the stomach and the discovery, after the removal of the skullcap, of some abnormality in the ventricles of the brain. Complex though his testimony was, there wasn't a sound in the courtroom during it.

When Dr Moore had finished his testimony, Redcar asked: "Is it possible to produce insensibility in someone by making them inhale during sleep?"

"It is."

"Have you done that yourself?"

"No. It's extremely dangerous."

"Danger apart, have you any doubt that it could be done?"

"As I say, with some risk."

"Is it possible to put liquid down the throat of a person who is in that insensible state?"

"Yes. You can put liquid down the throat of a person who is moderately under the influence of chloroform."

"Would there be any insuperable difficulty in putting liquid down someone's throat using a glass or a medicine bottle?"

"Not an insuperable difficulty. No."

"So, it would be possible, if someone was made insensible by inhaling chloroform, in that relaxed state, it would be possible to pour chloroform down the throat of that same person?"

"It would be possible. Yes."

"Thank you."

At the time, she hadn't given a thought to the possibility of failure. All she had thought about was the threat Stanley posed to Evelyn.

Henry Redcar resumed his seat to a murmur of excitement. All eyes, including Marie's, turned to Sir Herbert. He remained seated for a moment, as if deep in thought.

That morning, before the sitting, Sir Henry had called on Marie in the holding cell. He was in a buoyant mood.

"The next few hours are going to be critical for us," he said. "Everything will hang on how I handle things today. We're reaching the heart of the case."

She was already nervous and his visit was making her feel worse. "What do you mean?"

"While Mr Henry Redcar KC has been preoccupied with making arrangements for his holiday in Nice, I've been spending night after night pouring over medical books and consulting with experts, trying to make the effects of chloroform on the body clear to me."

"And are they clear now?" Marie asked.

"They are. I won't lie to you – this is a difficult case, Mrs Minton. One that many of my colleagues thought I was a fool to take on. But if I've judged things correctly, and if I win, with so much set against me, my already formidable reputation will be increased. I shall see you in court."

Without waiting for a reply, he whirled out of the cell, leaving her shaken.

Now, in the courtroom, as Sir Herbert slowly rose to face Dr Moore, Marie clenched her fists until her fingernails cut the palms of her hands. There wasn't a sound in court, apart from the rustle of Sir Herbert's papers.

"I would just like to clarify one or two matters, if you don't mind, Dr Moore, in layman's terms."

Marie, like everyone else in court, scarcely breathed.

"Of course."

"The trachea, or windpipe, is sealed by the epiglottis when swallowing occurs, so that what is swallowed passes into the mouth, down the pharynx or throat, and into the oesophagus and so on into the stomach. The epiglottis, by its closing, prevents whatever has been swallowed from going into the windpipe and then into the lungs and so on. Otherwise a person could choke. Is that correct?"

"That is correct."

"If a person were made insensible, would the normal act of swallowing follow? I mean; in such a relaxed state would the epiglottis still seal the windpipe?"

"If the person were so insensible that there were no involuntary reactions, probably not."

"In which case you would expect some of the liquid to have gone into the windpipe, which would have caused vomiting?"

"Yes."

"You would expect to see burning in the windpipe?"

"Ah, but if the person were only *partly* insensible, then the involuntary closing of the windpipe by the epiglottis may still take place."

"Partly insensible? I see. But chloroform burns, chloroform is bitter, would someone lie there, even if they were partly insensible, and allow such a liquid to be poured down their throat? Would they not cough; would they not react? Would this involuntary reaction, in itself, not open the epiglottis, and thus allow the liquid into the windpipe? Either way, wholly insensible or in part, there should be traces of burning in the windpipe and mouth?"

"Possibly, yes."

"And suppose you yourself had to deal with a sleeping man and it was your object to get down his throat, without him knowing it, a liquid that would cause great pain to his lips and throat. It would be a very difficult and delicate administration, wouldn't it?"

"It would be difficult. It would be very delicate. Sometimes it might fail, but equally, sometimes it might succeed."

"I ask you again, Dr Moore, with the knowledge you have, would you feel confident of being able to administer chloroform in this way?"

"No. Not confident."

"And we must remind ourselves that Mrs Minton knew something of medicine, so she would also understand the problems such a course of action would entail. Thank you, Dr Moore."

Mr Justice Pollard brought the proceedings to an end for the day and the silence that had held during Dr Moore's testimony was suddenly broken by a babble of voices. His evidence was sifted through, torn apart and then put back together again as neighbour argued with neighbour as to its meaning. Scarcely anyone noticed Marie being led out of the dock, down the stairs to the cells and out to the Black Maria that was waiting for her at the side entrance of the Town Hall.

★

Alone again in her cell in Armley Gaol, Marie sat on the bed and stared down at her hands, which were folded in her lap. They hadn't stopped trembling since Dr Moore had taken to the witness stand.

"Someone to see you."

Marie had been so deep in thought she hadn't heard the approaching footsteps. "Ten minutes, that's all." The wardress stepped back and in swept Daphne Senior, her hair shorter than ever, her skirt even more severely cut, her double-breasted jacket revealing a white shirt and brightly coloured tie.

Marie was so stunned to see her she couldn't speak. Daphne moved towards her, arms outstretched. "I was in the courtroom today. I came as soon as I could. To let you know you're not without friends."

Marie slowly rose and then, with a cry, flung herself into Daphne's arms. "I can't believe this. I really can't believe it. I never thought I'd see you again." Her voice was muffled against Daphne's shoulder. "I'm sorry." She pulled back and wiped her eyes with the sleeve of her dress. "I'm being so silly. I know you think it's stupid to cry."

"Cry away," Daphne said airily, peeling off her gloves as she took in the surroundings. "Just don't expect me to join in. Slightly better than my cell at Holloway, but not by much. I was in there for three days for breaking a window."

"Oh Daphne, how did you manage to persuade them to let you in?"

"I have my ways." She sat on the bench and pulled Marie down to sit beside her. "I'm sorry I didn't keep in touch. The WSPU has been taking up all my time. I read about the trial in the newspaper. I couldn't come here earlier because of my commitments, but Sir Herbert appears to know what he's doing."

"Yes, he does, doesn't he?" Marie had her emotions more under control now. "I didn't believe in him at all in the beginning. Now I think he's doing as well as anyone can be expected to do under the circumstances. And I suppose I should be grateful to Evelyn for sending him to me." She'd let the name slip out before she'd realised it and was angry with herself.

Daphne looked astonished. "Evelyn? Who's Evelyn? I sent Sir Herbert to you."

It was Marie's turn to look astonished. She was temporarily at a loss for words. "I'm sorry… I… Sir Herbert never said…"

"He's far too fond of mysteries, that man," said Daphne, with some irritation. "He really is annoying sometimes. He occasionally handles cases for the WSPU. That's why I chose him."

"*You* sent him?" She was bewildered. So Evelyn had nothing to do with it. Did that mean he'd turned his back on her after all? Daphne was oblivious of the impact of her words.

"You mustn't mind my interference," she said. "My father died a year ago and I inherited everything. I'm afraid I'm rather well off now, so I can afford Sir Herbert."

Marie drew breath to say that she couldn't accept her friend's kindness. Daphne mistook her intention and held up her hand.

"No, don't concern yourself about my father's death. He was no great loss to me. He always made it plain that he regretted having a daughter and if there'd been anyone else he could have left his money to, he would have done so. I really won't discuss it anymore."

Given the truth, Daphne's generosity was hard to bear. "I can't let you do this."

"I've done it and it's too late to stop it now," she said, dismissively. "It's tomorrow you give your evidence, am I right?" Marie nodded. "Are you feeling strong enough to face it?"

"Not really." Marie could hear her voice trembling. "At night, when I'm alone, I become very frightened. I start to imagine what it will be like to hang. I can't help it," she said, as Daphne pulled a face. "I wonder, is it painful? Is it quick?"

"Stop it. This is maudlin claptrap – you must snap out of it. Be positive. I come with good news. The WSPU is prepared to give you its full support. We will confront Parliament if necessary."

"No, Daphne. No. No. No. Stop." Marie stood up and put her hands over her ears. She couldn't drag anyone else into this pit she'd dug for herself. "Stop it. If you hired Sir Herbert on behalf of the WSPU so that you can use my case for the Women's Movement, then you've made a terrible mistake. I'm not worthy of it."

"Nonsense. You have to fight this, Marie."

"If the jury find me guilty," Marie said, quietly, "and if the world agrees with them, your movement will face public criticism for becoming involved with my case. It will be accused of clambering on the back of the trial simply to gain publicity. You mustn't let that happen. There are better causes than mine that need your help."

"It's you I want to help and I will not walk away," Daphne said fiercely. "I left you once before to fend for yourself after the fire, and see what a mess you've made of everything. I fled to my father's, my tail between my legs, and you ended up here."

"I'm not here because of you, and you've done more than enough to help me already. You sent me Sir Herbert."

"Do you know why I sent him?" Marie shook her head. "I've never forgotten that you helped me once. You risked your life to drag me out of the fire. You could have left me to fend for myself but you didn't. You stayed by me. Thanks to you I have a future, and I'm trying to repay that debt by giving you a future, too. Sentimental rubbish, I know, but there you have it."

Marie looked at her without speaking for a moment. "You make me feel very ashamed. I'm not a good person, Daphne. I can't seem to..." she hesitated. "I'm not a good person. I think

I was born with a badness inside me." Her voice became a barely audible whisper. "And I'm so frightened of it." Daphne placed an arm around her shoulders. "I have made terrible mistakes. Do you understand me?"

After a moment, Daphne said: "I understand one thing and it's the only thing that matters. Any badness is not of your making. You are a fine person and whatever you do, whatever you say, nothing will ever persuade me otherwise."

Marie was so moved that she couldn't speak. She could never burden Daphne with the truth, not now, although she wondered how much of the truth her friend suspected.

Daphne held her tightly. "I have seen people – lost souls – who, through no fault of their own, have been driven to extremes. But given a second chance, they have achieved remarkable things."

"If they hang me, I won't have a second chance," Marie said quietly.

"Which is precisely why you have to fight."

"Fighting comes naturally to you." Marie was remembering the march on the factory.

"Does it? Perhaps it does." Daphne released Marie and stared silently ahead for a moment. "You know, somebody else said that to me some years ago. Fighting comes naturally... well, something similar."

She paused as a wardress passed, her keys jangling. A distant door slammed shut with a metallic clang.

"It was Dora who said it to me, before she left for India. She said: "If you love me, you'll leave here and come to India with me. And when I said there were still too many battles to fight in England and that I couldn't turn my back on them, she said: "See, you don't really love me. You're only happy when you're fighting for some cause, and then you lose sight of the individual. It's only the fight that matters to you, not the person." And she was right. Only it's too late to tell her that now. I had a letter a few days ago telling me she had died in India. So, you see, I want to prove to her and to myself that I can care more about the person than the cause. And that's why I paid for Sir Herbert to represent you."

Marie took her friend's hand and held it for a while without speaking. "It gets inside your head a place like this, doesn't it?" she said. "In places like this, and at times like this, the past drags you by the heels into darkness."

They remained still, sitting in silence together, side-by-side.

CHAPTER TWENTY-FIVE

The next day Marie left the Black Maria at the side of the Town Hall as usual. As she was being led towards the prison entrance, Daphne suddenly emerged from the group of people who had gathered to catch a glimpse of her. Before she could be stopped, she hugged Marie.

"I'm here for you," she muttered. To her astonishment, Marie felt an envelope being thrust into her hand. Then Daphne was hustled away and Marie, with the envelope concealed in her hand, was ushered to the holding cell.

Once she was alone, she looked at the folded note. It was addressed to Mrs Marie Minton, but she instantly recognised the writing – it was Evelyn's. She tore it open. It began: *I believe in you. Be strong.* Those first two sentences were all she needed to know. *I believe in you. Be strong.* She quickly scanned the rest of the note.

> *As you will be aware by now from the bearer of this message, Daphne hired Sir Herbert to defend you. It had been my intention to hire counsel for you, but she was ahead of me. I have made enquiries and I am now reassured that Sir Herbert's only motive is to serve you well. I made contact with Miss Senior through John Pickard, who she believes is the author of this note. Miss Senior knows nothing of my involvement in this matter. However, if you ever need me, you only have to send me word and I will come at once.*

He hadn't signed it. He was right not to have signed it.

As she heard the footsteps of the wardress approaching the

cell, she thrust the note into the pocket of her dress. Just to know it was there would give her the courage to face what was to come.

★

As Marie entered the court, the first person she saw was Geoffrey Minton. He'd been absent since giving his evidence, but he was back and he'd found a seat that gave him a clear view of the witness box. To her relief, Sir Herbert was already in his place. She waited for him to acknowledge her as usual, but it seemed that he was far too absorbed in the papers in front of him to do that. Redcar was in deep conversation with his legal team and did not look up.

She saw Daphne sitting on the front row of the gallery. Her friend smiled encouragingly at her. Marie nodded an acknowledgement. She slipped her hand into the pocket of her dress to touch Evelyn's note. It gave her comfort. The court rose as Mr Justice Pollard entered.

It was now the turn of the counsel for the defence to call its witnesses, but first Sir Herbert stood to give his delayed speech outlining the case for the defendant. It was a short speech, but he made it with passion and conviction. He would show, he said, that far from being the perpetrator of a terrible crime, Marie Minton had been the victim of a family who had offered her their protection, but instead had taken her money and abandoned her to a husband who had destroyed her life by an evil act of self-destruction. He was a powerful orator and no one moved as he spoke.

"I call Mrs Minton," said Sir Herbert.

There was a stir of excitement through the court as people stood to get a better view of the accused. Her silence during the inquest meant that this was the first time anyone had heard her give a full version of events, and speculation was rife as to what she would say. Silence fell as Marie entered the witness box, extremely pale and visibly nervous. She took the oath, swearing to tell the truth.

When she was little, she used to cross her fingers behind her back so that God would know she had no intention of keeping any promise she was about to make. She didn't think it would help her today. She tried to speak clearly and calmly as she described how she was an orphan who had been brought up in a convent. How she knew nothing about her parents. How, when she'd left the convent and arrived in England, it was to find that a guardian had been charged to look after her and had arranged for her to marry Stanley Minton. She had no idea where the money came from. That was a bitter disappointment to the reporters.

"Would you say you were in love with Stanley Minton when you married him?" Sir Herbert asked.

"I respected him and I believed he respected me." She looked down at her hands, at the wedding band on her finger, at the diamond and sapphire engagement ring that she still wore. "He seemed a kind man and I wanted our marriage to work. You see, I was to be part of a family at last and as I had never known my own parents, that was important to me."

"You moved into The Laurels where Stanley Minton lived with his mother and father?"

"Yes."

"Describe life in The Laurels if you would, Mrs Minton."

She glanced towards Geoffrey Minton who was sitting on the edge of his seat, glowering at her.

"Stanley's family made it clear that they didn't like me. I hadn't realised at the time of our marriage that my husband had accepted money to marry me and that it was to be invested in his business."

She glanced up to the gallery and saw Daphne listening intently. So far, she had told nothing but the truth.

"And no one discussed the state of your husband's business with you?" Sir Herbert prompted.

"No."

"So there was no way you could know that your money was the only thing that was saving him from ruin?"

The judge leant forward to curb the line of questioning, so Sir Herbert changed the subject. He would like, he said, to ask her about her relationship with Peter Minton. The judge subsided and everyone else in court leant forward, eager to hear what she would say.

"Did Mr Peter Minton know that the relationship between you and your husband was in name only?"

She answered awkwardly: "Yes. He knew I was a wife in name only, at that time."

"Would you say that your relationship with Peter Minton was of an intimate nature?"

She paused. A lady in the gallery could be seen fanning herself in some agitation. "No. It was not."

"Did you seduce Peter Minton?"

"No, I did not. It was Peter who pursued me. The night that Mrs Minton died, he asked me to pay for his passage to America. He suggested we run away together, but I looked on him as a pleasant companion and nothing more – and I refused."

"When he left for America, did he write?"

"No."

"He had the money he needed from Geoffrey so he had no further use for you, I suppose?"

There was a ripple of appreciation from the listening crowd. The judge leant forward to admonish him. "Sir Herbert, you are asking her to speculate."

"I apologise, my Lord." He turned back to Marie. "Relations between you and your husband improved, didn't they? How was that?"

"It was the death of his mother that changed his attitude towards me. He missed her and he turned to me for comfort. I moved into his room. I became his wife in truth." Sir Herbert had warned her that he would have to ask questions of an intimate nature, but she felt deeply embarrassed at having to discuss something so personal in public. "I conceived, but the baby died. It was a great shock to us both."

"I am sorry to have to ask you this, Mrs Minton, but who was the father of your baby?"

"My husband, Stanley Minton," she said, clearly and distinctly. She looked straight at Geoffrey as she said it.

"Thank you, Mrs Minton, I wanted to clear that matter up. Your husband's business continued to fail, didn't it, despite the input of your money? Did your husband's health deteriorate at the same time?"

"Yes, it did. He had stomach pains and he said he had an ulcer that was causing his increasing ill health. After we moved to Leeds, however, I discovered that my husband had become addicted to chloroform."

A murmur ran through the court and Marie saw Geoffrey shake his head violently from side to side in denial. She turned away from him to look at the jury and described how she had found the bottle of chloroform.

"When I realised what it was, I went to look it up in *Farnsworth's Medical Dictionary* and what I read frightened me a great deal. I realised it could kill him. That it surely *would* kill him."

"What were your feelings about that?"

"I had committed myself to the marriage. My future lay with my husband. I didn't know how I would manage if he died. We had no money, and I had no other family but Stanley. I suspected I wouldn't receive help from his brother or his father."

"Did you talk to your husband about your discovery of the chloroform?"

"I tried. He refused to discuss it. He said it hadn't killed him yet and nor would it." She hesitated. "He insisted his illness was due to the ulcer, yet he refused to do anything about it. He rejected Dr Hornby's suggestion of surgery. When I challenged him about that…" She broke off and looked up to the gallery. She wasn't sure she could continue. Daphne leant forward willing her to go on.

"Yes, Mrs Minton," Sir Herbert prompted, gently. "You were saying?"

"Yes, I'm sorry." She tried to keep her voice steady. "When I challenged him, he became violent."

Geoffrey was on his feet. He couldn't keep silent any longer. "Lies! She's lying. Everything she has said is a lie. She wants to blacken Stanley's name"

Daphne also stood up, with the intention of saying that if anybody could be said to be blackening another's name, it was Geoffrey Minton and his family. However, Mr Justice Pollard was hammering on his desk and she didn't get the chance.

"Mr Minton, I will not tolerate this behaviour. Will you leave or will you be quiet?"

Geoffrey collapsed weakly onto his seat, where he sat for the rest of Marie's testimony with his head in his hands. She remembered what a shock it had been for her when she'd discovered Stanley's addiction – so how much worse must it be for him.

Sir Herbert continued with his questions. "Why didn't you seek help? Why not confide in Dr Hornby, for instance?"

"Stanley told me that decent people would reject us if they knew. We had very little money, but what we did have we would lose if it became common knowledge. He swore he was in control of the liquid."

"And you believed him?"

"I had no choice."

"And you continued to hide the truth from everyone?"

"Stanley said we would both go to prison if I didn't. I was too frightened to say anything."

"When it was obvious that Stanley was ill, you sent for Dr Hornby?"

"Yes. He said the symptoms suggested that Stanley was suffering from an ulcer and it could be about to burst. I accepted that, and saw no reason to mention the chloroform – for fear of the consequences I've just mentioned.

"In your own words, Mrs Minton, tell us what happened on the night of your husband's death."

This was the moment she'd been dreading. Until now, she'd spoken nothing but the truth – from now on, though, she would be lying under oath. She couldn't look at Daphne. Her hand slipped into the pocket containing Evelyn's note. She needed him to go on believing in her. She took a deep breath and began to repeat the story that Dr Hornby had introduced into the inquest in July.

"That night, my husband was ill, very ill. I sat by his bedside..."

Anyone who had come to court to wallow in the widow's emotions felt cheated. There were no histrionics, no tears, because forcing herself to remain detached was the only way Marie could get through the ordeal.

"And when I woke the next morning" – she was nearly at the end of the story now – if she could just keep going a little longer – "I went to his room to see how he was and..." She faltered mid-sentence and Manners swiftly prompted her.

"And when you found him at six o'clock the next morning he was dead?"

"Yes. He was."

"Mrs Minton, on the day of May 30th last year, did you

buy a bottle of chloroform from Jackson, the chemist?" She didn't reply. He said sharply, "Mrs Minton?"

With an effort, she said, "Yes, I did."

There was a mutter from the crowd. She saw a movement in the gallery. Daphne Senior leant back with a groan.

"Stanley asked me to buy it," she added quickly. "And a bottle of brandy."

"Was it the first time you'd bought chloroform for him?"

"The first and only time."

"Why did you agree to buy chloroform for him on that particular day?"

"At first I said no, but he insisted. He frightened me. He attacked me; he was choking me. Once I agreed to do it, he let me go. He gave me the address."

"You didn't tell anyone that he had become violent towards you?"

"Who would I tell? Besides, I'd heard that in this country a wife is considered her husband's property. No one will interfere between them."

"Well said!" shouted a voice, and Marie knew it was Daphne's.

"Why did you agree to the laundry woman's suggestion…" Sir Herbert glanced at his notes, "Mrs Wilkinson. Why did you agree to her suggestion that she should wash the bed sheets after she'd finished laying out Mr Minton?"

"I thought it was kind of her to offer. What else would I do with them?"

"You weren't trying to hide evidence, like vomit, on the sheet?"

"No."

Sir Herbert moved on to his next question. "There was a chloroform bottle in the bedroom when Mr and Mrs Gilpin arrived?"

"Yes."

"But not when Dr Hornby arrived?"

"No. I disposed of it, because I saw no reason why anyone should ever need to learn of Stanley's weakness."

"How did you dispose of it?"

"After Mr and Mrs Gilpin left the room, I saw the bottle and I panicked. As I said, I wanted to protect my husband's reputation, so I threw it in the river on my way to see Dr Hornby."

"Because you still believed it was the ulcer that had killed him and the chloroform had nothing to do with it? What was your reaction when you discovered from the post-mortem that your husband had died by ingesting chloroform?"

"I was shocked."

"Have you any idea how this chloroform came to be in his stomach?"

This was always going to be the hardest part, the direct question – the direct lie – but she'd come too far, been through too much, to lose her nerve now. "No."

"Knowing that you are still under oath – did you give your husband chloroform?"

She saw Daphne's white face staring down at her. "No," she said quietly.

"Thank you, Mrs Minton."

She turned to leave the witness box, but the judge stopped her. "Mr Redcar may have some questions for you, Mrs Minton."

Redcar was on his feet. "Yes, thank you, my Lord." Marie reluctantly turned back. "Mrs Minton, are you really trying to convince us that ill as your husband was, he still had the power to use violence against you?"

"Yes."

"You pride yourself on your medical knowledge, I believe. Are you seriously telling us that you didn't realise it was chloroform that killed your husband?"

"Dr McCullough had told Stanley he had an ulcer. Dr Hornby said it had reached a critical stage. Why should I doubt these men? As has been pointed out, I haven't had medical training."

"You were anxious for Dr Hornby to sign a death certificate before you notified his family. Isn't that the case?"

"No. Dr Hornby himself was anxious to sign the death certificate, to save me distress. It was very kind of him."

"Are you seriously telling us that it never entered your head that your husband died of chloroform? Having told us how frightened you were when you read in *Farnsworth's Medical Dictionary* that the narcotic could kill if used improperly?"

"It crossed my mind, of course it did, but Dr Hornby was so certain it was the ulcer." She looked at Sir Herbert, who smiled encouragingly.

"Wouldn't any innocent person have raised the question with the doctor anyway? That it may have been chloroform?

"I have said that I wanted to protect my husband's good name. I knew that mattered a great deal to him." She saw a look pass between the jurors.

"Mrs Minton, on oath, did you kill your husband?"

Her head was pounding and her heart was beating so fast she could scarcely breathe. "No."

"Thank you, Mrs Minton."

She returned to the dock wearily. There was absolute silence in the courtroom as she did so. It felt like an anti-climax when Sir Herbert called on Gladys Crawford, the Minton's housekeeper at The Laurels, to give evidence.

Gladys was extremely nervous, but she held her head up high and answered as clearly as she could. She had never, she said, seen anything in the behaviour of Mrs Minton that could have been called shocking or scandalous. She was a lady, and gentle and kind. It was true that she'd been friendly with Mr Peter Minton, but there was nothing surprising in that. They were of a similar age and the rest of the family had ignored her. She had no one else to turn to for companionship. "She was so young, a foreigner as well, but Mr Stanley Minton spent very little time with her."

Sir Herbert then asked about Marie's herbal remedies, to which Gladys replied that she considered Mrs Minton to have a great gift in such matters. She'd helped cure her boys on more than one occasion. No one had suffered any harm from them.

"Thank you, Mrs Crawford."

Redcar asked only one question: "Did you ever see Stanley Minton raise his hand to his wife?" To which Gladys answered truthfully: "No."

"No more questions," said Redcar.

Gladys received a nod from the judge and she made her way out of the witness box.

Dr McCullough was called next and Marie looked up in surprise. He had never been a friend to her, so why would he agree to give evidence in her defence? However, Sir Herbert didn't intend to detain him for long. His question was simple: "Had Stanley Minton suffered from ill health?" Dr McCullough confirmed that he had, continually. "And will you confirm that the deceased had an ulcer and that Mrs Minton knew of it?" Dr McCullough confirmed that Stanley Minton had had the beginnings of an ulcer, but he couldn't confirm whether or not his wife knew of it.

Redcar rose to ask if Dr McCullough had any reason to suspect that the deceased had taken to chloroform.

"I most certainly did not."

"Could he have concealed such an addiction from you?"

"If it's been proved that he took chloroform, then he must have concealed it from me. I've never been aware that I've treated anyone with such an addiction."

After a break for luncheon, Sir Herbert called his next

witnesses: three doctors, all eminent practitioners in the field of medicine. One after the other, Sir Arthur Fortescue, Dr Joseph Millard and Dr Royston Fields attested that the chances of someone successfully pouring liquid down the throat of another, whether that other was insensible or not, was highly unlikely without some of the liquid entering the windpipe and leaving signs of irritation. Despite Redcar's protests, Sir Herbert put the same point to all three.

"If Stanley Minton, distressed by his failure in business, with no prospect of recovering his former glory, his life ruined by a narcotic to which he had become addicted, if in this state, his senses dulled by alcohol, he took the chloroform himself, might he not have achieved the same results? That is, succeeded in swallowing it with no burning in the windpipe and no sign of vomiting? If he made himself partly insensible?"

All three reached the same conclusion. It was possible, but they would still have expected to see some irritation or burning in the mouth and windpipe, and signs of vomiting.

"So my suggestion as to how the chloroform got into the deceased's stomach is equally as plausible, or equally as improbable, as the prosecution's suggestion that Mrs Minton administered it herself," suggested Sir Herbert, before resuming his seat. Redcar passed on asking any questions.

"That completes the evidence for the defence, my Lord," said Sir Herbert.

The Prosecuting Counsel rose to make his closing speech. He believed, he said, that the testimony of the accused had been a series of lies from start to finish. She was no innocent convent girl, as the defence would have them believe. She'd had an intimate relationship with the brother of her husband, which was the cause of Peter Minton leaving in England.

"After Peter Minton left for America, she says that relations between herself and her husband were consummated and she had a baby – a baby that sadly died. Might this not have led to feelings of resentment towards her husband? He had made his wife wait for such a long time before the relationship was consummated and for that to end in the baby's premature death, would she not feel bitter? In such a state of mind, might her bitterness not have increased over the months that followed? Might not that bitterness have increased following the loss of her husband's business, which meant the loss of the money she had brought to the marriage? And, finally, there was the discovery that her husband was addicted to chloroform. Might she have seen in his addiction to chloroform a way to rid herself of the man she had grown to despise? Remember, on the day he died, she procured the chloroform that killed him."

Turning to the jury, Redcar went on to say that the defence counsel had made much of the fact that the accused had known enough of medical matters to realise the risk of failure involved in administering chloroform through the mouth. "Might it not also have given her the skill to ensure that it was done effectively? The defence has worked hard to suggest that it would be equally possible that Stanley Minton took his own life, but no man would pour such a liquid down his throat of his own choosing. We have been told it is a painful death."

She wanted to put her hands over her ears to shut out his voice – to shut out the image his words were creating. She closed her eyes, but the image wouldn't go away.

Sir Herbert was on his feet now. "Mrs Minton is not the perpetrator of a crime; she is the victim of it. You only have to look at the facts to realise that. Trapped in a loveless marriage that she struggled to make work, this young girl, who had lived all her life behind convent walls, had to fight off the unwelcome attentions of the brother of the deceased – a practiced seducer. Gentlemen, Peter Minton wanted money for his passage to America and as a result of his story, Geoffrey Minton gave him it.

"Stanley Minton's mother sadly died, but immediately

after her death the relationship between husband and wife improved. They had a child, the sad outcome of which we have already mentioned, but through all that followed Marie Minton remained faithful to her husband. No one has suggested otherwise."

Marie looked down at the floor. She thanked God that Evelyn's name had never been mentioned.

Sir Herbert's oratory had captured the court's full attention. "Even when Marie Minton discovered her husband's addiction – even then – she remained devoted to him. Dr Hornby has testified to that devotion. It's that devotion that has placed her here under suspicion. Believing her husband's name to be of so much importance to him and believing in Dr Hornby's diagnosis that Stanley Minton had died of an ulcer, Mrs Minton took steps to conceal her husband's disgusting habit from the world by getting rid of the bottle of chloroform.

"Let me ask you, what motive would my client have for killing her husband? No motive has been suggested by the counsel for the prosecution. It certainly was not money. Let me suggest an alternative to you. That Mrs Minton did not kill her husband. He killed himself. I have read that sometimes a drug begins to lose its effectiveness over a period of time. That the dose has to be increased, or a new way found to titivate a jaded palate. I have read that some addicts turn to drinking chloroform, no matter how painful, in the hope of a more intense sensation. He asked his wife to buy him chloroform and brandy. Brandy could perhaps help to alleviate the drugs taste and make it easier to swallow."

He saw that the jurymen were exchanging glances. "You may doubt a man would do that to himself. It's clear that you are men who have never sunk so low, never been dependent on such a foul habit. I am suggesting to you that my explanation is as likely to be true as the explanation put forward by the Prosecuting Counsel. They have to prove, beyond any reasonable doubt, that Mrs Minton killed her husband. They have to prove how it is possible for a person to pour a painful and bitter liquid into the mouth of another, whether that person is insensible or not, without leaving any sign of burning or irritation in the windpipe, the throat or the mouth. No one for the defence or the prosecution has been able to show, without any doubt, how that can be done. How then can Mrs Minton be proved guilty of the crime?" After one last glance at the jury, he sat down amid silence.

The atmosphere in the courtroom was intense and Marie kept her head lowered. She was terrified to look into the faces surrounding her for fear of what she would see.

The judge began his instruction to the jury. "Gentlemen, this is a most difficult case, full of contradictions. The question is how the chloroform entered into the stomach of the deceased. The prosecution is of the opinion that it was introduced by the accused after making her husband partially insensible, then persuading him, or making him, swallow the chloroform."

He looked down at his notes for a moment. "As we've heard, such an attempt is surrounded by so many difficulties, and open to so many chances of failure, that no skilled man would venture upon it unless he was a madman. Defence counsel has tried to persuade us that Mrs Minton had enough knowledge to be aware of those difficulties and so would not risk making such an attempt. But if she did succeed in that fashion, then it is not too much to say it was a cruel fortune, because the conditions and chances were all against it.

"One can speculate, as the defence counsel suggests, that Stanley Minton resorted to drinking chloroform to increase the effect on his jaded palate. A man who is a slave to narcotics is a man to be greatly pitied. His sufferings are greater than any person who has not gone through such an experience can imagine."

Mr Justice Pollard then highlighted the points and

contradictions put by both the defence and prosecution. "Gentlemen, if you have any doubts as to the role Mrs Minton played in her husband's death, then it is your solemn duty to give the prisoner the full benefit of such considerations. If you concur with the emphatic appeal by the learned counsel for the defence and believe his client to be innocent or, if falling short of that, you are unable to come to a decision, and you remain in a state of honest and conscientious doubt, then the prisoner should be acquitted.

Gentlemen, my task is done. I now leave you to yours, be pleased to retire."

The jury trailed out, throwing one last look toward the accused, as if trying to read in her face what their verdict should be.

★

Waiting in the holding cell underneath the courtroom, Marie sat on the bench with her head in her hands. How long would they take to decide her fate? One hour? Two hours? She rose shakily to her feet as she heard footsteps approaching. So soon? But it was only Sir Herbert, come to tell her that there was to be no decision today. The court would reconvene tomorrow.

"I don't think I can bear it," she whispered.

"You have no choice, Mrs Minton, and neither have I. It's out of our hands now. I will see you tomorrow."

She was returned to her cell in Armley Gaol and spent a sleepless night listening to the distant church clock chiming every quarter of the hour.

When morning finally arrived, she was taken to the side door of the Bridewell as usual, but today the street was full of people waiting to see her. Some jeered, some called her names and some just stood in silence staring at her. There was a small group of women, among them Daphne Senior. She tried to get close enough to Marie to say something to her, but she was stopped by a policeman this time. Marie tried to smile at her, but the muscles of her face were too taut and they wouldn't move. She was quickly ushered inside.

*

Evelyn, standing in the shadow cast by the Town Hall, moved further back into the darkness. He didn't want her to see him in case it unsettled her. He'd intended to stay away and he'd promised his mother he would stay away, but he couldn't. He'd travelled to Harrogate to ask John Pickard to discover who had provided the counsel for Marie. When he'd told him it was the Women's Social and Political Union and that Daphne Senior was an old friend of Marie's, he felt reassured.

With that question answered, he should have returned to London immediately, but he couldn't leave – not before the verdict was delivered. He had driven to Leeds and booked a room in the Metropole Hotel. He would stay there for as long as it took the jury to reach their verdict. He would be close by if she needed him.

*

Marie had no idea how long she'd been waiting in this cell underneath the court. She had no way of knowing. There were no chimes to be heard through these thick walls. All she did know was that this waiting was unbearable.

Sir Herbert was suffering the same agonies as he paced the marble corridor outside the courtroom. There should have been a verdict by now. Five hours had passed since the court had reconvened for the day. Lawler, his junior counsel, found him sitting on one of the steps outside the Town Hall, doing battle with despair.

"They're coming back, sir. They've reached a decision."

Everywhere were running footsteps as people scurried back to court, determined to be present when the verdict was given. Sir Herbert quickly took his place. As Marie entered, supported on both sides by wardresses, he rose and gave her a slight bow, and she was grateful for the courtesy. The wardresses sat either side of her, two doctors and a chaplain stood behind. The jury filed in and the judge took his place as silence fell.

The clerk of the court rose. "Gentlemen, have you agreed upon your verdict?"

The foreman replied: "We have."

"Do you find the prisoner, Marie Minton, guilty or not guilty?"

The foreman paused. Everyone leant forward. Marie didn't breathe.

"We've considered the evidence and we do not think there is sufficient proof to show how, or by whom, the chloroform was administered."

"Then you say the prisoner is not guilty?"

"Not guilty."

There were gasps from those who were convinced she was guilty. Cheers from the few who believed her to be innocent. Daphne sank back in relief as the women of the WSPU stood on the benches waving handkerchiefs.

Marie collapsed in tears. She couldn't take it in. Sir Herbert Manners crossed to her, his hand outstretched. She took it in a daze and muttered: "Thank you. Thank you. Thank you."

She caught sight of Geoffrey Minton sitting in the well of the court, the crowd milling around him. He was in shock; his face was white. She saw Daphne pushing her way towards her.

She flung her arms around Marie and hugged her. "Thank God," she kept saying. "Thank God."

*

Outside the Town Hall, Evelyn caught hold of the arm of a gentleman who had been attending the trial.

"What was the verdict?" he asked.

"Not guilty," he replied.

The man's wife joined him. "Only because they couldn't decide how she'd done it," she said. "If you ask me, it's obvious she killed him."

But Evelyn barely heard her because at that moment Marie came out of the Town Hall supported between two people. On one side was Sir Herbert Manners and on the other was a woman whom he recognised as Daphne Senior. They helped her down the steps and hurried her through the crowd into a waiting hansom cab, which sped its three passengers away from the throng of reporters.

He watched the cab disappear into the distance. It was over. She was free and that was the end of it. She could move on and put everything behind her. Forget about the past and concentrate on the future, as he must – but there was something he had to do first.

CHAPTER TWENTY-SIX

Daphne stood in Tilly Walker's front parlour viewing her surroundings with mock horror. "Red curtains and green wallpaper? How on earth could you bear living here?"

Marie smiled. "After the white walls of my cell, it seems like heaven. I'm grateful to Tilly for letting me stay on after the trial. I'd nowhere else to go. The Gilpins made it clear I wasn't welcome back there. While I was in Armley Gaol, they put all my belongings into storage. There's nothing of mine left in Garibaldi Street. Won't you sit down?"

"No, I can't stay. I have to return to London."

Marie nodded. "Thank you again for everything you've done, Daphne. I'll never forget it."

"No thanks needed." Marie could see that Daphne had something on her mind, something she was finding difficult to broach. "Look, I called because – well, to say goodbye, yes – but because there's someone who asked me to speak to you on his behalf. He's here, waiting, hoping you'll see him."

Marie covered her face with her hands. It could only be Evelyn. "He shouldn't have come here. Oh, he shouldn't have come."

"No one else knows he's here and you know *I* won't say anything. I haven't asked questions and nor will I. It's not my business, but he's in the kitchen talking to Tilly. He'll leave straightaway if you'd rather not see him."

"Oh Daphne, I'm not sure I can face him." How could she, after everything she'd done?

"I'll tell him to go then." Daphne turned towards the door.

"No." Marie stopped her. "No. Don't let him leave."

"Oh, my dear friend," Daphne turned back to her and hugged her tightly, "don't despair. Make use of the life you now have." She held Marie at arm's length for a moment, studying her. "You look so frail. Take care of yourself. Write to me often. You have my address now."

Marie nodded and, with one last hug, Daphne left. A moment later Evelyn entered, quietly closing the door behind him.

They stood at opposite ends of the room, facing each other, neither able to speak for the moment. Marie tried to read the expression on his face. All she could see was compassion. It was she who broke the silence.

"Your letter – the one Daphne gave me – means a great deal to me."

"I wanted to do more. So much more."

It was so good to hear his voice again. "You shouldn't have come here. If any reporters saw you."

"They didn't."

She wanted to run to him, to throw her arms around his neck, but he had made no move towards her and she felt too shy to take the initiative.

"Daphne tells me you're returning to France?" he said, eventually.

"Yes. I intend to train at a nurse's school outside Bordeaux, and to offer my services to one of the nursing orders once I'm trained."

"Do you have enough money to do that – if it isn't impertinent of me to ask?"

"I have enough. Tilly arranged for the sale of my furniture, and that will give me what I need to live on until I've finished my training."

He seemed so awkward; it was making her nervous.

"Marie, there's something you should know. Something I have to tell you." Whatever it was, she could see that it was difficult for him to say. "When I was in France, I did meet Father Connor." Her first reaction was one of delight, but that quickly dissolved because it was obvious he didn't share it. "When your mother saved my father's life they… fell in love. You were the result."

It took a moment for his meaning to dawn on her. The she almost laughed at the absurdity of it. She'd obviously misheard him. She waited for him to correct what he'd just said, but he didn't.

"It isn't true. It can't be." The feelings she had for him were not a sister's feelings.

He was standing stiffly, formally. "God help you, but you are my father's daughter, Marie, and my parents did you a great wrong by trying to hide that fact. It led me to misinterpret the… natural feelings I have for you."

"I'm sorry, I still can't believe it." She turned her back on him, unable to continue facing him.

"It's true. My parents hid you away in a convent – they hoped you'd stay there. There's more." She shook her head. She didn't want to hear any more. "My father cheated Henri Montrecourt out of a gold claim – not directly, but he was part of the group that did. He used the money to save the estate, but that money should have been yours. I want to give you…"

"No," she swung around to face him. "Is money the answer to everything in your family? It's because of your family's money that I married Stanley." He tried to speak. "Stop it. Don't say anymore. I don't want to hear any more and I don't want your money. I don't want anything from you – any of you. I just want to be left alone." Tears were streaming down her face and she couldn't stop them.

"I have to make amends; you have to let me make amends." He was pleading with her now, aware that he was close to tears, too. "Anything you need – anything. You have the right to ask for it. I swear I knew none of this before."

She believed him. "I want to put things right. Do everything I can to mend things."

She thought of Stanley, of what she'd done and she shook her head. "It's too late. Too much has happened." She wiped away the tears. She had to ask him something – it was important to her. "Did your father love my mother?"

He had no idea, but he sensed it mattered to her. "Yes." Perhaps he had. Evelyn had no way of knowing. "If I'd realised when we first met..."

"If – that's such a futile word, isn't it? It means nothing; it solves nothing." She was in control of herself again. "I know your intentions are good, Evelyn, and I thank you for them. But truly, there is nothing I want from you, except to beg you to leave me alone. Let me go with your blessing to find the freedom I never had before. I want to make decisions that are my own and not ones dictated to me by your family's interests."

"It's your family, too."

"No, you were never my family. Not really."

After a while, he nodded reluctantly. "If that's what you want. Will you keep in touch with me?"

"No. It wouldn't help. Daphne will always know where I am and what I'm doing. But take my advice, Evelyn, and let go of the past. It's nearly destroyed us both. Look to the future. Do wonderful things. I want to read in the newspapers about the great things you're achieving."

"I don't think I'm capable of achieving anything," he murmured.

"You are. I know you are. I believe in you," she added quietly.

Evelyn stood outside Tilly's house and fought back the urge to hammer on the front door, demanding to be let back in. He would never see her again, he knew that, and there were so many things he wanted to say to her. She was right to tell him to look to the future, but memories were not so easily forgotten. He would always remember his first sight of her. Her hair, the colour of amber, forming a halo around her face. She had worn a white lace waistcoat over a white dress, and a black shawl embroidered with roses was thrown around her shoulders. She looked like a painting by Rossetti, and that was the image of her that he would always carry with him.

★

Marie was staring into space when Tilly touched her on the shoulder. It made her jump. She'd been thinking about Evelyn. It had been hard, but she had been right to send him away. The past had to be amputated like a diseased limb.

"You going to that storage place now, Mrs Minton?"

"Yes, I'm just going there to pay the bill, Tilly."

"Want company?"

"No. I'll be all right. Thank you."

"You don't have to leave here, you know. You're very welcome to stay on. I've enjoyed having you about the place."

Marie was touched by her kindness. "Thank you, but I have to leave for France tomorrow."

Tilly hovered in the hall as Marie put on her coat. "It won't be the same without you," she said sadly.

★

The warehouse where her furniture was being stored was in the middle of a forest of chimneys and a labyrinth of narrow alleyways. She found it eventually, despite the fact that the sign on the wooden gate was caked with mud and dust. A bonfire was burning in the yard, the smoke creating a choking, grey fog. There was a small pile next to the fire, consisting of the bits and pieces left over from the sale of her furniture.

Beavers, the owner of the yard, was engrossed in a newspaper. He threw it aside as the gate creaked open. “Mrs Minton, is it?” When she nodded, he said: “There’s three months’ storage to pay.” He took the money from her. “And what do you want me to do with the rest of this stuff?” He indicated the small pile. “I’ve left it here in the yard for you to look over.”

“Burn it all,” she said.

She accidentally swallowed a lungful of acrid smoke from the bonfire and held a handkerchief to her mouth as she coughed.

“The wind’s changed direction,” he said, shuffling away. “Stand on the other side while I go and get your change.”

She did as he directed, looking down at all that was left of her belongings – at the notebook containing Sister Grace’s remedies, its leaves lifted by the wind, and Hortense’s tin box, which contained the tarnished silver button, the shiny lump of rock and the note that her mother had written. The flames from the bonfire reflected on something else among the jumble. It was the Bunsen burner. She shivered.

“Here you are, lady.” Beavers came back, holding out the few shillings of change in his grubby hand. “I suppose you don’t want to keep these?” He indicated another pile of jumble she hadn’t noticed until now. It consisted of the glass cases full of butterflies. “I could sell them if you’ll let me. Make a few bob for myself.”

“No. I don’t want you to do that.” The butterflies’ wings were stretched out – they were trapped in perpetual flight.

Ignoring Beavers’ astonished protests, she picked up the cases and smashed the glass against the stones of the yard, scattering the contents. Released from the pins that skewered them against the velvet, the butterflies were animated by the wind. It played with them and caressed them, lifting them up on damaged wings, twisting them in circles, like so many dead leaves. But they were free.

ACKNOWLDEGEMENT

Some of the incidents in this novel draw on events in real life but characters have been changed and action and relationships invented.

Any mistakes are my own, but I would like to thank all the friends who have encouraged and helped me. In particular the writer Carolyn S Jones for her guidance, without whom I am sure I would never have finished the novel.

Long after I began writing it, my sister was diagnosed with dementia. I decided to contribute whatever proceeds came to me from its sale to Alzheimer's Research UK, in the hope that in some small way it might help in the search for an understanding and cure of an illness that affects so many.